THE RUNAWAY

• • •

ALSO BY TERRY KAY

THE RUNAWAY

• • •

TERRY KAY

Perennial

An Imprint of HarperCollins*Publishers*

A hardcover edition of this book was published in 1997 by William Morrow & Company.

THE RUNAWAY. Copyright © 1997 by The Terry Kay Corporation. All rights reserved. Printed in the United States of America. No part of this book may be used or reproduced in any manner whatsoever without written permission except in the case of brief quotations embodied in critical articles and reviews. For information address HarperCollins Publishers Inc., 10 East 53rd Street, New York, NY 10022.

HarperCollins books may be purchased for educational, business, or sales promotional use. For information please write: Special Markets Department, HarperCollins Publishers Inc., 10 East 53rd Street, New York, NY 10022.

First Perennial edition published 2000.

Designed by Leah S. Carlson

The Library of Congress has catalogued the hardcover edition as follows:
Kay, Terry.
    The runaway / Terry Kay. — 1st ed.
     p. cm.
   ISBN 0-688-15033-0
   I. Title.
  PS3561.A885R86 1997
  813'.54—dc21   97-16737
                                                 CIP

ISBN 0-380-81342-4 (pbk.)

00 01 02 03 04 ❖ / RRD 10 9 8 7 6 5 4 3 2 1

I believe that every writer needs an agent who is part counselor, part editor, part lawyer, part liar, part arbiter, part seer, part dreamer, part irritant, and part believer. And because the agent who handles my material, as well as my fears and my occasional (but gentlemanly) outbursts of frustration, is all of the above—which, in sum, makes him a special person and a sensitive and caring friend—I dedicate this book with admiration and appreciation to

HARVEY KLINGER

And, further, because they have taught me much over the years and because knowing them inspired many thoughts concerning this book, I wish to acknowledge my brothers-in-law, each a veteran of the armed services, either in World War II or in Korea.

Army

Harry Francis Patat (killed in action; France)
James Luther McBath
Gwyndol Duvall Phillips (deceased)
Fred Lester Skelton

Air Force

Edwin H. Holmes
James Paul Huskey

Navy

David William Nix
Jimmy A. Carey

FOREWORD

When I was twelve years old, or thereabout, a young black man I knew, also twelve, or thereabout, called me *Mr. Terry* one day. It was a great shock, one of those moments that is boldly tattooed to the skin of memory. I did not understand it then, but I accepted it. (I think people who are beneficiaries of mystifying experiences *always* accept them.)

Many years later I realized that being called *Mr. Terry* was a ceremony in my rite of passage into young adulthood as a Southerner, a kind of cotton field bar mitzvah. It was the ceremony of Logan's Law.

Logan's Law is from this book. It means "the law of the way things are."

Logan's Law is why the civil rights movement began.

And why it continues.

And why we may never get things right, for Logan's Law is enforced in one form or another by every race and culture on earth.

Still, it interests me that things—and people—do change, sometimes so subtly there is little, or no, cognizant awareness of those changes.

Desegregation in the South, for example.

Historians of events and dates have it wrong about desegregation. It did not begin in the fifties with court-ordered mandates belligerently opposed by southern politicians firing mouth-loaded weapons in a war of words that still echo faintly in small rural communities.

Desegregation began after World War II when soldiers and war workers—men and women—returned home.

They were not the same people who had left farms to answer the drumbeat call of patriotism.

They had been to Europe and to the Pacific, or to factory cities in the United States.

They had met people from New York and New Mexico, from Pennsylvania and California, from every other state in the nation, from foreign countries barely familiar to them.

They had heard accents and languages that were, to them, mostly unintelligible babble, spoken by people with names bafflingly unpronounceable.

And though they did not know it consciously—not all of them, at least—they had returned to their homes as different people. There was strut in their step, stories on their tongues. Ghosts slept with them.

They had changed.

Part of that change was an intuitive understanding that freedom was not a select experience for a select few, and it was that door crack of tolerance (a serious discomfort for many, I suspect) that first prepared white Southerners for the shock of the civil rights movement.

From that time, desegregation was as inevitable, as inescapable, as any prophecy God might have whispered to wise men about upheavals on the horizon.

I write this opinion realizing it is the perspective of a white Southerner, and I know that the end of World War II did not bring an end to bigotry. In some cases, that bigotry was escalated, made uglier and more insulting than indignities that blacks had suffered before the war.

I realize also that the majority of white Southerners returning from World War II—given the influence of Logan's Law—reacted passively to the changes invading their environment. Yet that reaction eventually became an important contribution to desegregation. When push came to shove in the civil rights movement, they *remained* passive, which greatly weakened the assumed presence of a United White Southern Front. Such a front simply did not exist.

But there were some white people who stepped across the line, thumbed their noses at Logan's Law. World War II was a passionate memory for them, and in their homes, a quiet, private lesson was being taught in the aftershock of a war ignited by tyrants hell-bent on destroying races of people as well as conquering land: *Don't put anyone down. Anyone.*

I have written this book because that period of time has always fascinated me and because I am of that generation of Southerners born to segregation and to Logan's Law, one who became a passive member of a passive transition period, and one who has lived his adulthood balanced on the still-shaky highwire hanging between then and now.

I write of then, hoping to better understand now.

THE RUNAWAY

●　●　●

PROLOGUE

Conjure Woman walked in a steady step, her white wrap dress and white head turban glowing under the moon. She walked down the middle of the road, and the drivers of the cars that came upon her suddenly out of the darkness steered to avoid her, knowing who she was.

The drivers of the cars slowed to a stop and looked back down the road and whispered in awe of seeing her.

"Conjure Woman . . ."

"Conjure Woman . . ."

"Conjure Woman . . ."

At the side-by-side shanty houses along the road where Conjure Woman walked, dogs whimpered and slithered into hiding, and the people who lived in those houses peeked from behind ratty curtains at the large, white-shrouded figure in the middle of the road, and they muttered to one another in startled voices, "Conjure Woman's walking." They crept outside and whispered across their yards to one another, saying, "Look yonder, look yonder. Conjure Woman's coming down the road."

Hootie Veal came out of his tar-paper shanty, followed by three of his eight children. Hootie and his children were thought to be addle-brained, the way they behaved. Hootie skittered up to Conjure Woman, mocking her step, playing the fool. His children laughed and played the fool with him.

"Where you going?" Hootie bellowed.

Conjure Woman did not answer. Her step did not change.

Hootie ran in a circle around her, lifting his knees high, swinging his arms low. His children laughed and leapt in the air and beat their hands together.

"Where you going off to?" Hootie said again, shoving his face close to Conjure Woman's.

"Be out of my way," Conjure Woman told him. Her voice was like the blade of a cold wind.

Hootie threw his head back and howled a dog howl. His children howled also and giggled.

Conjure Woman did not stop walking. She raised her hand and pointed her finger at Hootie, and Hootie's legs began to wobble, wobbling like Charlie Chaplin's before a fall, and then Hootie crumpled to the ground as though his bones had been jerked from his legs. His children laughed at the comedy and began circling Hootie, still dog-howling. Hootie rolled on the ground, slapping at the air with his hands. His tongue hung from his mouth in a wad of flesh.

Conjure Woman did not look back.

"Goda'mighty," whispered the people who saw Hootie fall as they watched from the windows of their homes and from their cars.

"Damn fool," they said of Hootie. "You don't go messing with Conjure Woman when she's out walking at night."

The drivers of the cars and the people behind the curtains could not see Conjure Woman's face. Her face was coal-dark, darker than the night, and against the night it was invisible. But they all knew the face they could not see—huge and round, a flat nose, eyes that were fire-hot in temper and shiver-cold in disdain, eyes that were like the dreams of demons.

When Conjure Woman walked at night, something was about to happen. Everyone knew that. Everyone. The stories of Conjure Woman were too many and too remarkable, and no one made light of them. Haiti woman, the stories said. A voice that spoke in a clipped accent, her words rising at the ends of her sentences. Older than anyone knew, but never aging. Always dressed in white, toe to turban. In league with the spirits, the stories said. Conjure Woman could find lost things behind her closed, fire-hot, shiver-cold eyes. It was her trade. Dollar readings in the bare room of her home in Softwind. Lost jewelry. Lost money. Lost souls. She could look into the clear bubble of a stone that she kept in her pocket and see the future. She could command birds from the limbs to sit on her shoulder. Poisonous snakes curled peacefully in her hands.

The Klan had tried to run her off, hadn't it? That's how the story went. All sheeted out in their white robes with eyehole hoods, the Kluxers were, even some who had been to her with their dollar bills, asking their anxious, dollar-bill questions. They went to Conjure Woman's house liquored-up brave, carrying a Jesus cross made out of heartwood pine and wrapped in grain sacks soaked with gasoline. And they called her out: "Get yourself out here, Conjure Woman, and keep on going! Don't want the likes of you around here, nigger witch!" Conjure Woman stepped onto the porch, smiling. She slowly raised her hand, the story went, and suddenly, for no reason at all, the Jesus cross burst into flames, blistering those who held it. The men dropped the cross and yelped and ran, their white robes and white hoods fluttering across the field and down to the road where they had left their cars and trucks. And the last thing they heard was a maniacal laugh. One of them—Chester Murphy—looked back, the story went, and saw the burning cross sizzling on the ground. Until he closed his eyes in death three years later, that blue-heat image was in Chester's eyes like cataracts.

The stories of Conjure Woman were many. Only a fool would scoff at them.

Now Conjure Woman was in the middle of the road, her steady step falling like a heartbeat, her coal-dark, unseen face aimed toward Crossover.

"Wonder where she's going?" whispered the people who saw her.

"Something's happening," they said. "Conjure Woman don't leave her place unless something's happening."

"Crazy goddamn Hootie and them crazy goddamn half-wit kids. Playing the fool. You don't play the fool with Conjure Woman."

"Cold out there. She must be freezing," they said.

Conjure Woman did not feel the cold of the February night. She willed the space around her to be warm, and it was warm.

She did not pause to rest. Each step was the same, step after step.

After she passed by them, the people came out of their homes and their cars and looked down the road where Conjure Woman had been. They inspected the powdery, red-clay ground for her footprints, but they saw nothing.

"Wonder where she's going?" they said.

"Something's happening," they said.

It was a long walk from Softwind to Crossover, many miles to hold the touch in her hands. The touch trembled to be released.

• • •

At early morning—a purple bruise of light on the muscle of the hills that rose up behind Sweetwater Swamp—Conjure Woman topped the knoll above the tenant farmhouse where Rody and Reba Martin lived. And there, at last, she paused. A broad smile flowered on her face. She reached into her pocket and pulled out the clear stone and rubbed it with her fingers, then she pushed it back into the pocket.

• • •

At the farmhouse, Reba moved painfully and carefully down the side of the barn toward the milking stall. Her abdomen billowed with the child that had stopped moving inside her the day before. Getting ready, she guessed. Already dropped some. She touched her abdomen with her fingers, then eased on toward the milking stall. Rody better get use to milking the cow, she thought. Don't matter if he don't like doing it, he better get ready. It'd take some time—a few days—before she could bend at the milking stool after the baby.

She went into the stall where the cow stood at the feed bin, hungrily eating the cottonseed hull and meal mix she'd dumped through the feed slot from inside the barn.

"You be still, old cow," she said aloud. "Reba don't feel like running you around today."

She took the milking stool and placed it beside the cow, and then she sat and tilted the milk pail and poured the small pool of water she had warmed in the kitchen into the palm of one hand, and she cleaned the cow's teats and massaged them.

"Don't you go kicking over the bucket," Reba said.

She reached for the teats. And then the pain hit—a sudden, violent pain, erupting inside her, a pain that imploded in her body and in her soul. It threw her up from the milking stool and thrust her across the milking stall and slammed her into the wall.

She heard the voice before the pain took her senses: *"His name will be Son Jesus."*

She did not know how long she had been unconscious. She knew only that when she turned her head and opened her eyes, she could feel the baby dangling from her, bathed in a covering of fluid. She looked. The baby writhed on the inside of her dress.

"Praise Jesus," she mumbled.

She reached for the baby and wiped her hands over his face, clearing the mucus from his nose. He turned, like someone yawning, and then he cooed.

"You come out of nowhere," she said softly. She slid her hands beneath him and pulled him up and wrapped the button-up sweater she was wearing around him, and she cuddled him in her arm. She saw the umbilical cord and the faint pulsing that ran like a gentle trembling through the cord.

"Got to get up," she said.

She struggled hard, pushing with her free hand against the wall. She could feel the dampness of the aftermatter on her legs. She struggled mightily and stood. The cow at the feeding bin turned her head and gazed at Reba, then turned back to her food.

"Gon' miss being milked this morning," Reba said to the cow. Then she began her weak walk to the house.

● ● ●

Conjure Woman watched from the knoll. She saw Reba move from the barn into the house. The smile deepened. She closed her eyes and moved her mouth in a soundless incantation. The sun was now in the trees, a paint stroke of red. The fogbank of the swamp rose up into the sun like cool smoke.

● ● ●

Dr. Jake Arlington fluttered the match dead with a whip-shaking of his hand and drew hard on the pipe he held between his teeth. A string of blue wiggled out of the pipe bowl and curled toward the ceiling. His face was still flushed from the work, a coat of perspiration still glittered on his forehead.

"Well, Hack," Jake said, "you've got a live wire in there. Damned if I don't think that boy's got the best set of lungs I ever heard. Almost dropped him when he turned loose with all that bellowing."

"Just glad he's all right," Hack Winter said.

The doctor picked up the cup of coffee that Hack had placed on the kitchen table for him. "He's fine. Got all his fingers and toes and the other equipment he needs." He sipped from the coffee. "Ada's fine too," he added. "She's about got this baby business down." He winked at Hack. "That could be dangerous, you know. Gets easier every time."

"This is it," Hack told him. "Four's enough. Hard enough to feed the ones I got, and if things get much worse, I guess I'll be hiring myself out to sharecrop for somebody. Four's enough."

"Well, I won't argue with that," the doctor replied. "These days, it is."

"I appreciate you coming out, Jake," Hack said earnestly.

Jake Arlington smiled. Having been born in Baltimore, Maryland, and still an outsider in the Deep South, he had always found the people guarded but genuinely grateful for his help. Hack and Ada Winter were good people, like most of the people of Overton County. Hard workers of small farms. Year-to-year survivors. All of them alike. All of them holding on. "It's my job," he said, after a moment.

"Well, I'm glad you were here. You remember how it was with Troy."

The doctor laughed. "Almost didn't make it on time."

"Ain't that the truth," Hack said. "Thought I was gon' have to do it myself."

"You could've, I guess. I expect you've brought a few calves in the world."

"Calves ain't babies."

"No, they're not. What're you going to call him?"

"Ada wants to name him after her daddy and my daddy," Hack answered. "Thomas Alton. Thomas was her daddy's name; Alton was my daddy."

"Sounds like Ada," Jake Arlington said. "She ever finish finding all the limbs on the family tree?"

Hack chuckled and shook his head. His wife had become interested in genealogy following the death of her father. Now she was obsessed by it. They had taken summer driving trips from Virginia to Louisiana to visit cemeteries with headstones carrying the Fitzgerald name, and during the trips he had found himself searching for markers with the name of Winter.

"She's still at it," Hack said. "Must have a dozen tablets filled with names. It's like a jigsaw puzzle. Now she's doing it for half the people in the community."

"Keeps her mind active," Jake suggested. "I like that. I tell you one thing, Hack, she's got spirit. More than anybody I've met since I've been down here." He stretched and felt the strain in his muscles. "Don't let them girls stay in there too long with her."

"I won't."

"Where's Troy?"

"Still in his room. Said he wadn't coming out until he knew everything was all right."

Jake chuckled. "Boys just naturally don't like being around babies, I guess."

◉　◉　◉

Reba lay on her back in her bed, holding the baby on her abdomen, the umbilical cord still linking them. Her daughters, Cecily and Remona, were busy cleaning her, bundling blankets and towels and sheets and wedging them around her body. In the main room, her husband, Rody, shoved oak firewood into the fireplace. He was nervous. A burning, finger-rolled cigarette dangled from his lips.

Rody did not hear the door open. He felt a rush of cool air and he turned from the fire. The cigarette fell from his mouth when he saw Conjure Woman standing at the door. He did a funny foot dance and stepped on the cigarette.

"Where's she at?" Conjure Woman said in a sharp voice.

Rody nodded toward the bedroom.

Conjure Woman closed the door and crossed to the bedroom. She stepped inside.

"Mama—" Cecily whimpered. She was staring toward the door.

Reba raised her head from the pillow. Conjure Woman seemed to fill the room.

"Move," Conjure Woman said to Cecily and Remona.

The two girls looked at their mother. She nodded and they stepped aside quietly.

"Why you here?" Reba asked weakly.

Conjure Woman walked to the bed. She looked at the baby curled on Reba's stomach. "Him," she said.

She leaned over the bed and over Reba and studied the baby. The smile returned—not broad, or deep, but gentle. She reached into her pocket and took out a silk handkerchief and unfolded it and lifted two white strings and draped them over the flesh of one hand.

"Get me the sharp knife, child," she said across the room without looking toward Cecily and Remona. "Put it in the boiling water."

Cecily and Remona rushed from the room.

"Now we take him from you," Conjure Woman whispered. She took one of the strings and tied it around the umbilical cord near the baby's stomach, then she tied the other string around the cord a few inches down.

"Say his name," Conjure Woman commanded.

Reba lay back into the pillow. She closed her eyes and remembered the voice. "Son Jesus," she said quietly.

"You heard?"

Reba nodded.

Conjure Woman bent close to Reba's face. "There be a white boy too," she whispered.

Reba frowned in confusion.

"There be a white boy too," Conjure Woman said again. "They be bound."

"Bound?" Reba whispered anxiously.

"They make the change," Conjure Woman said.

"Change?"

Conjure Woman raised her hand, swept it through the air over Reba's face. "Sssssssh," she said. The sound was like the sound of a bird's wings.

"Mama," Cecily said timidly from the door of the room.

"Come here, child," Conjure Woman commanded without turning from Reba.

Cecily came back into the room, holding a knife by its handle. She looked at her mother and then Conjure Woman.

"Give it to me, child," Conjure Woman said.

Cecily handed the knife to her.

"Watch me, child," Conjure Woman told her.

She sliced the umbilical cord between the strings in a quick stroke and then she gave the knife back to Cecily. She lifted Son Jesus from his mother's body and held him up like an offering.

"He call me here," Conjure Woman said in a loud, singing voice. "My hand be on him."

●　●　●

Ada Winter tried to rest. It was midafternoon, February 7, 1937. Her son had been born at twenty minutes after six in the morning and had finally stopped his noisy complaint over the experience at seven-thirty. The birth had not been difficult, but still she was tired. It was as though she had given up an energy that her other children had not demanded in their birth. He was now in the crib near the bed, sleeping calmly. She remembered his first cry, so sharp it had made the doctor jerk in astonishment.

Elly had hovered over him, touching him, whispering to him. Not Miriam or Troy. Miriam and Troy lingered at a distance, peering over the walls of the crib. Their faces said they were on guard against the loud intruder in the crib.

It's the way of things, thought Ada. Elly had claimed him. Elly would be his other mother. It had been the same with her younger brother, Spencer. When she had seen Spencer in the bed beside her mother, Ada had known immediately that he would be special to her. She sighed silently, prayed a quick prayer that Tom would not burden Elly as Spencer had burdened her. More than once, she had wanted to prune Spencer away from the family tree, lob him off like a decayed limb, but she could not. Spencer was still special.

Elly had given the first gift—a book of nursery rhymes. She had scratched through her own name on the flyleaf of the book and had begged Miriam to print TOM on the page, and Ada knew that would be his name, though she preferred Thomas.

"Can I read to him, Mama?" Elly had asked excitedly. "Can I hold him and read him a story?"

"If you let Miriam sit with you," Ada had answered. Elly was four and had only learned to mimic the reading of the nursery rhymes, but she knew the words by memory and that was close enough to the real thing.

And Elly had recited from the book, with Tom nestled in a blanket, his head resting against her chest.

The first words from a book that Thomas Alton Winter ever heard were:

Hickory, dickory, dock . . .
The mouse ran up the clock.
The clock struck one . . .
The mouse ran down.
Hickory, dickory, dock . . .

But the reading had worked. Tom had drifted into sleep and Miriam had taken him from Elly and placed him in the crib and covered him with a blanket.

"Did I do good, Mama?" Elly had asked.

"You did fine, honey. Real good. I guess you're going to have to be the rocker and reader for him. I think he likes your voice."

• • •

In the afternoon, Rody hitched the mules to the wagon and drove Conjure Woman back to her home in Softwind.

Those who saw her sitting in the back of the wagon, on a chair Rody had taken from the kitchen, said among themselves, "Conjure Woman walked last night, and there she is, going home."

They said, "Who's that colored man driving the wagon, taking Conjure Woman home?"

They said, "Wonder what happened?"

They said, "Whatever it was, it was something. Always is when Conjure Woman walks at night."

ONE

His family called him a runaway, and Tom guessed that he was.

He did leave home a lot, and if leaving home was running away, well, yes, he was a runaway. But he never went far, and someone always found him, which was easy enough since he usually stood around waiting for someone to show up.

And if he had to tell the truth, Tom would confess that part of the reason he ran away was that he knew someone would always find him. It was like hide-and-seek, but better. He played hide-and-seek only with Son Jesus and, sometimes, with Elly, when Elly thought he needed attention. But Son Jesus and Elly gave up too easily. Especially Son Jesus. Son Jesus wouldn't look for more than a minute before quitting the game. He would call out, "Where you at, Thomas? I give up." And Tom would come out of hiding, declaring victory over Son Jesus, and that, too, was aggravating; Son Jesus didn't care if he lost to Tom. Playing the game was enough. Besides, Son Jesus believed that with Tom, whatever happened between them was meant to be. "It's done been planned," his mother, Reba, had preached. "Ain't nothing nobody can do about it."

Few people believed Reba. They thought she was simply a yammering religious lunatic who did not know a vision from a headache.

But Son Jesus believed her. And Tom believed her.

They had reason to believe.

The story of Conjure Woman's nightlong walk from Softwind to Crossover was part of their heritage. Conjure Woman had proclaimed that her hand was on Son Jesus, and she had whispered to Reba, "There be a white boy too. They be bound. They make the change."

When she learned of the coincidence of timing in the births of Son Jesus and Tom, Reba accepted what Conjure Woman was telling her—that it was a sign, that God had a plan. It had to be, she reasoned. She did not understand it, did not know what was meant by being bound, or by making the change, but she did not have to understand it; she only had to believe it.

To Tom and Son Jesus, hearing the story many times from Reba, it meant they were special, and being special was worth more than hidden treasure.

• • •

The first time Tom ran away from home was on a September afternoon in 1944. He was seven years old. It was a high-sky day of bleached blue, a cloudless, airless day of heat blistering the earth, a day that smelled of cooking topsoil and of cotton drying on weighing sheets where it had been piled by the pickers. Tom had been eager about the picking. He had said to his father and mother, "Lots of cotton out there. Can't we start picking it?" And finally his father had said, "Well, I guess we can," and he had led Tom and Troy and Miriam and Elly into the field. Tom had picked for a half hour before wandering off to play. "Damn it," Troy had muttered to Miriam and Elly. "Can't wait to get us out here, and then he takes off to lay around on his lazy little butt."

Tom was sitting on a sheet of the cotton that had been pulled under the shade of an oak tree beside the road. A book was open in his lap. The name of the book was *The Gingerbread Boy*. Elly had brought it to the field from the house after lunch. Tom had read it a hundred times, he guessed, but he read it again because Elly mothered him and he knew it would please Elly.

Son Jesus was beside Tom, buried in the cotton, playing with four large maypops fashioned into play soldiers, with stick arms and stick legs. From the back of his throat, he was making the rat-tat-tat sound of a machine gun followed by the pinging of bullets hitting rocks.

Tom watched Son Jesus with disinterest, then brushed a fly away from his face and stared across the field at the pickers. His brother, Troy, who was fifteen, was working furiously, crawling on his knees between two rows, picking both. Miriam and Elly were near him, each picking from one row. Miriam was thirteen; Elly, eleven. Farther back was Reba and her two daughters, Cecily, who was fourteen, and Remona, who was twelve. Reba lived with her children in a crowded tenant house on Harlan Davis's farm, but they did not sharecrop, not since the murder of Rody Martin a year earlier. They worked as maids for

Harlan Davis's wife, Alice, and for other white women, or as hired hands for fieldwork. No one had ever been arrested for Rody Martin's murder, though everyone knew the killer was a mysterious man who was known only as Pegleg.

Hack Winter was not in the field. Earlier, he had hitched the mules to the wagon and had driven away to the cotton gin with a wagonful of cotton.

"Keep picking," Hack had said to Troy. "See if we can't get another bale done by tomorrow morning."

"Yes sir," Troy had replied. "We'll keep at it."

Tom hated it when Troy was left with the responsibility for work. Troy was too bossy. His father could get irritated, but his father never raged. Tom rolled in the cotton and made a pillow for his head. He imagined his father at the cotton gin, waiting his turn for the great vacuum to suck the cotton out of the wagon and spit it into the machinery that stripped the lint from the seed. His father would be drinking a Coca-Cola, cold as ice, from the ice-packed drink box. He would be drinking his Coca-Cola and listening to the stories of the men who waited in line for the ginning.

Tom had begged to go to the gin. "Me 'n' Son Jesus," he had whined. "We won't ask for nothing." But his father had said, as he almost always did, "Not this time." His father knew that Tom and Son Jesus would leap from the wagon at the gin and begin pleading immediately for money for a drink from the drink box at the store. "Them two," he had complained, "aggravate me to death. It's like trying to hold hornets in your hand."

"You dead," Son Jesus exclaimed suddenly. He flicked a finger and knocked over one of the maypops.

Tom turned to look at him. "Who's dead?" he asked.

"The Jap," Son Jesus said. He balled his small, dark fist and slammed it into the maypop, crushing it. A *pfffft*, a sigh of maypop life, escaped from the green, egg-shaped bulb.

"That wadn't the Jap," Tom said. "That was General MacArthur."

Son Jesus picked up the squashed maypop and held it delicately by one of the stick arms. He examined it carefully.

"No, it ain't, Thomas," he argued. "It's the Jap."

Tom stretched his leg and pointed at another maypop with the toe of his foot. "That's the Jap."

"Don't look like no Jap to me," Son Jesus whined.

"Does to me."

"Don't to me."

"Son Jesus, you couldn't tell a Jap from General MacArthur if they hit you on the head and told you who they was. I found them maypops. I guess I know which one's a Jap and which one ain't."

Son Jesus put the maypop down gently. A worried expression clouded his face. He looked toward the pickers, then back to the maypop. He pulled the sticks from the pulp of the bulb and pushed them back in, rearranging them.

"He ain't dead," Son Jesus mumbled. "Just hurt some."

"Shoot, that don't matter," Tom said authoritatively. "General MacArthur's been shot lots of times. It don't mean nothing to him. They was a story in the *Grit* newspaper about it. I read it."

Son Jesus smiled relief.

"Yeah, me too," he said. "I read that story too."

"Son Jesus, you ain't got no newspaper," argued Tom.

Son Jesus frowned in thought. "Read it up at your house, Thomas. Out on the back porch."

Tom nodded. "He's got them Japs running."

"Got them running," echoed Son Jesus.

"I'm gon' join the army," said Tom, after a pause.

"Me too," said Son Jesus.

From across the field, Troy called out, "Tom, you and Sonny go get us some water."

Son Jesus stood, but Tom did not move.

"Tom! You hear me?" Troy bellowed.

Tom stood slowly. "I ain't gon' go get no water," he said quietly.

"You get a whipping, you don't," Son Jesus warned.

"Well, they gon' have to catch me first," Tom vowed.

"Where you going?"

"I'm gon' run away from home."

"Why you gon' do that?"

"I'm gon' join the army. I'm gon' fight the Japs."

"When you gon' do that?" Son Jesus asked.

"Right now."

Son Jesus stared at the face of his friend. Tom was gazing at the road, his eyes blazing with anticipation.

"Right now?" Son Jesus asked timidly.

"Right now."

"Uh, 'bye," Son Jesus whispered.

" 'Bye," Tom replied. He stepped off the sheet of cotton and began striding toward the road. Then he began to run.

Son Jesus watched him for a long moment before he turned and started across the field toward his mother.

Reba saw him approaching. She straightened from the stooped-over position of the picker and arched her back to relieve the ache.

"What you doing?" she asked sharply. "You supposed to be helping Thomas get the water."

"He done run away," Son Jesus answered.

"He done what?"

"He done run away," Son Jesus said again.

"Where he run to?" Reba asked, her voice rising to the shrill it always reached when she became excited.

"Down the road," Son Jesus said. He added, "He gon' join the Army, gon' fight the Japs."

Reba's hands flew to her face. She turned toward Troy, who was far ahead of her in the field. "Mr. Troy! Thomas done run away," she screamed.

Troy stopped his picking. He looked at Elly.

"What'd she said?" he asked.

"She said Tom run away," Elly replied in a worried voice. She slipped the cotton sack from her shoulders.

"Ah, shit," Troy muttered. He ducked his head through the band of his own sack and dropped it to the ground. "Com'on, let's go get him." He waved to Miriam. "Y'all keep on working. We'll be back soon as we find him."

Reba was wringing her hands. "They's snakes out there," she wailed. "That little boy get lost, he's gon' get snakebit."

Troy crossed to Reba and Son Jesus, followed by Elly. "He gets snakebit, it'll kill the snake," he said bitterly. Then, to Son Jesus: "Which way did he go, Sonny?"

Son Jesus pointed toward the road. "Down yonder," he answered. "Said he was gon' join the army."

"We ought to let him," Troy grumbled. "Maybe they could get him to do some work."

"Mr. Troy, you go find that baby," commanded Reba. "He get down in that swamp, ain't nobody never find him."

"We'll find him, Reba," Troy said. "If Daddy comes back, tell him where we are."

He started a slow jog across the field, with Elly beside him.

"Y'all run," shouted Reba.

"I'm gon' whip his little butt," Troy mumbled.

"No, you ain't," Elly snapped. "He's just mad because Daddy wouldn't take him to the gin."

"That ain't got nothing to do with it," Troy argued. "He didn't get his way, that's all."

At the road, they stopped and looked in both directions.

"I see him," Troy said.

"Where?" asked Elly.

"Down about the turnoff to the Elder house. The little shit."

Elly started running. She cried, "Tom, Tom, come back here."

In the distance, she saw Tom sprinting faster, his arms churning in the air.

Troy was in a race with Elly. He called, "Tom! Tom! You better stop."

In their own field, picking their own cotton, Ollie Elder and his wife, Brenda, and their three children stood watching Tom and Troy and Elly.

"Little scooter's fast, ain't he?" Ollie drawled.

"Wonder what he's done now?" Brenda said from the sunbonnet that covered her face. She was five months pregnant and her faded dress stretched tight against her abdomen.

"Ain't no telling," Ollie replied. He shrugged the cotton sack off his shoulders. "But we better try and get him before he gets down to the creek. Ain't no telling where he'll head off to if he gets down in them woods." He wagged his head. "Com'on," he said to his children. "Brenda, you keep on picking."

"Ho, Tom!" Carl Elder shouted. "You better put your little butt in gear, 'cause I'm gon' catch you." Carl was fourteen, but he had the look of a man.

Tom glanced over his shoulder. He saw the Elder family dashing across the field, knocking cotton from the bolls with their legs. Behind him, he could hear Troy and Elly calling for him to stop.

I'm the Gingerbread Man, Tom thought. *Run, run, as fast as you can. You can't catch me, I'm the Gingerbread Man.*

He rounded the curve leading to the downslope going to the bridge of Sweetwater Creek. His legs were working like pistons and his heart was pounding with the gladness of the game. He saw the bridge below him and remembered in a flash the day that he fell into the creek while fishing with Troy. Troy had jumped in after him and pulled him out of the gurgling water. He remembered Troy's trembling body, and the angry flood of tears, and the tongue-lashing: "Damn it, Tom, you could of been drowned and I'd of had to think about that all my life, you little shit." He remembered also how Troy had held him to his chest, stroking his back with a powerful, loving hand.

He listened to the echo of his feet on the wood planking of the bridge, then he was across the bridge and headed up the hill toward Charlie Goodlove's farm. He could still hear the voices behind him.

"Tom, stop!"

"You can't outrun us, Tom!"

"You better stop it, Tom! And I mean right now!"

Tom was at the edge of Charlie Goodlove's cornfield. He jumped from the road and scrambled up the gully and dove into the field. The heavy blades of the corn slapped at his chest and shoulders, and the dust from the stalks flew up into his eyes. He could hear the voices and the footsteps getting closer.

Suddenly, he collapsed, breathing hard. In a moment, he was scooped from the ground by Troy.

"What you think you're doing?" Troy demanded.

Tom did not answer. He ducked his head pitifully.

"You gon' get your little butt whipped," Troy declared. "And this time, if Mama don't do it, I'm going to."

"Shut up, Troy," Elly hissed. She pulled Tom from Troy's arms and held him. "What's the matter, honey?"

Still, Tom did not answer.

"What you running away from home for, Tom?" asked Carl Elder.

Tom lifted his face to Carl, and he knew immediately and instinctively that one of the joys of being a runaway was the joy of being pitied. From Elly's shoulder, he whispered, "They won't let me have nothing to eat."

Ollie Elder's face turned to a frown. He glared at Troy.

Troy's mouth opened in disbelief. He snapped, "That's a lie, Tom, and you know it. Why you want to tell a lie like that? You eat like a pig. You gon' get your little butt whipped for telling lies like that. You wait and see."

"Ask me, the boy does look a little poorly," Ollie said. He motioned with his head to his children. "Com'on. We got work to do."

Elly stood holding Tom for a moment, waiting for the Elder family to reach the road, then she said, "Tom, you can't go saying things like that in front of people. They'll be talking about us all over the place before sundown."

"He's gon' get his little butt whipped, and I guarantee it," Troy predicted.

● ● ●

Troy was not wrong.

Tom was punished, a mild paddling from his father when he returned from the cotton gin.

But it was a punishment delivered over the objection of his mother, who had scooped him into her arms and soothed him with whispers and with her own tears over the imagined pain of losing him in Sweetwater Creek.

And then he was fed from a hot marble cake that Reba had left the field to bake for him.

All of it amazed Son Jesus, who shared the cake with Tom. "When you gon' run away again, Thomas?" he asked.

"Before long, I reckon," Tom answered seriously.

"Next time, tell your mama you hungry for some ice cream," urged Son Jesus. "I like ice cream better'n marble cake."

That night, in bed with the windows open, he heard his mother and father on the front porch, arguing about him.

"You should of tore his little tail up the minute he got home," his father groused. "Can't have that kind of behaving. You let him get away with it, he'll be doing it every other day."

"I couldn't do it," his mother sighed. "It's not his fault."

"Whose fault is it, then?" his father demanded.

"More'n likely, it's from your uncle."

"Who?"

"That sorry Doyle Winter," his mother said.

"What's he got to do with it?"

"He was a runaway, wadn't he?" his mother said with disgust.

"Good Goda'mighty, Ada, nobody's seen or heard from Uncle Doyle in twenty years or more," his father protested.

"That's because he run away from home one time too many."

"Ada, what in God's name are you talking about, anyhow?"

"I've read about it, mister. Yes, I have," his mother answered stiffly. "It's in the blood, running away is. It's something that's passed on."

"Well, unless I been blind drunk or asleep for a few years, it seems to me that boy's my son, not Uncle Doyle's."

"Don't matter. It's in the blood. It skips over generations, then shows up," his mother said.

Tom heard his father snort in astonishment. "Well, damn. I guess that's it. I must be as dumb as a knot on a log not to see it. Lord knows, we don't want to give out a spanking for something that's running around in my blood."

"Well, nobody in my family's ever run away," his mother proclaimed.

"What if he turns out to be a drinker?" his father said. "We gon' say it was Spencer's fault? He's your brother and he ain't been sober since Hitler was a paperhanger, and unless I miss my guess, I'd say brother-and-sister blood was thicker than uncle-and-nephew blood."

There was a pause. Tom knew his mother was trapped, but he knew also that she would have a final word. He heard the scraping of a chair on the floor of the porch, and in his mind's eye he could see her standing defiantly, glaring down at his father, her hands planted firmly on her hips.

"It's not Spencer's fault," she said in an angry whisper. "You know all that got started after he got kicked by that mule."

His father laughed once—a short, sarcastic laugh of pity.

TWO

Ada Winter's forgiving Tom for running away was a mistake.

After that September day in 1944, with his mother attempting to understand his moods and to be patient with the sickness he surely had inherited from Doyle Winter, running away became a compulsion for Tom, a kind of innocent adventure to be played with his family, who yodeled his name in the woods, and with the yard dogs, which romped gladly in search of him. The dogs and Tom loved the game. After each runaway, and each finding, he was dutifully spanked by his father and anxiously embraced by his mother. Tom was troubled, she insisted. It was a sickness. He had wanderlust blood, tainted blood, corrupt blood, blood low in the iron will to keep his feet planted in one place.

"He ain't got nothing but gall," his father argued. He added, irritably, "And his mama's apron to hide behind."

But it did not matter what Hack Winter said, or how often and how firmly he said it; he could not break through the stubborn shield of his wife, or of his daughters, Elly and Miriam, or, finally, of Reba, who believed adamantly that part of God's plan for Tom and Son Jesus involved her vigilant mothering of both. Hack Winter had a son the size of his leg, who was more protected than Winston Churchill had been in an underground bunker in London.

"I got to give it to him," Hack confided one day to Troy when they were looking for Tom in the woods behind Ollie Elder's farm. "He's a smart little cuss. Ain't but eight, and he knows how to play all the angles. Probably wind up in politics."

"He's got everybody in Crossover talking about him," Troy complained. "It's like he was a midget in a circus playing the fool."

"Like I said, he'll probably wind up in politics," Hack replied.

● ● ●

Over the next three years, it became part of the legend, and the humor, of Crossover that Tom Winter was on the run, and on bright Saturdays when the men of Crossover gathered at Dodd's General Store and Cotton Gin to tell their men-stories about the war they had fought in strange places with strange names and to cuss freely and to make reasons for laughing after so many years of fear, there was always someone willing to reward Tom's adventures with prizes of candy or soft drinks.

"Hey, Tom, where you been lately? Heard tell they caught up with you over in Goldmine last week. Somebody was saying you was going over to South Carolina to join up with the railroad."

"Ain't what I heard tell. I heard tell you was caught going over toward Pleasant Grove. That where it was, Tom? Shoot, boy, you gon' make it to the highway one of these days."

"Next time you take off, Tom, how about taking my old lady along? She keeps griping she don't never go nowhere. Stays on my back because I went off to the war. Says I wadn't doing nothing but sightseeing. You take her next time you light out. See if you can lose her somewheres along the way."

To the men of Dodd's General Store, Tom was an amusement but also an emissary to possibilities that baffled them. After the killings of the war and the somberness of believing the world might blow apart from so many explosions, Tom provided for them gossip and the giddiness of childhood dreams. They loved the stories that he took from books and translated with eager exaggerations—stories of giants and midgets, of flying horses and magic swords.

The only person at Dodd's General Store who worried about Tom was Arthur Dodd. Arthur claimed that he knew Tom's problem: "Boy reads too damn much. That's it, plain and simple. Never saw nothing like it. He was reading real words when he was three. Great God'amighty, they's some things a boy ought not be doing. Reading too much is one of them. Sets your mind to wandering, and pretty soon you gon' find out the feet ain't far behind. I know. My ex-wife, Hilda, was that way. Always reading them moving picture magazines, primping in front of the mirror like she was Betty Grable, or somebody. Well, by God, she up and left, didn't she? Took the Greyhound out to Hollywood, California, and, far as I know, took to humping every Tom, Dick, and Harry she could. Don't tell me about reading. I seen what it can do to a person, and that little scooter must read three or four books a week from the town library. Enough to blind a man, and that's what's wrong with him. Sure as God. Ain't nothing else. I was talking to Ada after they found him that time down in the Sweetwater Creek bottomlands, pretending to be Robinson Crusoe. He was down there writing notes on Blue Horse tablet paper and stuffing them in bottles and plugging them up with cork fishing floats and then throwing them in the creek. I feel sorry for his mama. She was telling me he believes everything he reads, and he reads everything he can get his hands on, except the Bible. Says she can't get him to read a word of it. It's like the Devil's got ahold of him. I guaran-damn-tee you all that reading's bound to get that boy in trouble."

But to the men who gathered at Dodd's General Store on bright Saturdays, Tom's running away was not a matter of being troubled or under the devil's thumb, or even of too much reading. To them, Tom was merely spirited, and they liked him.

"Damned if he ain't a mess. Little scooter's got rabbit in him. Ollie Elder says he ain't never seen nothing like it, way he gets gone."

"More like fox, you ask me."

"Troy was telling me them dogs they got know exactly where he is, every time. Said the last time he took off and headed over to that old hay barn over on the Grill place, them dogs was waiting on him when he got there. Them dogs take on over that boy like he was one of their pups, or something. It ain't nothing but a game to them."

"What was he supposed to be this time? Some Indian? Damned if that boy can't tell some tales."

"I liked it that time he got on that old mule and took his mama's butcher knife and told Ollie's boy, Carl, he was gon' have to go get his head cut off by the Green Knight. Said he was one of them Knights of the Round Table."

"His mama come close to having a fit that time."

"I heard tell his daddy wears his little butt out every time, but his mama takes on over him like he ain't never coming back one day."

"She says it's from his daddy's side, anyhow. I never heard tell they was nobody crazy in that Winter clan, but if anybody knows, Ada would. I reckon she's got the history on everybody that ever took breath on both sides of her family. Maybe they was somebody in Hack's family that don't nobody never talk about."

"You ask me, that's where the boy gets his spunk from—his mama. That woman's heard Eleanor Roosevelt speak one time too many."

Sometimes the men half believed Tom.

The story of the old man in the swamp they half believed.

Tom was ten when he told the story.

He had met an old man wandering around the swamp like he was lost, Tom said, and the old man had told him about a gold mine nobody knew about—one the Indians had dug. The Indians had pulled gold from the ground like plowed-up sweet potatoes and they had fashioned the gold into Indian things—arrow and spear heads, bracelets, war shields, bowls, cups. And then some white men from Spain had traveled through and they had learned of the gold and had tried to get the Indians to tell them where they'd hid it. But the Indians wouldn't say a word and the white men had killed them. Still, there was a map, and the old man had a copy of it that he had shown Tom.

"What'd that map look like, Tom?" Keeler Gaines had asked, half joking, half curious.

And Tom had knelt in the dirt under the oak outside Dodd's General Store and he had scratched out a map that looked amazingly map-like, with the bends and curves of Sweetwater Creek and the woods and fields of the farms that were beside the creek. When he finished the drawing, Tom crossed an X in a spot near Tanner's Bridge, and Keeler had exclaimed in disbelief, "Well, I be damned. That's right near where them two old gold mines was being worked before the Civil War."

"Right along there is what that old man said," Tom had assured them.

"Wonder who that old man was?" someone had mused.

"Could of been old man Pete Logan," someone else had suggested. "Lives off in that old run-down shack over on the ridge. I used to hear tell he was always digging around them old gold mines, looking for gold."

"I ain't seen that old man in years."

"Me neither. I thought his kids had moved him away to Athens, or somewhere."

"Hell, he's been crazy for fifty years."

"Tell you what, Tom, why don't me 'n' you go up there and take a look around?" Keeler had suggested. "Shoot, maybe we'll find us some gold."

And the men at Dodd's General Store had laughed robustly and made a joke of it, and then they had all crowded into Keeler's truck and Keeler had driven them to Tanner's Bridge and they had spent their

Saturday afternoon wandering up and down the banks of Sweetwater Creek, poking around with sticks to find an ancient Indian cave filled with gold.

To Tom, it had been as good an adventure as running away from home. He did not tell Keeler or any of the men about the story he had read of the Inca king Atahualpa and of the legend of the lost gold of the Incas. None of them would have understood it.

The men laughed and wagged their heads in pleasure over Tom.

"That's boy's a mess."

"Got to watch him. Got to watch him every minute. Little scooter's liable to take off anytime you got your back turned."

And it was true. Tom did have to be watched.

In the beginning, running away was a game to be played, a way to enjoy the rewards of being pitied. Even Tom did not know that Arthur Dodd was right: he ran away only after he had finished reading a book, with the sights and sounds of the adventure of that book still blazing in his mind. To Tom, it was a whim, a carnival mood that rode the back of a carnival breeze, one that crooked its finger in Tom's face and whispered teasingly, "Come on, Tom, let's be off." And Tom would leap up from a closed book and follow the whim, and hours later, off somewhere, he would hear the yodeling calls and he would sit down and wait for the happy, barking dogs to find him.

But for Tom, there was little artistry in a whim, and the older he became, the more he became intrigued with artistry. Artistry required preparation and resolve. Artistry required a plan. In June of 1949, the summer of his twelfth year, Tom created a plan, schemed it patiently and in detail, watched it performed again and again in the silver tube of vision that is seen only with closed eyes. His plan needed a river, a boat, and Son Jesus. The river and the boat would be easy, but Tom knew he would have to be persuasive to convince Son Jesus. Still, he did have an advantage: Son Jesus was with him constantly, a result of Ada Winter's efforts to rid her son of the demons that called him to the woods in a finger snap.

"Maybe he won't be running away if Sonny's with him," Ada had proposed to her husband after the Robinson Crusoe episode on Sweetwater Creek. "Seems like Sonny's the only one that can keep his mind from wandering off. Besides, we can use more help in the fields, and I don't want to see Sonny working for Harlan Davis. That man's as sorry as they come. Works Reba and the girls like slaves. One of these days, I'm going to find Reba another place to live, get her off Harlan's place."

"Now, Ada, you can't go stirring up trouble just because you don't like somebody," Hack had cautioned. "I don't think he'd take too kindly to us using Sonny."

"Well, I don't give a flip what Harlan Davis thinks," Ada had snapped. "That boy needs to be someplace where he's cared for, and that means with us, and that's all there is to it."

Hack knew when it was useless to argue with his wife. "They ain't gon' do nothing but sit on their butts and throw dirt clods at one another," he had predicted in resignation. Hack Winter was a wise man.

•   •   •

It was on Friday, June 17, that Tom told Son Jesus of his plan. They had been hoeing grass from a flourishing field of cotton, near a stand of pine trees. The pines offered shade from the heat, and Tom and Son Jesus had slipped into them on the pretense of having to pee.

"Run away?" Son Jesus said, worried. "I ain't running away, Thomas."

"Son Jesus, you gon' run away if I run away," Tom said emphatically. "Ain't we always done things together?"

"I ain't never run away, Thomas. You the one's always running away. I ain't never."

"You ain't never been around when I got ready to go," Tom said. It was a stretch of the truth, but Son Jesus did not argue.

"No sir. My mama whip my tail, I do that," Son Jesus protested. "Just like you always getting a whipping," he added.

"She ain't gon' whip you if you run away," Tom countered. "How's she gon' do that, when you ain't around?"

"She gon' catch me, like they always catching you."

"They ain't gon' catch me this time," Tom said. "I got me a plan."

Son Jesus edged close to Tom. He picked up a cluster of fallen pine needles and began to roll them between his fingers. He looked through the trees to the cotton field. He had never heard Tom speak of a plan, not even when they badgered Tom's mother for special favors. "What plan you got, Thomas?" he asked in a whisper.

Tom smiled. He knew Son Jesus was curious. "We gon' take old man Ben Carlen's flatbottom fishing boat and float off down the river," he said.

"Where we going to?"

"I don't know, Son Jesus," Tom answered irritably. "Wherever the river winds up, I reckon. Maybe down to Florida. Maybe out in the Gulf of Mexico. I ain't never been, so I don't know where we going."

"What we gon' do when we get down there where you ain't never been, Thomas?"

"Whatever we get a notion to. Why you asking all them questions, Son Jesus?"

Son Jesus shook his head in despair. "I don't know," he mumbled.

"You going, or ain't you?" Tom demanded.

Son Jesus shrugged weakly.

"What's that mean?" Tom said.

Troy called from the cotton field: "Tom, what y'all doing?"

"We coming," Tom yelled. "Son Jesus had to do number two."

Son Jesus rolled his head in embarrassment. "What'd you go say that for?"

"Takes longer to do," Tom told him.

"What'd you say it was me for?"

"If it was me, he'd come down here to see if I was making it up. What you gon' do, Son Jesus?"

Son Jesus was puzzled. "About what? I ain't even got to pee."

"About running away with me."

"I guess so," Son Jesus said softly. "I just ain't never run away from home."

"Ain't hard," Tom announced. "I done it a hundred times."

"They done found you a hundred times too," Son Jesus said.

"Son Jesus, you don't know nothing, do you?" Tom replied in exasperation. "I was just practicing all them times. Now it's for real."

Troy yelled again, and Tom and Son Jesus moved reluctantly, at a funereal pace, back to the field.

"I ain't never gon' hoe no cotton no more," Tom said. He picked up his hoe and leaned against it.

"What you gon' do, Thomas?"

"I was thinking maybe I'd be a robber," Tom answered. "Rob from the rich and give it over to the poor."

"Like Robin Hood?" asked Son Jesus.

"Yeah, like Robin Hood. You like that story, don't you?"

Son Jesus nodded his head eagerly. He looked up, to see Troy standing on a terrace, glaring down at them. Son Jesus lifted his hoe and sliced lazily at a head of grass growing at the base of a stalk of cotton. He missed the grass and cut the stalk off at the ground. He knelt and picked up the stalk and poked it back into the ground and then he pinched dirt around it to make it stand.

"I don't know, Thomas," Son Jesus mumbled. "They was always after Robin Hood, shooting arrows at him. Ain't nothing wrong with hoeing cotton. Ain't hard work. Somebody gon' kill you, you go around robbing people like Robin Hood."

"Ain't nobody gon' kill me, Son Jesus."

Son Jesus' voice was soft, lonely: "They killed my daddy, Thomas."

"But he wadn't robbing nobody, Son Jesus."

"Pegleg done it," Son Jesus replied somberly. "Took my daddy off, where nobody couldn't find him." He struck monotonously at the ground and the grass with his hoe.

"Com'on, Son Jesus," Tom pleaded, "I ain't gon' wait all day. I been reading about it. Ain't nothing to it. You coming or you not? That's all I want to hear."

Son Jesus wagged his head in thought. "I don't know," he mumbled. "I ain't never done nothing like that." He paused and corrected himself. "I ain't never done nothing."

"There you go again," Tom complained. "You ain't never done nothing. Well, you the only person I know that got named by God, and what about that time two or three weeks ago over at the store? You beat everybody saying the multiplication table. Me, the Darby twins, Keeler Gaines, Mr. Dodd—everybody. They was saying they never saw anything like it."

"That ain't nothing," Son Jesus said.

"You ask me, it was," Tom argued. "If you smart enough to rattle off eleven times twelve without ever thinking about it, you smart enough to know what I'm saying. What's eight times nine?"

"Seventy-two," Son Jesus answered quickly.

Tom's eyes narrowed, checking the answer in his mind. It sounded right. He stared at Son Jesus. "You going?" he asked.

The smile that was always on Son Jesus' face, even when he was worried or afraid or sad or angry, deepened. "I reckon so," he replied. "But I ain't gon' rob nobody."

"You don't have to," Tom told him. "Anybody does any robbing, it'll be me." He looked across the field to Troy, saw that Troy was busy working, then he buried the blade of his hoe into the gray earth and leaned against it. He said, in a whisper, "We gon' leave in the morning. You put some clothes in a feed sack. Maybe get some sweet potatoes and whatever else you can find to eat. And some fishhooks and sinkers and fishing line."

"Mama's got some soda crackers," Son Jesus said.

"Get them. I like soda crackers."

"I got that Boy Scout canteen you gave me on my birthday," Son Jesus added.

"We can always use a Boy Scout canteen," Tom assured him. "I got that army mess kit and I been putting away some lard in tobacco tins I been picking up at the store. We'll have us some grease to cook with. And I put some wax on some kitchen matches to keep them dry. You got a knife?"

"Ain't sharp," Son Jesus answered.

"Don't make no difference. Bring it."

Son Jesus stopped his hoeing. The smile faded slightly from his face. He looked at Tom seriously. "What's Mr. Carlen gon' do when he finds out we took his flatbottom boat?"

"Make him another one," Tom said. "It ain't much of a boat, like it is."

Son Jesus shifted on his feet. He dug his toes into the soil and stared at the ground. Finally, he asked, "What about them suckholes in that river?"

"Ain't no suckholes in that river," Tom replied arrogantly. "You believe anything anybody tells you, don't you, Son Jesus?"

Son Jesus shook his head in disagreement. "My mama says they's suckholes in that river big enough to swallow up a cow."

"That don't mean nothing," Tom snorted. "My mama says the same thing. They just don't want us playing out on that river, that's all."

"Uncle Jule, he says they's suckholes out there, Thomas."

Jule Martin was Son Jesus' uncle, the older brother of Rody Martin. He stayed in a run-down sharecropper house on land belonging to Merle Whitfield, who lived in Athens and had a loose agreement with Jule to watch over his herd of beef cattle in exchange for the house. It was the perfect job for Jule. The cattle did not bother him and he did not bother the cattle. Jule's house was a lazy-walk mile from Reba's house, and he was often there, pretending that he was needed, when, in fact, he showed up mostly at mealtime. Son Jesus and Tom liked Uncle Jule more than any other adult they knew.

"Uncle Jule ever been down that river, Son Jesus?" asked Tom.

Son Jesus shrugged away the question. He lifted his hoe, slapped the blade into the ground, lifted it, slapped it.

"Son Jesus, I ain't gon' say it no more. You ain't coming with me, you say so. I'll go find me somebody else to go."

"No, you ain't," Son Jesus said quickly. "I'm gon' go."

"All right," Tom replied. "But we got to do it right. What we gon' do is camp out tonight and take off early in the morning, before anybody starts looking for us."

"I don't know, Thomas," Son Jesus mumbled. "My mama says I'm gon' have to quit doing all that camping out with you. She says we getting too old to be doing all that camping out all the time."

Tom was astonished by what Son Jesus said. "That don't make the first bit of sense," he argued. "We been camping out since we was—what? Since we was eight years old, I guess."

Son Jesus inhaled slowly, deeply, like someone accepting a tragedy. "I don't know, Thomas. My mama just say I'm gon' have to start cutting it out."

"Tell her you'll start it some other time. Tell her we camping out tonight to do some fishing. Tell her we gon' catch a string of catfish just for her."

Son Jesus rubbed his hands over the handle of the hoe. His smile flickered in his face. "I guess it'll be all right," he said softly. "Mama likes catfish."

"Know what, Son Jesus?"

"What, Thomas?"

"I got to do number two."

Son Jesus cackled.

From across the field, Troy heard the laugh and turned. He shook his head in despair.

"What's the matter?" asked Miriam.

"I just wish Mama would keep them at the house," Troy answered. "They ain't hoed ten feet in an hour, and I guarantee you they ain't a stalk of cotton left standing anywhere they been."

THREE

Troy had tried to join the army in 1947, the day after his eighteenth birthday, but he had been rejected because he had flat feet, and he had returned to the farm. At nineteen, he lived in the same bedroom he had occupied since the age of five. He helped his father and he farmed forty-five acres of his own land that he had purchased from Charlie Goodlove. He also owned one of the few tractors and combines in Crossover, and he often hired out to plow land or harvest wheat and oats. He had a reputation as a hard worker and a good businessman. Arthur Dodd swore that Troy was the only man he knew who could squeeze piss out of a buffalo nickel.

More than anything, Troy had pride. Because he was the first child and the oldest son, he had been taught to believe he had special responsibilities, and nothing meant as much to him as living up to those real, and imagined, expectations. During the war years, with the cry of patriotism as fervent as an altar-calling hymn at a revival, Troy and others like him—the workers of the farms—were as dedicated to victory as generals in war rooms. It took a man to stand and fight a far-off enemy in the furrow of a corn row, and to everyone who knew him, Troy had been a man since he was thirteen.

Though he never complained about it, Troy's lost childhood affected him greatly, and there were times when it seemed that he wanted to stop being a man and start over. He played pasture baseball with boys who were years younger than he, or he went with Tom on Saturday afternoons to see cowboy movies and action serials that featured the Phantom, or Batman and Robin, or Flash Gordon. It was as though the instinct of the child would emerge in Troy and he would make claim on the years that he had sacrificed to the fields. Once, he even joked with Tom that he wished he, too, could run away and see things no one else could see.

It was during one of those periods in his life, after he had been rejected by the army, that Troy constructed the campsite Tom and Son Jesus used when camping. As a boy, Troy had wanted to be a Boy Scout, but there were no Boy Scout troops in the community and he had settled for reading the Scout manual and dreaming. One of the merit badges called for camping forty nights, and that is what Troy did. The badge meant nothing to Troy; earning it mattered.

The campsite was on a high bank beside a small, nameless branch that ran into Sweetwater Creek. It was in a cluster of oak and pine trees that provided a soft flooring of leaves and needles. Troy had constructed a lean-to of black gum slabs he had picked up from Jed Carnes' sawmill. He had nailed the slabs together and covered them with tar paper to keep the wind out. The lean-to was large enough and deep enough to sleep three people. In front of the lean-to, there was a stacked circle of rocks for a cook fire, and Troy had taught Tom and Son Jesus how to keep the fire from spreading to the needles and the woods. "Pour sand on it if it gets outside the rocks," he had instructed. A bucket of sand was kept nearby.

Tom and Son Jesus did not sleep in the lean-to if the weather was clear. Once, they had found a scorpion scurrying across one of the walls, and they knew, with Tom's embellishment, that a scorpion bite would make their bodies shrivel up like helpless old people's before it killed them. After that, they slept outside, under the stars, crammed into one bedroll.

It was a favorite game to lie on the piled pine needles, in their bedroll, and trace faces from the stars and clouds and tree limbs above them. Tom, inspired by the books he had read and by the stories he had heard on radio, saw images of heroic men of adventure. Son Jesus saw men of the Old Testament—Abraham and Moses and Daniel and Samson—that his mother talked about incessantly.

"Where you see Samson in that, Son Jesus?"

"Right yonder, Thomas. Got that long hair hanging down his neck. Where he got all his muscles from."

"That ain't Samson, Son Jesus. You don't know nothing. That's Tarzan."

"Look like Samson to me."

"Where does it say in the Bible that Samson had an alligator snapping at his feet?"

"What alligator, Thomas?"

"Right there at his feet. Plain as day. Got his mouth open. See them stars? Them's his teeth." He moved his pointing finger to another ball of leaves. "And what does that look like? Some kinda angel? That's Tarzan's monkey. That's Cheetah."

"Uh-huh . . ."

Tom loved the nights camping with Son Jesus. It gave him a chance to invent facts about the world around them—wars never fought, heroes who never existed, ghosts who had never fluttered up from their earthly graves—and to listen to Son Jesus' mumbled replies. Son Jesus did not believe any of the stories, but he suffered them politely because he liked hearing them. Hearing them lulled him to sleep.

On those nights, watching Son Jesus sleep under the lemon light of the moon and stars, Tom marveled at the one thing he knew about Son Jesus that no one else seemed to recognize: the tint of Son Jesus' skin changed color. He was not black—not just black. He was bronze and chocolate, red as sun tea, rich as honey. He was the color of the light that was on him. And at night, outside, the tint of color on Son Jesus, asleep under the moon and stars, was lemon.

●　●　●

During his years of running away, Tom had mastered the art of manipulating his mother. It would begin with the pretense of restlessness, of pacing the floor, of staring out the window, of opening and closing books, of emitting long, sorrowful sighs. And then he would stop talking and fix his gaze on something—a chair, the ceiling, anything—and his mother would begin to creep around him, her forehead furrowed in worry. His behavior was a sure sign of his urge to run away, she believed. She had read of it in books, had researched evidence of it in the unnatural behavior of her ancestors and her husband's ancestors—especially her husband's people—and she had talked at length to Dr. Jake Arlington about it. Dr. Arlington had agreed that Tom's moods could be a prelude to his actions. He called it psychological behavior. "It's like using a thermometer to take his temperature," he explained. "If he acts the same way every time, then that should be a serious indication that something is happening, perhaps some chemical reaction that's not easy to define by existing medical technology. My advice is to give him some room, trust him, let him feel that he already has the freedom he thinks he wants."

"Like what?" Ada had asked.

"Well, you tell me he enjoys camping with his little friend," the doctor had answered. "Permit it. Encourage it. It means they're outside, in the woods where Tom always seems to go. Think of it as taking the place of running away."

Tom did not know about Jake Arlington's advice; he only knew that whenever he played his game with his mother, she suggested that he should go camping with Son Jesus.

And that was how he got the blessing to camp with Son Jesus on the June Friday of his master plan to run away.

"Mama, them boys didn't do nothing today but kill good cotton," Troy protested. "I looked at what they was doing. They cut down more cotton than they left standing. Tried to stick it back in the ground, like it was gon' take root and grow. Ain't nothing left but some withered stalks. You can almost expect it out of Tom. He ain't big enough to pick up the hoe hardly, but Sonny's almost a man. You let them camp out tonight, and Tom won't be worth a plugged nickel tomorrow. He'll say he stayed awake because he was scared, or he slept wrong on his neck and he's got a headache."

His mother made signals of distress with her face. Troy was right about the difference in size. Tom and Sonny looked like Mutt and Jeff in the comic strips, and she knew that it was Tom who did the lagging in the field. Sonny merely stayed with him, as he had always done. She said, "I'm sure they'll be up and out in the field by the time you get there, Troy." She smiled at Tom. "Won't you, son?"

"We'll be there at sunup, Mama, ready to hoc," promised Tom.

"Daddy, you gon' let him get away with this?" asked Troy.

"Son, that's between him and his mama," his father answered wearily. Over the years, Hack had learned to treat his wife's stress over Tom with caution, though it often tested his patience—and he was a patient, forgiving man.

"Don't be so mean, Troy," Elly said.

"Yeah, Troy," echoed Tom.

Troy glared at him, then stormed out of the room.

"Now, honey, you made a promise," his mother said. "You know you have to keep it."

"Yes, m'am."

• • •

Tom was squatting before the cook fire, cooking hot dogs on a stick, when Son Jesus arrived at the campsite at sundown, carrying a feed sack and a bedroll over his shoulder. His smile was like a banner. "I'm gon' run away," he said proudly.

"What you got in that sack?" asked Tom.

"Everything I could put my hands on when they wadn't nobody looking," Son Jesus said. "Got us some sardines."

"What you got sardines for, Son Jesus? We gon' be living off catfish."

Son Jesus shrugged. "They was there," he said in a small voice.

"Well, that's all right," Tom told him. "Can't never tell. We might not catch nothing." He pulled the hot dogs away from the fire and examined them, then he said, "I tied my sack up there on a limb. Keep the rats and possums out of it. You better do the same." He held up the stick speared with hot dogs. "I got us some hot dogs cooking."

Son Jesus laughed and winked at Tom. "I could smell them a mile away."

• • •

Ada sat in the rocking chair on the front porch and felt the breeze of the night slithering over her face. She was holding her genealogy tablet, adding the offspring of a long-forgotten great-aunt named Nellie Barton, who had married a sailor and moved to Seattle, Washington, never again to return to the South. The letter she had received from the granddaughter of Nellie Barton had contained a photograph of Nellie. The photograph was startling. Nellie Barton could have been Ada's twin. The only difference was the sparkle in Nellie's eyes. Little bright stars. Eyes that had seen much of the world and had found it spectacular.

Ada leaned wearily against the chair back. She was forty years old, but she felt ancient. Four children and a lifetime of farmwork, of failed crops, of days too hot to bear and days so cold the chill ached in her bones, of thousands of meals cooked on the heated steel of a woodstove and tons of dirt-encrusted clothes boiled clean in an iron pot before the coming of the electricity. But even the stove and the washing machine that the electricity operated had made little difference. The work was never-ending, and too little money from it. It was not the life she had wanted for herself or her children. She had wanted to live in a town, in a nice house with neighbors so close the families would have to be separated by a fence. She had wanted to wear cool dresses and work in a store that had the smell of perfumes and body powders. She had wanted to see her children playing on lawns of soft grass, riding bicycles on concrete sidewalks. She had wanted to hear the hope of laughter, filling the air like flowers growing in a garden. She had wanted to see the world as Nellie Barton had seen the world.

She smiled and closed her eyes. The wishes always relaxed her, always made her mind swim back to snapshots of moments with Hack and with her children. The moments were sweet, good. The moments made her dreamy wishes vanish. God knows, she had a good husband in Hack. So honest, he made other men uncomfortable. Made them look away. Made them mumble. Took a straight line dealing with everybody. White or colored, it didn't matter. If he had been a talker—as she was—he would have been called a troublemaker, a rabble-rouser. He would have been accused of trying to play God. But he was not a talker. He was a listener, patient and attentive, who had a way of making other people see things his way, and his way was always as simple as the Golden Rule. Be fair. That was Hack's way. Be fair. Little wonder that other men deferred to him, elected him to office in school and church. Hardworking, he was, and tolerant of her temper and her thinking, and of her dragging him cemetery to cemetery, searching for something that always seemed lost to her. Loved her too. She knew he loved her. Could see it in his face, feel it in his touch, even if the touch appeared to be accidental. Sometimes he was clumsy that way. Trying to show what he felt but could not express.

She thought of Troy, who had chosen the life of the farm, and of Miriam, who was at nursing school, and of Elly, who was a senior in high school and would go to college in a few months, and of Tom, who was bright and cheerful. She had watched them working in the fields, sun-browned, lost in their own dreams. Her children. Her good and beautiful children.

Tom.

Ada sniffed. She felt a chill and hugged the genealogy tablet to her body. Tom, her baby. Tom, who suffered from the bad blood of his great-uncle, a sorry man no one had seen in twenty-five years. No one knew how much she ached for her baby son.

"What you doing out here?"

It was Hack.

"Just sitting," Ada said.

Hack sat in the rocker beside her. "Cooler out here," he said.

"A little."

"Ada..."

"What?"

"We got to talk about Tom."

She turned to look at him. Her eyes narrowed. It was the look he dreaded.

"What about Tom?"

"We just can't let him get by with all he's getting by with," Hack said.

"What's he getting by with?"

Hack stared at her incredulously. "Everything," he said. "He ain't worth nothing working in the field."

"Don't talk that way, Hack Winter."

"Well, he ain't."

"He's just a baby."

"Troy and Miriam and Elly did five times as much work as he does at the same age," Hack argued.

Ada fought against the tears that bubbled in her eyes. She whispered, "Nothing's wrong with their blood."

"Please, Ada, don't start that," Hack said. "I love the boy too, but he ain't doing nothing but pulling a fast one on you, having a high old time. Only thing wrong with Tom is he's too smart for his own good, and if you want to talk blood, that ain't from my side of the family. He's more like your daddy than you are."

"Don't you talk about my daddy," Ada snapped.

Hack rocked forward, then back. He wedged his feet to the floor and stopped the chair and looked at his wife. "Good Lord, Ada, what I just said was a compliment. Your daddy was the smartest man I ever met."

Ada turned her face from him. He was right about her father, she thought. Her father had been the principal of Crossover Junior High School and the most respected man in the community. Sometimes she believed it was because of her father that her husband tried so hard to be a leader. There had been more than five hundred people at her father's funeral. And Tom did remind her of her father. His eyes, his love of reading, his easy, childish storytelling, his energy.

"You think they're all right?" Ada asked.

"Who?"

"Tom and Sonny."

"They're fine," Hack said. "And that's another thing we've got to get a handle on—him and Sonny."

Ada inhaled slowly. She looked toward the pasture and the cover of trees where Tom and Son Jesus were camping. After a long moment, she said, "I know."

FOUR

Tom saw Bluebeard the pirate in a bundling of oak limbs that stirred softly in the night breeze. Two stars that glittered through the leaves were Bluebeard's eyes. Son Jesus said the face looked more like King David to him.

"There you go again, Son Jesus," Tom said. "I swear, you must be blind."

And then Tom began a story about Bluebeard's raid on Crossover more than two hundred years earlier, when there were many Indians living there. It was another version of the story of Atahualpa that Keeler Gaines had half believed. The Indians, Tom said to Son Jesus, were gold miners and they had a roomful of gold that Bluebeard wanted, but the Indians had hidden the gold in a cave and Bluebeard killed them all before he could find out where the cave was located.

"Uh-huh," Son Jesus mumbled sleepily.

"Ain't nobody ever found that cave," Tom said. "It's still around here somewhere."

"Uh-huh."

"If we wadn't running away, I'd look for it," Tom added.

"Uh-huh."

"Bluebeard finally gave up," Tom said. "He had his ship anchored down on Sweetwater Creek, and he got in it and sailed off back to the ocean."

Son Jesus did not reply.

"You reckon Uncle Jule knows where that cave is?" Tom asked.

"Don't know," Son Jesus answered. He giggled. "We ask him, he gon' be thinking on it."

"He knows about babies, I bet he knows about that cave," Tom said.

They both laughed. They knew Jule well.

Jule believed that every task to be done, every problem to be solved, could easily be accomplished if a person would only take the time to consider the possibilities.

"The trouble with peoples is they in a hurry," he had preached to Son Jesus and Tom. "Like y'all boys. Y'all don't know nothing about thinking a thing out. No sir, y'all don't know nothing at all. Take that old creek down yonder. How y'all gon' cross over it when y'all got to? Gon' wade it? Gon' swim it? Or y'all gon' take y'all's time and go alongside the bank to y'all comes to a tree that's fell over it? No sir. What y'all's gon' do is the first thing that comes in y'all's heads. Y'all gon' jump right in, that's what. Gon' jump right in and not give a hoot about how deep that water is, or where they's a copperhead up under a root, or where they's a suckhole and y'all can't see it. Boys like y'all don't take no time to think nothing out. That's y'all's trouble."

Because Jule pondered more than he worked, there were many in Crossover who believed that he was lazy. Son Jesus and Tom thought he was a remarkably wise man.

He had taught them about where babies came from, about sex.

"They don't come from no bird with no long legs, like everybody lets on," he had explained one day while fishing with Son Jesus and Tom.

"Now, all y'all got to do is think on it, boys. What y'all reckon them dogs is doing when they get all hung up out yonder in the yard? What y'all think that old bull's doing when he rises hisself up on that old cow out in the pasture? Y'all put some thinking on it, boys. What they doing is making babies."

Son Jesus and Tom were startled when they heard the news.

"They making baby dogs and baby cows," Jule had elaborated. "That's how babies like y'all is made. A man gets hisself up on top a woman and puts his thing in her thing and they both like what's going on, and that's how it's done, boys. Y'all stop and think on it."

"What about chickens?" Tom had asked.

It was a question that had baffled Jule. "Well, now, boys, I ain't rightly figured chickens out," he had confessed. "They got all them feathers. Can't see nothing. But I'll think on it some more. Maybe it'll come to me."

Tom pulled up in the sleeping roll and cupped his hands behind his head. "Yeah," he said, "I bet Uncle Jule knows where that cave is."

"Uh-huh," Son Jesus muttered.

"You going to sleep, Son Jesus?"

"Uh-huh."

"Yeah, I'd go looking for that gold," Tom said. "If I wadn't running away, that's what I'd do."

*   *   *

They awoke before sunrise, in the washed-pale color of dawn, and they packed their bedrolls in the feed sacks and ate a biscuit and poured water over the weak coals of the fire.

"You ready?" Tom asked.

Son Jesus nodded hesitantly.

"Com'on, let's push in the side of the lean-to."

"What for?" asked Son Jesus.

"I told you, I got a plan. We got to make it look like somebody's took us off," Tom said. "That way, won't nobody think about looking on the river for a while. They'll be looking in gullies and culverts and caves and old houses for where we been killed and hid away."

Son Jesus sighed. He said, "Thomas, I ain't wanting nobody to go looking for me in no gully."

"They ain't gon' look long," Tom assured him. "It'll keep them busy a little while, that's all."

"Gon' scare my mama, Thomas," Son Jesus whispered.

"We gon' write her a letter soon as we get down to the end of the river," Tom promised. "We gon' tell her we all right. Same with my mama."

"They gon' put your mama in the hospital, Thomas. She gon' be scared to death."

Tom thought of his own mother crying hysterically. "She'll be all right," he said to assure Son Jesus. "Maybe we'll stop before we get to the end of the river and mail them a letter."

"I'd like that, Thomas."

"Well, com'on, we got to get this done right," Tom said.

They pushed with their shoulders against the wall of the lean-to, and one of the corners fell forward.

"We done tore it up," Son Jesus said with regret.

"It ain't bad," Tom judged. "Troy can fix it up in no time. Now lie down on the ground."

Son Jesus looked at him suspiciously. "What for?" he asked.

"I got to drag you across the pine needles, up the edge of the woods."

"Why you gon' do that, Thomas?"

"What you supposed to do, Son Jesus," Tom said irritably. "Got to make it look like somebody's drug us off."

Son Jesus began to back away.

"Com'on, Son Jesus, we ain't got all day. We got to be going."

Son Jesus looked at the lean-to.

"I mean it, Son Jesus. You got to lie down and let me drag you by the feet up to the edge of the woods. That's the way it's done."

Son Jesus shook his head and sat down on the ground and lifted his feet. Tom caught him by his heels and pulled him over the needles up to the trees, leaving a ripple like the racking of a brush broom.

"Thomas, they's rocks," Son Jesus complained.

"They ain't gon' hurt long," Tom assured him. "Hurry up. We got to make another drag."

"What for?"

"How many of us you see, Son Jesus? Two, that's how many. You got to have two draggings."

"I done been drug. You lie down and I'll drag you," Son Jesus protested. "You ain't as big as me. They's got to be a difference in the dragging."

Tom glared at him. "Son Jesus, who thought about this? It was me, that's who. I do the dragging. If you'd of thought about it, you'd be doing the dragging and I'd be the one that was drug. Fair's fair."

Son Jesus surrendered. He closed his eyes and grumbled as Tom pulled him again over the needles and rocks to the edge of the woods.

"That looks good," Tom declared proudly, inspecting the furrows. "Looks like somebody come up on us and took us off. Looks like something a escaped convict would be doing."

"My mama's gon' be scared, Thomas."

●   ●   ●

Tom and Son Jesus knew the trail through the woods and Sweet-water Swamp by memory, like animals on prowl at night. It was two miles to the east fork of Sweetwater Creek, but they reached it quickly and crossed it on the trunk of an oak that had fallen over the water during the washout of summer flooding. They climbed the steep, slick hill of Pilgrim's Ridge behind the Carnes place and then followed an old logging road, cushioned with layers of pine needles, until they reached the opening to one of Jed Carnes' abandoned sawmill camps.

Son Jesus stepped closer to Tom and pulled nervously at Tom's shirt. He bobbed his head toward the camp. "Look at them, Thomas," he whispered.

"Look at what?"

"Them—them sawdust piles," Son Jesus muttered. "They's—they's like graves."

Son Jesus was right. In the woods, in the dull wash of morning, the heaps of sawdust piles were like mounds in a forgotten cemetery. Tom could feel a shudder fly through Son Jesus and into him, and from him into the ground.

"Ain't nothing but sawdust piles," Tom said in a trembling voice that pretended bravery. "I swear, Son Jesus, you beat all, you know that? You keep seeing things, they gon' think you crazy."

"We—we ever been here, Thomas?"

"I ain't," Tom said. "I heard some of the men over at the store telling about this being a shortcut to the river."

"Something bad about this place, Thomas. Something bad."

"Well, com'on, let's get out of here," Tom said.

Son Jesus did not move. He was staring at one of the mounds.

"Com'on," Tom said again.

"What—what's that, Thomas?" Son Jesus muttered. He pointed to the mound.

"I don't know," Tom answered. He stepped forward. He saw something white, like a twig, sticking from the sawdust. He knelt and brushed away the sawdust and pulled it out.

"What's that?" Son Jesus asked.

"A bone," Tom said.

"Uh-huh," Son Jesus whispered.

Tom laughed. "Shoot, Son Jesus, it ain't nothing but a bone from a bear, or maybe a cow." He stood and examined the bone. "It's good luck finding a bone. We run into any ghosts, we just wave that bone around and they gon' take off running."

"Who you hear that from, Thomas?"

"I read about it," Tom said. "Ghosts just don't like bones of no kind. Makes them think of when they was alive." He made a cross in the sawdust pile with the bone.

"How come you do that?" Son Jesus asked.

"It's a good luck mark," Tom explained seriously. "You get a piece of good luck, you got to mark the spot you got it or it don't work. Now com'on. We got to get to the river."

They passed through the sawmill camp and slipped under a fence into Ben Carlen's pasture. Ten minutes later, they were at Scrubgrass River and the wet-water inlet below a steel-and-wood bridge where Ben Carlen kept his boat tied to the exposed root of a black gum tree. The gray light of morning slithered down the wax face of leaves on laurel and scrub brush growing at the riverbank. Tom and Son Jesus could hear the flutter of bird wings in high limbs. A fish rolled against a log. Downriver, in the trough of a rock shoal, the water gurgled softly. Tom knew that his father, or Troy, would soon be at the campsite and the wrecked lean-to, ready to wake him and Son Jesus. It was too late to turn back. His plan to run away forever had begun.

"Let's go," Tom said.

"Thomas, that old boat don't look like much," Son Jesus said in a whine.

"Son Jesus, I ain't waiting. You get in that boat," Tom said angrily.

"Thomas, I'm scared."

"You don't get in now, they gon' think you killed me, Son Jesus. They gon' hunt you down."

Son Jesus stepped quickly into the boat and sat on the plank bracing that was nailed side to side. He held tight to the feed sack in his lap.

"Hold on," Tom said. He threw his sack into the boat and untied the tie-line and jumped in beside Son Jesus. The boat begin drifting slowly over the slick skin of the water.

"We going," Son Jesus whispered like a prayer. He turned his head to look back at the riverbank and the dark ripples of water trailing the boat.

"Shut up, Son Jesus," Tom commanded. "You get you a paddle and start to paddling. We got to get down below Reed's Bridge before they start looking on the river."

"We ain't never coming back," Son Jesus moaned sorrowfully. "We gon' wash right out in the ocean, Thomas. We gon' be swallowed up by a whale, just like Jonah."

"We ain't going nowhere, you don't start paddling some, Son Jesus," Tom said.

●   ●   ●

Troy stood at the kitchen window, looking out toward the pasture. He held a cup of coffee in his hands. The dome of the sun was cuddled to the base of the trees like the coals of a simmering fire. "I'm telling you, Mama," he said. "Them's the two laziest boys in north Georgia. At least Tom is. Sonny might be all right without Tom around."

"Now, Troy, you need to remember what it was like to be that young," his mother said.

"I never was, Mama," Troy replied quietly.

"Well, just go on down there and tell them they made a promise and I expect them to keep it."

Troy swallowed the last of his coffee and put the cup on the table. "You got to quit spoiling him, Mama," he warned. "He won't be worth shooting when he's a man if you don't."

Ada sighed heavily. She turned the water on at the sink and began to rinse the breakfast dishes. She was tired of arguing with Hack and Troy about Tom.

"I'll go get them, Mama," Elly said.

"I'll do it," Troy countered. "Daddy wanted to put an edge on the hoes," he said to Elly. "You better get them for him." He walked out of the kitchen, letting the door slap hard behind him.

Ada watched from the kitchen window as her older son crossed the yard toward the pasture. He walked with a heavy step, his powerful, wide shoulders bobbing in the plodding rhythm of a field-worker who had followed the plow. He resembled his father, Ada thought. Strong body, a determined, serious face. But there was a difference. Troy's eyes flashed moods that sometimes promised anger and sometimes offered tenderness. The anger often spilled from him in bitter, resentful words; the tenderness was swallowed, turned away. Her husband was seldom angry. He almost never raised his voice in complaint. To Hack, there was too much good about life for one to let the bad interfere with living it. A smile was better than the spewing of threats. It was the thing she loved about him—his sensibility, his belief in goodness. He had courted her with it, had persuaded her to marry him with the soft light of his smile. Sometimes his even nature irritated her. Sometimes she wished she did not win all their arguments.

"Are you going to town today, Mama?" asked Elly.

"I guess. This afternoon," Ada answered. "I've got to pick up some things at the grocery store. You want to go with me?"

"I want to see if they've got some new shoes in at Belk's," Elly said. "Mary Beasley said they were expecting some."

"All right," Ada replied. She thought of Mary Beasley. She and Mary had been girls together in Crossover. Mary had always wanted to live on a farm, but instead she lived in the town, working in Belk's department store, where there was an aroma of perfume and body powder, swirled in the air by the ceiling fan.

"Will you tell Troy when he comes back?" Elly said. "He'll want me to be in the field all day."

"I'll tell him. Now you better get the hoes for your daddy."

"Okay," Elly said. She glanced out the window and saw Troy running toward the house from the pasture. "Mama," she whispered.

Ada knew instantly that something was wrong. She turned off the faucet at the sink and dried her hands on a dish towel. She could feel her heart beating furiously. She heard Troy calling, "Daddy! Daddy!" She moved from the window at the sink to the window beside the breakfast table. Elly stood with her, touching her on the arm. Ada saw Hack come out of the barn, saw Troy run up to him and begin to talk excitedly. Troy's hands were describing something terrible. She saw her husband nod seriously and start for the house in long strides, with Troy beside him.

"Oh, God..." Elly sighed.

Ada did not speak. She stepped away from the window and waited beside the door. The pounding of her heart thundered in her ears.

The door opened, and Hack and Troy stepped inside.

"Ada, Elly," Hack said, "sit down."

Ada and Elly moved to chairs and sat, their eyes fixed on Hack's face, their eyes watching for the words they knew they would hear.

"Looks like something's happened to the boys," Hack said seriously. "They ain't there—"

"The lean-to's been pushed in," Troy sputtered, interrupting his father. "And it looks like something's been drug across the ground."

A gasp, a cry, flew from Ada's throat. She covered her mouth with her hands.

Hack motioned with his head to the living room. He said to Troy, "Go call the sheriff, and then start calling around to the neighbors. Tell them to come on down here. Bring their guns."

Elly began to sob. "Tom, Tom, Tom . . ."

"Get hold of yourself, Elly," Hack ordered. "We got to start looking."

He turned and walked briskly through the house and took his shotgun from its rack in his bedroom. He opened a drawer and caught a handful of shells and slipped them into his pocket, then he returned to the kitchen.

"Ada, you stay here," he instructed. "Wait for the sheriff. Show him where the campsite is. Blow the car horn a couple of times when he gets here." He turned to Elly. "Honey, you go get Reba and stop by Jule's house and tell him what happened."

He did not wait for an answer. He pushed open the kitchen door and stepped outside and started running toward the pasture.

FIVE

The sun was a glare in the canopy of river fog as Tom and Son Jesus passed quietly under Reed's Bridge, and by midmorning they were far downriver, floating in the current like driftwood. They were relaxed.

"You ready to do some fishing?" Tom asked.

"Been ready," Son Jesus replied. "What we gon' use for bait?"

"Grasshoppers," Tom said.

They paddled the boat into the mouth of a small branch and pulled it up on a sandbar and tied it to the limb of a drooping cottonwood, and then they went into an open field of grass and caught grasshoppers and bundled them into a handkerchief. A half hour later, they were back on the river, fishing from the boat. It was a warm, lazy morning, a fish-biting morning, and in only a few minutes they had caught more than a dozen catfish and Son Jesus complained there was no more room for them on the stringer Tom had rigged from a loop of binder twine wrapped around his bedroll.

"We got so many, they dragging the boat sideways," he said.

"We might as well quit," Tom told him. "We got more'n we gon' eat, anyhow."

"Not more'n I'm gon' eat," Son Jesus argued. "We can let out some more binder twine." He dropped his hook back into the water.

"I been thinking, Son Jesus," Tom said languidly.

"What you thinking about, Thomas?"

"We done gone so far ain't nobody gon' know us down around here," Tom said, "but there's bound to be some stories about two boys who been stole, or run away—one white and one colored."

Son Jesus nodded. He watched his cork float gently on the surface of the water.

"I was thinking, maybe we ought to change our names," Tom said.

"Uh-huh," mumbled Son Jesus. He added, "I got me a bite, Thomas."

"Looks like it's dragging bottom to me," Tom said. "You hear what I was talking about, Son Jesus?"

"What was you saying, Thomas?"

"How we ought to be changing our names."

"What we gon' call us, Thomas?"

"I was thinking I'd call you Jim and you could call me Huck."

"I like Huck better'n Jim, Thomas."

"Won't work that way, Son Jesus. You got to be Jim and I got to be Huck."

Son Jesus lifted his pole and examined the bait on his hook. The speared grasshopper dripped with water. "Where'd you get them names, Thomas?"

"Book I been reading," Tom said. "About this boy named Huckleberry Finn, but they call him Huck. Didn't I tell you about that?"

"Don't know," Son Jesus answered lazily. "Don't remember it."

"Huck and Jim run away too," Tom said.

"Uh-huh. They get found out, Thomas?"

Tom shifted in the boat, remembering the story. "They did," he said after a moment, "but that don't mean nothing. That was a book. This is real life."

The answer seemed to satisfy Son Jesus. He dropped his hook with the grasshopper back into the water. "Don't care what you call me, Thomas," he said. "Jim's all right with me."

"Then that's what I'm gon' do," Tom told him. "I'm gon' call you Jim and you can call me Huck. Them's our new names."

Son Jesus smiled. He reached his hand over the side of the boat and dipped it into the river and scooped a palmful of water and splashed it over his face. He said, "Getting hot, ain't it, Huck?"

"Sure is, Jim. Hot as all get-out."

"Maybe we ought to go swimming, Huck."

"Let's wait to we bank the boat, Jim."

"Yeah, Huck, I reckon you right."

They laughed.

"Tell me about that book," Son Jesus said.

They floated and talked and Tom told the story of Huckleberry

Finn—how Huck had been taken away by his father and locked up and how he had escaped and was thought dead, and of Jim appearing on the island where Huck was hiding.

"They was after Jim because they thought he was the one that'd done the killing," Tom explained.

"Jim?" Son Jesus said. "Jim didn't kill nobody."

"Well, I know that, but they didn't," Tom said impatiently. "They was after him and they was gon' put him in jail."

Son Jesus looked suspiciously toward the riverbank. He slipped down into the boat.

"It didn't matter, though," Tom continued. "They got them a raft and took off down the river, just like we doing."

He told Son Jesus of the adventures that Huck and Jim had on the Mississippi. Son Jesus especially liked the story about the King and the Duke. He thought he would have enjoyed knowing them.

"They wadn't much," Tom said.

"Sounds like they was always acting up," Son Jesus replied. "I bet they was something."

Of all the people in the story that Tom told him, Son Jesus liked Tom Sawyer the least.

"Like his name," Son Jesus said. "Like Tom. Same name you used to have, Huck, but I don't like him."

"Why not?" Tom asked.

"What you was saying about the way he done Jim," Son Jesus said. "Putting them rats and snakes and spiders in that room with Jim. Sure wouldn't like that. Not this Jim."

"It was just a book," Tom assured Son Jesus, "but you right about it. Huck was better'n Tom. Wadn't as mean."

"They ain't gon' be no Tom Sawyer on this trip, is there, Huck?"

"Ain't nobody but me'n you, Jim."

"Ain't gon' be no rats and snakes and spiders?"

"We might see a snake in the river," Tom said.

"He ain't gon' get in the boat, is he?"

"He does, we getting out," Tom promised. He stretched his head and shoulders across his bedroll and propped his feet over the plank that was in the middle of the boat, serving as a brace and a seat, and then he dangled his hand over in the water. At the opposite end of the boat, Son Jesus mimicked him.

• • •

Within an hour of Troy's discovery of the caved-in lean-to and the evidence of bodies being dragged away, there was a gathering of men at the campsite on the branch—somber-faced, huddled in groups, building stories and courage in whispered guesses that passed among them like fraternal secrets.

Were there any signs of blood?

"Ain't nobody said, and that means they must of been some."

Anybody remember hearing any sounds of shooting down this way last night?

"Could of been. I heard some dogs barking and not like they was chasing something, but like they was scared."

They ever catch that convict that escaped over near Athens last week?

"Come to think of it, they ain't. Not the last time I heard."

You reckon it's just Tom running off from home again?

"Not with that little colored boy with him. No way Sonny'd go along with running away. His mama'd blister his little butt."

You think maybe somebody got pissed off over a white and colored camping out together?

"Could be. Them boys getting too old for that kind of stuff."

What if it was Pegleg?

"Ain't nobody found him yet. He killed Rody, maybe he was after Rody's boy too."

Anybody tell Reba what happened?

"She's up there with Mrs. Winter. I come up just as she got there. Half the colored people around here is up there. They all standing around under the pecan trees with that old colored preacher, Doodlebug Witcher."

The men whispered among themselves and smoked their cigarettes and waited for Frank Rucker, the sheriff of Overton County, to begin the search.

"Well, Frank, what we standing around here for?" said Keeler Gaines irritably. "Let's go do it." Keeler loved Tom's stories. He added, "If anybody's hurt that boy—him or Sonny, either one—I'm gon' knock his dick up in his watch pocket."

Frank Rucker was thirty-eight years old, tall, powerfully built in the lean, muscled way of athletes. He had fought in the Second World War in Europe and had returned to Overton County as its most decorated hero, had been celebrated with a parade and then, in the after-parade enthusiasm, he had been given a deputy's job over his own misgivings. He had been appointed sheriff after the death—an unresolved murder— of Logan Doolittle, who had been sheriff of Overton County for more than fifteen years. There were many days when Frank wished to be back in the army, off somewhere new, someplace he had never been, listening to the voices of people he had never met.

"Keeler, that's what we're about to do," Frank said patiently. He knew Keeler well, respected him. Keeler was ten years younger than Frank but looked as old, or older. He had also returned from the war, from the Pacific, with ribbons dangling from his chest.

Frank kicked the ground hard with the heel of his boot, like an animal declaring its territory. It was unfamiliar ground. Overton County was not large, but each community was like a small nation, with its own pride and personality, its own walled-in boundaries. Frank had been reared in the Oakland community, which was at the opposite end of the county from Crossover, and though he knew many of the people from Crossover—knew them and knew their stories—he did not know its fields and woods and streams. Crossover was, in many ways, the most unusual community in the county. The Pegleg killings had all occurred there, and yet it was considered a friendly, progressive place to live— discounting a few absolute assholes. But there were absolute assholes everywhere, Frank thought. He looked at the men gathered around him, waiting for him to issue orders, their worried faces peering at him anxiously. None of the absolute assholes that he knew from Crossover were there, but he had not expected to see them. You could not be an absolute asshole and care what happened to other people. But the men who were there cared. Frank could see the caring in the brave-skittish shine of their eyes, and he could hear it in their mutterings. The men liked Tom Winter, liked his outrageous stories, and they liked Sonny Martin—*Son Jesus* Martin. He privately believed the disappearance of Tom and Son Jesus was nothing more than another of Tom's runaways, but there was the nagging question of a maniac on the loose, someone like Pegleg. Pegleg—whoever he was—was still free.

Frank motioned with his head to Hack and Troy. "Mr. Winter and his boy, Troy, have been to most of the places they think the boys could of gone off to, but they're nowhere to be found. So that means we got to cover every square foot around here." He reached for a stack of papers that one of his deputies held. "Fletcher's been making up some maps. This way we won't be walking all over one another."

Fletcher Wells was Frank's first cousin. "I used to do some surveying," he said proudly. "I learned map drawing from that."

Frank glared at Fletcher and Fletcher ducked his head. Frank began to hand out the sheets of paper with the crudely drawn maps. "Here, y'all split up and take one of these."

The only black man in the crowd was Jule. He reached for one of the maps. "We'll take this one," he said.

"Who's going with you, Jule?" asked Frank.

"They's some men up to the house," Jule said. He added, "They's *two* boys missing here."

"You got any guns?" Frank asked quietly.

"We got some," Jule told him.

"If it was somebody that took them boys, he could be close to going off the deep end," Frank warned. "He thinks he's being pushed, he's liable to do anything."

Jule did not reply. He turned and began walking away, clutching the map.

"You find them, fire off two rounds," Frank called.

"Them niggers ain't gon' find nothing," a retired deputy named Arlo Lewis mumbled.

Troy whirled on Arlo. His face flushed with anger. "They got a right to look, damn it."

"Son," Hack said in soft caution.

Arlo stepped back and smiled nervously.

"They got a right," Frank said.

• • •

Reba sat at the kitchen table in the Winter house, with Remona and Cicely sitting on each side, their hands touching her. Ada and Elly sat across the table. Three neighbor women moved silently around the kitchen, making coffee, nervously washing dishes that had already been washed. Reba railed in loud declarations, in a lamentation that was not of sorrow but of anger. God would strike the heart of the man who had taken her boys away, she wailed, and if God overlooked the punishment, she would attend to it. She would not spill tears, Reba declared; she would spill blood.

And Reba's mood was a signal to the other blacks who had gathered at the Winter house and who waited anxiously under the pecan trees with Dooley Witcher, listening for the occasional outbursts of Reba from the kitchen. They had assembled in trembling, in tears, praying mournful prayers, begging God, but they had seen Reba, had heard her voice of temper, and they, too, had become angry and restless. Only Dooley Witcher seemed willing to turn everything over to God. "Lord, you done mighty works," he intoned. "You done took the children of Israel out of Egypt and you done delivered Jonah from the belly of the whale and you done took Daniel out of the den of lions and you done rose up Jesus from the tomb. Now, Lord, we ask you to bring back them boys to us, safe as the day they was borned!"

●　●　●

And as Dooley Witcher made his eager prayers, Tom and Son Jesus floated and talked of cooking fish over a campfire in Tom's mess kit, using the lard Tom had stuffed into tobacco tins when no one was looking, and of how to hide the boat at night and what they would do if it rained. Tom cautioned Son Jesus to watch for a raft drifting on the river. "We find a raft, we'll get on it and tie the boat behind it and we'll have us a floating house," Tom said confidently.

Tom called Son Jesus *"Jim"* and Son Jesus called Tom *"Huck."*

"You know what I get to thinking about sometimes, Jim?"

"What's that, Huck?"

"I get to thinking about when me 'n' you used to play Brer Rabbit and Brer Bear."

Son Jesus mumbled, "Uh-huh." His smile shimmered in the reflection of the water. "I liked that," he said. "We ain't done that in a long time, Huck."

"No, we ain't, Jim. But I been reading some of them stories about Uncle Remus. I sure like them stories."

"Don't think I never read about none of them stories, Huck," Son Jesus said slowly, thoughtfully. "Me 'n' my mama and Cicely and Remona went over to Athens to see the picture show. Uncle Jule took us."

"Picture show?" Tom said.

"One about Uncle Remus," Son Jesus replied. "Thought I told you about that, Huck."

"I forgot, Jim," Tom said, and he had forgotten.

"What you been thinking about them stories, Huck?"

"I just like reading them. I like Brer Rabbit and Brer Bear. But every time I read one, I get to thinking about you, Jim."

"What for, Huck?"

Tom baited his hook with a grasshopper and dropped it into the water and watched the grasshopper flutter out of sight below the boat. "Well," he said deliberately, "I keep thinking about how you talk, Jim."

"What you mean, how I talk, Huck?"

"I keep thinking you don't talk colored, Jim," Tom said.

Son Jesus looked at Tom indignantly. He said, "I talk colored good as anybody else does."

"No, you don't, Jim. You talk just like me."

"Ain't so."

"Is."

"Ain't."

"You ought to sound more like Jim does in *Huckleberry Finn*," Tom said. "Or like they do in them Uncle Remus stories."

Son Jesus stared at the water for a moment, then lifted his head to face Tom. He squinted his eyes, and a frown of bewilderment crossed his forehead. He asked, "What they sound like, Huck?"

"I don't know," Tom mumbled. "They sound—they sound, well, colored. They say 'I's.' You don't say 'I's.'"

"Eyes?" Son Jesus said. "What you talking about, Huck? Eyes you see with?"

"No, Jim. *I's. I's.* I is. I is in a boat. *I's. I's* in a boat."

Son Jesus nodded knowingly. "Say it if I want to," he declared.

"You say you gon' do something, just like me," Tom continued. "Colored people say 'gwine.'"

"Gwine? What's gwine?" Son Jesus asked in exasperation.

"It's colored talk, Jim," Tom explained. "You ought to be saying, 'I's gwine go fishing.' You don't. You say, 'I'm gon' go fishing,' just like me."

"I ain't never heard 'gwine,'" Son Jesus offered.

"Well, that's what you supposed to say. It's a African word, where you come from," Tom said.

Son Jesus shook his head seriously. He tilted his face up and stared studiously into the trees drooping over the river. He let his hand trail in the water. Finally, he opened his mouth and thrust his jaw forward and stretched his lips painfully over his teeth, and he whispered, "I's. I's gwine. I's gwine." He looked at Tom and the smile billowed over his face. "Shoot, Huck, I can say that. Ain't nothing to it. What else they say?"

"Lots of things, Jim," Tom told him. "We'll work on it some tonight."

"I's gwine do it," Son Jesus said in proud exaggeration.

SIX

By noon, the vigil for Tom and Son Jesus at the home of Hack and Ada Winter had begun to resemble a political gathering. Whites and blacks not in the search parties—older men, women, children—waited anxiously under the shade of pecan trees, mingling awkwardly, gazing like fretful birds toward the pasture. They were whisper quiet, uncomfortable, afraid.

When they did speak, they spoke of ominous possibilities. Was it Pegleg? Could a bear have wandered from far away in the mountains and found them and devoured them? Were there moonshiners around, planning to set up another still?

Inside, Ada and Reba sat listlessly at the kitchen table and waited.

"They all right," Reba said again and again. "It's God's plan. My babies, they all right."

To Ada, it was always strange hearing Reba speak of Tom and Son Jesus as her babies, but it was an old expression and one spoken always with love and with the assurance that God's plan was at work, and, dear Jesus, if anyone had the need to believe in divine power, it was Reba— her husband beaten to death and then carried off by a man with a hood over his face, never to be seen again, while Reba and Son Jesus and Remona and Cecily watched in terror. But that was only the beginning of it. After Rody's death, Reba and Remona had had to give more time in housework to Harlan Davis's bickering, spoiled wife, Alice. Many people in Crossover considered Reba a lunatic because she had claimed a vision in the naming of Son Jesus and because Son Jesus—and, to a lesser degree, Tom—had been anointed by Conjure Woman, but they also respected her. She was diligent and honest, and if anybody needed help—white or black—she was there with her children, announcing, "Want to do what little bit we can. Neighbors got to help neighbors."

Ada had tried to sense how it would be to live with Reba's burdens, or her faith. Perhaps it was like a seesaw, she had thought. Burdens on one end of the plank, faith on the other end. When burdens tilted the plank down, the faith rose; when faith became heavy with neglect, the burdens rose. It would have to be something like that. She wondered if she could take losing Hack the way Reba had lost Rody. Never having a body to bury. Never being able to prove the murder, though everyone knew Rody had been murdered and the murderer was the man known as Pegleg.

She remembered being at Reba's house on the day after the attack, waiting with Reba while Sheriff Logan Doolittle went through the motions of finding some piece of evidence to identify Pegleg, something stronger than Reba's loud, angry insistence that Logan was protecting someone. "Got to have more'n seeing a man with his face covered up and him walking with a limp," Logan had said cynically. "Hell, they ain't even a body. How I know he didn't just up and leave? You got to have something to go on." But there had been nothing. On that day, Ada had held Son Jesus and he had buried his small head against her chest—not moving, not crying—and on that day she, too, had felt something special in his presence. It was as though he understood something none of the rest of them knew—that his father's death was part of the destiny of the plan God had in store for him.

"Want some more coffee, Reba?" Ada asked.

Reba shook her head. She was staring out the kitchen window. "They all right," she said again.

A chill struck Ada. Reba's voice was like a whisper that echoed inside her.

Elly came into the kitchen. "Mama, Miriam just called," she said softly. "I told her about Tom being gone. She's on the way home."

Miriam had been away for less than a year, studying nursing in Augusta. Her absence was both pain and pride for Ada.

"Oh, honey, we'll find them before she can get here. You better call her back and tell her to stay there. Tell her I'll call her as soon as we know something."

"Yes m'am," Elly said. Then: "Why don't you eat something."

"I'm not hungry, honey."

"Reba?" asked Elly.

Reba waved her hand. "No, baby, Reba don't want nothing to eat."

"What about everybody outside?" asked Ada.

"Some of them went over to the store and brought back sandwich stuff, and we got what people been bringing in," Elly answered. "Everybody's all right."

"There's gon' be some people coming in from the woods pretty soon," Ada said. "They'll be hungry."

"Mrs. Carnes is taking care of that," Elly explained.

"Oh, Lord," Ada sighed. "I hope she's not being too bossy." Evelyn Carnes lived two miles away by the road, a mile by a straight line through the woods north of the swamp. She was the widow of Jed Carnes and a good, caring woman, even if her late husband had been as evil as Satan himself.

"No m'am," Elly said. "She's just making some sandwiches."

"Oh, I know it," Ada said, annoyed with herself. "She's as good as they come, but sometimes she gets a little flighty, that's all. But I don't guess she can help it. After all she's put up with in her life, she deserves going overboard once in a while, and Lord only knows, it's time she quit pretending to grieve over that sorry husband of hers."

•   •   •

Tom and Son Jesus ate lunch from the food in their feed sacks—biscuits and baked sweet potatoes—and then they banked the boat on a sandbar and swam naked in the pool of water that curled in a cup above the sandbar.

"Let's make us a campout here, Huck," Son Jesus suggested as they sat in the sun, drying. "We must of been here two hours, anyhow."

Tom peered at the sun through the trees. "Too early to stop now, Jim," he judged. "I been seeing some corn in the bottomland. Means people around somewhere. We better go on down the river a while longer."

"Uh-huh," Son Jesus agreed. Then: "Some corn sure would taste good with them fish, Huck."

"Maybe we'll stop by a field and pull us two or three ears, if they full enough," Tom said.

"Can't do that, Huck. That'd be stealing. They gon' throw us in jail for stealing."

"That ain't stealing, Jim."

"Why ain't it, Huck?"

"Don't nobody call it stealing when boys do it. It's like watermelons.

Boys just plain expected to get in a watermelon patch if somebody's got one around."

"My mama says the sheriff come get me if I get caught doing some stealing," Son Jesus said firmly.

"What my mama says too, Jim. That's the way mamas talk."

"My mama says the Lord looking down on what's going on. Says he don't never sleep. Says he's keeping one eye aimed on me—why he named me Son Jesus, before you named me Jim. My mama says it don't do no good to lie or nothing like that. Says the Lord knows it, anyhow."

Son Jesus sounded somber and frightened. He crossed his arms tight over his chest. In the sun, under the haze of the trees, his body was the color of dark clay.

"Well, Jim, I done some reading about the Lord," Tom said confidently. "Now, one thing the Lord liked was babies, and we ain't much more'n that. Time or two in the Bible, he told the grown-ups to leave him alone and let him play with the babies that was hanging around. What the Lord didn't like was grown-ups doing what they was doing. Grown-ups supposed to know better. We ain't, Jim, and that's a fact. The Lord ain't gon' get mad at us for doing what boys supposed to do."

"I guess you right, Huck," Son Jesus said softly. "I ain't never thought of it like that." He paused. "Grown-ups is mean," he added.

"Some of them," Tom agreed.

"Mr. Davis, he mean," Son Jesus whispered.

Tom could see tears beginning to well in Son Jesus' eyes. "What's he done?" he asked.

"He mean to Sister."

"What sister you talking about?" Tom asked.

"Remona."

"I like Remona," Tom declared.

"Mr. Davis mean as anybody I know, Huck," Son Jesus said.

"Why don't your mama and Remona quit working for him?" Tom asked.

"Can't," Son Jesus answered. "We live on his place."

"We'll write a letter to the sheriff, or to my daddy," Tom replied. "Tell them about it. Get the sheriff to go down there and put Mr. Davis in jail."

A nervous smile fluttered across Son Jesus' face. He nodded vigorously.

"Corn sure would taste good with them fish," Tom said.

"Uh-huh."

•   •   •

Frank Rucker brushed the fur of a dandelion whisker off his sheriff's badge and rubbed his mouth with the thumb heel of his hand. He took another drink from the jar of iced tea that Evelyn Carnes had handed him. It was cooler under the shade of the pecan tree than in the bowl of the swamp, where the humidity swam through the brush like a steaming, invisible rain. Frank's shirt and pants were stained with perspiration, turning the pale tan to a dark fudge color. The wide gun belt around his waist and the heavy revolver that hung from it chafed the skin on his stomach and hips. He could feel a rash clawing at his testicles and wondered if he had accidentally walked through a field of chiggers. He wanted to drop his hand discreetly and scratch, but Evelyn Carnes was standing there staring at him, smiling sweetly, offering a ham sandwich that had a sheet of lettuce growing from the bread.

"Thank you, m'am," Frank said. He took the sandwich and looked at it. He hated lettuce in a sandwich.

"You poor men must be exhausted," Evelyn said sympathetically.

"Well, it's a little hot out there," Frank admitted. He bit into the sandwich. He thought he could feel the grit of sand from the lettuce on his tongue, working its way to the tender roof of his mouth.

"It's so sad, them two little boys being lost," Evelyn sighed. "I don't know what gets into people. World's changing, Sheriff." She smiled. "But I guess you know that better than anybody, with all you must see in your job."

Frank nodded and chewed. If he didn't answer, maybe she would go away, he reasoned. The apple-odor cologne she wore, baking on her skin in the heat, made his mouth dry.

"I was telling Ada that it wouldn't surprise me a bit if it wadn't one of the boys who came out of the war shell-shocked, or something," Evelyn said. "I know my cousin Albert never has been——" She paused. "You know Albert, don't you, Sheriff?"

Frank nodded again. Of course he knew Albert Hixon. Albert was a regular inhabitant of the Overton County jail.

"Albert never has been right since he came back from the war," Evelyn continued. "Poor boy. Drinks all the time. Aunt Rita worries to death about him."

Frank swallowed his food and sipped again from the tea. He said, "Albert's all right. He just likes to drink a little too much, but if I remember right, he was that way some before the war."

Evelyn blushed. She lowered her voice. "Well, that's what I keep trying to tell Rita, but she won't listen. Thinks Albert got wounded some way in the war, some way you can't see."

Frank pulled his damp handkerchief from his pocket and wiped his face. He wanted to tell Evelyn Carnes that her cousin had not been anywhere near the front lines, that Albert had worked in a supply unit, where the greatest physical danger he faced was cutting his finger on a can of Spam, if he couldn't con somebody into opening it for him.

"Well, I wouldn't know, m'am," Frank said. He smiled again. "If you'll excuse me, I need to talk to my deputies."

"Oh, of course," Evelyn replied. "You want another sandwich?"

"Maybe later," Frank told her.

"I'll keep some put away special for you," Evelyn whispered. She smiled girlishly.

Frank nodded and crossed the yard to Fletcher Wells. He was certain he could feel the grit of sand from the lettuce scraping at the roof of his mouth. His hip was raw from the weight of his revolver and the perspiration. His testicles burned. He could feel people staring at him, asking with their looks if he knew what he was doing, or was he just another red-faced joke wearing a sheriff's badge.

"Looks like you got you a girlfriend there, Frank," Fletcher said to him.

"Don't start it, Fletcher."

Fletcher grinned. He said, "That's a widow lady, and not too long ago. Just coming out of mourning, the way I hear it. And I guarantee you, you ain't seen bumpers like that since we ran that hootchy-kootchy show out of the county last year."

Frank glanced back over his shoulder at Evelyn. She was in her mid-thirties, he guessed. Would have to be, though she looked younger since Jed had died. Fletcher was right. She did have a body that held a man's attention. Thin, but big-breasted. Lips that pouted. Hazel eyes under auburn hair. She smiled pleasantly, and he nodded and turned away.

Wouldn't be bad, he thought. He had been divorced for two years, but he did not date. Once a month, on his four-day weekend, he went to Anderson, South Carolina, and visited a good-natured woman named Hilda Dewberry. Until now, looking at Evelyn Carnes, Hilda had been all that he cared to fool with.

Fletcher coughed away his giggle. "She's got a mouth that could suck the pit out of a peach without breaking the fuzz," he whispered.

"Not another word," warned Frank. "Not one. You understand me?"

Fletcher cleared his throat. He looked away, toward the swamp. "Guess I'd better get back," he said.

"I was thinking about bringing in the bloodhounds," Frank said.

"What for? Them other dogs didn't find them, and from what Hack was saying, they go to his boy like he was leftover barbecue."

Frank sniffed and sighed. He was tired, bone-tired. "They just ain't bloodhounds, that's all."

"We'll do what you want," Fletcher said, "but I'd give it a little more time if I was you. We got people all over the place. Likely as not, they done messed up any chance for tracking."

"I guess you're right," Frank grumbled.

"I was talking to Hack's girl—Elly, I think they call her," Fletcher said. "She told me that Troy and the Oglesby boy, and two or three of their buddies, come in about a half hour ago. Said they were heading on up the creek."

"I hope they have better luck than us," Frank muttered. "Anybody say they'd seen Hack and Hugh?"

"Not that I heard," Fletcher replied. "I heard somebody talking about Jule and that bunch of colored men he had with him. Said they come by earlier. Said Jule was hobbling pretty bad."

Frank glanced back toward the house. He did not see Evelyn Carnes. He wiped his brow with his handkerchief. "Everything we doing is probably a waste of time, anyhow," he said. "Ten to one that boy ain't done nothing but run off again and talked Reba's boy into going along with him. And we out here sweating our tail off." He shook his head in disgust. "All right, let's get going." He started across the yard, avoiding the stares of the gathered crowd.

"Sheriff! Oh, Sheriff!"

Frank and Fletcher stopped and turned to the voice. It was Evelyn, rushing toward them. She had a paper sack in her hand.

"You forgot your sandwiches," she enthused. She handed the sack to Frank.

"Uh-huh," Frank said. He bobbed his head. "Appreciate it."

"Hope y'all find them," Evelyn said.

"Me too, m'am," Frank mumbled.

SEVEN

Tom was on his knees in the boat, holding a paddle in his hands, playing it lazily through the water. It was the same pose he had seen in a drawing of Huckleberry Finn from the book he had read. Son Jesus was nestled against his bedroll, a thoughtful, peaceful look on his face, an expression of understanding that always baffled Tom. It was as though Son Jesus knew something that no one else could quite comprehend, that he had a secret he had never told anyone.

"How many books you got in your school, Jim?" asked Tom.

Son Jesus tilted his head to look at Tom. "Teacher, she got some books," he said.

"Don't you got some books in the school?"

"Got a spelling book and a arithmetic book," Son Jesus answered. He added, almost gladly, "Teacher got a storybook she read, but she ain't good as you at telling stories, Huck."

Tom spit over the side of the boat. He wondered if he had read as many books as Son Jesus' teacher. Probably, he guessed. Maybe more. And then he remembered something about Son Jesus that always confused him when he thought of it.

He was in the second grade. It was a cold winter day, storm-wet, the red-clay roads slippery with mud. He was on the school bus, cuddled beside Elly trying to keep warm. Troy was the driver of the bus. They were nearing Herman Crawford's house when he looked out the window and saw Son Jesus and Remona and Cecily and the Cater twins walking along the road. He jumped up from his seat. "Troy! Troy, there's Son Jesus."

Elly pulled him back in the seat. "Be quiet, Tom," she said in a hushed voice.

"Where's he going?" Tom asked anxiously.

"Going to his school," Elly answered.

Tom was stunned. He did not know that Son Jesus had a school. "Where's it at?"

Elly pointed to a small, dark house off the road, tucked under the limbs of two giant oaks. "That's where the colored go to school," she explained.

"Where's their school bus?" Tom wanted to know.

Behind him, Joe Elder giggled. Elly shot him a look of warning.

"They ain't got a school bus," Elly said. "They get to walk."

Tom wiggled from his seat and ran to the back of the bus and peered out the back window. He thought he could see Son Jesus standing in the road, gazing at the bus.

"Tom, get back in your seat," Troy demanded in a harsh voice.

That afternoon, when he asked his mother why Son Jesus had his own school and why he did not have to ride the school bus, his mother turned her face away and said, "Honey, it's the way things are." He thought his mother's voice sounded sad.

He still did not understand why Son Jesus had his own school, or why Son Jesus did not ride to school on a school bus.

"Guess it's about time we started looking for a place to camp out," Tom said. "River's getting narrow down this way."

"Getting fast too, Huck," Son Jesus said. "We going faster than we was."

Tom glanced at the water. Son Jesus was right. He had not noticed the current. He lifted his head and looked downstream. He could see the water whipping off walls of mud and rock banks, folding into a flat, simmering center with spits of white curls spewing up from it.

Son Jesus' body stiffened suddenly. He lifted his head like a listening bird. "You hear that, Huck?"

"What?"

"Listen."

Tom heard it: a roar, a closing storm of sound. He grabbed his paddle and cried, "Paddle, Son Jesus. We got to get to shore."

"What's going on, Thomas?" Son Jesus asked. His voice quivered. He sat as still as a statue.

"Waterfalls," Tom snapped. "Com'on, Son Jesus, help me with the paddling."

"Suckhole? It a suckhole, Thomas?"

"Waterfall and suckhole, both," Tom screamed. "Get to paddling."

"Oh, help me, Jesus," Son Jesus moaned. He grabbed for his paddle and began slapping at the water.

They paddled furiously, crying out to each other, but the boat was seized in the exact middle of the river, in a waterslide that flew uncontrollably into the mouth of a deafening roar. The river streamed between steep banks of granite, turned abruptly left, and fifty yards away, Tom saw the spray and foam of the waterfall.

"Hang on, Son Jesus," Tom shouted.

"Hang on," Son Jesus echoed.

Tom grabbed his feed sack and the seat plank and bent forward toward the center of the boat. Opposite him, Son Jesus did the same. They looked as though they were praying to each other.

Tom did not see the boat hit the waterfall. He felt the sound swallow him, felt the boat leave the water in the gullet of the spill, felt it tilt downward, splash hard. He felt his body rolling in the air, free of the boat. He was underwater only a moment and then he was bobbing on the surface, pushed up by the force of the swell. He could see Son Jesus ten feet away, maybe closer. Son Jesus was trying to pull his face out of the water, but he did not seem able to move his neck. His eyes were closed. His shoulders were arched.

Tom yelled across the water: "Son Jesus!"

Son Jesus rolled like a lazy fish and slipped beneath the surface. Tom lunged forward, pulling frantically at the water with his hands. He could see Son Jesus' back turning up. He ducked under the water and kicked at the sand on the bottom and then he touched Son Jesus and pushed his shoulder under Son Jesus' stomach and shoved him up. He was limp in Tom's arms. He's dead, Tom thought. He's dead and I'm going to die too. Then he realized he was standing in the water, holding Son Jesus above the surface.

"Son Jesus, you all right?" Tom whimpered. Son Jesus' eyes were still closed. Tom could see blood spreading from a small cut on his forehead, at his hairline. "Son Jesus..."

Tom looked downstream. Below him, in the middle of the river, was a small island, and Tom began to walk-swim across the sand bottom of the river, holding Son Jesus around his chest, under his arms, dragging him, feeling for a heartbeat.

He did not know how long it took him to pull Son Jesus from the river—minutes that were like hours. He could barely see Son Jesus' chest rise and fall in breathing. The smear of blood on Son Jesus' forehead caked above his eyebrow. Tom leaned close.

"Don't you go dying on me," Tom begged. He began to cry. "Don't you go dying," he said again.

• • •

Hack Winter stepped from the woods, followed by Ollie Elder and Hugh Joiner. He cupped his hand over his eyes and gazed at the sun. Late midafternoon.

"We near the house," Hack said wearily. "Let's go on up and get us a bite and then drive up toward the Pleasant Grove road."

"Guess that's as good as anything," Hugh said. "They ain't in that swamp. We'd of heard somebody's gun going off if they were." Hugh was one of Frank Rucker's deputies, a pleasant, handsome man in his early thirties who had served on an aircraft carrier with the Pacific fleet. Hugh was smart and likable, and being in the navy had given him an air of confidence and the dignity of good manners. Smart enough to go to college on the GI Bill if he wanted, but he had chosen to stay in Overton and take a job as a deputy. People trusted Hugh. It was believed that he would be sheriff when Frank decided he had had enough of the job.

"Maybe we ought to look on the creek, behind my place," Ollie suggested. "My oldest boy Carl used to say that's where Tom liked to play, sliding down them hills on sheets of cardboard."

Hack fanned his straw field hat in front of his face and rocked agreement with his body. Ollie had been a neighbor for twenty years. He was a good man. Ollie was one of the men at Dodd's General Store who urged the stories from Tom, and Ollie knew the pain of losing a child. Carl had been killed in a car wreck on Christmas Eve in 1947.

"Sounds like a good idea, Ollie," Hack said quietly.

• • •

The crowd was not as large at the Winter home as it had been. Many of the people had left to cook more food for the waiting, or to do their Saturday shopping, or to gather at the Old Spirit Baptist Church, where the Reverend Dooley Witcher pitched prayers in the direction of heaven for the safe return of Son Jesus Martin and Thomas Alton Winter.

Hack and Hugh and Ollie sat under the pecan trees, eating from Evelyn Carnes' sandwiches and from the food-gift platters of the Sympathy Committee of the Crossover Methodist Church, where Hack served as the Sunday school superintendent. They had answered the only question that could be asked—"You see anything?"—with the only answer they had: "Nothing."

Ada stood near them, staring at the woods in the distance. Her arms were crossed tight against her chest, as women do when they are trying to embrace something that is missing from them.

"Where's Reba?" Hack asked.

"Out on the front porch with Cecily and Remona. I plugged the fan in. It's a little cooler out there." She looked at her husband. "You better take the time to call Miriam while you're here. She called earlier and Elly let it slip what was going on. She's worried to death. Said she'd be sitting by the phone until she heard something."

Hack nodded. "In a minute," he said.

"Reba say anything about going to see Conjure Woman, Mrs. Winter?" Hugh wanted to know.

"Not yet. I been expecting it," Ada said. She paused, chewed on her lip nervously, then added, "But I don't think she'd do that unless she has to."

Hugh nodded his understanding. "They was some of the colored talking about it before we started looking."

"I just wish I knew Tom was running away again," Ada sighed. "Pretending to be somebody he'd been reading about. I'm almost used to that."

Hack looked up from his plate. He frowned suspiciously. "What's he been reading, anyhow?"

"I don't know," Ada told him. "It'd be under his bed."

Hack stood. "Be back in a minute," he said.

When he returned from the house, he was holding a book. "They're on the river," he said.

"How you know?" Ollie asked.

Hack dropped the book on the table. It was Mark Twain's *The Adventures of Huckleberry Finn*. He said, "This, that's why. I should of known it. Tore-up campsite, places where it looked like bodies had been drug." He walked over to the tree where his shotgun was propped, and he raised it in the air and fired it twice.

From the woods and the swamp, the search parties of men paused and raised their heads as though they could see the pellets of the shells that called to them.

"Must of found them," the men said among themselves.

◦   ◦   ◦

Tom had managed to pull Son Jesus from the sandbar of the island to a plate of land that was covered with black gum and scrub pine. There was still sunlight from the late afternoon, but on the river the day was cooling, and Son Jesus, unconscious, shivered. Tom removed his shirt and squeezed water from it and covered Son Jesus' chest.

"I'm gon' make us a fire, Son Jesus," he said nervously. "You gon' be warm."

Tom circled the top of the island and found pieces of the broken boat and his feed sack and both bedrolls, which had washed up on the narrow shoreline. He dragged them under the trees and then he gathered an armload of twigs and small limbs that had been dropped by the trees and he cleared away leaves and needles from a spot close to Son Jesus and stacked them in a pyramid. The week before, making his plans, he had waxed the tips of matches and put them into a tobacco tin to keep them dry, and he found them and scraped away the wax from one and struck it on a piece of flint rock. In a minute, the fire bloomed under the stack of dry wood.

"You gon' be warm, Son Jesus," he whispered. "Won't be but a minute."

And then he sat beside Son Jesus and took his arm and began to rub it, hoping for the healing that his mother practiced when he did not feel well.

"You feeling better, Son Jesus?"

Son Jesus did not answer.

The sun nestled in the top of the riverbank trees, spilling orange-red over the leaves. Tom listened to the drumming of the waterfall and the lapping of the river against the sandbar and the hiss of the fire and thought of the nights of camping with Son Jesus at Troy's campsite. Son Jesus loved the monotonous swirl of the water. "We gon' sleep good," he said always, before falling asleep. "Water sounds like rain on a roof."

"Don't you go dying on me, Son Jesus," Tom said in a loud, fearful voice.

● ● ●

It was Troy's guess that Tom was in Ben Carlen's flatbottom boat. It was the boat they had borrowed a month earlier when Troy took Tom fishing on the Scrubgrass River.

"Should of thought of it earlier," Troy said gravely. "I could tell he was taken with that old boat. Didn't fish hardly at all. Kept moving around, touching that boat all over. Had that look in his eyes when he gets to daydreaming. I kept trying to get him to pay attention, since he'd never been on the river, but he acted like he knew everything about it. Told me that was the river where steamboats used to be."

Troy was kneeling below the bridge at the inlet where Ben Carlen's boat was always tied off, examining the dull footprints that Tom and Son Jesus had made. Hack and Frank and Fletcher and Ollie were beside him, looking into the river. Other men waited at their cars, smoking cigarettes. Ada and Elly were with Reba and Remona and Cecily in Ada's car.

"I'd say they been drifting most all day," Hack judged. "Maybe they stopped off some, but not for long, not when he's got his raft."

Frank did not know why Hack called a flatbottom boat a raft, but he did not ask. He said, "If they have, they probably gone over the falls."

Hack nodded gravely. "Guess we better go on down there and see. We don't find some sign, we can work our way back up, but we got to get going. It'll be dark before we know it."

"They went over them falls, they could be in trouble," Frank said bluntly.

"They ain't that high," Fletcher said. "Shoot, I been over them on a tire tube."

Frank looked at him incredulously. "They're boys," he said. "You were probably drunk."

Fletcher shrugged away the comment. He glanced toward Jule and a group of black men standing near Jule's car. "What about that bunch of colored?" he said in a low voice. "Reba says she's gon' look for her boy if he's on the river. She's scared to death about suckholes."

"It's her boy, ain't it?" Frank replied. "Let her look."

• • •

At sundown, Son Jesus opened his eyes, then closed them again. He whispered, "I hurt, Thomas."

Tom knelt beside him. "You all right, Son Jesus," he said. "You all right."

"Where my mama?" Son Jesus asked.

"We'll be going home soon," Tom promised. "You'll see her soon."

Tom knew it was a lie. They were on an island in the middle of the river, in a place where he had never been. They were lost.

"You hungry, Son Jesus?"

Son Jesus shook his head slightly. "I hurt, Thomas," he said.

"They coming to get us," Tom said. "They'll be here soon."

"They ain't," Son Jesus mumbled.

"Yes, they are," Tom insisted. "I'm just waiting to it gets dark enough and I'm gon' build up the fire so they can see it and find us."

"Dark now," Son Jesus said.

Tom looked around. The sun was dimming through the trees. "Well, almost, I reckon," he said. "Dark enough. You just lie there and I'm gon' get some sticks and throw on the fire."

Tom worked frantically to gather sticks from the trees of the island, stacking them in a pile beside the fire. He threw some of the sticks on the fire and watched the tongues of the flame lick high into the thickening dusk of evening and the sparks of the dying ash spew like exploding firecrackers against the limbs of the trees above them.

"They gon' see us," he said to Son Jesus. "I read a story one time. It was just like us. It was about a pirate out in the middle of the ocean. He was shipwrecked, been there for years, and one night he saw a ship way off in the water and he built him up a fire. Got to burning as high as the trees and they saw it on the ship and sailed in and took him off that island. That's what we gon' do, Son Jesus."

The expression did not change on Son Jesus' face. He lay under the trees, where Tom had pulled him. He stared at the fire as though hypnotized.

"I'm right here, Son Jesus," Tom said. "Know what we ought to do? We ought to sing us a church song. Like your mama's always singing to us. Like you always singing. You know the one I like the most?

'Swing Low, Sweet Chariot.' That's the one. I like the way you sing that. Shoot, you do that better'n anybody I ever heard. Come on, see if you can help me."

Tom tried to sing, but Son Jesus did not move his eyes from the fire. Tom did not think Son Jesus could hear him. The sun paled, then vanished, and the night seeped around them. Tom sat beside Son Jesus, watching the fire burn itself into embers.

● ● ●

It was a voice like a far-off singer, or a singer's echo: "Son Jee-sus. Son Jee-sus."

Then, from another direction, far off: "Tom. Ho, Tom."

Tom sat up and pulled at Son Jesus.

"You hear that, Son Jesus?"

Son Jesus did not answer. His eyes were closed.

"I heard something," Tom said in a whisper.

"Son Jee-sus!"

"Ho, Tom! You out there, Tom?"

Tom scrambled to his feet and listened. The voices were coming from both sides of the river, riding over the hissing of the waterfalls and the loud bubbling of the shoals. Tom grabbed a handful of pine needles and threw them on the dying coals. The flame flickered, spewed a ribbon of orange, then burned brightly. Tom stacked a tepee of twigs over the flame and knelt and blew into the fire.

"Son Jee-sus!" The sound of the voices was nearer.

"Here we are," Tom yelled. "On the island." The fire blazed.

"Yonder they are," someone shouted from the riverbank. "They got a fire."

Tom knelt beside Son Jesus. "I told you they was coming," he said. But Son Jesus did not answer.

● ● ●

Tom and Son Jesus were carried from the island by men who were weary but relieved. Reba cuddled Son Jesus in her arms and cried mournfully. Tom explained that Son Jesus had been hurt going over the falls and that he couldn't stay awake. Hack told Troy to call Jake Arlington and have the doctor go to Son Jesus' house.

It was dark and, on the riverbank, cool. Tom could hear the waterfall and the high-pitch hum of nightbugs. He knew he would be severely disciplined for running away from home and for persuading Son Jesus to go with him, but there, on the riverbank, it did not matter. He and Son Jesus had been Huck and Jim, Jim and Huck, and Tom knew it was something he would never forget.

EIGHT

Jake Arlington took the call from Troy about the runaway and the injury to Son Jesus. Yes, he said, he would drive immediately to Reba's house. He asked Troy about Tom.

"Guess his butt's burning a little bit," Troy told him, "but he wadn't hurt when they went over the falls."

"That's good," the doctor said. "I like that boy. He's got spirit."

"You don't have to live with him," Troy replied sourly.

Jake drove quickly and eagerly to Crossover. He suspected that Son Jesus had a concussion, but it could be worse, and maybe that was why he was called instead of Harper King, the black doctor. Harper was a good general practitioner and a tireless worker, but he was old now and too overwhelmed to keep up with the changes of medicine. It was sad, Jake thought. There were three doctors and eighteen nurses at the Overton County Hospital; Harper worked alone, with two nurses to assist him.

But there was another reason that made Jake Arlington drive recklessly over the narrow country roads with tricky curves. He had never seen Son Jesus Martin, yet he had heard the story of Son Jesus' birth and of Conjure Woman from Ada and Hack, and he had determined that Son Jesus and Tom must have been born at the same time—perhaps the same minute of the same hour. If Ada's declaration was true, Conjure Woman knew about Tom as clearly as she knew about Son Jesus. Such things fascinated Jake. It was part of the fundamentalist Deep South that seemed, to him, mysterious and, in its way, grand. He had made discreet inquiries about Conjure Woman. She was a con-artist fortune-teller, some said, a Halloween carnival act who made money off the colored and down-and-out white trash with her outlandish tales. Those who scoffed at her were few, however. Others—most others—believed Conjure Woman was an agent of another world: heaven, they guessed, as the prophets of the Old Testament had been. The reports Jake had received—the stories of healing and psychic visions—were too bizarre to believe, but still he wondered: Was there really a power that could peer into the future, a power that did not need scalpels and drugs to heal the ill? And if so, was it a power selectively given? Were there people blessed with gifts too spectacular for anything but myth? And if Conjure Woman had such gifts, had she passed them on to Son Jesus Martin with her touch? The stories said she had. The bizarre, chilling stories.

Ada and Hack were at Reba's house with Frank Rucker when Jake arrived. He was led by Ada to Son Jesus. Reba was at the bedside with Cecily and Remona.

"Give me a few minutes," he said gently to Reba.

"You need me, you call," Reba said. She left the room with her daughters and Ada.

Jake stood for a moment, studying the boy on the bed. He was startled by the face. It seemed beatific, as though the face at least resided in another place. If there was pain in the body, it was not in the face. Jake touched Son Jesus' forehead.

"Let's see what happened to you," Jake said in a soft voice.

●　●　●

It was a concussion, Jake told Reba, something like a bruise on the brain.

"He'll need to rest quietly and give the brain a chance to heal itself," he explained. "I don't know how long it'll take, but it's about all you can do."

"I feel terrible," Ada said. "If it wadn't for Tom—"

"He's a boy," Jake cautioned. "They were just having a little adventure. You can't blame him for that."

"Son Jesus gon' be all right," Reba said confidently.

"I'm sure he will," the doctor replied. "But you keep a watch on him."

"He's gon' be fine," Reba insisted.

"Just keep him quiet," Jake advised. "If you need me, have Mrs. Winter give me a call."

Ada followed Jake out of the house, where Hack and Frank were waiting.

"How's he doing, Doc?" asked Frank.

"Hard to tell," Jake answered. "Didn't want to say much about it inside, but it looks like he's got a pretty bad concussion."

"Didn't know there was any such thing as a good one," Frank said.

Jake chuckled softly. "Well, you got me there, Sheriff. There's not. Some are worse than others, that's all. I'd say the next few days should tell us something, but it could go bad."

"I appreciate you coming over," Hack said. "I figure I'm responsible since Tom started this whole thing. You send the bill to me."

"Glad to do what I can," Jake told him. "Funny. He doesn't even look like he's hurt. More like he's just taking a nap."

"Uh, Doc," Frank said hesitantly.

Jake turned to him. "Yes?"

"Mind taking a look at something?" Frank asked.

"Not at all."

Frank led Jake to his car and opened the door and took a bone from the front seat. "Got any idea what that is?"

The doctor took the bone and turned it in his hand to catch the light of the moon. He shrugged. "It's a fibula." He glanced at Frank. "The leg bone, from the knee to the ankle." He handed the bone back to Frank.

"Then it's human?" Frank said.

"Sure is. Where'd you get it?"

"Just turned up. Appreciate you telling me what it was," Frank replied. He tossed the bone back into his car and closed the door.

"Well, there's a lot more of him to show up, if that's all you've got," Jake said.

"Yeah," Frank mumbled.

● ● ●

Tom was punished for running away from home, as he knew he would be. His father whipped him with a belt—harder than before, but not with violence. The real punishment was greater than the stinging slaps of a belt across the back of his legs. There would be no more games from Tom, no more running away. If he left, no one would come looking for him. And the business of spending all his time with Son Jesus was a thing of the past. He would go to the fields, and he would work, not dawdle.

Tom had heard such threats before, but they had never mattered. He had only to perform his act of melancholy and great distress in front of his mother, and the threats became meaningless. But Tom knew intuitively that his long-running act—his perfected mime of sorrow and his soliloquy of sighs—was over. His mother's anguish had hardened to anger. She insisted that he would go with her on Sunday afternoon to Son Jesus' home and he would apologize to Reba.

"I want you to take a long, hard look at Sonny," Ada said harshly. "They don't know if he's ever gon' wake up. I want you to keep that in mind when you see him. You better pray that he does. You better fall down on your knees right there at his bed and pray he gets better, else you'll be living the rest of your life thinking about it. You don't learn to start behaving, you'll wind up in jail somewhere and there won't be a thing in the world that anybody can do about it. You'll be a convict, wearing striped clothes, working out on a road gang, with somebody holding a shotgun on you day and night, and it'll serve you right. Much as I hate to say it, there's been more than one person in this family who's been on the chain gang, but you don't ever hear me talking about them, do you? That's because nobody wants to remember somebody who wouldn't do right."

When Tom saw Son Jesus from the doorway of the room—Son Jesus in his bed, on his back, his head against a pillow, his eyes closed like Tom imagined a dead person would look—his mother's words taunted him. He remembered the convicts who appeared occasionally on the dirt road leading to his home: mean-faced men shouldering shovels and picks and sling blades, following road-scraping machines. The convicts' clothes were black-and-white-striped stories of crime. Troy had told him about it, that each white stripe represented a bank robbery, or something equally mean, and each black stripe was a counting of the number of people the convict had murdered. The convicts with leg chains were the meanest, Troy had declared. They had so many stripes they were called zebras, and they had killed so many people the sheriff had stopped counting. Watching Son Jesus' motionless body in his bed, his eyes closed, looking like a dead person must look, Tom had a sudden, sickening image of being fitted with a shirt with one black stripe.

"Mama?" Tom said uncomfortably.

"Go on over there and take a close look," Ada commanded.

Tom crept slowly, reluctantly, across the room to the bed. Son Jesus' face seemed faded. In the room's dim light, he was the color of ash. Tom could not see his chest move in breathing.

"Dear Jesus and God and all the holy angels," Tom mumbled in a single quick breath, "make Son Jesus like he used to be."

"What was that?" Ada asked sharply.

"I was praying, Mama."

"You better be."

Reba sat in a rocker beside the bed. She said to Tom, "Come here, honey."

Tom eased to her cautiously. She took his hand and began to rub it.

"It's all right, baby," Reba cooed. "Son Jesus, he gon' be fine. You'll see. He gon' be fine. Lord's looking after him."

Tears bubbled in Tom's eyes. He apologized for talking Son Jesus into running away with him and accepted the responsibility for Son Jesus' injury. Reba continued to stroke his hand, assuring him that she was not angry, that she knew they were just boys and boys were always doing things they weren't supposed to do, which is why God had a special group of angels looking out for them. Besides, Reba insisted, God meant for Tom and Son Jesus to be together. It was in his plan. No matter what happened to pull them apart, God would find a way to put them back together again.

"Way it is, honey, and ain't nothing nobody can do about it. It's the Lord's doing," Reba declared.

"You gon' spank Son Jesus when he wakes up?" Tom asked.

Reba laughed. "Lord, no, honey. I'm gon' make him a marble cake."

Tom thought that Reba was far more sensible than his own parents had been in regard to the incident.

"He'll like that," Tom told her.

Ada promised Reba that Tom would return the following morning, prepared to do Son Jesus' work. "He's got to learn he can't get away with things. You work him until he drops, Reba. Long as Sonny's sick and unable, he'll be over here making up for what he's done. And I promise you something else: he'll be reading the Bible and praying tonight, and every night from now on, even if I have to stand over him with a switch, making him do it. This boy's got to get some religion in him, or he'll wind up on the road gang sure as I'm standing here."

"Not my Tom," Reba said gently. She fingered the hair off his forehead. "Not my baby. They ain't never gon' put him on the road gang. But I'd like him praying for Son Jesus. That'd make Son Jesus feel good."

"Well, he's gon' be," Ada said, "or he's gon' be needing somebody praying for him."

● ● ●

That night, in his bed, Tom read aloud the story of Cain and Abel to his mother, and she explained to him that God was more angry with Cain than he had been with Adam and Eve. "That's why he put a mark on him," Ada said.

"Like the clothes that convicts wear?" asked Tom.

"Something like that," Ada agreed.

"Mama?"

"What?"

"Why didn't God like what Cain was giving him? Why'd he think what Abel was giving him was better?"

"I don't know," Ada replied irritably. "That's what it says in the Bible. That's all you need to know."

"Don't sound like God was being fair."

"Tom!"

"Well, it don't."

"You'll not go questioning what God does, young man," Ada snapped. "The point is, you better think about Cain and Abel and learn something from it. You almost got Sonny killed out there on that river, and that's just about the same as Cain killing Abel. Not a whole lot of difference at all."

"Mama, did God know that Cain was gon' kill Abel?"

"God knows everything."

"If he knew it, why didn't he stop it?"

"Tom, I'm warning you. Don't go questioning God."

"Seems to me like he was egging it on," Tom said.

"You go testing God and you'll live to regret it," warned Ada. "Your great-grandfather on your daddy's side found that out. He got struck by lightning because he was mad at God for sending a hailstorm during cotton-picking season." She stood from the chair where she had been sitting. "Now you roll over and do some serious praying."

"Yes m'am."

Tom prayed until he fell asleep. He prayed for Son Jesus to be well. He prayed to be spared a life as a convict. He prayed for Cain's soul. He prayed for a new softball glove. He prayed that Troy would repair the lean-to. He prayed that Rachel Jarrett would quit telling people she was his sweetheart. He prayed that Reba would save some marble cake for him. He prayed to know where the cave of Indian gold was located.

In his sleep, Tom dreamed of being alone on the river in Ben Carlen's boat and of hearing God's voice asking, "Where's Son Jesus?"

"I don't know, God," Tom answered in his dream. "I'm just out here catfishing, but I ain't catching nothing."

"Don't lie to me, Tom Winter," God roared. "You got catfish hanging over the side of that boat you stole. I can see underwater just as well as I can see up in the air."

"I ain't got many," Tom whined.

"I can hear Son Jesus calling out," God said.

"Where, God? Where is he?" Tom asked timidly.

"I can hear his blood crying out from the ground," God thundered. "You killed him, Thomas Winter, and I'm going to put my mark on you."

"No, God, no—"

"Hold still, Tom Winter!"

And Tom could see a branding iron, sizzling from a fire hotter than the sun, flying through the sky, falling across his forehead. He could feel a terrible burning. He could see the smoke from his flesh filling the space of his dream.

He awoke, crying in panic, "Mama! Mama! I'm on fire."

NINE

Frank Rucker was uncomfortable. What he was doing was not under-handed, but he knew there was more to it than official business. He could have sent Fletcher, or Hugh, to make the inquiry, but he had decided to make the trip himself.

It was a matter of coincidence, he reasoned, as he turned the steering wheel of his car and pulled off the main road onto the drive-up leading to Evelyn Carnes' home. That was it: coincidence. It wasn't his doing. It was something that happened and there was nothing he could do about it. Seeing Evelyn Carnes again was only part of it, even if he had dreamed about her on Sunday night. He had a job to do.

He had found the bone in Tom's bedroll by accident. On the island, Troy had lifted Tom and waded across the river with him, and Claude Capes, who was mule-strong, had gathered up Son Jesus and carried him to the riverbank, to Reba. Frank had picked up Tom's bedroll and feed sack, and the bone had slipped out of the bedroll. He had almost left it there, had taken a few steps away from it and then had returned for it. Later, he had asked Tom about it, and Tom had told him that he and Son Jesus had found it at the old sawmill near Ben Carlen's pasture.

"Where was it?" Frank had asked.

"Under some sawdust that looked like graves," Tom had told him. "Not far from the fence. I marked where we found it with a cross for good luck."

The old sawmill had been owned by Jed Carnes, Evelyn's late hus-band.

Frank stood at the door of Evelyn Carnes' home and knocked gently. He held his hat in his hand, fingering the rim. He wondered if he had splashed on too much aftershave lotion. He sniffed as the door opened.

Evelyn was in a faded green summer dress, the kind that women wore for housework. The top of the dress was unbuttoned one button more than was proper for greeting someone at the door. Her abundant breasts pushed proudly against the cloth. Her hair had a windblown look. She wore only a touch of makeup.

"Why, Sheriff, what a surprise," she oohed.

"Morning, m'am," Frank replied politely. "Sorry for the interruption."

Evelyn smiled. "You're not interrupting a thing. Come in, come in." She opened the door.

Frank stepped inside. He could feel the blush that glowed on his face. He wanted to keep his eyes above Evelyn's chest, but he raised only his head. He looked like a man trying to see a fly on the end of his nose.

"What brings you out?" Evelyn said. "Reba's little boy's all right, I hope."

"Sonny? Yes m'am, I think so. Uh, I won't take but a minute—"

"Fiddle," Evelyn sang. "You come on in and have a glass of tea with me." She started toward the kitchen and Frank followed hesitantly. "I'm glad for the company. I always get the Monday blues after seeing so many people at church on Sunday. And besides, I must have three gallons of tea left over from the other day, when everybody was off trying to find Tom and Reba's boy."

"Yes m'am."

"I swear it gets hotter every year," she babbled. "My late husband, Jed, used to say it was from all the wars all over the world, but I can't hardly believe that, can you?"

They were in the kitchen and Evelyn was waving him to a seat at the table.

"Well, I can't say as I ever thought about it that way," Frank told her. "Could be, but I wouldn't know."

Evelyn popped ice from an ice tray and filled two glasses, and then she poured tea over the ice. She talked as she worked: "I just think the weather goes in cycles. Cool a few years, hot a few years. Seems like I've read something along those lines somewhere, or maybe I heard it on a radio program. Hot a few years, cool a few years." She placed the tea in front of Frank and gazed at him and smiled. "I like it cool," she added, "but I don't mind being hot, either."

Frank could feel the blood rushing to the pit of his groin. He swallowed quickly from the glass of iced tea. Evelyn sat opposite him at the table. She had made no attempt to button her dress. She looked very much like a young French girl he had met in a village near Paris. The girl had thrown her arms around his neck, laughing deliriously. She had said something in French, repeated it joyfully, something bright and lyrical, like a playground song, and though he could not understand the words, he had known intuitively what she meant: *You're here, you're here, you're here.*

"So what brings you out, Sheriff?" Evelyn asked lightly.

Frank licked his lips subconsciously. He said, "When we took them boys off the island the other night, I found something in Tom's bedroll and he told me he'd picked it up at that old sawmill site Jed used to run on the back of your property. That's where they cut through to get to the river."

"What was it?" Evelyn asked.

"It was a bone."

"What kind of bone?"

"It was human," Frank said.

A question clouded Evelyn's face. "Oh, my," she whispered.

"I just wanted to ask if you could tell me how to get out there, and if you'd mind if I look around some," Frank said.

"Why, of course you can look around, all you want to," Evelyn replied. "I'll be happy to show you where it is."

"I don't want to mess up your day," Frank told her.

"I wadn't doing anything but piddling around. With nobody here but me, I hardly have to do anything at all."

Frank nodded. He swallowed again from the tea. "Well, I'd appreciate it. Can we drive to it?"

"Almost," Evelyn said. "We'll have to walk a little bit. Just give me a minute to get into some walking clothes."

Frank smiled foolishly. He knew he should stand when Evelyn stood, but he also knew it would be too embarrassing.

Evelyn sprang from her chair. "You want more tea, just help yourself," she said.

"Yes m'am."

"And stop that m'am stuff. I may be a widow, but I'm not old enough to be a m'am," Evelyn ordered playfully.

Frank grinned and nodded foolishly and watched her wiggle off. She did not close the kitchen door leading down the corridor and he could see a hall mirror that caught a narrow angle of her bedroom. That door was open too, and he saw her skinning out of her dress. He squirmed in his seat. A film of perspiration coated his forehead and neck. "Oh, Lord," he muttered.

He tried to keep his eyes from the mirror, but it was impossible. He caught an eyeblink glimpse of her in the nude as she crossed the room, holding a blouse. Her breasts quivered with her step. His mouth was dry, and he swallowed the rest of the tea.

"Won't be but another minute," Evelyn cried from her bedroom.

"Yes m'am . . . uh, all right," Frank called back. "Take your time."

When she came back into the kitchen, Evelyn was dressed in tan pedal pushers that were cuffed calf-high and a white blouse that had been more discreetly buttoned. She wore white canvas shoes. The curves of her body were like those Frank had seen on pinups in the war.

"Ready at last," she said.

"You sure I'm not taking you away from something?" Frank asked.

"Oh, hush, Sheriff. I already told you. I wasn't doing anything."

•   •   •

The drive to the old logging road took no more than ten minutes.

"It could be a little rough," Evelyn warned. "I haven't been up this way in years."

Frank eased his car along the road, rolling over grass beds and the pine seedlings that took root every year and then died in the hard clay. The road curved under trees and across gutted washouts. Finally, they could go no farther. A fallen tree blocked the way.

"It's not far now," Evelyn said. "We can walk it easy."

They climbed over the tree and followed the road. The day's heat was rising, and Frank stole glances that told him Evelyn was also perspiring, her blouse beginning to cling to her body. He fought to concentrate. He was on the job. There was duty to be done, maybe even finding the remains of a body. But he also had needs, and since his divorce, those needs had taunted him terribly. He remembered his dream of Evelyn. Her body writhed over him, her great breasts shimmering with the slippery moisture of the night's heat.

"Well, it wouldn't surprise me, whatever you find," Evelyn said in a chatty tone. "No telling what sawmill hands will do. That's the only thing I never liked about Jed's work. The kind of men he had to work with. I know they played cards at the sawmills all the time, and they did a lot of drinking. Jed told me about it. Always having fights. Jed used to say it was because of the sound of the big saws, said it was enough to drive a man to do anything after a while."

"Guess so," Frank said.

"I've never told anyone, and you have to keep it to yourself," Evelyn said, "but I could always tell what kind of men they were when they'd come to the house for something that Jed would send them after. I could tell it by the way they looked at me. You knew that looking was not all they had on their minds."

"Could have been dangerous," Frank said seriously.

Evelyn stopped walking and looked at him. "You sound concerned, Sheriff."

Frank swallowed. Her eyes were covering him. He could see the outline of her breasts cupped in the bra under her clinging blouse. "A person has to be careful," he mumbled.

"That's sweet," Evelyn said. She turned and waved her hand to a clearing. "We're here."

Frank knew immediately from the piles of sawdust and shavings that the mill had been abandoned only a few years. There was still a faint odor of pine that seeped up from the sawdust. Little windblown mounds—Tom had called them graves, and they did look like graves—dotted the grounds.

Tom had tried to describe the location of the mound for Frank—near the fence, marked by a good-luck cross. The description was as accurate as a map. Frank found it easily.

He knelt at the mound and reached with his hand and began to scrape away the sawdust. In three deep pulls, he touched a bone. In five minutes, he had uncovered enough to know a body was there. Evelyn stood nearby and watched with fear and fascination.

Finally, Frank stood and dusted his hands and looked down at the emerging skeleton. Evelyn stepped close to him and looped her hand into the cradle of his arm. Frank could feel the globe of a breast against his side.

"Who do you think it is?" she asked in a frightened voice.

"No telling," Frank answered. "There's been two or three people missing from the county for the last few years. Could be one of them, or it could be a drifter."

"Last person I know that's been missing from around here—and it's been five or six years now—is Reba's husband," Evelyn said. "I can't remember what they called him."

"Rody," Frank said.

"You don't think it could be him, do you?" Evelyn asked.

"I don't know," Frank admitted. "When was it that Jed quit sawing back here?"

"Well, it was right before he got sick," Evelyn said. "Two or three years ago, I guess. He moved the mill around some, but he came back here and worked a little while just before he stopped for good."

"Uh-huh," Frank mumbled. He studied the hole that he had scraped away. It had been a deep grave when first dug, he believed, heavily packed with new wood shavings and sawdust. And that was probably why the body had not been dug up by animals—the smell of resin. Over the years, the wind had blown away layers of the sawdust. He began to rake the sawdust back over the bones with his foot.

Evelyn tugged at his arm. "Why you doing that?"

"Got to keep it covered up until we can come back and dig it all up," Frank told her.

"It scares me," Evelyn whispered. "It's so close to the house."

"Don't worry about it. Whoever did this has been long gone."

"I can't believe people can be so mean," Evelyn whimpered.

Frank nodded agreement. He pulled away from Evelyn's arm and continued covering the bones, carefully raking the sawdust back into a mound. He thought about Jed Carnes. Jed had had a reputation as one of Overton County's most difficult men. A complainer. A cheater. A man with a dangerous and intimidating nature. People had whispered in dismay for years about how he fooled his wife. There were those who believed he had married Evelyn only to have a trophy, or to somehow improve his reputation, and others had said, "Well, good Lord, he could of married a snake and done that. Wadn't no need to drag down something that fine." And being called fine was a high compliment for Evelyn, or women like her—women from sharecropper homes, fieldhand women who wrinkled quickly under the burning of the sun. Fine meant more than physical beauty. Fine meant unusual, unique. Fine meant *fine*. Frank knew he might have to question Evelyn about her late husband. There was no doubt in his mind that Jed could have killed one of his workers and left him there to rot, but Jed had been dead for over a year and

Frank had no idea how long the body had been in its sawdust grave. Still, if it did get down to business—official business—with Evelyn, he would have to do it. It was his job.

"Evelyn, I got to ask you not to say anything about this for a while," Frank said.

"Why—why, of course not, Frank," she replied. "And thank you."

"For what?"

"You called me Evelyn. That's much better than m'am."

Frank blushed.

TEN

Son Jesus had not regained consciousness by Monday morning, and Reba and Remona and Cecily had stayed beside his bed, bathing his face with cool towels and singing soft prayers to him. Elly had driven Tom to Reba's house early, leaving him to help Jule repair a plank fence that circled a small pasture near the barn. She knew the day would be wasted, with Tom yammering nonstop and Jule pondering the right way to do the job. And she was right. For most of the day, Tom daydreamed under the shade of a chinaberry tree, while Jule smoked finger-rolled cigarettes and droned about the many ways a fence could be repaired and about the danger of Son Jesus' condition. He was fearful that Son Jesus might die in his sleep.

"He don't wake up by in the morning, or he ain't dead, Reba's gon' have me going after Conjure Woman," Jule moaned. "She is and that's a fact. Lord, Conjure Woman scare me. She look you in the eyeballs and you feel like you done been throwed in the pit."

"What pit, Uncle Jule?" asked Tom.

"Pit of hellfire and damnation, that's what pit."

"She can't do that, can she?"

Jule shook his head slowly. He said, "Hooo, boy, you don't know nothing, do you? Don't know nothing a-tall. That woman can do what she sets her mind to do. Shoot, I seen her make things float in the air, just like they was feathers hung up on the wind."

Tom was intrigued. "What did she make float?"

Jule's face pinched in thought. "Seen her make a ax float," he said after a moment.

"She did?" Tom said in amazement.

"Uh-huh." Jule thought another moment. "Seen her setting out on her front porch and she was making that ax cut her some stovewood. It was out there by the woodpile, just chopping away. Wadn't nobody holding it. Just hanging out there in the air."

Tom was astonished that something so grand had happened in the same part of the world where he lived and he did not know about it. "I never heard about that, Uncle Jule."

Jule covered a grin behind his cigarette. "Uh-huh. White folks don't know about them things," he answered.

"Why don't they, Uncle Jule?"

"They white folks," Jule answered.

"Mama says Conjure Woman knew I was being born," Tom said.

"Uh-huh. Now, that says it, don't it?"

"Says what?"

"Says what white folks don't know nothing about."

"How's that, Uncle Jule?"

Jule cocked his head and stared at Tom incredulously. He said, "Conjure Woman—she white or she colored?"

Tom had never seen Conjure Woman and he had never thought about her color. "Colored, I guess," he answered.

Jule laughed. "Well, there you go. Course she colored. She black as roof tar," he said. He rocked his body in the kitchen chair he had taken from the house and placed under the tree. He said again, "White folks don't know nothing about them things."

"Why'd Conjure Woman know about me, Uncle Jule?" Tom asked.

"Well, now, I don't rightly know. Have to do me some thinking on that," Jule mumbled. "Why don't you go in the barn and get me the hammer and some nails. We got to get busy on that fence."

"You figured out how we gon' do it?"

"Uh-huh. We gon' nail the planks back up to the fence post."

• • •

By late afternoon, Frank and Fletcher Wells had removed the bones from the sawdust pile on Evelyn Carnes' farm and had bagged them carefully, as Pug Holly, the county coroner, watched. It was almost a full skeleton. The only thing missing was the foot that had been attached to the fibula Tom had taken.

"Who you reckon it is?" Pug asked. Pug was short, round, ugly. He had attended school with Frank and had inherited Holly's Funeral Home from his father, who had also been the county coroner.

"I'd say it's Rody Martin," Frank answered honestly. "I pulled the case when I got back to the office this morning, and read everything I could find about it. Way he was described, he had some missing front teeth, just like we got here. And he was the same size, from what I'd guess."

Pug bobbed agreement with his head. "I'd say he's been here a few years, judging from the condition of the bones. That's about the time that Martin fellow was missing, wadn't it?"

"Killed," Frank corrected.

"Well, maybe. They never found a body."

"Have now."

"If it belongs to the right person," Pug said.

"Good Lord, Pug, everybody knows damn well that Pegleg killed him. Just walked in there and bashed him over the head and took him out," Frank said irritably. He pointed toward the bag of bones. "That's another thing we got: a crushed-in skull."

"Just a nigger fight," Pug mumbled.

Frank turned to glare at him. "What'd you say?"

"Just a nigger fight. Happens all the time. Always killing one another."

"Were you born this way, Pug, or did you have to study to get so goddamn dumb?" Frank demanded.

"What's eating you?" Pug snapped.

Frank stepped directly in front of Pug. He hissed, "What color was them bones?"

"Kiss my ass, Frank," Pug growled.

"What color?" Frank said again, his voice rising.

"White, like they supposed to be," Pug said.

"What we doing right here, right now, is investigating a bunch of bones—white bones—that look like they belonged to somebody who may, or may not, have been killed by some kind of blow to the head," Frank said angrily. "I think that man was Rody Martin, but I don't know, and I don't care what kind of skin they were wrapped in. You understand me, Pug?"

Pug huffed a sneer that he tried to twist into a smile. "Sounds to me like you getting your balls all in a wad over some dead nigger," he said arrogantly.

Frank sighed in disgust and turned away and looked at the hole that had been dug in the sawdust. He saw Fletcher carefully gathering some pieces of clothing from the grave. Finally, he said to Pug: "You didn't fight in the war, did you, Pug?"

"You know damn well I didn't," Pug said. "Bad heart. But what's that got to do with anything?"

Frank laughed sadly. "If I told you, you wouldn't understand it, anyhow. Now get your ass out of here and go do your job—and one other thing, Pug: Keep your mouth shut about this out here. I want us to have a chance to look around before half the damn county comes snooping around."

Pug walked away in an offended strut.

● ● ●

Frank had persuaded Evelyn to stay at her home during the removal of the bones. He did so in part to keep anyone from asking questions of her and in part to keep their minds on the right body. Evelyn standing around in her pedal pushers would have been more than a distraction; it would have been a disaster.

She was waiting in a rocking chair on the front porch of her home when he stopped his sheriff's car and got out. She stood immediately and came to the steps. She had changed clothes again, back into the faded green cotton dress with the top unbuttoned one button too low. Frank thought: Damn.

"You got it?" Evelyn asked.

"Most of it," Frank answered. "Couldn't find the right foot. Guess it must have been drug off."

"Well, come on up and sit down," she said. "I've got some tea."

Frank followed her to the chairs on the porch. She had a pitcher of tea on a foldout serving tray and, beside the tea, a silver bucket filled with new cubes of ice, leading Frank to believe that she had been watching for his car, and when she saw it coming from the creek road, she had hurriedly filled the bucket with the ice and brought it to the porch. The bucket was sweating cool drops of water. He sat in one of the rocking chairs as Evelyn fingered ice into a glass and poured tea over it.

"Are you hungry?" she asked.

"No," he answered. "Thank you, though."

She sat near him and leaned her arm over the armrest of the chair and gazed at him. She said, "You know who it is?"

"I think so," Frank told her. "Reba's husband. We found some clothes—rags mostly—and there were some things about the bones that match what we know about Rody. Just got to check out a few other things."

"That's terrible," Evelyn sighed. "Her boy being hurt like he is, and then this."

"I expect she'll be glad to know he's been found," Frank said. "Give him a decent burial, or what's left of him."

"You got any idea who did it?"

Frank cupped his hand around the glass of tea, feeling it cool his palms. "Pegleg," he said after a moment.

"I been hearing about him for years, but that's the only name I've ever heard him called," Evelyn said. "Jed used to say he was the meanest man in Georgia."

"Well, he was right," Frank admitted. "Somebody that likes to play games is all I know. Puts him on a hood made out of a sack, best I can figure, and shows up out of the blue. Walks like he's got a wood leg, or something. Why they call him Pegleg. I don't know much about him. All the killings he was supposed to do took place while I was still in the army. All I've done is hear about him and read what little there was in the files."

"He must be crazy," Evelyn said.

"Wouldn't argue that," Frank agreed.

"If he's got a wood leg, he ought to be easy to find."

"Seems that way," Frank said, "but there's not but one man in the county that's got a wood leg that I know of, and that's old man Abe Ingram. He's eighty-seven years old and he lives twenty or thirty miles away from Crossover."

"Then Pegleg must not be from around here," Evelyn said.

"Don't know. Still a lot of people tucked off in the foothills that don't nobody know much about. People moving in and out all the time since the war."

Evelyn leaned back wearily in her rocker. "Scares me to death, thinking he's still out there and could show up anywhere. Think I'd better oil up Jed's shotgun, just in case—especially at night." She looked at Frank. "Be so easy to break in my bedroom through the back."

Oh, Lord, Frank thought. Don't even mention it.

"Guess it's a good idea, but he ain't never bothered whites," he said, "and I suspect whoever it was is long gone, anyway."

"Well, I'd appreciate it if you'd drop by once in a while, just to take a look around and see if you see anything I might not notice," Evelyn said.

Frank cleared his throat. "Be glad to," he said. He stood. "Well, I got to be going on. Need to stop by Reba's house and tell her what we found."

Evelyn did not rise. She twisted her body in the rocker. "See you later, then?"

Frank smiled, did a half-nod, and walked away.

●　●　●

Cecily stared out the window of the small bedroom where Son Jesus lay. She was watching Uncle Jule and Tom at the fence. She did not know which was lazier. It had taken them almost an hour to nail two boards between two posts. They were like dawdling children trying to fill time until something more engaging came along. She could hear Tom's laughter across the yard and she knew that Uncle Jule was telling him something outrageous. The two were a perfect match, she thought. Both were happiest when telling lies that were interesting, or amusing, even if they were unbelievable. But the lies were mostly harmless—not even lies, really; more like absurd stories. The only difference was that Uncle Jule liked only to talk, but Tom wanted to act things out, like the *Huckleberry Finn* runaway on Scrubgrass River, and that made Tom dangerous. Son Jesus was in bed, unconscious with a concussion because of Tom. Still, she loved Tom. He had been around since Son Jesus was a baby and he was like a noisy extra member of the family. And that, too, was strange. Tom was white and most of the time he acted like other whites, but he did not seem to recognize, or care, that Son Jesus was black.

Since she had been away from home, living on her own and working in Overton at Higginbottom's Funeral Home as a receptionist and some-time embalming assistant for Reeder Higginbottom, Cecily had found it difficult to explain Tom to people she knew. "He sound dumb, you ask me," they said. And they laughed giddily over what they imagined as a performing jester, much as many of them had been treated by whites they knew. But when she told them about Conjure Woman's appearance at Son Jesus' birth and about her declaration of a white boy—whom her family believed to be Tom—their laughter turned to surprise and then to frowns. Conjure Woman was not anyone to challenge with behind-the-back snickering.

Cecily moved from the window and sat again in the chair beside Son Jesus' bed. She felt uncomfortable, as though she were sitting with one of the corpses in the receiving room of the funeral home, the at-peace look fixed permanently on their faces by Reeder Higginbottom's talented fingers. Son Jesus breathed easily, with a slight nasal hissing, like a repeated sigh, coming from his mouth and nose. That was the only difference between being dead and being alive. Tomorrow, she would have to leave him and go back to work, and she wanted to see him awake, to know he was all right. She knew her mother was more worried than she pretended to be.

And there was the nervous, moody behavior of Remona. It was more than fear over Son Jesus. There was something else, but Remona would say nothing when asked about it. She would merely leave—fade away— as though she had not heard the questions.

"Honey, she seventeen," Reba had tried to explain. "She ready to go, just like you was ready to go. She tired of the field and Miss Alice's kitchen. Honey, she tired of Miss Alice. And Mr. Harlan, he just make her be sick to her stomach. Harlan Davis, he a sorry white man, honey."

"Mama, I know," Cecily had replied. "I had to put up with him too." She had added, after a moment, as though speaking to herself, "I know."

"He worser now, honey. He's took to drinking bad. He a sorry man."

Another year of school, and Remona would be with her, Cecily thought. There was a job waiting. Reeder Higginbottom had promised it, and with the two of them working, they could rent a place for their mother, since their mother refused to leave Crossover. Maybe the sharecropper house on Doyle Allgood's farm. Since he had quit row crops and started raising beef cattle, Doyle Allgood had had no need for sharecroppers. The house had been empty for two years.

She took the cloth from the washbasin and squeezed the water from it and then she patted it gently over Son Jesus' forehead. He did not move.

"Come on, baby, wake up," Cecily whispered. "Wake up for Cecily."

From outside the house, she heard the sound of a car door closing, and she got up from the chair and went to the window and looked out. She saw Frank Rucker strolling across the yard toward Uncle Jule and Tom. She called, "Mama, the sheriff's here."

● ● ●

"Looks like y'all about wore out," Frank said to Jule and Tom.

Jule took off his hat and slowly, painfully wiped his shirt sleeve across his forehead. He wagged his head in agreement. "Well, Sheriff, the boy, he try, but he ain't learnt what it's like to do a man's work. Have to keep on him just to get a nail put in the fence now and again."

"Uncle Jule, I done all the nailing," Tom protested.

"Well, course you have," Jule countered. "Somebody got to hold up the board, and a little-bitty thing like you ain't strong enough to do that. Man's got to do it."

Frank laughed. "Looks like you two make a match," he said. Then: "How's Sonny?"

" 'Bout like he was," Jule answered sadly. "Ain't woke up yet."

"Reba's gon' get Conjure Woman," Tom volunteered.

"That right?" Frank asked Jule.

"What she say," admitted Jule. "He ain't woke up by the morning, she gon' make me go bring that old witch woman over here."

A screen door opened at the back of the house. They all turned, to see Reba holding the door open.

"Yonder she is," Jule said. He lowered his voice. "Tell her they ain't no need of that old witch woman coming over here."

"I ain't about to get caught up in that, Jule," Frank said. "You know Reba. She wants Conjure Woman, well, I expect you gon' go get her." He turned toward the house.

Jule nodded surrender.

"Don't y'all work too hard, now," Frank added. "A man could get a heatstroke out in the sun."

"We ain't got to worry about that," Jule said. "This little-bitty boy can't do much of nothing, nohow. Leave me to do everything."

"I done the hammering," Tom reminded him.

"Hammering? That ain't nothing. . . ."

Tom and Jule were still arguing when Frank crossed the yard to Reba, who had come out of the house and was standing in a corner of shade from the roof. Her hand was propped on the framing of the door and she was half leaning against it. Frank knew she had not slept.

"Afternoon," Frank said in greeting. "How you holding up, Reba?"

Reba inhaled deeply. "He's still not woke up," she replied. "Just laying there, like he was taking a nap."

"Sorry to hear that. You need the doctor?"

Reba shook her head. "He's gon' be all right," she answered.

Frank started to ask about Conjure Woman but changed his mind. "I need to talk to you about something," he said.

Reba's face pinched in worry.

"Hate to bring it up now, but I can't put it off," Frank continued. He paused, looked back to Jule and Tom. They were measuring the distance between two posts by walking it off in toe-to-heel steps. He turned back to Reba. "I think we found the remains of Rody."

Reba pushed away from the door framing. Her eyes filled with tears. She began rubbing her hands together in a washing motion. She said in a trembling voice, "Where at?"

"At Jed Carnes' old sawmill, under a sawdust pile," Frank answered. He did not want to tell her about Tom having Rody's leg bone on the runaway. Later, he would. At the right time.

Reba sagged to the steps leading from the kitchen door. She bowed her head and closed her eyes, and the terrible memory filled her mind in white-hot strobes. She was at the supper table, laughing with Cecily and Remona at a thin mustache of mashed potatoes that caked Son Jesus' face. "Lick them off," Rody said, and he demonstrated the licking with his own tongue. Suddenly, the door flew open and the Pegleg man filled the doorframe. A shriek flew from Cecily's throat—sharp, shrill. Rody turned to look. The Pegleg man was over him, raising his hammer. She tried to stand, but the Pegleg man threw her aside, into Son Jesus, and then he slapped the hammer once across Rody's head. Rody's hands rose feebly, then dropped, and his face fell forward over the table, knocking his plate to the floor. The room filled with cries, with the scraping of falling chairs, with the shattering of broken tea glasses. She grabbed for Son Jesus and rolled across the floor to a corner of the room. Her daughters threw themselves over her like sudden clouds, and for a mo-

ment she could not see what was happening. But she could hear. The
hammer fell again and bone cracked, and she pulled Remona aside to
watch the Pegleg man lift Rody over his shoulder. He stood for a moment and glared across the room, and then he turned and left, slamming
the door behind him. And the screams began, screams loud enough to
pierce the walls of the house and ride the nightwind that had taken
Rody's soul away from them.

"I can't be sure, since all we got is the bones," Frank said gently.
"But we found some rags of clothes that look like what you said he was
wearing."

"It's him," Reba whispered with certainty. "Now I'm gon' put him
to rest, praise Jesus."

"He did have some missing front teeth, didn't he?" Frank asked.

Reba nodded. "Didn't have none. They was knocked out cutting
trees for Mr. Jed Carnes. Crosscut saw jumped up and hit him in the
mouth." She looked at Frank. "Why'd that Pegleg man take him off like
that? That's what I ain't never been able to get out of my mind."

"Wish I knew," Frank said. "I guess he was just trying to scare
people."

"When can I get him?"

"Pretty soon, I guess. I'll take care of that."

"What about Pegleg?"

"We got a body now," Frank said. "I'll take care of that too."

Reba struggled to stand and Frank reached to help her. From inside
the house, at the window, Cecily watched. She knew something was
wrong and somehow, from some bewildering sensation—like a voice that
did not speak words—she knew it had to do with her father.

"You want me to tell your girls and Jule?" Frank asked Reba.

"Don't go worrying about that," Reba answered. "I'll take care
of it."

"Anything I can do?"

"Will you go by Miss Ada's and tell her?" Reba said. "Maybe she
can drive me over to see him."

"You sure you up to that?" Frank asked.

"I been waiting a long time to see him," Reba whispered.

"What about Jule?" Frank said. "Maybe he can drive you over. Y'all
can follow me."

"I'd rather Miss Ada."

It was a thoughtless suggestion, Frank realized. Of course Reba would prefer Ada Winter's company over Jule. Ada Winter would take control. She would ask the right questions, make the right demands. If Pug Holly got on his high horse, Ada would have him cowering in one of his own coffins. "All right," he said.

Reba looked across the yard to Jule and Tom. Jule was rolling another cigarette, while Tom sat on a sawhorse.

"He come to his rest now," she said quietly. "We done found him. Thanks be to Jesus, we done found him."

ELEVEN

That night, after their supper, Tom was told about the discovery of the bones that were thought to be Rody Martin. He said nothing. He sat at the kitchen table and listened to his mother's anxious, sad story, or half listened. He gazed out the window and remembered pulling the bone from the sawdust mound, and he remembered also how Son Jesus had been afraid of the sawdust mounds. Son Jesus had asked, "We ever been here, Thomas?" Tom wondered if Son Jesus had sensed something from the grave of his father. Had Son Jesus' father called his name while he was dying and did Son Jesus hear that voice, all those years later? And was it Rody Martin's bone in his bedroll that had kept Son Jesus from dying on the river?

Such things were possible, Tom imagined. Spirits were everywhere. He had read such stories and he had heard Reba talk about the Holy Spirit, saying you couldn't hide from it and nothing on earth was more powerful.

In fact, that was why he did not like reading the Bible. None of the stories about God and Jesus and the Holy Spirit that he read were as wonderful as Reba's telling of them. On rainy days when he played at Son Jesus' home, they would go inside and Reba would give them butter biscuits with brown sugar or she would pop popcorn for them, and then she would have them sit close to her in front of the fireplace and she would tell them stories of Daniel or Jonah or Samson or Joshua or David or dozens of other familiar names, and to Tom, her telling was far grander than the Sunday school teachings of those ancient writings that he impatiently endured each week in the Crossover Methodist Church. Reba had a voice that celebrated words in a range of whisper to rage, and each story had precisely the same moral—that man floundered until God decided to intercede personally and do something unforgettable. In man's floundering, Reba's voice was quarrelsome, bickering, irritating. When God appeared, her voice became a magnificent echo—happy and rhythmic, sweet, purring. When God appeared, Reba's face became flushed with laughter and tears, and often she would pull Son Jesus and Tom to her in an embrace that quaked with joy and she would sing out, "Oh, my babies, my babies, my babies. God loves you. Jesus loves you." The way Reba said it, in a declaration like great music, Tom knew it had to be true. When Keeler Gaines' wife, Corrine, said it in Tom's Sunday school class, reading from a lesson book in her monotone, nasal whine, it sounded like God had the sense of a chicken.

Reba's favorite stories were of Abraham and Moses and Job and Noah. Especially Noah. The story of Noah was a grand story on days of rain, and to Tom and Son Jesus, being close to Reba, eating butter biscuits heaped with brown sugar, was as good as being on the ark.

"Babies, everybody thought ol' Noah done took leave of his senses. They laaaaugh at him. They say, 'Look at that ol' fool out yonder, making him a boat on dry land. Ain't no water nowhere around here, nothing but that ol' wet-water spring, and that ol' fool out there with them crazy sons of his, tarring up a gopherwood boat. Ain't even got him no oak, ain't got no cypress.'

"They laaaaugh, babies. Oh, they laugh when ol' Noah start to load up that boat with every kind of animal they is. They say, 'Noah! Ho, Noah! What you gon' do, Noah? Start you a zoo?' But when it start to rain, babies—wadn't no more'n a sprinkle to start off with—they kind of quiet down, and they wadn't but a giggle once in a while. And then it rain down harder 'n' harder, and the sky it turn blacker 'n' blacker, and it rain so hard you can't see across the yard, and the water it start to rise up higher 'n' higher, up to the toes, up to the knees, up and up.

"And the people they start to beating on the sides of Noah's boat and they yell out, 'Noah! Noah! Let us in, Noah! You ain't crazy, Noah! The rain's gon' drown us, Noah!' But God done told Noah what to do and Noah he don't pay no attention to all that yelling, babies. Noah, he don't turn his head. Noah done told them they better be changing they ways and they ain't listened. Noah done say, 'Don't go mocking God. He gon' bring a flood. You go on mocking God, you be swallowed up by the flood God's gon' bring.'

"Noah, he listen to God, babies. Noah, he high and dry."

"Now, Tom, you understand you're not to say anything about this until they know for certain," Ada Winter cautioned. "The sheriff said he was pretty sure, and from what I saw when I drove Reba over there, I don't have the slightest doubt about who it is, but they'd have to wait until they can prove it."

"Yes m'am," Tom said.

"You can't go making up any stories about it, either," his mother added. "You do and it gets back to Sonny, it could hurt his feelings. You don't want to do that, do you?"

"No m'am."

His mother sniffed. She said in a pitiful voice, "I just hope he wakes up, so he can know they found his daddy. Sometimes when people get hit on the head, they just sleep on and on until they die."

Tom felt a flush of guilt. "Uncle Jule's gon' go get Conjure Woman," he said.

"Oh?" his mother replied. "When?"

"In the morning," Tom told her. "If Son Jesus don't wake up tonight, Uncle Jule's gon' go get her."

Ada frowned sadly. During the trip to and from Overton, Reba had said nothing about getting Conjure Woman. She had said almost nothing, in fact. Some mumbling. Incoherent, almost. Prayers, Ada had guessed. Prayers watered by a spring of tears, prayers growing like new sprouts to God.

"You think Conjure Woman can wake Son Jesus up, Mama?" Tom asked.

His mother patted his arm. She said, "I think praying can wake him up just as well," she answered. "So you pray real hard, and maybe when we go over there in the morning he'll be sitting up and feeling fine."

"Yes m'am."

●　　●　　●

Before he went into his bedroom to pray and to sleep, Tom walked down to the barn, where Troy was tinkering with the motor of his tractor under the glare of an overhanging work light. His first words to Tom were, "Don't you touch nothing, turdface."

Tom ignored the warning and picked up a screwdriver. It felt like a sword in his hand, and for a moment, a flash, he imagined himself and Troy being two of the Three Musketeers. Son Jesus would be the third, and Son Jesus was being held against his will in a dungeon. He balanced the screwdriver in his hand like a rapier and thrust it gently against the tractor tire.

"Damn it, Tom, I mean it," Troy growled. "You put a hole in that tire, you'll be having a choice about which butthole you gon' use to take a dump."

Tom put the screwdriver down.

"You ever seen Conjure Woman, Troy?" Tom asked.

Troy picked up a cloth grimy with oil and wiped his hands. He said, "Why'd you ask that?"

Tom told him about Uncle Jule going for Conjure Woman if Son Jesus did not regain consciousness during the night.

"Shee-it," Troy muttered. Then: "Yeah, I seen her. One time."

"Where?"

"At her place," Troy explained. "Me 'n' Ned Oglesby went over there. He'd lost his billfold. Damn fool. Had every penny he'd made for six months in it. She told him exactly where it was. Said it'd fell out of his pocket when he was on a date with Shelia Franklin."

"How'd that happen?" Tom asked.

Troy laughed and wiped his rag across the top of the tractor, leaving a shining film of oil. "Ned got carried away."

"What's that mean?"

"It means Ned got to wallowing around with Shelia on the sofa and his billfold popped out of his pants about the same time his goober did. Shows what a woman can do to you, boy. By the time Ned got his billfold back, about six months of work had somehow wiggled out of it and got swallowed up by that sofa."

Troy's explanation was confusing, but Tom did not question him. He did not care that Ned Oglesby had lost his money, or his goober, in Shelia Franklin's sofa. He wanted to know about Conjure Woman.

"What'd she look like?" he asked Troy.

"Big," Troy answered. "Ugly. Dressed up in white. Scary woman. Got a voice that could drive tenpenny nails through concrete."

"You think it's so, what she said about me and Son Jesus being born at the same time?"

Troy laughed. He turned off the work light, and the barn was swallowed by shadows. The only light was from the full moon rolling in through the opened door.

"Naw," Troy said. "That's just talk, and you ought to quit thinking about it, turdface. You don't, and everybody in north Georgia is gon' think you're as crazy as that old woman. Lord, Tom, you got to start growing up. You know what it's like having a brother that's read more books than the whole damn school system, teachers included? Goda'mighty, Arthur Dodd's right. All them books is enough to wilt the brain. You got to quit being cowboys and Indians. I mean, you don't really think you're Tarzan, do you? Everybody knows damn good and well that Tarzan lives down in Africa. You think this is Africa?" He put his huge hand on Tom's shoulder and squeezed it. "Tell you what," he said gently. "What about me teaching you how to drive the tractor tomorrow?"

Tom could feel the blood draining from his face. He had always known that one day Troy would scoop him up and put him on the seat of the John Deere and try to make a farmer of him.

"Uh, yeah," Tom muttered. "But I got to go over to Reba's house in the morning and help Uncle Jule finish putting up that fence."

Troy bellowed a laugh. He said, "You and Jule. Ain't a ounce of difference between the two of you. That fence'll rot before y'all get it nailed up." He dragged at Tom's shoulder and walked him from the barn, still laughing.

And from the dark canopy of the side porch, where she sat with her husband, Ada watched her two sons crossing the yard.

"They're so different," she said quietly. "So different."

"Ain't that the truth," Hack sighed.

•   ●   ◉

In his bed, before he slept and began dreaming, Tom prayed that he and Troy would get to Son Jesus on time and that none of them would be wounded in the swordplay with the dungeon guards. He said, in his mind's voice, "The Three Musketeers are on your side, God." Then he thought, "Amen."

In his dream, Conjure Woman sat on the porch of Son Jesus' home and watched an ax cutting away at the fence he and Uncle Jule were frantically trying to build. No one was holding the ax. Blood was on its blade.

And then Conjure Woman was at the sawdust pile, standing over a pit that held the bones of Rody Martin. She lifted her arms in front of her and turned the palms of her hands down and spread her fingers, and Rody Martin's bones clattered together and rose out of the pit and danced in the night air like a puppet—white bones jerking wildly against the dark velvet of night. His right foot and his right leg bone, from the knee down, were missing. He opened his toothless skeleton mouth and uttered the word "Pegleg." And the word echoed throughout the woods, skimming air currents that were curling in heat: "Pegleg...Pegleg... Pegleg..."

And then Conjure Woman was beside Tom's bed. Her face was close to his face. Fire burned in the pupils of her eyes. She hissed, "Why'd you try to kill Son Jesus?"

Tom awoke in a convulsion of fear. He could feel the perspiration coated to him. He whispered, "God, where'd you go?"

• • •

Jule had already left in his ancient Ford car for Softwind and Conjure Woman when Elly arrived at Reba's house with Tom the following morning.

Reba was outside, gathering wood for the cookstove. "He ain't no better," she reported sadly to Elly. "Uncle Jule, he gone for Conjure Woman."

"Where's Cecily and Remona?" Elly asked.

"Cecily had to go back to work, honey," Reba answered. "Mr. Harlan come for Remona early on, just about sunup. Said Miss Alice wasn't feeling good."

"Miss Alice is just too lazy to get up and make her own breakfast," Elly grumbled.

Reba nodded. "Honey, that Mr. Harlan Davis, he a mean man."

"He's worthless," Elly replied bluntly. Then: "Mama sent over a sweet potato pie for Son Jesus when he wakes up."

"That's sweet of your mama," Reba said. "Real sweet." She touched Elly on the cheek. "I swear, honey, you get more like your mama every day. You got her same ways."

Elly blushed. She was not at all like her mother. Her mother was strong, aggressive; Elly was shy, skittish, awkward. "Thank you," she said softly, then turned to Tom. "Help take in some wood," she told him.

"He a good boy," Reba cooed. "Been helping out a lot around the house."

"He better," Elly said. She followed Reba into the house, carrying the pie. Tom trailed, his arms cradled around two small sticks of wood.

"Son Jesus, he got to wake up," Reba said to Elly. "Conjure Woman, she gon' help him." She took the wood from Tom. Tom knew by the strain in her face and eyes that she had not slept.

"I'm sure he'll be up before long," Elly said. "We been praying for him, Reba."

Reba crossed her arms and looked toward the room where Son Jesus lay. "Lord's watching over him, honey," she said softly.

Elly left after a few minutes, warning Tom against pulling any of his tricks to skip the work Reba expected of him.

"You get caught goofing off on the job, you know what Daddy's gon' do," she said. "You can't hide behind me and Mama anymore. You've got to grow up."

Tom watched the car fade into the tornado of red dust that flew off the wheels, and he crept back into the house to see if Reba had cut the pie. She had not. It was covered with a white cloth. He crossed to Son Jesus' room and stood in the doorway and watched Reba sitting on the bed, stroking Son Jesus' face with the tips of her fingers. He could hear her soft weeping, her whisperings to God. Son Jesus' body was heaped in quilts, his hands folded over the top of his chest. Tom could not see the up-and-down of Son Jesus' breathing. He's dead, Tom thought.

Reba looked up at Tom and smiled. She read the fear in his face.

"No, baby. Son Jesus ain't dead, he just resting," she said. "Jule gon' bring back Conjure Woman. She close to the Lord, baby. She make Son Jesus better."

"What's she gon' do?" Tom asked timidly.

"Why, baby, she gon' call up the Lord."

"What if she calls up the Devil by mistake?" Tom said.

Reba motioned from the bed and Tom went to her and she took him in her arms. She said, "No, baby. Conjure Woman a good woman. She done fight that ol' Devil to he's tired of fighting. He done tuck that old fork tail of his and sneaked off to find somebody else to pick on. Conjure Woman, she strong." She stroked Tom's head and added, "Why don't you go on outside, down by the barn, and wait for Jule. Maybe see if you can find me some eggs in the hen nest."

Tom went outside to the barn and looked for eggs, but found none. He was sitting in the shade of the barn, leaning against it, when Jule arrived with Conjure Woman. She was exactly as Troy had described her—huge, dressed in white, scary. She turned when she got out of the car and she looked at him. Tom could feel the air suddenly freeze around him. Then she walked into the house. Tom watched Jule open the door of his car and get out. He closed the door and leaned against it and rolled a cigarette. His hands were shaking. He lit the cigarette and crossed to Tom.

"That old Conjure Woman, she scare me," he confessed. "She look like she burn your head off with them eyes she got. Don't go around that house, boy. Don't go messing around with that ol' Conjure Woman."

"What's she gon' do, Uncle Jule?" Tom asked, expecting a more detailed answer than Reba had given.

"Don't know, boy. Say some words, I reckon. I'll do me some thinking on it. She scare me, that old Conjure Woman."

"You tell her about the sheriff finding Son Jesus' daddy?"

"Don't go talking to me about that, boy. That my brother you talking about. Gets me all choked up, talking about my brother."

"I'm sorry," Tom said softly. "I just wondered—"

"I ain't told that old woman nothing," Jule countered. "Ain't no need to. She know it. She know whatever she want to know."

Jule sat in the shade of the barn next to Tom. He smoked his cigarette nervously and fanned his face with the brim of his felt hat. His face furrowed in worry.

And then they heard Conjure Woman's voice from the house. It was a deep rumble—rising, falling, rising, falling. It droned, grew louder. They could hear Reba crying, "Help me, Jesus!" Jule sat frozen, holding his hat in his hand, his face lifted, cocked toward the house.

"Oh, Lord . . . ," Jule muttered.

Tom did not know how long the healing of Son Jesus lasted. He watched the house and he watched Jule, watched Jule roll and smoke many cigarettes, watched him pace under the shade of the chinaberry tree, fanning his face with his hat. Conjure Woman's voice was hypnotic, and Tom became sleepy, and he lay in the shade of the barn on a seed sack and closed his eyes and slept a dreamless sleep.

When he awoke, Reba was standing over him, tugging at his arm. She was smiling. Conjure Woman was standing beside Reba.

"He better, baby," Reba said happily. "He open his eyes and guess what he say, honey? He say, 'Where Thomas?' "

Tom sat up. Conjure Woman glared at him. Uncle Jule had been right, he thought. Her eyes were pits of fire.

"Who you, white boy?" Conjure Woman asked sharply.

"He Thomas," Reba said proudly. "He the white boy you seen when Son Jesus was born."

Conjure Woman bent over, close to Tom. She whispered, "I know who he be. White boy, you want me turn you black?"

Tom could not answer. Her face was like a weight pressing down on him, choking him. He could see the branding iron of fire flung from the hand of God.

Reba laughed. She said, "She trying to scare you, baby. Don't go listening to that."

Conjure Woman's lips curled into a slow, spreading smile. She leaned over and reached out her hand and touched Tom's arm with the tips of her fingers. Her eyes blinked lazily, like a lizard's eyes, then she pulled her hand away.

"I know who he be," she said again. Her voice was deep, even. She stood erect and closed her eyes and for a long moment she did not seem to be breathing. Then she added in a whisper, "I see the time for the change. The time for the change be coming."

"Change?" Reba asked. She remembered Conjure Woman's words on the day of Son Jesus' birth: *They make the change.* She asked, "What you mean, change?"

Conjure Woman did not answer. She turned and walked to the car, where Jule waited nervously, smoking a cigarette.

Tom stared at his arm. He thought he could see his skin changing color, changing from the brown of his summer tan to a dark almond.

"Com'on, honey, let's go see Son Jesus," Reba said. She started walking toward the house, with Tom following. "I'm gon' cook him some butter biscuits and cover them up with brown sugar," Reba added happily. "Won't that be good?"

"Sure would," Tom agreed. "You gon' cook some for me too?"

Reba laughed. "Honey, you know that. Sure, you know that."

Son Jesus was sitting up in his bed, his head propped against pillows. He grinned when Tom entered the room with his mother.

"You all right?" Tom asked timidly.

"Feel like I been sleeping a week," Son Jesus answered.

"Almost have," Tom said.

"He fine now," Reba cooed. She touched Son Jesus on his forehead with her fingers, brushing her fingers over his skin.

"Uh-huh," Son Jesus said.

"Thomas been here helping out while you was sick," Reba said.

Son Jesus giggled.

"Me 'n' Uncle Jule been fixing up the fence," Tom said proudly. "I been doing most of the work."

"He been working hard," Reba said.

"You see Conjure Woman?" asked Tom.

Son Jesus wagged his head against the pillow. "I seen her. Didn't have to open my eyes, but I seen her."

"She scare me to death," Tom admitted.

"Now, I done told you they wadn't no need to be scared of Conjure Woman," Reba said. "She done wake up Son Jesus, ain't she?"

"I guess," Tom mumbled. He looked up at Reba. "You tell Son Jesus about finding his daddy?"

Son Jesus' body jerked in the bed. He pulled up from the pillow, gazing at Tom.

"Not yet, child," Reba said gently. She sat on the bed beside Son Jesus. A look of sadness settled into her face.

"Mama——" Son Jesus whispered.

"They find him, honey. Find out where he done been buried."

The question trembled from Son Jesus: "Where at?"

"Over in them sawdust piles on Mr. Jed Carnes' place," Reba told him.

Son Jesus settled back into his pillow. His eyes blinked with moisture.

"It's all right, honey," Reba said quietly. She stroked his face with her hand. "Praise Jesus, it's all right. Jesus done led us to him and we got him back. Now we gon' bury him like he supposed to be."

Son Jesus turned his head and looked away. A bubble of tears rolled over his cheeks.

"You the man of the family now, honey," Reba said.

For a moment—fleeting, bright, surreal—Tom could see the sawdust mound and the bone sticking from it.

"You found him, Son Jesus," Tom said.

"Like it supposed to be," Reba added. "Your daddy show up for you." She leaned to him, kissed him tenderly on his cheek. "You the man of the family now," she said again.

TWELVE

Frank Rucker wondered if he was being too obvious. The uniform he had on was starched and dry-cleaned, not machine-washed and hurriedly pressed by Lucy Hix, who came to his house once a week to clean and wash and iron. Lucy was not a great improvement on his own habits, and it was difficult to tell if she had done anything except keep him in a supply of uniforms. Every couple of months, Frank would spend a day piling the junk of his haphazard living into paper sacks, and then he would take the sacks to the county dump, and Lucy would invariably claim to have done the work.

She would say, "You ever see this place look this good, Mr. Frank?"

And Frank would answer, "You did a good job this time, Lucy."

Still, Frank could not complain to Lucy, or about Lucy. She was the best source of gossip he had ever met—black or white. She jabbered incessantly and when he wanted to know something about someone without it appearing like an investigation, he would simply ask Lucy and Lucy would go to the scent of the question. She was better than blood-hounds or the FBI.

He had said nothing to Lucy of Pegleg, however. He thought that he would, but not so quickly after finding the bones of Rody Martin. Frank needed to do his own investigating, needed to check out certain leads.

And one of those leads was Evelyn Carnes.

It was early Wednesday morning, a morning of bright cerulean sky and yellow sun, when he pulled into the front yard of Evelyn's house. The starch in the collar of his uniform cut into the back of his neck and gouged at the fleshy part of his chin. He could smell the Old Spice he had slathered on after his shave. In the rearview mirror, his hair glistened with Wildroot. He wondered if Evelyn would be wearing the summer dress and if the dress would be unbuttoned down her chest. Blood rushed to his loins.

He got out of his car and stood for a moment and looked across the land to the main road. Frank had not seen anyone and no one had seen him. Good, he thought. Won't be so damn many questions about why I'm back over here. He glanced at himself in the murky glass of the car window. He knew he looked as handsome as it was possible for him to look. He had watched Hugh, had learned from Hugh the proper dress code of an officer of the law. It was something like army brass in parade dress. He glanced in the window again. The starched creases in his uniform pants were sharp enough to cut cheese. His gun belt was polished and level.

He crossed the yard to the front porch and knocked softly on the door. Waiting a few seconds, he knocked again. From behind the door, he heard Evelyn Carnes say, "Who is it?" Her voice was small and frightened.

"The sheriff, m'am," Frank said.

Frank heard a nervous, excited laugh. The door opened.

"Why, good morning," Evelyn said. She was dressed in a robe that fit tightly around her body. Her hair was wrapped in a towel. "What a nice surprise."

Frank could feel his blush. His eyes blinked to Evelyn's chest. Her breasts were like living things calling to him, daring him, begging him.

"Uh, sorry to disturb you," Frank said. "But I was just back over this way to do some checking on them, ah, them bones, and I thought I'd stop by to make sure you were okay."

Evelyn reached for his arm with both hands and squeezed it gently, milking it with her fingers. "That's sweet of you, Frank. I did have some dreams that made me pitch about a little bit last night, but no visits from Mr. Pegleg."

"Glad to hear that," Frank said.

"Come on in," Evelyn said, dragging him forward into the house. "I've got coffee on. Did you have breakfast?"

"Ah, yes m'am. Before I left."

Evelyn led him through the house, toward the kitchen. "Now, I've told you, and I mean it: none of that m'am stuff. Do you want me to think I'm old and decrepit? Good heavens, I'm only thirty-five, and I know that's a few years past sweet sixteen, but it's not like I've got one foot in the grave. You've got to learn: it's Evelyn."

"Evelyn," Frank said.

Evelyn sniffed the air delicately. "Old Spice, right?"

Frank nodded. A shimmer of heat rose up the stem of his neck.

"I love it," she purred. "It's my favorite." She looked at him and smiled. "Sit, sit," she ordered. "I'll get you some coffee."

Frank sat at the kitchen table and Evelyn poured the coffee.

"I hope you don't mind, catching me in this old robe and this towel around my head." She chatted easily. "I just got out of the tub a few minutes ago and was about to get into something cool. I just know it's going to be too hot to breathe today."

Frank could feel his blood pumping hard. "I didn't mean to, uh, barge in, or anything," he stammered. "Just thought I'd stop by."

Evelyn waved away his apology with a light flip of her hand. "Well, I'm glad you did. Now, you sit there and drink your coffee and talk to me while I dry out my hair."

Frank bobbed his head.

"It won't embarrass you, will it?" Evelyn asked. "I suspect you've seen women dry their hair before. You were married, weren't you?"

"For a little while," Frank answered. Then: "Go right ahead." He added, "I only got a couple of minutes."

Evelyn pulled away the towel, and her hair—thick, auburn-colored— fell free in damp curls. She took the towel and began to scrub at the curls. Her breasts quivered with the motion.

"I heard you'd found out them bones did belong to Reba's husband," Evelyn said.

"What they said," Frank answered. "Reba made me show her the bones and the clothes. She said it was what Rody was wearing and said they wadn't no question about the teeth. She said it was Rody. I'm gon' turn him over to her and they're gon' have a funeral."

"Well, maybe now he can rest in peace." Evelyn sighed. "I was talking to Ada about it. She said it was the saddest thing she'd ever seen, watching Reba just standing there, looking at them bones." She flipped her hair back over her head and put the towel on the table and sat across from Frank. "I guess you're after Mr. Pegleg."

"Doing our best," Frank told her. "Not easy, since nobody's ever seen his face, and it's been a long time since Rody was killed."

Evelyn shook her head sadly. "My late husband, Jed, told me it was some crazy colored man," she said. "The way Jed was around the colored, I was just glad it wadn't him."

"Heard he had a temper," Frank said cautiously.

Evelyn picked up her cup and sipped from it. "Well, you heard right," she admitted. "I suspect the only thing he liked about the colored was their women."

Frank frowned with interest. "That right?" he said.

A playful smile broke across Evelyn's face. "Oh, fiddle, Frank, surely you must of heard the stories: Jed and his colored women. You could fill a book with all those stories."

Yes, Frank thought, he had heard the stories, but he had never known if there was any truth to them or if they were just stories told by bragging men with too much liquor in them. And Jed Carnes had not been the only white man said to have taken young black girls and forced them to have sex.

"I never pay much attention to loose talk," Frank said.

"Well, mind you, I never saw Jed do anything," Evelyn replied. She smiled at Frank. "I always thought that I was enough."

Frank squirmed uncomfortably. He looked away from her, reached for his coffee, but did not pick up the cup. He could see his hand tremble and he dropped it in his lap. The gesture made Evelyn lean forward, over the table.

"But there was one time," Evelyn continued, "that made me think different, even if Jed did deny everything."

Frank cleared his throat. "What was that?" he asked.

"You remember that old man they call Amos Whitley, the one who lives on that farm down near the river?"

"Amos?" Frank said. "Sure do. Must of had twenty kids. Owns that farm, I hear. He's a good man."

"That's him," Evelyn agreed. "I guess six or seven of his boys worked for Jed at one time or another. Anyway, one night, right after dark, he came up to the house, right up to the front door, and knocked on it, and Jed went to the door. I was in the front room there and heard everything."

"What happened?"

"Amos said he'd heard that Jed had been fooling around after one of his daughters. He told Jed that if he ever found him around any of his people—any girl or woman that was in his family—he'd kill him. Said it just as calm as could be, but I knew he meant it, and so did Jed. Jed didn't even raise his voice. He said that whatever Amos had been told was a lie, and he promised he'd find the man who was spreading such rumors and take care of it."

"That don't sound like Jed," Frank said.

Evelyn's eyes lingered on Frank. A smile was balanced in the corners of her mouth. "It *wadn't* like him," she said. "He was scared. Scared of what Amos might do to him and scared of what I might say."

"Did you?" Frank asked. "Say anything, I mean?"

The smile turned to a laugh. "Heavens, no. Why should I? It'd have just been a fight and he'd have won. Not saying anything, I had him where I wanted him. Anyway, listen to me, will you? Rattling on like this. Want some more coffee?"

"Uh, no, thanks," Frank said. "I got to be going."

"Well, I expect you to keep Mr. Pegleg from my door," Evelyn cooed.

Frank smiled and blushed.

"You going to be over this way all morning?" Evelyn asked.

"Don't know. Maybe."

"Why don't you come back for lunch?" Evelyn urged. "It's been a long time since I've cooked for anybody."

"I—I don't know."

"You can call me."

"Well, thank you. If I can make it, I'll do that."

Evelyn stood. She said, "Just give me a minute to slip into something and I'll walk you out. Wouldn't want anybody driving by to see me at the front door with you, and me being dressed in nothing but my robe. No telling what people would say." She laughed and rushed away, down the corridor to her bedroom. Again, she left the door open. Again, Frank watched her from the angled mirror. She slipped from her robe and stood for a moment, nude, in the perfect spot to be seen in the mirror. Her body was better than any hootchy-kootchy dancer Frank had ever seen. Then she dressed, slowly, seductively.

"Damn," Frank muttered. She's got to know what she's doing, he thought. She's got to know I can see her.

• • •

He drove idly along the road leading through Crossover. The day was already building heat, and the steam-cooking of road grass and corn and cotton stalks from the fields flowed across the road and into his car.

He slowed the car when he passed the cutoff going to Hack Winter's house. The thought of Tom made him smile. Great God, that boy could tell some outlandish stories. What was it he had heard from the men at Dodd's General Store? Something about a wagon caravan of dwarf Gypsies with a girl they had kidnapped. She would be sold off into slavery, Tom had vowed.

Frank chuckled aloud. The little turd. Had Keeler Gaines out with his shovel and pick looking for gold on Sweetwater Creek, over near the old gold mines.

Nothing wrong with the boy, though, Frank decided. Just high-spirited. He'd do fine when he got older, unless, of course, he got caught up in all that talk about Conjure Woman's predictions. And the business with Reba's boy, with Sonny, that would have to change. Kind of sad too, Frank thought. He remembered a friendship with a black playmate named Moody. They'd had good times together when they were boys. Fishing. Hunting. They had had rabbit boxes together one year, had built them from scrap lumber left over from repair work on his daddy's barn. Frank shook his head wearily. Moody had moved to Detroit when he was seventeen or eighteen. Word was that Moody had been killed in the war. Nobody knew for sure. It was only gossip, but such gossip was almost always correct.

Four miles later, he approached Harlan Davis's farm. Harlan's home was old but well-kept. The clapboard was painted a gleaming white, the shutters at the windows were forest green. Lightning rods were at opposite ends of the roof line, like small, sharp horns. The yards were perhaps the finest in the county. Islands of small shrubs fanned out between the oaks that waved tall over the house, and the flower gardens that Alice Davis loved bloomed in spectacular colors. It was a place that should have belonged to a gentler man than Harlan Davis.

Frank slowed his car, watched the house grow larger as the car rolled toward it. Harlan Davis was a part of his youth that he would never forget. A football game on a Friday night. Harlan was there, with some of his friends. They had stormed the field, attacking the

other team, and the fight had become a riot. He remembered standing
on the sideline, being pushed back by his coach, as Harlan gleefully
assaulted a parent who had rushed to the aid of his son, and he had
wondered how a man—in his late twenties then, Frank guessed—
could be so uncontrolled, how he could find such pleasure in causing
trouble. Harlan Davis had not changed much, according to the stories.
He was fifty, or almost fifty, and his face wore the scars of many
fights, but his eyes glittered with the merriment of their memory. Harlan had not changed; he had merely aged, had taken a wife—Alice—
who once had been portrait pretty but was now a nervous and sour
woman, with only a trace of the beauty of her youth. Frank remembered hearing Fletcher talk of Harlan and Alice Davis. "Damn good
thing they didn't have no kids," Fletcher had said. "They ain't fit to
raise pigs, much less kids. I've known that old boy a long time. He
don't bother me none, since I don't pay him no attention, or get in
his way, but he's got a bad streak in him."

At the narrow sideroad beside Harlan's house, the road leading to
the sharecropper home where Reba Martin lived, Frank braked to a stop
and turned his car. Wouldn't hurt to talk to Reba again, he reasoned.
Plenty of time until lunch. Maybe the younger girl would be there.
Remona, that was her name. He had not talked to Remona about Pegleg,
and Remona had been in the room, at the table, when Pegleg kicked
open the door and forced his way inside.

And maybe he would talk to Sonny, if Sonny was up to it.

Word was, Conjure Woman had talked Sonny out of his coma. And
the word was from Ada Winter, which meant it was right, or close
enough to being right that arguing the point would be a waste of breath.
She had called to urge a quick release of Rody's remains. "He needs a
decent burial," Ada had insisted. She had added, "Tom was over there
when Conjure Woman was with Sonny. He said Conjure Woman said
something about a change coming. I don't know what that means, and
I've got to say that I've had my doubts about that old woman—but if
she can do what modern medicine can't, then I think we all better start
paying attention to anything she says."

Frank could feel a shiver slide down the back of his arms, under his
starched shirt.

●   ●   ●

It had been a persuasion that Hack Winter could not deny, or debate. Even Troy had shrugged and nodded agreement.

Tom needed to be with Son Jesus. Especially now, Ada had argued, now that Son Jesus had been told about the bones of his father being found in the sawdust pile.

"Reba asked for him," Ada had said sadly. "She said if Tom and Sonny could spend some time playing around the house, and maybe helping Jule finish putting up the fence, she thought Sonny wouldn't be thinking about his daddy all the time."

"Well, I hate to say it," Troy had muttered, "but she's right. If anybody on earth can keep a person from thinking, it's Tom."

"How can you talk that way about your brother?" Ada had demanded.

"Mama, how can you even ask me that question?" Troy had replied. "You know good and well that he'll be butt-deep in some kind of mess before suppertime."

Troy had been right. That morning, while Frank Rucker gazed at Evelyn Carnes' naked body, Tom and Son Jesus had made a bow from a poplar limb and arrows taken from the new growth of a pecan tree, and Tom had convinced Son Jesus to sneak a sweet potato from his mother's kitchen.

"What you gon' do with this sweet potato, Thomas?" Son Jesus asked, handing the potato to Tom.

"Ain't nothing to it, Son Jesus," Tom told him. "I'm gon' put this sweet potato on top of your head and shoot it off with a arrow."

Son Jesus grinned as though amused by a fool.

"You ever hear about William Tell?" Tom asked.

Son Jesus shook his head. He stared at Tom suspiciously, his eyes wandering from Tom's face to the bow and arrow and sweet potato that Tom held.

"I swear, Son Jesus, you ain't never heard about nothing," Tom complained.

"Uh-huh," Son Jesus mumbled. He stepped back from Tom and put his hands in his pockets. He leaned against a pecan tree.

"William Tell was a man who put a apple on his little boy's head and shot a arrow straight through it. Cut it clean in half. And I bet a nickel I can do the same thing," Tom said smugly.

"You ain't no William Tell, Thomas."

"Ain't nothing to it. All you got to do is stand still. Anyhow, this potato's bigger'n a apple."

"Ain't it supposed to be a apple, Thomas?"

"Ain't no apples big enough this time of year, Son Jesus. You know that. Besides, this sweet potato's flat on one side. It'll fit on top of your head just like a hat."

Son Jesus stared at Tom. "I ain't gon' do it, Thomas," he said stubbornly. "I ain't gon' put no sweet potato up on my head and let you shoot at it."

"If I'm gon' be William Tell, you got to be the little boy," Tom insisted.

"You be the little boy. Let me be William Tell," Son Jesus suggested.

"You already got the name," Tom argued. "Sometimes William Tell called the little boy 'Son,' just like you."

Son Jesus shook his head. "Ain't gon' do it. Cecily say I got to quit doing everything you say for me to do."

The argument ended quickly. Son Jesus was unrelenting in his refusal to play the little boy, reminding Tom of the trip on the river and his near death.

"You gon' get me killed," Son Jesus vowed.

They agreed at last on a substitute—a scarecrow that Uncle Jule had erected a year earlier in an old garden spot.

The scarecrow was on a pole and crossarms, dressed in a throwaway shirt and pants and stuffed with wheat straw. Its head was bundled and tied at the tip with binder twine. Remona had taken an old sock and tied it around the scarecrow's neck and she had driven nail holes in tin can lids and dangled them from the arms like gaudy jewelry. In the wind, the tin can lids twirled against one another in sun flashes and made dull, clacking noises. Son Jesus and Tom had named the scarecrow Uncle Jule, and Reba had agreed with them. "He ain't moved a lick, just like Jule," she said.

Son Jesus and Tom took the sweet potato and pushed it into a nest of straw on the scarecrow's head.

"You ain't gon' hit nothing," Son Jesus predicted, giggling.

"I'm gon' hit that sweet potato," Tom said confidently. "I'm gon' cut it right in half."

Tom stepped away a few feet and took an arrow and fit its notch into the bowstring of binder twine and pulled on the string and aimed.

"You gon' shoot, or ain't you?" Son Jesus asked.

"Shut up, Son Jesus."

"You ain't gon' shoot," Son Jesus said. "You ain't gon' do nothing but look."

"Son Jesus, didn't nobody say nothing to William Tell when he was taking aim," Tom snapped.

"Uh-huh."

Tom inhaled, steadied his hand, then released the arrow. He could feel the shaft skim over the fingers that were gripping the bow. He heard the singing of the bowstring snapping taut, the brief whistle of the arrow, a hard thump, a sigh from Son Jesus. He looked up. The arrow had buried itself into the face of the scarecrow, exactly where a mouth might have been.

"Thomas, you done killed Uncle Jule," Son Jesus said softly.

"It ain't nothing but a scarecrow," Tom said.

"You was wanting me to do that," Son Jesus mumbled. "You was gon' kill me. They was gon' find my bones like they find my daddy's bones." He looked toward the road and saw Frank Rucker's car. "Yonder come the sheriff," he said. "I'm gon' tell him you was trying to kill me again."

THIRTEEN

Frank saw the boys approaching from the garden as he stopped his car under the shade of an oak. Son Jesus was stalking ahead of Tom, shaking his head, and Tom was dancing to keep up with Son Jesus' step, jabbering frantically. Frank knew they were arguing and he smiled. God only knows what that's about, he thought. Some stunt of Tom's, probably.

"How's it going, boys?" Frank asked as Son Jesus and Tom got to the car.

"He trying to kill me," Son Jesus said emphatically.

"Ain't so," Tom countered angrily.

"Whoa, whoa," Frank said. "What's this all about? What're you talking about, Sonny?"

"He done killed Uncle Jule," Son Jesus declared.

Frank blinked in surprise. "He killed Jule?"

"It ain't Uncle Jule," Tom argued. "It's a scarecrow that's named Uncle Jule."

"It was gon' be me," Son Jesus said. "Then he was gon' bury me and wait to somebody find my bones." He looked away, toward the scarecrow. "Thomas, he want me to put a sweet potato on my head and he was gon' shoot it off with a bow and arrow."

"I wadn't, neither," Tom snapped. He looked sheepishly at Frank. "I was just carrying on."

Frank tried to cover his smile. He nodded seriously, cleared his throat. "Well, now, boys, that's dangerous, playing with bows and arrows. You can't go aiming arrows at people. It could slip and somebody could get hurt."

"Uncle Jule, he got hurt," Son Jesus said. "Thomas done killed him."

"But it was a scarecrow, wadn't it?" Frank asked.

Son Jesus nodded. He folded his arms across his chest and stared at the ground.

"Where's the real Uncle Jule?" Frank said.

"He went over to the store to get some nails," Tom answered, "so we can finish the fence."

Frank looked at the fence. It was the same as it had been two days earlier.

"Well, you can't hurry some things," Frank said. "Takes time to put up a good fence."

"Ain't nothing good about that fence," Tom corrected. "Already had some boards fall off of it."

A chuckle rose in Frank's throat. He said to Son Jesus, "Is your mama home?"

Tom answered for Son Jesus: "She's in the house."

"Is Remona here?"

"She up at Mr. Davis's house," Son Jesus replied quickly. He looked at Tom triumphantly.

"Uh-huh," Frank mumbled. He started across the yard to the house.

"You gon' make Thomas quit trying to kill me?" Son Jesus said bravely.

Frank turned and looked at Tom. "You quit trying to kill Sonny. I got to give my Tom Winter posse a rest."

A smile broke across Tom's face. "You got a Tom Winter posse?" he asked.

"Got to have one," Frank told him. "You the most wanted man in the county."

◦ ● ◦

Frank did not stay long with Reba. She was folding the few clothes that Rody had owned and putting them into a paper sack. There was no reason to keep them, she told Frank.

"He been found now," Reba said sorrowfully. "Won't be needing them things. Maybe Jule can use them."

She asked Frank when she could get Rody's remains, and Frank told her he would have them delivered as soon as he got a release from Pug Holly.

"I'd say tomorrow," Frank judged. "Maybe this afternoon. Guess you want them taken over to Higginbottom's place."

Reba bobbed her head. "Cecily's taking care of things over there. We gon' have the funeral day on Saturday."

"Sorry you got to go through this," Frank told her. "But at least you'll know where he's resting."

"Thank the Lord," Reba mumbled.

"How did Sonny take hearing about his daddy?" Frank asked.

"Almost break his heart, but he better now. He growing up," Reba answered. She gazed out the window, watched Son Jesus and Tom with the bow and arrow. Tom's hands were waving frantically as Son Jesus aimed the arrow at the scarecrow. "Sometime he be just like a boy. Sometime he be just like a man. Just like my Rody. I tell him he the man of the family now."

"Well, he'll make a good one," Frank said. Then: "You reckon it'll be all right to stop by the Davis place and talk to Remona a few minutes?"

A frown wiggled into Reba's forehead. "Don't know," she replied. "Mr. Harlan, he don't like for that girl to stop working. Says Miss Alice too weak to do anything."

"Well, I think I'll see if I can take a minute or two away from Miss Alice," Frank said firmly. Harlan Davis would not tell him how to do his job.

"Hope Remona don't get in no trouble," Reba sighed. "That Mr. Harlan, he get mad real easy."

"Don't you worry about it," Frank said. He looked through the window. Tom and Son Jesus were examining the arrow buried in the stomach of the scarecrow. "Glad to see your boy's feeling fine," he added.

"Conjure Woman wake him up," Reba said.

"What I heard," Frank told her. He tipped his hand to his hat and started to walk away. Then he stopped and turned back. "Mind if I ask you something?" he said.

Reba shook her head numbly.

"You ever ask Conjure Woman where somebody might find Rody?"

Reba crossed her arms tight around her thin chest and nodded.

"What'd she tell you?"

"She say to wait. She say he be found. Say his bones gon' walk out of the ground."

• • •

Remona was at the back of the house, hand-wringing a mop over the side of the porch, when Frank stopped his car in the yard and got out. She paused in her work and watched him crossing to her. He knew that she was nervous.

"Morning," Frank said easily. "You got a minute or two?"

"I'm mopping the floors," Remona answered timidly. "Miss Alice—"

"Won't take but a minute. I'll tell Miss Alice."

Remona shook her head. "She taking a nap now." She turned her body from Frank, pulled her arms close to her. Her face was the face of a child—small, slender, bright-eyed, caramel-colored—but her body was that of a girl-woman. Muscled. Full-breasted. Graceful, even in her awkwardness of standing before the sheriff of Overton County.

"Where's Mr. Davis?" Frank asked.

"He went off."

"How long ago?"

"Not long," Remona said. "He be coming back soon."

"I won't be but a minute," promised Frank.

Remona did not reply. She squeezed weakly on the mop and held it.

"Just trying to make some sense of this Pegleg thing," Frank said. "You were there when he came in the house, wadn't you?"

Remona nodded.

"You heard what your mama told me about him," Frank continued. "Was there anything else you might have seen that she didn't tell about?"

"No sir."

"Nothing at all?"

Remona fingered the damp cords of the mop. Her eyes darted toward the door leading into the kitchen. She shook her head.

"Your mama said he picked your daddy up and walked off with him. How big a man was your daddy?" Frank asked gently. He knew the answer to the question, but he needed for Remona to keep talking.

Remona shrugged shyly. "He was little," she said.

"What'd he weigh? You got any idea?"

Frank waited for an answer. Remona ducked her head. She lifted her shoulders. The gesture told Frank she did not have an answer.

"Was he as big as me?"

Remona looked at Frank. For a moment, she had a curious expression of amusement. "No sir. He wadn't big as you."

"What about the Pegleg man? Was he as big as me?"

Remona looked away. Her forehead wrinkled. "Yes sir. I guess."

"And you didn't hear Pegleg say nothing? Nothing at all?"

"No sir."

"How bad did he limp, this Pegleg man?"

Remona shrugged slightly.

Frank saw Alice Davis's movement against the window in the kitchen before he heard her from inside the house: "Remona." Her voice was hard-edged.

Remona's body jerked. She turned quickly toward the door as Alice opened it and stepped outside.

"Yes m'am," Remona said nervously.

Alice smiled pleasantly at Frank. She said, "Well, now I see why I can't get anything done around here this morning."

"Morning, Mrs. Davis," Frank replied. "Just doing a little checking on the Pegleg man." He nodded to Remona. "Appreciate you talking to me, Remona."

Remona ducked her head and took the mop and rushed past Alice and went inside the house.

"Goodness, Sheriff, don't you think you could pick a more appropriate time to talk to people?" Alice said. She played irritably with the neck buttons on her blouse. To Frank, she had a frail, used look, the look of embarrassed alcoholics whose drinking was an escape from fear, their faces always betraying them with sudden twitches. "Hard to get any work out of the colored anymore as it is," she added.

Frank could feel a rush of anger. "Wadn't her fault. Guess she knows if a sheriff wants to talk to her, he's gon' do it."

"Well, she owes me a few extra minutes this afternoon for lollygagging," Alice said with a sniff. She added, "You know Harlan won't like it, you talking to her while she's supposed to be working."

"Well, m'am, I'm just doing my job."

Alice threw her hand up suddenly, waved it erratically. "Don't know why you're wasting taxpayers' money to look for somebody that's probably a thousand miles away by now," she said. "Good Lord, that killing took place years ago. I can't understand why finding a bunch of bones

has made you start acting like J. Edgar Hoover. It's over and done with.
Next thing we know, you'll have all the colored in the county just sitting
around, waiting for somebody to stop by and gab away with them, and
they won't a thing get done."

"I can't look at it that way. Wouldn't be fair," Frank said.

"Good Lord," Alice sighed. "Fair? Why, Sheriff, if it wadn't for
people like us, people like Reba and her bunch wouldn't have a place
to sleep or a stitch of clothes on their backs. What's fair is their doing
a little bit of work for it." She touched the buttons at her throat again,
laughed frivolously, then turned and went back into the house.

• • •

Frank knew that Remona would suffer from his visit. She would
have to give an extra hour of work to Alice Davis and she would take
a tongue-lashing from Harlan. He twisted his hands on the steering wheel
of his car. "Goddamn it," he whispered. But it was his doing, he thought.
If he had waited to talk to her, it would have been better. Still, there
was no reason to treat people as Harlan and Alice Davis treated Reba
and her family. The way Hitler treated people was not much different.

He saw a lone figure in a garden on a hill off the road, an older
woman wearing a long dress and a sunbonnet. She was leaning on a hoe,
grasping the top of the hoe with both hands. Her shoulders were narrow
and stooped. Her head turned slowly under the beak of the sunbonnet
as she watched his car pass. Her face was chalk white. To Frank, she
had the appearance of an odd and ancient bird, its claws locked on a
limb, its wings tucked to its neck. He wondered who she was and how
she lived and what she thought. Did she worry about Pegleg? Probably
not, he guessed. Pegleg's hammer would be nothing to her. She had been
pounded by the hammer of wars and the Depression and, most likely, a
parade of funerals that were as dulling as life had become for her.

• • •

Keeler Gaines was at Arthur Dodd's General Store, escaping his wife,
as he confessed to Frank.

"Damn woman drives me crazy when she's got her time of the
month," Keeler griped. "Yaps about everything she sees, and that's why
I find me something else to do, someplace else to be. She can't see me,
she can't yap at me. I swear, if I'd of known what I was coming back

to, I'd of stayed in the army. Between that woman and the boll weevils, I'm about to go slap crazy." He looked up at Frank and grinned. "You wadn't married when you come home, was you, Frank?"

"No, I wadn't," Frank answered.

"I been telling you, Arthur, we got us a crazy man as the sheriff," Keeler said. "I guaran-damn-tee you, if I'd of been Frank I'd of stayed over there in France, playing parlez-vous with them big-titted French girls and drinking that high-quality French wine. You'd of have to have had a team of mules to drag me back here. Ain't nothing here but worked-out dirt and women with their legs crossed at their knees. At least that the way mine is."

"She's a woman," Arthur said flatly. "Ain't one in ten of them worth a pinch of owl shit, but they rule the damn world. I swear they's something missing in the Bible. Adam done something we don't know nothing about, but whatever it was, it ticked God off, and that's why he jerked out a rib and made woman."

"That was one good-looking old lady you had, Arthur," Keeler said, teasing.

"Well, good Lord, Keeler, I know that," Arthur snorted. "But you said the right word—had. I ever even talk about getting married again, I want you boys to tie me down and cut my peter off."

Keeler laughed, then he asked Frank, "You got any ideas about Pegleg?"

Frank rolled the Coca-Cola he was holding over his palms, feeling the frost from the ice in the drink box. He shook his head in answer.

"How many was it he killed?" Arthur asked. "Two, wadn't it?"

"Three, by my count," Frank said. "Counting Rody Martin."

"I forgot how many it was," Arthur said. "All I know is, all of them lived around here."

Keeler lit a Camel cigarette. He said, "Well, they must be some mean-assed colored man right here in our own backyard that we don't know nothing about."

"Maybe he ain't from here," Arthur suggested. "I reckon I know everybody in this community, white and colored, and they ain't a colored man around that sounds like who Reba kept talking about. Only people I know that limps even a little bit is Jule Martin and Ed Cooley. Sack of fertilizer rolled off the wagon and fell on Ed's leg a few years ago. Jule's too lazy to kill a gnat, much less a man."

"Well, it ain't Ed," Keeler said. "He ain't as big as a minute, and he ain't colored, and I kind of doubt if ol' Ed can lift his goober, much less a hammer."

Frank sat and listened as Keeler and Arthur ran through a directory of names they had memorized from their years in Crossover. They did not know they were doing it, but Keeler and Arthur took the names from a mental map of the roads that spread out in five directions from Arthur's store. Name after name, white and black. They leaned back in the cane-bottom straight chairs that Arthur had placed on the front porch of the store and they gave history to Crossover. Tragic history. Funny history. Family by family, name by name. Those who had gone off to war, some killed, some returned. Those who had left the farms for work in textile mills or to study under the GI Bill. Those who had married and moved away, never to be heard of again. "Ain't like it used to be, before the war," Keeler observed, and Arthur concurred: "Hard to keep up with so much change. Drive down a road one day, and you'll see a yardful of kids—half of them in diapers, dirty as hogs—and the next week, there ain't a soul in sight. It's like they packed up in the middle of the night and lit out."

Being with Keeler and Arthur was like taking a walking tour of Crossover, and Frank listened intently, trying to connect a man covered in a sack mask, a man with a limp, to a name that Keeler or Arthur mentioned. Nothing matched.

He shifted uncomfortably in his chair when Arthur mentioned, with a smile that was almost evil, the name of Evelyn Carnes.

"She's a woman, which means she's as sneaky as a damn copperhead, but she's got a set of jugs on her that'd make a cow blush," Arthur drawled.

Keeler laughed. "Ain't that the truth. Remember when Jed died? Wadn't a month before every single man in the county was finding some reason to stop by there and talk to her. I hear tell that Kenny James kept going over there to give her money that he said he'd owed Jed. Said he kept finding bills for lumber. Almost broke Kenny, and all she'd do was take his money and send him off dragging his goober between his knees. But I reckon she's over Jed's dying now. She quit wearing black."

"How long's Jed been dead now?" asked Arthur.

"Little over a year," answered Keeler.

"I wish could understand why she married Jed in the first place," Arthur said. "Lord, that woman could of had anybody she wanted." He grinned. "Shit, she could of had me."

"Good God, Arthur, Jed had more money than anybody around here, that's why," Keeler said. "I've known Evelyn Carnes since she was twelve or thirteen years old. She was old man Cale Welborn's girl. Sharecropped a farm down near Shiloh. They didn't have enough money to rub two nickels together, and what they got, Cale drank it away. When Jed come along, Evelyn jumped at the chance to get out of there. Can't blame her for that, even if it meant living with Jed."

"I reckon she never got over being scared of him," Arthur suggested. "He was a mean little bastard."

"Yeah, but he damn well knew who not to mess with," Keeler declared adamantly. "You remember how he used to stay clear of that old colored man Amos Whitley?"

Frank could feel the hair on his forearms bristle. "What for?"

"Well, if you know that Whitley clan, you'll know why," Keeler said. "You mess with one of them, you had the whole damn bunch down on you, and I guaran-damn-tee you they ain't nobody, white or colored, that wants them Whitley boys pissed off. I seen two of them pick up a wagon one time and turn it around in the road." He turned to Arthur. "Ain't I right? I was fighting the Japs, but I've heard stories of how riled up Amos got the first time Pegleg showed up."

"Pegleg?" Frank said.

Arthur stood and stretched and rubbed his back against the four-by-four column that held up a corner of the roof over the porch. He said, "Well, you would of still been in the army, Frank, but Keeler heard it right. Amos was one more pissed-off man." He nodded thoughtfully. "That first Pegleg killing happened when three or four colored fellows were sitting around a campfire playing cards one night, and this man just come out of the woods, wearing his mask. Started swinging that hammer, scattering people right and left, except for the one he was killing. Anyway, them other old boys hightailed it out of there. It was them that said the fellow with the hammer looked like a colored man with a pegleg, and that's how he got named Pegleg. Amos went through the house of every colored family around here, looking for somebody who was limping. If they was a pegleg man around, by shot, old Amos would of found him."

"Why?" Frank asked. "The boy that was killed wadn't a Whitley, if we talking about the same one."

"The first one that Pegleg killed is the one I'm talking about," Arthur said.

"According to what I read, he was a Conley. Blue Conley, they called him," Frank replied.

Arthur nodded vigorously. "That's who it was. Blue Conley. Had that color skin—blue-black. I knew his daddy real good. Asa. That was his name. He could pick four hundred pounds of cotton a day. But his boy, Blue, was married to one of Amos Whitley's girls and that made him one of them, and Lord, that family was thick as fleas. Keeler's right. Don't nobody mess with them."

Son of a bitch, Frank thought. He remembered Evelyn's rambling, almost casual story about Amos Whitley appearing at the front door of her home, telling her husband to stay away from his daughter.

Frank glanced at his watch. It was ten forty-five. He could feel the sensation of knowing, the whispering of instinct, singing its true note. He stood. "You care if I use your phone, Arthur?" he asked.

"Help yourself," Arthur replied. He added, with a grin, "Just don't steal nothing while you're in there."

●　●　●

Forty minutes after calling Evelyn Carnes from Dodd's General Store, apologizing for not being able to have lunch but promising to return soon, Frank was in his office, reading old newspaper reports on the death of Blue Conley. It took him only a few minutes to find what he was looking for: the description of Pegleg by the men who were playing poker with Blue on the night of the killing. One line puzzled him: *None of the men involved could give an accurate account of the size of the intruder.* He called Fletcher Wells into his office.

"You were around when the first story about this Pegleg fellow came up, wadn't you?" he asked Fletcher.

"Sure was," Fletcher said. "First year I was a deputy."

"Tell me what you remember about it."

"We couldn't find the first trace of him, but didn't nobody never question the fact that he was killed. Them boys that was with him said they could hear his skull cracking, even when they was running off," Fletcher replied.

"Blue Conley," Frank said.

"Who?"

"Blue Conley, that was his name."

"Yeah, that's right," Fletcher said.

"Were you around when they were talking to the other fellows that were with Blue?" Frank asked.

"Sure was," Fletcher replied proudly. "Hell, Frank, I was pretty much in charge of it. You know how old Logan was. Niggers killing niggers. He didn't pay no attention to that."

"You remember anybody saying anything about how big Pegleg was?" Frank said.

Fletcher frowned in thought. He fumbled a cigarette out of its package and lit it from the spewing end of a kitchen match. "Well, best I can remember, they wadn't much description that they could give us. Wadn't too big, though. Why?"

Frank waved away the question with his hand. "What do you mean, he wadn't too big?"

"Well, one of them old boys that was in that card game—can't recall his name right now—was about the biggest nigger I ever seen," Fletcher explained. He grinned in memory. "Son of a bitch looked like a horse, Frank. I swear he did. Anyhow, he was saying Pegleg was big as he was, but the rest of them said he was lying, said Pegleg wadn't much bigger'n that old boy's leg. I remember making them tell me which one he come closest to matching, and they picked the littlest one in the bunch. Hank Oldfield. That was his name. I see Hank all the time now. You know him, don't you?"

Frank nodded. He did know Hank Oldfield. Hank was so small he looked almost deformed.

"Shit," Frank muttered.

"What is it?" asked Fletcher.

Frank ignored Fletcher. He leaned his elbows on his desk and rubbed his face in the palms of his hands, as though to clear a murky picture in his mind. It was puzzling how everyone could describe Pegleg, except for his size. His size ranged from molehill to mountain.

"What is it?" Fletcher asked again.

"Nothing," Frank muttered. Then he added, "You ever wonder if Logan knew who this Pegleg was?"

Fletcher shrugged. "He could of. All them killings happened in

1943, clumped together in a few months. That's when Logan ran just about everything in the county—you know, with the war going on. For a while there, we lost more men out of the county to Pegleg than we did to Hitler, but Logan didn't do much more'n pass it all off to one of us. Said he wasn't gon' waste his time looking for somebody who was doing everybody a favor."

Frank inhaled—slow, deep, sad—and shook his head wearily. "I'm surprised somebody didn't kill the son of a bitch," he said.

"Somebody did," Fletcher reminded him.

Frank looked up. He remembered going to Logan Doolittle's house on the morning that Lucy Hix had found Logan's body in his bed, shot once through the head. Frank had investigated it thoroughly, exhaustively, but no one had ever been arrested. There were too many suspects, with too many motives. Out of the murder, Frank had gained the sheriff's badge and Lucy Hix.

"I mean sooner than they did," Frank said. He pulled himself from his chair and picked up his hat.

"Where you going?" asked Fletcher.

"Out for a little while."

"What for?"

"I got somebody I want to talk to."

•   •   •

Higginbottom's Funeral Home, the only black mortuary in Overton County, was an imposing two-story house on Compton Street. The first floor had been converted to a waiting room for grieving families, and the back porch had been framed in as an embalming room. Reeder Higginbottom and his family lived in the rest of the house, though, by habit, they seemed to huddle upstairs. Frank had been to Higginbottom's on three or four occasions to question Reeder, or sobbing family members, over a suspicious death. He had been struck by two almost eerie impressions—the odor of embalming fluid, which had permeated the walls of the house, and a silence that seemed to be suspended in the air, drifting ghostlike from room to room. To Frank, it was a house of subdued horror.

Cecily Martin sat composed in an armchair in the waiting room, her hands crossed in her lap, her chin lifted. If she was nervous, she did not show it, and Frank quickly realized that Cecily was in an environment that pleased him. At Higginbottom's, Cecily had discovered something valuable—her dignity. It was impossible to believe she had worked in fields for most of her life.

"Just wanted to ask a few questions about the day your daddy was carried off," Frank said gently.

Cecily nodded. She licked her lips and swallowed. She would not let her eyes waver from the sheriff's face. "Just look him in the eye and answer quiet-like," Reeder Higginbottom had advised. "I done talked to him lots of times. He ain't gon' try to scare you."

"I talked some to your mama and to Remona," Frank continued. "They were telling me that this Pegleg man was somebody maybe my size, but all the reports I've read said he wasn't too big. Can you tell me about that?"

"He was bigger'n my daddy," Cecily answered.

"Uh-huh," Frank said. "Maybe as big as me?"

Cecily's eyes flashed over him. "Yes sir."

"One thing I can't figure out," Frank said, "is why he might have picked out your daddy. From everything I know, your daddy was a fine man."

Cecily swallowed again, but she did not reply. Frank could see a film of tears coat her eyes.

"You got any thoughts about that?" Frank asked. "You ever see your daddy get mad at anybody?"

Cecily blinked, and in the blink her memory flashed to a cotton field on a late June afternoon. Her father had been plowing cotton for Harlan Davis and she had brought him water in a glass jar. Harlan Davis had stopped his truck on the side of the road and walked across the field, inspecting the plowing.

"Can't get it done leaning against the plow," Harlan had said roughly.

"Yes sir, Mr. Harlan," her father had answered, handing the jar back to Cecily. "Just taking a little drink of water."

Harlan had let his eyes drift over Cecily's body, and a smile had cracked on his hard face. "This girl's growing up, ain't she? Almost a woman."

"Yes sir," her father had mumbled. "She thirteen now."

"Last time I saw you, girl, you was skinny as a fence post," Harlan had said. "Getting some tits now, ain't you?"

Cecily remembered the wave of embarrassment that soured in her stomach. She remembered feeling her breasts against the thin pullover blouse she wore. She remembered staring down at the ground to avoid Harlan Davis's gaze.

"Come here, girl, let me get a look at them things."

"Mr. Harlan," her father had said sternly, "don't want you bothering my girl, now." He had looked pleadingly at Cecily. "Go on home, honey."

"Goddamn it, Rody," Harlan had snapped. "Don't you go talking back to me." He had turned to face Cecily. "Pull up that blouse, girl. Let me see how big them tits are."

"Go on home, honey," Rody had ordered firmly, his voice rising in anger.

Cecily remembered backing away warily, her eyes flitting from Harlan Davis to her father. She remembered turning suddenly and running down the freshly plowed furrow of the cotton row. She remembered hearing Harlan Davis's laugh.

"What about it, Cecily?" Frank asked again. "You ever see your daddy get mad at somebody?"

Cecily shook her head. Her eyes did not move from Frank's face. "No sir."

Frank stood and nodded. "Well, I took enough of your time. Appreciate you talking to me."

Cecily's head bobbed once. Her hands stayed crossed in her lap. "Yes sir," she said. Then: "Why you looking for him? My daddy's been dead a long time."

"I know," Frank told her. "I guess it just bothers me, knowing there was somebody going around killing people."

"Colored people," Cecily corrected calmly.

"Yeah, you right. Colored people," Frank answered. "And every one of them lived in my county."

FOURTEEN

Tom did not understand why Remona ducked her face toward the ground and cupped her hand over her eye when she got out of Harlan Davis's car and hurried into the house. He saw Harlan Davis glare at him and at Son Jesus and Uncle Jule from the opened window of his car, and he saw Son Jesus step back under the power of the glare. Harlan Davis turned the car slowly in the yard, his eyes locked on them, then he drove away.

From inside the house, Tom heard Reba cry out.

"What's the matter?" Tom asked.

"Y'all boys stay here," Jule ordered. He crossed the yard cautiously and went into the house.

"Why's your mama crying?" Tom said softly to Son Jesus.

Son Jesus shook his head. He turned from the house, toward the road, and watched Harlan Davis's car disappear.

They sat without talking under the shade of the chinaberry. Tom doodled in the ground with a stick, making round faces with hole-punch eyes. Son Jesus gazed at the road. His face was as peaceful as it had been when he was unconscious on the river.

They were still sitting, still not talking, when Ada drove into the yard. She saw them and called, "Come on, Tom, we need to get on home."

Tom pulled himself from the ground and moved hesitantly to the car. He leaned in at the opened window and said quietly, "Mama, something's happened to Remona."

Ada's eyes widened in surprise. She thought about trouble coming in threes. First Sonny, then finding Rody's bones, now this, whatever this was. How much could Reba take? She opened the door and got out of the car quickly.

"What, honey?" she asked.

"I don't know," Tom said. "They in the house. I heard Reba crying."

"You stay here," Ada ordered. She rushed away into the house.

Tom turned to Son Jesus. He said, "I guess I better wait in the car. I'll see you tomorrow." Son Jesus did not look at him.

It was only a few moments before Ada pushed open the door to the house and stalked across the yard. She was mad, and Tom knew it. It was in the way she held her head—proudly, defiantly. Her eyes were burning with fury. His father had called it the Eleanor Roosevelt look, when Eleanor Roosevelt got mad. She stopped at the car and turned to Son Jesus. "Don't you worry, Sonny, we're going to take care of this," she said in a voice that was a cry and a promise. She got into the car and sped away.

"Mama," Tom said.

"Hush, Tom, don't talk to me."

"Why you so mad?"

"I hate fools, that's why."

"Who's a fool, Mama?"

"Harlan Davis, for one. He's a fool."

"He scares me," Tom admitted.

"Well, he don't scare me. Not one bit. No sir, not one bit. He just made a big mistake."

"What'd he do?"

"He just made me mad."

◉ ● ◉

Frank was sitting in a rocker on his back porch, having a glass of iced tea left for him by Lucy Hix, thinking of his conversation with Cecily Martin. She had not told him everything, and he knew it. There had been a moment when her eyes had glazed over, when she had left the waiting room in Higginbottom's Funeral Home and had flown away to a distant memory. And wherever that memory had taken her was where he would find the answer to many questions. Frank was sure of it.

From inside, he heard the telephone ring, and he rocked up from his chair and went into the house. The call was from Ada Winter, angrily reporting the beating that Harlan Davis had inflicted on Remona. "You got to do something about it, right now," Ada demanded. "If you don't, we might as well turn this county over to him and that bunch he runs with."

"Yes m'am," Frank told her. "I'll handle it." Then he put down the receiver and muttered, "That son of a bitch." He felt a rush of guilt. It was his fault, stopping to talk to the girl, knowing what kind of man Harlan Davis was. He picked up the phone again and dialed. Hugh Joiner answered. "I'll be by to pick you up in a minute," he said to Hugh.

"What's going on?" Hugh asked.

"We're fixing to throw somebody's ass in jail," Frank told him.

● ● ●

There was only a smear of day left on the horizon, a single red-bellied cloud holding a nail-scratch of light from the sun, when Frank crossed the bridge at Sweetwater Creek, going into the Crossover community. The only thing Frank had said to Hugh on the drive was that Harlan Davis had beaten Remona, had maybe broken her jaw. Hugh did not ask any questions. He could feel the rage that simmered in Frank. It was like the sizzling of a fuse, fire-spitting and dangerous. He touched his hand to his revolver and let his fingers rest on the steel. Frank Rucker was not a man easily understood, Hugh thought. Frank had left his farm in 1942 to join the army, a friendly and gentle boy-man who had earned a reputation as a star athlete at Overton High School, and he had returned an uncomfortable war hero and a man who seemed surrounded by a restless aura. It was that aura, the inexplicable sense of difference, that had appealed to Hugh, had inspired him to apply for a deputy's position after his service in the navy. Frank was not like other men in Overton County. He would not turn his back on anyone, and he would not sell his soul to the highest bidder. Whatever had happened to him in the war, it was good.

Hugh also knew Harlan Davis. Harlan was bull strong. He would not go easily or quietly to jail.

Harlan was walking from his barn to his house when Frank wheeled the car into the yard and braked to a hard stop and got out of the car, shoving the door closed angrily. Hugh got out of the passenger's door and stood, waiting.

"What you want, Frank?" Harlan demanded.

"I want your ass in jail," Frank said evenly.

Harlan laughed. "What for?"

"Assault," Frank told him. "And I hope to God there's two or three other things I can think of—like resisting arrest." He started walking toward Harlan.

Harlan raised his hand and took a step back. "Well, by God, you may have that if you think you're gon' take me off to jail," he sneered.

"Suit yourself," Frank said. He motioned with his head to Hugh, and Hugh crossed to him.

"Now, Hugh, I'm gon' put the cuffs on this man, and if he gives me any trouble at all, I want you to take your gun and blow his head off," Frank added calmly. "And I mean it. Shoot the son of a bitch right between the eyes."

Hugh pulled his revolver from its holster and raised it toward Harlan. "You got it," he said.

Harlan's face paled. He stared in disbelief.

Frank stepped toward him, unsnapping the handcuffs from his gun belt. His eyes cut into Harlan's face, daring him. His voice was barely controlled: "You low-life asshole. I'm the sheriff of this county. When I decide to talk to somebody, I, by God, will do it, and not you, or nobody on this earth, is gon' make a mockery of it."

"What the hell you talking about?" Harlan said.

"Reba's girl," Frank answered. "Remona. You slapped her around because I stopped to talk to her today."

Harlan laughed nervously. "Shit, Frank, she got a backhand for sassing. What the hell's wrong with you? Why you so riled up over some colored girl being kept in her place?"

Frank stopped walking. He could feel his lips trembling. His heart was pounding. "I killed some men in the war," he whispered angrily, "and I wadn't near as pissed off at them as I am at you, Harlan."

A sneer curled over Harlan's lips. "Well, General, you ain't in the war no more, are you?"

There was a pause, a daring that became heat in the space separating the two men. And then Frank growled, "Shoot the son of a bitch, Hugh."

Harlan's eyes darted wildly toward Hugh Joiner. He heard the click of the hammer on Hugh's revolver.

"Let me get this right, Frank," Hugh said. "You telling me to kill him?"

"You damn right I am," Frank snapped. "The lying son of a bitch." He turned to Hugh. "Shoot him," he ordered.

Hugh tilted the barrel of the gun up. "Just remember, Frank, you the one who told me to do it."

"All right, all right," Harlan said in a rush. "Hell, I didn't mean nothing by it. I thought she was lying. They always lying. Shit, you know how niggers are. I thought she'd stopped you at the road when you come by. Alice said—"

"I don't give a damn what Alice said," Frank barked. "The girl didn't even want to talk. She was scared to death."

"Well, hell, that ain't what Alice said."

"I told you, I don't care what Alice said," Frank growled. "Nothing on earth gives you the right to beat up on people, especially people that can't fight back. Turn your sorry ass around and put your hands behind your back."

Harlan did as he was told and Frank snapped the handcuffs on his wrists.

"You gon' be sorry you done this," Harlan said bitterly. "I guaran-damn-tee you, you gon' be sorry."

"You got another one," Frank said.

"Another what?"

"Charge," Frank replied, pushing Harlan roughly toward the car. "You just threatened an officer of the law."

"Kiss my ass, Frank."

Frank's hand flew up and caught Harlan in the flat of the back. He shoved. Harlan stumbled and crashed into the side of the car.

"Well, I swear, you must be drunk too," Frank hissed. "Hugh, put that down. The son of a bitch couldn't stand up."

● ● ●

From the window of her house, Alice Davis watched the sheriff's car drive away. She felt faint and frightened. She wondered what Frank knew about her husband, besides the beating of Remona. She wondered if Frank knew what she knew, that her husband would take Remona down into the barn and tie her and rape her. Once, she had seen it. By accident. Through a loose plank in the barn when she had gone out to cut gladiolus from her flower bed. She had heard her husband's rough, loud breathing as she passed quietly by the barn, carrying her cutting shears. It was a sound like a pig's grunting when a pig has been running. She looked through the loose plank and saw him—her husband pounding himself into the forced-open legs of a young colored girl. She had wanted to kill him with her cutting shears, but knew she could not, even if she had had the strength. She had not mentioned the rape to her husband, but she had never let him touch her again.

● ● ●

The anger that surged in Frank did not begin to subside until ten o'clock. He had calmed his jitters by buying a package of cigarettes after being off them for two years, and he had chain-smoked a half-pack. He had also downed a half-pint—maybe more—of bourbon, diluting it with water and cracked ice.

Sitting in the dark on his back porch, his face tilted up to the breeze of an overhead fan he had installed only two months before his wife left him—a last gesture of trying to appease her, a failure for the marriage but good for him—Frank let the night and the breeze and the cigarettes and the bourbon stroke him. He needed to think clearly, to reason about what he had done and what would be the end of it.

On the drive from his home to the jail, Harlan Davis had railed about the end of Frank's career. It was a vow Harlan had made before God. A white man arresting another white man for slapping a black girl who needed slapping might as well take his own pistol and blow his brains out. He would be dead, politically if not literally, as soon as the word got out. "Before I post bail," Harlan had promised, "your ass will be on its way out. You done forgot where you are, boy, and who you owe."

And maybe it would be that way, Frank thought. He'd seen such times and known such men. Logan Doolittle had been that way. There was no law governing a white man beating a colored when Logan Doolittle was sheriff. Logan had called it the law of nature, and the law of nature always superseded the law of the book. Logan's Law, Logan Doolittle had called it. Frank remembered hearing someone ask him, "What's that? What's Logan's Law?" and Logan had answered, "It's the law of the way things are."

Frank clucked his tongue, rolled his head to stretch his neck. How many stories had he heard about the law of the way things are, about Logan's Law? But Logan's Law was just a name. You could scratch Logan's name out and put in the name of almost every other sheriff, or peace officer, in the South, and you came up with the same thing, he guessed. Lynchings still gravely remembered, still talked about by men who daily took their places on the benches surrounding the courthouse on Courthouse Square. Arrogant stories, told with a coward's pride, the kind of stories that always ended with, "Wish I'd of been there." But not only lynchings. Stories of arresting colored men for nothing more than having a pint of liquor in their house, and sending them to the chain gang for six months because there was roadwork to be done. The stories were endless, and he had heard them since his childhood. When he asked about the stories, his parents had warned him with regretful voices about such men as Logan Doolittle. Bad apples in every barrel, they had said. No reason to treat people that way.

And there was one story that caused a chill each time he thought of it. In Columbus, after the war, a colored soldier who had helped liberate Jews at one of the death camps—Frank could not remember which—had been met at the railroad station by a mob of men who forced him to remove his uniform and flee for his life, wearing only his underwear. The law had watched, or so the story said. The law had watched the assault with smirking disregard, had watched the burning of the uniform.

He had read of the story in a magazine given to him by Logan Doolittle. "Now, by God, *that's* a parade." Logan had laughed. "Uppity nigger. I ain't never seen a nigger come back from the war that wadn't uppity, strutting around in that uniform like he was a hotel bellboy."

Frank had said nothing. He had simply walked out of the office, with rage filling his mouth like bile.

On that day, he could have killed Logan. Wanted to. Wanted to kill Logan and then drive to Columbus and kill the men who had burned the uniform of a soldier. A few phone calls, and he could have recruited a small force to go with him.

But maybe the story of the soldier, and Logan's snickering glee over it, had been the reason he had accepted the sheriff's badge, Frank thought. Maybe he had had to accept it.

One thing was certain: Logan's Law—the law of how things are— was more powerful than armies of men doing their killings in wars. Wars ended. Logan's Law did not. Logan's Law killed from the inside out.

Still, everything had its limits. Maybe Harlan had pushed Logan's Law too far. Harlan was a cheat, and everybody knew it. Few men liked him. Beating a young girl, white or colored, would not be easy to put aside, to excuse. And, also, there was Ada Winter. Ada was angry. Ada would not be pushed around. Not Ada. Not in her Eleanor Roosevelt mood. She was the type who would match Harlan word for word, one of the few women in the county who could rally support. She had done it in the war—organizing scrap-metal drives and church suppers to sell bonds. She had helped illiterate farm mothers write letters to their sons and had read to them the letters their sons had laboriously scrawled on tablet paper in foxholes. After the war, Ada Winter had been written about in the *Atlanta Constitution* in a column called "Home Front Heroes," one of only four women from the county to be recognized by the governor in a postwar campaign to celebrate citizenship during an election year.

Frank drank from his bourbon and smiled. He could see Ada leading a parade of women on the county courthouse, ready and willing to burn it to the ground if they were not heard. Harlan had better be careful. Not even Fuller Davis—Harlan's father—could save him from Ada, and Fuller Davis was one of the finest men in the county. It was a mystery how Fuller could be the father of Harlan and George and Mason— especially Harlan and Mason. George was different. Not as mean. Quieter. Almost everyone thought George simply copied his brothers, stood up for them. Maybe because he was afraid of them. No one could understand what had happened to the sons of Fuller Davis. The times, maybe. The Depression and the war. Meanness following meanness. And the long illness of their mother, a slow-eating cancer that had left her helpless for years. That, too, could have had something to do with it, not having the strong presence of a mother.

Frank shifted in his chair and stretched again, a long full-body stretch. He could see the moon coating the leaves of the oaks that grew in his backyard. Earlier, drinking his bourbon, he had listened to cicadas and tree frogs rehearsing for the night, like the instruments in the orchestra pit of the Broadway musical he had seen after the war. Now the cicadas and the tree frogs, and the night insects no one could ever see, were performing, and their music was good to hear. It calmed Frank. He thought of his friend Jabbo Lewkowicz, who had led him on a tour of New York City after the two mustered out of the army in 1946. To Frank, New York City had been like Jabbo—too loud, too hurried, too much. It had been worth following Jabbo around for a day or two, just to see the happy fool enjoy himself, but then the need for some quiet—some peace, a slowed-down pace—had set in, and Frank had taken the Greyhound home.

Jabbo had sent him a ballpoint pen from Gimbel's—the most advanced invention in the history of writing, Jabbo had boasted—and he had used the pen to exchange letters with Jabbo for a few years. Once, Jabbo and his new wife—Frank could not remember her name; Glenda, maybe—had even stopped by to visit on their way to Florida, but it had been more than a year since he had written to Jabbo, or Jabbo had written to him. It was the same with Jack Cason, who was from Pennsylvania, and Galen Pitts, who was from California. A few letters exchanged—promises kept from moments when dying was as likely as living—and then the letters stopped coming or being sent. And that was a sorry way to celebrate friendships. He should have kept writing, no matter what, Frank thought. It had been men like Jabbo and Jack and Galen who had taught him that people were very much the same, no matter where they had been reared, or what shape and color their faces were, or how odd their names sounded when spoken. Jabbo and Jack and Galen had spent some foxhole time talking about it—wanting to know from Frank what it was like living in the South. They had asked him straight out why the colored were given such a hard time. Frank had not had any good answers. He had sounded a lot like Logan Doolittle: "That's the way things are." He remembered what Galen had said: "Well, time changes everything. I never thought I'd see the day I'd waste my breath on one of you redneck crackers, and now, by God, I'm in a foxhole with one."

Galen was right. Time did change everything. Even foxhole promises of friendship made when dying was as likely as living.

Frank closed his eyes and listened to the orchestra of tree frogs and cicadas playing their night music, and he was not aware of the telephone ringing inside his home until the third or fourth ring. The ringing blended with the music.

He glanced at the clock as he answered the phone. It was ten-fifteen. "Hello," he said.

The caller was Evelyn Carnes. There was a sleepy, whispering sound to her voice. She said, "Hi. It's me—Evelyn. Were you sleeping?"

"Oh, no. Just sitting outside on the porch, trying to keep cool," he answered.

"I know. I feel like I'm baking," she said. She inhaled slowly. "I hope I'm not calling too late."

"Not at all. Is everything all right?"

"Fine. I talked to Ada Winter a little earlier and she told me that you had arrested Harlan Davis."

Lord, thought Frank. He did not want to talk about Harlan Davis. "That's right."

"Well, I'm not surprised," Evelyn said lightly. "I don't care if he and my late husband were friends. I never liked him. He's a crude man. Mean and crude. Is it true that he beat up on Reba's little girl?"

"Yeah, it's true."

"They'll be giving you fits, you know. I don't know when a white man's ever been arrested in this county for doing whatever he wants to to the colored."

"I had to do it," Frank told her.

"Oh, I know you did," Evelyn said. "It's about time somebody took a stand on how people get treated around here, white or colored."

Ada Winter had begun recruiting her army of women, reasoned Frank. If she had a tank, she could start a war.

"Anyway, I don't want to go on about all of that," Evelyn said lightly. "I was just sitting here drinking some iced tea that I'd made for our lunch and got to thinking about you and wondered if I could talk you into making up for it tomorrow."

Frank smiled. He thought of Evelyn sitting nude on her sofa, swirling the ice in the tea glass while a fan blew a warm breeze across her body.

"Don't think so," he said. "Not tomorrow. I'll probably have my hands full with Harlan's kinfolk. Maybe Saturday. I'm coming over for Rody's funeral. Fact is, I was thinking about talking to you, anyhow. Got a couple of questions running around loose."

"Well, I'm here." Then: "You sure it can wait until Saturday?"

Maybe she's drinking something besides iced tea, Frank thought.

"Well, if you're talking about tonight, it's kind of late—"

"I was just teasing you, Frank. I'm about to go to bed myself. A woman has to have her beauty rest, you know."

"I wish it could help a man," Frank said.

"Oh, I'm sure it can," Evelyn whispered.

● ● ●

Tom's head was buried into his pillow, which was shoved against the headboard of his bed. He stared at a water stain on the ceiling, a billowing, cloudlike stain that had puddled on the Sheetrock at the corner of the room and then had seeped through it from a rainstorm so strong it had ripped up shingles from the roof. Tom believed the stain looked like Captain Marvel. Once, he had shown it to Son Jesus. Son Jesus believed it looked like Pilate, or maybe Judas.

A book was opened and turned down across Tom's stomach. It was Robert Louis Stevenson's *Kidnapped*. Troy had taken one look at the title and said, "Oh, shit," and Tom had understood, but he knew also there was no reason for Troy to be concerned. Tom's runaway days, playing out the stories in books, were over. He would not go out and kidnap anyone. In a way, he had already done that to Son Jesus while pretending to be Huckleberry Finn.

He had finally heard the story of Harlan Davis's beating Remona from his mother. Rather, he had pieced it together, listening to her rave to his father about the beating. His mother seldom shouted, seldom let her temper spill over the banks of reason and flood everything around her. But the beating of Remona would not be contained. Ada had called Harlan Davis a coward, a low-life redneck, worse than the poor white trash he usually bribed to do his dirty work. She had alluded to Harlan Davis's cheating ways—against his fellowman and against his wife. There was enough rumor surrounding Harlan Davis to drag him down a greased chute to hell, she had declared, but hell was probably too nice a place for such a man.

The high boil of his mother's ranting had not simmered until his father forced her to take a long walk with him, a walk around the road that circled the pecan grove in front of their home. Tom did not know what his father had said, if anything. His father had a way of bringing calm to anger simply by his presence. When they returned from their walk, his mother was almost normal. At least she had seemed that way. She had stepped into his room and had said to him, "Son, I want you to remember what happened today. It's wrong. It's got to change, and the people of your generation have got to change it."

Tom had known she was talking about the way whites treated the colored, and maybe even the way whites treated each other. His mother's sense of justice was like a knife—no, a sword: a sharp-edged sword. It cut a sweeping path whenever she raised it against evil. And her sense of justice was as contagious as the flu.

There had been a time, Tom remembered, when he had begged his mother to drive him and Son Jesus to the county fair. They were seven, or maybe eight, and they had been given a poster advertising the fair by a man who was tacking them to utility poles on the backroads of Crossover. The poster was magnificent. It was large and colorful, with thick, dark lettering, lettering bold enough to be read from a passing vehicle, and with an artist's montage of a spectacle promising laughter and danger. The face of an orange tiger, its teeth bared, a glitter of light beaming from its black eyes, was in the exact center of the poster, and around the face of the tiger there were sketches of people and rides and games floating in the white space of the poster board. There was a man in a top hat and tails, a woman with a beard, another woman in a dancing garment that fit low over her hips, a Ferris wheel, a merry-go-round, a dwarf dressed in a cowboy suit, a man licking fire from a torch, a boy throwing a baseball at taped milk bottles, a girl with her face buried in cotton candy.

Tom and Son Jesus took the poster to the barn, to a cave they had burrowed into the loose hay, and they propped it against a wall of hay and talked about going to the fair.

"I ain't never been to no fair," Son Jesus confessed.

"I went to one," Tom bragged. "Couple of years ago. I was too little to do much, except look around."

"That'd be something, Thomas. It sure would."

"I don't remember nothing much about it, except that little cowboy," Tom lied. "He was something."

Son Jesus was impressed. "He real?"

"Yeah, he's real," Tom said. "That's his picture, ain't it?"

And then Tom improvised for Son Jesus the story of the dwarf cowboy—that he had been born in Texas, near a place called Tombstone, that he had a horse no larger than a dog, and that his pistols, also real, were the size of clothespins and shot bullets that looked like the heads of nails. The story delighted Son Jesus. If he could be anyone he had ever seen, he would be that cowboy, he told Tom. Later, they tried to saddle Micky, Tom's collie, with a feed sack and ride him, but Micky trotted to safety under the house.

His mother had tried to dissuade Tom from going to the fair with Son Jesus.

"I don't think you and Sonny ought to be going off over there together," she said.

"Why not?" Tom asked.

"I just don't think you ought to. Somebody might say something."

"About what?"

"About you and Sonny being together. I can take you, and Reba can take Sonny."

"They ain't got no car, Mama."

"Maybe Jule can take them."

"Can I go with them, then?" Tom asked.

Tom's mother's face sagged in exasperation. "No. No, you can't," she said. "Maybe you'll get to see Sonny over there if we go on the same day."

"Mama, I want Son Jesus to go with me."

"Well, honey, he can't."

"Why not?"

Ada Winter understood she did not have an argument for her son's question. She knew he did not think of white and black at his age. Son Jesus was his friend. They had been given the poster together, had planned the trip together. She knew the relationship would change with time. She knew that, someday, there would be something that would break Tom and Son Jesus apart like a killing. She also knew that on the day Tom pestered her about going to the fair, Tom and Son Jesus were inseparable.

"All right, Tom. Sonny can go with you," she said sadly. "But there won't be many little colored boys over there. Anybody says anything about the two of you being together, don't either one of you pay it any attention."

A week later, Troy drove Tom and Son Jesus to the fair. Both believed it was one of the grand days of their childhood. The sounds of it—the calliope-whistling sounds of it—and the smells of sawdust and cotton candy and popcorn, made them giddy with joy. They bounded from tent to tent, ride to ride, with Troy fast-striding behind them, annoyed, cursing his duty. There was only one moment of tension, but it was a moment that had lodged like a tumor in Tom's memory. As they were buying a bag of peanuts, a white boy, older than Tom and Son Jesus, pried between them and snarled at Tom, "What you doing here with a nigger?" Troy caught the boy by the shoulder, spun him roughly, and snapped, "Shut up."

Tom thought he saw the stain on the ceiling move. The stain did not look so much like Captain Marvel as it once did. Maybe Son Jesus was right. Maybe it was Pilate, washing his hands of sin.

• • •

Sometime during the night—though she did not know when—Son Jesus slipped into the bed with Remona. She knew he was there even before she consciously became awake, and at first her body jerked in fear under the covers, like a nerve bolt shooting through her, betraying her mind. The memory-weight of Harlan Davis on her, driving the stem of his blood-filled penis into her in rough, spastic thrusts, flashed quickly, made her legs pinch together, made her arms cross over the small, hard mounds of her breasts. And then she knew that she was in her bed and that the person beside her, balanced dangerously on the side of the mattress, his back turned away, was Son Jesus.

She slid one hand across the mattress and touched his arm. He did not move. She tried to open her mouth to lick the dryness from her lips, and a sharp pain, like a surprising burn, stabbed at her. Her mother had said her jaw was not broken, but she thought that it was, that it was cracked at the exact place where Harlan Davis's fist had struck her.

Harlan Davis would not have done such a thing, her mother had declared forcefully, if their daddy had been alive, but Remona knew it would not have mattered. What would her daddy have done? Fought Harlan Davis? Killed him? Then what? Colored men did not fight white men over such things as beating, or raping, their daughters or their wives.

Remona touched her abdomen, ran her fingers across it. Harlan Davis had taken her many times, and she wondered if she would become pregnant with Harlan Davis's baby, and if she did, would she try to jab it to death with a stick from a chinaberry tree, as Kippy Powers had done when a white man—Kippy never said who—made her pregnant. Kippy had died of bleeding, and the white man's baby had died with her.

She would not want Harlan Davis' baby, Remona thought. If Harlan

Davis had made her pregnant, she would kill him. She would take one of his guns and walk into the kitchen as he was eating supper and she would put the gun at the back of his head and pull the trigger.

Son Jesus stirred in the bed and Remona rolled her head to look at him. He had said nothing about the beating from Harlan Davis. He had simply come to her and embraced her and touched her face with his fingertips, and then he had walked away, out of the house, to sit in the edge of the woods and stare off somewhere beyond the fields and the woods. Their mother had said that Son Jesus had the gift of forgiveness, like it said in the Bible to have. Had said Son Jesus was special. Didn't Conjure Woman show up when he was born? But maybe Conjure Woman was wrong. Maybe Son Jesus was like everybody else. Maybe he would do nothing.

It was not unusual for Son Jesus to slip into bed with her, she thought. Since Cecily had left home to live in Overton, Son Jesus had sensed the loneliness she felt in dark moments—especially those moments when Harlan Davis had had his way with her in the barns. She knew that Son Jesus had seen him lead her away into their barn, and maybe Son Jesus even knew what was happening, because, after those times, he would come to her bed at night and sleep beside her, not as a child needing comfort, but as a child *offering* comfort. Always, in the morning, when she awoke, he was gone. They did not speak of his being in bed with her. It was as though they shared a secret too private even for them to understand.

She closed her eyes and listened to the even sleep-breathing of Son Jesus. And then she slept also.

FIFTEEN

Alice Davis sat at her kitchen table and watched the sun bubble out of the earth through the net of trees that ran along the border of the field at the sideroad leading to the sharecropper house where Reba lived. She had been awake for an hour. A cup of coffee was on the table before her. The coffee was cool now and had a thick, bitter taste, and it rolled on her stomach like an acid, making her queasy. She had not slept well, not since watching her husband being handcuffed and driven away by Frank Rucker. Not even the vodka, stirred with orange juice, had helped, and the vodka, the little sips that she took in secret from Harlan's abundant supply, had always helped. She had called the Overton County Sheriff's Department and been given the reason for the arrest, and she knew it was the truth, that Harlan had slapped Remona. No. Not that, not a slap. He had hit her with his curled fist. She had even tried to stop him, but he had shoved her aside and he had struck Remona again.

Harlan had been arrested many times, but he had never stayed long in jail. And he would not stay this time. His father and his brothers had been called, the deputy at the Sheriff's Department had told her, and she knew they would gather early in the morning at the courthouse and post bail for his release, and then he would return home angry and maybe he would take it out on her. He'd hit her before. Drunk, he had hit her. His own father had bailed him out of jail for hitting her, and she had listened to Fuller pleading for peace and had dropped the charges against her husband. Dropping the charges had been wrong.

She heard a noise outside, realized it was a car, and looked through the window. It was Ada Winter, on the sideroad to Reba's house. By road, it was four miles to Ada's home, or close to it, the way the roads looped through Crossover. Through the woods, it was two miles, Alice guessed. She was always seeing the Winters' car on the road, going to and from Reba's house, and it was annoying. The road was on the Davis property, no matter what the county said. Ada Winter was like an irritating trespasser, going to and from Reba's house all hours of the day. It was like they were sisters, or something, Ada Winter and Reba. Harlan had called Ada a nigger-lover, and it was true. The deputy had told her that it was Ada who had called the sheriff about Harlan's hitting Remona. She leaned up in her chair. She could see the boy with Ada, in the front seat. What was his name? Tom. Always running away from home. What's Ada doing, going to Reba's house so early? she wondered. Maybe to talk to Remona. If that was it, Harlan could find himself neck-deep in hot water. Ada would not stop asking Remona questions, not until Remona told about the rapes.

Alice pushed the coffee cup away from her. A sense of panic struck her, then a rush of anger, and she inhaled sharply. She blinked rapidly, and a shower of small purple dots floated across the membrane of her eyes. The sun inched its way between the two oaks growing near the sideroad. Somebody's got to feed the livestock, she thought. And he'll want food when he gets home.

She stood and pulled the thin terry-cloth robe around her.

Reba could feed the livestock, she reasoned. Or her little colored boy, her Sonny. Or that other colored man, Jule. And Remona would need to come and get started on the food. Harlan would not be so angry if he came into a house smelling of food. She would have to get to Reba's house quickly, before Ada Winter claimed Reba or Remona for the day. It was not fair that Ada Winter could use Reba or Remona at all. Reba and her bunch did not live on Ada Winter's land, in Ada Winter's tenant house. Anybody who knew anything knew that colored help was first obligated to the people who owned the home they lived in, and that meant anytime of the day, any day of the week. Ada Winter was jealous that she did not have her own colored family to call on. Let her do her own work. She was used to it. Ada did not have the weakness that caused a woman to take long periods of rest.

She gathered the keys to the car and went outside and got into the car and started it. She sat for a moment, her hands clasped on the steering wheel, feeling the puttering engine massage her fingers. Yes, she thought. Have everything right when Harlan comes home, and he won't be mad. Not at me. No, not at me. Get Remona. Stop her from saying too much. She drove away quickly.

• • •

It was Jule who saw Alice Davis's car rolling into the yard. He said, from the window, "Yonder comes trouble."

"What?" asked Reba.

"That Davis woman. She out in the yard."

Reba and Ada were at the kitchen table, examining Remona's bruised, swollen face. Tom and Son Jesus were also at the table, leaning on their elbows over the opened first-aid kit that Ada had brought—a white, snap-down tin box with a bold red cross painted across the top. The box smelled of gauze and alcohol and iodine and adhesive tape.

"What for?"

"How I know what for?" Jule answered. "I ain't her."

Reba and Ada moved to the window and looked out. They saw Alice get out of the car.

"Lord, she ain't even dressed," Reba said. "She looks mad." She sighed. "Oh, sweet Jesus, that woman's got a temper."

"Alice Davis?" Ada said in disbelief. "She's scared of her shadow."

Reba wagged her head. "You don't know that woman. She go slap crazy when she get mad. Wonder what she wants?"

"She's probably come to get Remona," Ada replied.

"Well, she gon' go home empty-handed," Reba mumbled. She crossed to the door and opened it and stepped outside. Ada was behind her.

Reba's voice was so sharp it startled Alice Davis. She said, "What you want?"

Alice blinked, then blushed. She had never heard Reba use such a tone with her. "Somebody's got to feed the livestock," she said. "And Remona's got to come and start the cooking. They'll be letting Mr. Davis come home and—"

"She ain't going nowhere," Reba said firmly. "Jule, he can go feed the livestock."

Alice looked beyond Reba to Ada Winter. It was Ada, she thought. If Ada wasn't here, Reba wouldn't talk to me that way.

"You got no right to be here, Ada," Alice said hatefully. "Reba and Remona's my colored women. Not yours. You got no right to come over here. This house belongs to my husband."

A surge of energy flew through Ada. She stepped past Reba, toward Alice, "You hear me, Alice Davis, and you hear me good," she snapped. "I'm over here to take a look at a little girl your husband almost beat to death, and I don't care whose house it is. And I can tell you that little girl can barely stand up, much less work. So if you want some food on the table when your husband gets out of jail, you better try to remember how to cook, because that's the only way he's going to get it."

The words slapped at Alice. She pulled her shoulders up and glared back at Ada and Reba. She could see the faces of Tom and Son Jesus in the background, peering out. Their eyes were wide in awe. She licked her lips, imagined the taste of orange juice and vodka, then she pulled the terry-cloth robe up under her chin.

"Reba, you come with me," she ordered.

Reba wagged her head. "I got a hurt child," she said. "I got to take care of her."

There was a pause. Alice aimed a long, daring gaze at the face of Ada. She wheeled suddenly and marched back to her car, then she turned. "You'll hear about this, Ada Winter," she shouted. "You think you can tell my colored what to do, you got another think coming. You wait to my Harlan gets home." She opened the car door and slipped inside and started the car and drove away, leaving two whirlwinds of red dust spinning from the wheels.

"That a mean woman," Reba whispered.

"No," Ada said quietly. "No, she's not mean. She's just scared."

"She ain't the only one," Reba said. She turned back into the house and motioned with her head toward Jule. "You go on up and feed the livestock," she said. "Take them boys with you."

Jule cocked his head. His forehead furrowed in concern. "She gon' take a gun to us, we go up there," he whined.

"Jule," Reba said sharply.

Jule's body slumped in defeat. He mumbled, "Com'on, boys, let's go get ourselves shot."

● ● ●

Frank did not know what Fuller Davis had said to his son, but it must have been effective. Temporarily, at least. From his office window, Frank had watched Mason Davis driving away from the county jail quietly at eight o'clock in the morning, with Harlan and George in the car. Frank had expected the car to stop at the courthouse and Harlan to fling himself out of it and bellow threats from the sidewalk, but nothing had happened. Harlan had left with Mason and George. Left without a look toward the courthouse. Fuller stayed behind, lingering in the waiting room of the Sheriff's Department until Frank finished reviewing the paperwork on the arrest, and release, of Harlan.

Fuller Davis was an old man—in his early eighties, Frank believed—but he had the hard, knotty body of the farmer, strength tempered in the furnace of the fields, and he had pride. His father had been wounded in World War I, his grandfather had been a major in the Civil War, and his great-grandfather had been one of the original settlers in the county, moving from South Carolina in the late 1700s. The Davis name had always been highly honored, even part of the history classes of Overton County—that is, until Fuller Davis's sons began to coat it with shame. The shame had greatly bothered Fuller. He could not explain it. His sons were arrogant. They did not know, or practice, honor. They did not care whom they offended. Only Fuller could keep them controlled, and he was certain that after his death, his sons would be justifiably killed by the people they hurt without feeling.

Still, they were his sons.

Fuller did not stay long with Frank. He stood before Frank's desk and spoke in a voice that quivered from age and anger. He said, "You tell Reba she's got nothing to worry about. That's not my boy's land. Not yet, it ain't. It's mine. And that house Reba lives in is my house. My boy just thinks it's his. Her daddy used to help me with the farming when I was getting started. One of the best men I ever knew. That's why she's there as long as she wants to be. Tell her I'm sorry about her girl. Send me the doctor bill, if there is one."

"Sorry about this, Mr. Davis," Frank said kindly. "I had to do it."

Fuller did not speak for a moment. His eyes wandered from Frank to some place in memory. "Ain't your fault," he said finally. "You just doing your job."

"Maybe Reba'll drop the charges," Frank suggested.

"Not asking her to," Fuller said.

"I know," Frank told him.

Fuller turned to go. He paused at the door. Without looking at Frank, he said, "I got a sorry lot for sons. Harlan and Mason was old for the war, and I kept George out to work the farm. Maybe if they'd gone to war and been killed, I could of said they died for something worthwhile." Then he left.

● ● ●

Alice Davis did not come out of her house with a gun to shoot at Jule and Son Jesus and Tom as they fed the livestock. She watched from the shadows of the window, deep enough in the room not to be seen, as Jule waved his arms in instruction and Son Jesus and Tom forked hay to the cows and shucked corn for the two mules that Harlan kept in the fenced lot next to the barn. She could see Jule cast worried glances toward the house as he hid behind trees and fences, and she knew he was trying to hurry the task; Jule did not want to be there when Harlan returned.

Alice did not want to be there, either.

Maybe she *would* leave, she thought. Go to her mother's home. She could say to Harlan that it was only for a visit, only for a few hours. And it would be that. Only long enough for Harlan to return home and have his fit. Her mother had warned her against marrying Harlan. Her mother had said that Harlan had the temper of a madman, that it was something she could read in Harlan's cold, glaring eyes. "Don't let your body tell you something that your mind's bound to argue someday," her mother had advised. "You don't know the first thing about love. You're just letting your blood get too hot."

Alice had not listened. Her hot blood had boiled at the touch of the muscled body of Harlan Davis, who had laughed at her mother's bitter prophecy. "Just jealous," Harlan had said teasingly. "Can't stand to think you're getting what she ain't never had." And Alice had come to believe her mother was a hard, unforgiving woman who had lost her own husband to drink and, finally, to the call of the road—"the whore's call," her mother had declared. "And you take after him," her mother had added bitterly. "Don't think I don't know that you been drinking. I smelled enough liquor in my life to smell it a mile away. Wouldn't surprise me one bit to hear you been whoring."

And she knew her mother was right: she was like her father. The taste of the vodka was good. Calming.

She had not seen her father in twenty years. No one else had, either.

Now she wished her father's blood ran more thickly in her. She, too, would leave and never be heard from again.

• • •

"Y'all boys hurry it up," Jule scolded as Tom and Son Jesus shelled dry corn from the cob and scattered it to a gathering of chickens. The chickens quarreled among themselves over the corn, clucking, pecking, spreading their wings like shields, flying their clumsy few feet before landing hard and off balance. Tom had named one rooster after Captain Hook in the *Peter Pan* story, and he was trying to keep it away from the rest of the chickens. Son Jesus was trying to free Captain Hook.

"I mean it," Jule said roughly. "Ain't catching me staying around here with that Mr. Davis getting out of jail."

"You ain't doing nothing, Uncle Jule," complained Tom. "Me'n Son Jesus doing all the work."

"Somebody got to make sure you doing it, ain't they?" Jule said. "Y'all boys wouldn't do nothing if they wadn't somebody around telling you to do it. I guess y'all the two laziest boys I ever seen."

Son Jesus grinned and threw his last handful of corn at the scratching feet of Captain Hook.

"Com'on," Jule said. "Let's be going on back." He started striding out of the yard, toward the road. He stopped when he saw the car slide into the driveway. "Oh, Lord," he muttered. He could sense Tom and Son Jesus cuddling beside him as he watched the car doors fly open and Harlan Davis, with his brothers, Mason and George, step out.

Harlan stood, glaring at Jule and Son Jesus and Tom.

"You niggers get out of my yard," Harlan hissed. "Goddamn it, right now." He took one step toward them, then stopped and looked at Tom. "I don't let niggers put foot on my land, unless I tell them to," he added. "And that goes for nigger-lovers too. You hear me, boy?"

Tom knew Harlan was talking to him. He nodded.

"You tell your mama and daddy the same goddamn thing, you hear me?"

Tom nodded again.

Jule broke into a nervous smile. He motioned toward the barn with his head. "I was just feeding the livestock, Mr. Harlan," he whined. "Them boys just come along with me."

"Well, you finished, now get your black ass out of my yard," Harlan growled. He whirled and stalked across the yard, toward his house. Mason and George lingered in the yard, threatening Jule and Son Jesus and Tom with their haughty stares.

"Com'on," Jule mumbled. He turned and walked away toward his car. Tom was amazed at his quick step. A run, almost. His short leg did not seem short.

"Wait up, Uncle Jule," Tom called.

Jule did not wait up. He did not slow down.

SIXTEEN

The funeral for Rody Martin was on Saturday morning at ten o'clock in the Old Spirit Baptist Church. It was the only church in Crossover for black families. Dooley Witcher, who was called Doodlebug by the less reverent members of his congregation and by all the whites in the community, was the fourth in a family line of preachers at Old Spirit Baptist that went back to the Reconstruction period, following the Civil War. Curiously, it had been his great-grandfather, the first Dooley Witcher, who had given Crossover its name—a fact that whites disputed for the sake of argument, though they knew it was true. According to Dooley's great-grandfather, Crossover was the place where people *crossed over* to the land of glory. It was, therefore, the place where everybody wanted to be on Judgment Day.

"And ain't that right!" Dooley Witcher would shout when recalling the extraordinary insight of his forefather. Every death, every funeral, invited the story. The dead were in the land of Crossover, and that was what they had done—crossed over. They had crossed over Georgia, crossed over the Atlantic Ocean, crossed over Jordan, crossed over showers of mystic light, crossed over clouds and skies and stars, crossed over the sun and all the other heavenly bodies, crossed over from the cramped space of a coffin, into the broad arms of Jesus.

"Hallelujah! They done crossed over and they resting in the bosom of the Lamb!"

Dooley called himself Pastor Witcher. During the week, he worked for Porter Clinton on his pig farm, a job he claimed as the source of his inspiration. "You work with swine, you know how to preach about swine," he reasoned loudly and profoundly. In his pulpit, or in Porter Clinton's pigpens, or on the streets of the small towns near Crossover—depending on where he was when the spirit seized him—Dooley often engaged the Devil himself (the Devil that to him looked like the picture on the Red Devil lye can), and he would shout and abuse the Devil with proclamations so mighty, he would exhaust himself.

Dooley Witcher was an unusual instrument of God. To many, he was comic relief; to others, he was a warrior whose tongue was one of God's swords on the blood-bathed battlefields of humanity.

Yet even Dooley Witcher was not prepared for Rody Martin's funeral.

Reba had insisted that her husband would be buried with dignity. She had instructed Reeder Higginbottom to wire Rody's skeleton together and to dress him in a new, deep-blue gabardine suit that she bought on credit from Belk's department store.

"Just a waste of money, putting such a fine suit on him," Reeder had said in his funeral-whisper voice, "especially since the coffin's gon' be closed."

Reba had wagged her head stubbornly. "Won't be closed. That's my husband in there, or what's left of him. He gon' be seen."

And the coffin for Rody Martin was left open. In it was a skeleton with missing teeth and a crushed-in skull, dressed in a fine, deep-blue gabardine suit.

"Why you gon' do that, Mama?" Cecily had asked. "Everybody's gon' get scared, looking at that."

And Reba had answered, "Everybody's gon' remember it, honey. Everybody's gon' think about what Pegleg did to your daddy."

Reba was right. The people who attended Rody Martin's funeral passed slowly before Rody Martin's open coffin and gazed in horror at Rody's dressed-up skeleton. Three people fainted. A singsong wailing, a lamentation of fear and sorrow, filled the small church, billowed out of the open windows, and drifted over the church grounds to the dug-out grave where Rody Martin would be buried.

It was the first time Tom could remember that he was truly in awe.

He sat on the back row of the crude benches of Old Spirit Baptist Church with the only white people at the service—his mother and father, Elly and Troy, Sheriff Frank Rucker, and, curiously, old Fuller Davis— and he stared wide-eyed at the opened coffin in the front of the church. He remembered the bone he had pulled from the sawdust pile, the leg bone of Rody Martin, and he wondered again if that was what had protected him and Son Jesus on Scrubgrass River.

He had not spoken to Son Jesus at the church. Son Jesus did not seem to be there. His *body* was there. Tall, lanky, looking older in his pieced-together Sunday suit. His body was there, but Son Jesus was somewhere else. There was an expression on his face—a calm, yet sad, expression—that Tom had seen before. Camping out with Son Jesus, he had seen it. He would be in the middle of a story about some made-up constellation, some quirky alignment of stars that held the faces and figures of cowboys and Indians, pirates and knights, and he would turn his head on the bedroll to look at Son Jesus and Son Jesus would be gazing toward the night sky, yet it was as though he was looking not *at* the stars but *through* them, *past* them. It was as though Son Jesus could see planets no one had ever seen. And Tom had always felt a surge of envy. He could make up stories about the stars, but Son Jesus could see into them.

"Them's just bones," Dooley Witcher cried from the pulpit of Old Spirit Baptist. "Brother Martin's done crossed over!"

The service lasted for an hour. When Dooley finished his sermon and his praying, when the glorious singing was over—*"Swing low, sweet chariot, coming for to carry me home . . ."*—the mourners filed from the church and staggered across the churchyard to the cemetery, following the coffin, which was carried on the strong shoulders of black men who were used to lifting the weight of burdens.

And there they lowered the dressed-up bones of Rody Martin into the ground.

Reba sobbed in a loud, anguished voice, and her daughters folded her into their arms. Son Jesus stood away from them with Jule, watching the men begin to shovel the dirt over his father's coffin. The expression on his face had not changed.

"Mama, is Son Jesus all right?" Tom whispered.

"He's fine, honey," Ada said. "He's just sad. Wouldn't you be sad if your daddy was being buried?"

Tom bobbed his head. He could feel tears stinging at his face.

"Why don't you come on with me and Elly, and let's go speak to Reba," his mother said.

"Yes m'am."

Tom took his mother's hand and followed her and Elly through the crowd of mourners. He could feel eyes watching him. Even without looking into the faces, he knew what the eyes were saying: *That's the boy that was with Son Jesus. He's the one that took Rody's leg bone.*

He turned to look back at his father and Troy. They were standing away from the crowd, under an oak tree, with the sheriff and old Fuller Davis.

"Come here, honey, give your Reba a hug," Reba said.

Tom stepped to her, gave in to the crushing embrace.

"You sweet to come," Reba cooed.

"Uh, yes m'am," Tom muttered. He added, "Son Jesus looks sad."

Reba bent close to him. "He is, honey, he is," she whispered. "He sad since they didn't find his daddy's foot bone. He think his whole daddy's got to be buried together."

Tom moved his head to look beyond Reba to Son Jesus. Son Jesus gazed at the dirt being shoveled over the coffin of his father. His eyes were damp.

"Wadn't for you, we wouldn't never of found my Rody," Reba said. "You special, baby. You special."

Tom knew it was a lie, an embarrassing lie. He had not found the bone; Son Jesus had. He nodded awkwardly and stepped back, and Reba turned to embrace Ada and Elly.

Behind Tom, a heavy woman named Grace Whitman began to sing, very softly, *"Nobody knows the burden I've seen, nobody knows but Jesus..."*

And Grace Whitman's voice was joined with other voices, and the space around Rody Martin's grave was crowned with the poetry of sorrow.

● ● ●

Frank had had the sheriff's car washed for the funeral, but a thin coat of red dust from the backroads leading to Old Spirit Baptist Church had dulled the gleam of the hood and the windows. The red dust on the car was a lot like his life, Frank thought: there was always something covering the few shining moments.

Still, there was something good about the red dust. Frank remembered returning home from New York on the Greyhound bus after the war, and the stirrings of joy that raced through him when the countryside from the window of the bus began to fade from gray to brown and then to red. Home. Spindly pines and hardscrabble, eroded fields that had been muscled from hillsides by men with little more than pride and a year-round charge account at a local store to keep them going season to season. Red was the color of the dirt in northeast Georgia, and the red dust of summer had an odor about it, like a fine earth powder, a talc that rubbed into a man's skin as he worked in it. His ex-wife, Sharon, had called it a sex scent. In the good days, that is. In the good, early, sex-filled days of their marriage. She would nuzzle her face into his chest after a workday, and she would say she could smell the earth on him, and in him. The smell of the earth had made her blood run hot in the good, early, sex-filled days of their marriage.

Frank shifted in his seat and slowed the car. He thought of Evelyn Carnes, and a surge of want shimmered through his abdomen. He looked at his watch. It was eleven thirty-five. He had promised Evelyn that he would be at her house at twelve-thirty for lunch and a few more questions—the questions were his excuse in case unexpected visitors dropped by. He had almost an hour to kill.

He crossed the railroad tracks below the large house where Fuller Davis lived, and turned left on Crossover Road, heading for Dodd's General Store. It was Saturday, and he knew the store would be crowded with men, and where there were men, there would be gossip, and the gossip would surely be of finding Rody Martin and Rody's funeral, and of the arrest of Harlan Davis. One of the things Frank had learned early as a law officer was that, many times, gossip told him more than facts.

He glanced in the rearview mirror and saw Fuller Davis's house disappear in the distance. He had been surprised that Fuller attended the funeral. Fuller's way of trying to apologize to Reba for the beating of Remona, he guessed. And maybe it had worked. He had watched Fuller speak softly to Reba, had seen Reba nodding her head slowly, as in surrender. He felt sorry for Fuller. Fuller could not live in peace, and he would not die in peace.

There were a half-dozen cars and trucks parked at Dodd's General Store. Men drinking cold soft drinks and smoking cigarettes were gathered on the front porch. Some were sitting in the few chairs Arthur Dodd always placed outside for the summer and inside, around the potbellied stove, for the winter. Others sprawled lazily on the steps, or leaned against the support posts holding up the roof of the porch. Laughter was dying among them when Frank opened the car door and stepped out. A good joke, he thought, something about a woman, for sure.

The men gazed at Frank as he crossed to them.

"Damn, Frank, you still alive, I see," Keeler Gaines said jovially.

"Any reason I shouldn't be, Keeler?" Frank replied.

"Well, I'd of thought Harlan and his brothers would've ambushed you by now," Keeler drawled. "Talk is, they pissed off."

"Don't think I ever arrested anybody that wadn't," Frank said easily.

"Ain't that the truth," Charlie Hazelgrove mumbled. He ducked his head and smiled. Frank had arrested Charlie for being drunk and disorderly at the last county fair.

"You get over it, though, don't you, Charlie?" Frank said.

"Ah, yeah. Shit, I had it coming," Charlie confessed. "Ain't no hard feelings."

Arthur sat forward in his chair. "You want a cold drink, Frank?" he asked. "On the house. Any man that'd take on Harlan and his brothers deserves a free Co-Cola."

Frank shook his head. "Just stopped by for a few minutes," he said.

"You been over to Rody's funeral?" asked Arthur.

Frank nodded.

"It true what I heard tell?" Keeler asked. "That Reba had old Rody's bones dressed up in a new suit?"

Frank nodded again.

"Don't that beat all?" Keeler said. "Just like the colored, ain't it?"

Frank shrugged. He pulled his handkerchief from his pocket and wiped the ribbon of perspiration that coated his forehead. "I don't know," he said slowly. "In the long run, I guess they ain't much difference in people when it comes to funerals. I remember one of my uncles died when I was about knee-high to a grasshopper. They put a fishing pole and a can of live worms in the coffin with him. All he ever did was fish."

Arthur laughed in memory. "Damn, I'd forgot about that," he said. "My daddy told me about it. I bet them worms had a feast."

A gentle laughter rolled across the porch.

J. D. Epps waved his straw hat in front of his face. He said, "When I was over in Germany, in the war, they was this old boy—I reckon he was Italian—that kept telling us if he was killed, we was to tie one of them little American flags around his goober before we dumped him in a foxhole and covered him up with dirt. Said that was why he was fighting, so he could be free enough to bed down any woman he had a mind to."

Another roll of laughter crossed the porch.

"Y'all do it?" asked Charlie.

"Well, I damn well didn't," J. D. snorted. "Only dead goober I ever had anything to do with is mine, and I don't do nothing with it but shake the pee off three or four times a day."

The laughter grew to a cackle, then died away.

"You got any ideas about Pegleg?" Keeler asked Frank.

Frank shook his head. "Nothing new."

"Yeah, well, I can tell you what makes me uneasy about it," Keeler said seriously. "Makes me uneasy that all of them killings took place around here. Only man I ever knowed that stayed pissed off at the colored enough to kill them was Jed Carnes."

Frank's forehead wrinkled into a frown. He thought about Evelyn. He could feel his stomach tighten.

"You talk about a goober you could hang a flag on," J. D. said, "it was Jed's." The laughter rose again. The blood flushed red over Frank's face.

"How you know that, J. D.?" asked Keeler.

"I seen him take a leak once over at his sawmill—over there where you dug up old Rody's bones, Frank—and Lord, I thought he was holding a ax handle," J. D. declared. "I bet you a dollar to a dime that old Jed had women standing in line for him from here to Athens."

"Well, he left one behind he must not of been able to handle," Charlie said comically. "Y'all see her prissing around when we was over at Hack Winter's place, looking for that boy of his?"

The men muttered agreement.

"Looked to me like she had her eye on you, Frank," teased Keeler. "I seen her trying to stuff you like she was feeding you a Sunday dinner."

The blush deepened in Frank's face. He wiped his forehead again with his handkerchief.

"Well, you saw something I didn't," Frank said dryly. "But I'll look for it. I'm about to head over that way, to ask about digging around them old sawdust piles some more. Could be that's where the rest of them bodies were put."

Frank studied the faces of the men on the porch. He saw their faces change quickly from merriment to frowns.

"Now, by God, that could be right," Arthur suggested. "If that's so, it could of been somebody who used to work for Jed, but I don't remember none of them boys walking with no limp."

The men nodded.

"Well, y'all hear any talk, I'd appreciate letting me know," Frank said. He pulled his hat back on his head.

"You take care, Frank," Keeler said.

"Yeah, you watch out from them Davis boys," warned J. D. His tone was serious.

"I will," Frank said.

•   •   •

Evelyn stood at the window of her living room and looked out on the stretch of road that led from Crossover. A hot flush covered her face and neck and chest. It seeped down her arms from her shoulders. She opened her mouth in a round O and slowly sucked in the warm air of the room. She could feel the heat of her tongue escaping from her mouth.

"Oh, my," Evelyn said aloud. She waved a hand in front of her face, as though her hand were an exquisite fan, and then she turned away from the window and drifted back to her bedroom.

"Well, Frank Rucker, you better not be late," she said to herself in a playful voice. "I don't keep dinner in the warmer for nobody."

She paused at her dresser and thought about Frank. He was forty years old, or close to it, she guessed, and though he had gained a few pounds since returning from the war, he was still hero-handsome. She remembered a story in the county newspaper about him, about how he had been given a field commission and how he had almost personally stopped a German assault. The newspaper had printed a picture of him in dress uniform. His muscular chest had been covered in enough battlefield ribbons to wallpaper a house. And then she had seen him at the parade given in his honor, a loud, giddy ride around Courthouse Square in one of Joe Harvey's new Ford convertibles. Frank smiling shyly, waving weakly to the crowd that cheered for him like they had cheered when he was on the football field for the Overton High School Purple Panthers. Even then, on that parade day, with Jed still alive and standing beside her as the convertible passed in front of them, she had felt a blush of infatuation for Frank Rucker. But she had put aside that infatuation, believing it was a fantasy. Compared to Jed, Frank Rucker was straight out of Hollywood, and Hollywood was all make-believe.

But that was then. Now was now.

She looked at her reflection in the dresser mirror. She was prettily dressed in a new summer cotton dress—gloriously yellow—that she had taken in at the waist on her sewing machine. The dress lifted her breasts and held them like gentle hands.

"Oh, I do like you, yellow dress," she said gaily. She leaned forward, toward her own image in the mirror. "And I like *you*, Evelyn Welborn Carnes. You do look pretty today, and Mr. Frank Rucker is going to think so too." She giggled and picked up a small cut-glass cologne bottle. She opened the bottle and tilted a single drop onto her finger, and then she pushed her hand inside the unbuttoned top of her dress and whisked her finger across her chest, under the top of her bra. She could smell the sweetness of the cologne. A shiver spilled down the heat of her shoulders.

"Ummm," she sighed.

●　　●　　●

The yellow dress that Evelyn wore startled Frank. He had never seen anyone dressed so obviously, not even Hilda Dewberry or the other bedtime women he had known, not even the streetwalkers in Rome, Italy. But Evelyn's dress was not an advertisement for sex. It was an advertisement for sensuality, a dress to be removed carefully, tenderly, not ripped from the body.

Frank stammered a hello and an apology for being five minutes late. His mouth was dry.

"Oh, don't even think about it," cooed Evelyn, taking his arm and pulling him inside the house. "Come on in. I was about to take the chicken out of the oven." She looked at him, forcing her eyes to be soft and inviting. "I decided to bake it, instead of frying it. It's so hot, standing over an open skillet."

"Yes m'am."

"Stop it, Frank, or I'll start calling you Sheriff Rucker."

Frank nodded. He placed his hat on a chair in the living room and followed Evelyn into the kitchen, listening to her chatter, breathing in the airwave of cologne. His eyes were locked on her body as she moved.

"How was the funeral?" she asked lightly.

"It was different," Frank said.

"Sit down right over there at the table," Evelyn ordered. "I've already poured the tea. The weather's so hot, you must be about dried out." She opened the door to the oven and removed the chicken. "I know I am," she added. She turned to Frank and giggled. "Dried out, that is. I must of changed clothes twenty times already this morning, trying to find something cool enough to wear. I finally just settled on this old thing. I don't even know if it's cooler than anything else I've got, but it seems like it is. I think it's the color. Yellow's my favorite color. So springlike, when it's really nice and cool. Like jonquils, don't you think?"

"It's—it's nice," Frank said. He sat at the kitchen table and picked up the glass of tea and swallowed deeply. The tea was sweet, with a hint of mint.

At the kitchen counter, Evelyn ladled beans and squash and field peas onto plates and then she speared the pieces of chicken with a long fork and placed them on the plates. As she worked, Frank stared at her body. In the yellow dress, it was remarkable.

"I do hope you're hungry," Evelyn said. "I almost never get a chance to cook for anybody, and when I do, I always seem to overdo it." She giggled girlishly. "Jed used to say I didn't have a lick of sense in my head when it came to cooking. Said I was cooking enough to feed half the field hands in the county, colored included."

The mention of Jed's name clicked in Frank's mind. He could hear the laughter of the men at Dodd's General Store as J. D. Epps talked about the size of Jed's penis. J. D. had made it seem grotesquely large, and Frank wondered how anyone as thin-waisted as Evelyn had managed to have sex with someone like Jed. But maybe it was a trick that only women understood, a thing as mysterious as a circus magician's illusions. Besides, Evelyn had round, strong hips. Not large, but full. And maybe that was the wrong word, he thought. Full sounded fat. Perfect, he decided. Like her breasts. Perfect.

"Well, you've got gracious plenty," Frank said. "Smells good."

Evelyn turned to him. Her eyelids blinked in a seductive flutter. "I hope you like what I've got," she purred. "Everything," she added.

SEVENTEEN

Perhaps there would have been more than lunch between them—as Evelyn wished—if she had not talked so much, if she had not asked the question about Frank's renewed investigation into the murder of Rody Martin.

It was a question deliberately innocent, deliberately calculated, a trail-of-crumbs question easy enough to follow back to safe ground if anything went wrong along the weaving pathway to her bedroom.

She said, "Anything new about that poor Rody Martin?"

Frank wiped his face with his napkin. The taste of peach cobbler was still on his tongue. He shook his head. "Nothing," he answered. "But I still got some looking to do." He remembered his announcement to the men at Dodd's General Store. "Thought maybe I'd do some more digging around in them sawdust piles before long—if you don't mind, that is."

"Oh, fiddle, Frank, do whatever you want to," she said, with a wave of her hand. "I doubt if you'll find anything, but dig all you want to."

"I appreciate it," Frank mumbled. "It'll probably be a few days. That's a lot of shavings. I been wanting to get it done, but I'll have to use some convicts, and they're out road-scraping right now."

"Do it whenever you want to," Evelyn prattled. "I'm just glad Jed's not alive. He'd have a fit."

"Why's that?"

Evelyn smiled over the tea glass she held in her hand. "I'd say of all his shortcomings—and there was plenty of them—the worse thing about Jed was his meanness about bothering anything that belonged to him." She sipped slowly from the tea, keeping her eyes on Frank. It amused her that the blush had not left his face throughout the meal. "It all went back to when he was a little boy, I suspect. The way he told it, his older brothers were always taking things away from him and there wadn't nothing he could do about it. And then when he came back from army training after he got wounded, there wadn't nobody in his family but his sister who came to see him. Do you know he never went to a single funeral when his brothers died off, one by one, three in three years? Well, I guess you could say there were four in four years, counting Jed. That was last year, in 1948. He had the cancer, you know. The first one died late in 1944. Jed was the only one of the lot of them that went in the army. Now the only one left in that whole family is Irene, and Lord help her, she's about dead. Do you know her, Frank?"

"Don't know that I do," Frank admitted.

"Irene Pilcher. Her late husband used to carry the mail."

"Oh," Frank said. "Ed Pilcher. I knew him. Sure did. Always smiling. Died of a heart attack out on the mail route."

"That's him. Irene is his widow." Evelyn sighed.

"I do know her," Frank said. "I thought she was dead."

"Oh, Irene's still kicking," Evelyn assured him. "She's always sniping at me about one thing or the other. Don't think she's ever liked me too much."

"You said that Jed was wounded in army training?" Frank said. "Guess I didn't know that."

"Oh, yes," Evelyn answered. "It was in 1942. September. That seems like a long time ago now."

"I didn't get out until '46," Frank told her. "Guess that's why I never heard of it. What happened? If you don't mind telling me."

"Of course I don't. Why should I?" Evelyn said lightly. She pushed a slice of the peach cobbler across her pie plate with the tip of her fork, playing with it. "Well, the way Jed told it, he was just in the woods on some kind of training thing, minding his own business, waiting for somebody to tell him what to do, when bullets starting hitting all around him, like it was raining. Said the next thing he knew, he felt like his leg was burning off, and he looked down and saw blood everywhere."

"He was hit in the leg?" Frank asked.

"Right above the knee," Evelyn answered. "But to tell you the truth, I think he shot himself."

"Is that right?" Frank said.

"I heard him laughing about it to Harlan Davis one time, when the two of them got to drinking. Jed said they were about to ship him out to Africa, and that was one place he wadn't about to go. Said there was enough colored people back home."

"Can't say them kind of things didn't happen," Frank said. "Saw one or two cases like that myself." Then: "How bad did it hurt him?"

Evelyn made a mugging motion with her face. "He walked with a cane for two or three months after he got back—you know, before he built back up the muscle in it. He was like a baby. Had to have everything done for him." She put down her fork and patted her lips with her napkin. "That's why he took up with Harlan. Harlan helped him get the sawmill back up and running. I always told Jed not to have anything to do with Harlan, but Jed said it wadn't none of my business." She forced a smile. "And I guess he was right. It just didn't seem right, somehow. Harlan was a lot older than Jed, you know. Lord, Jed wadn't but a few years older than me, but I always thought he looked a lot older. I think he was that way even when he was little. From all I can gather, he was a sickly child."

Frank's mind was racing. To slow it, he returned Evelyn's smile, then drank again from his glass of tea.

"My granddaddy used to walk with a cane," Frank said easily. "When he got old and needed to steady himself. He used to make them out of dogwood and laurel bush. I still got them. Every one of them's got some kind of knobby handle."

"Men never throw anything away, none of you," Evelyn said. "Jed kept his cane too, the one he got from the army. I'd give it to you, if I still had it. Jed had it in a trunk of things that he kept out in the barn. Just junk, you know. Mostly stuff he brought back from the army—his uniform, his helmet, a gas mask, a bayonet, stuff like that. Probably stole all of it." She snickered. "I looked in it one time when he was away. He'd left the key on the dresser and forgot about it. Guess what I found?"

"What?" Frank answered.

"Well, it's a little embarrassing to talk about . . ."

"That's all right. You don't have to if you don't want to."

"Oh, no, that's not it. It's just—well, it's just kind of personal, you know," Evelyn whispered.

"I don't mean to pry," Frank assured her.

"Well, you're not. Just promise me you won't say anything about it. No need to go smearing Jed's name, no matter how good or bad it was. And if anybody knew I was even talking about it, they'd have me dancing with the Devil before sundown."

"I promise," Frank said.

Evelyn leaned forward at the table. A slight blush colored her face. She said in a whisper, "He had one of those decks of playing cards. You know, the ones with men and women on them, doing all sorts of things."

Frank knew about the playing cards. He had seen them in the army. Men and women having sex. Morale boosters. The kind of happy propaganda that made men declare—and believe—that what they were fighting for could be found on everything from the queen of hearts to the ace of spades. It had always seemed ironic to Frank that men in war carried a Bible in one pocket and playing cards of men and women having sex in another.

"Oh," he said quietly.

"You promised," Evelyn chided.

"You got my word," Frank told her.

Evelyn fanned her hand in front of her face. "I feel myself turning red as a beet." She giggled. "You sure you had enough?"

Frank patted his stomach. "Too much," he said. "What happened to the trunk?" he asked.

"Oh, he gave it away to Harlan Davis before he died," Evelyn said. "Said Harlan liked all them army things and didn't have any himself, since he didn't go off to war. Said he owed Harlan for helping him out. He almost cleared out the barn, giving Harlan stuff."

"That's kind of strange," Frank said. He could sense something—a suspicion, a question—swimming inside him. It had to do with Jed Carnes being wounded, and with his friendship with Harlan Davis.

"Not for them two," Evelyn replied. "Lord, I remember how Jed used to try to get me to be friends with Harlan's wife, Alice, but I just can't abide that woman. And it wadn't the fact that she was older than me. I get along with Ada Winter like she was a sister. I guess the Christian thing would be to feel sorry for Alice since she's married to Harlan, but I never met anybody that mealy-mouthed. I don't know how she stands to look at herself in the mirror. And on top of that, she's got a mean streak a mile wide. I remember one time when we went to their place for supper. She had that little colored girl of Reba's cooking—the one that works over in the colored funeral parlor now—and all she did was complain about everything."

"That right?" Frank said.

"Oh, gracious, I'm jabbering like a jaybird," Evelyn said. She reached for Frank's plate. "Now, I know you can eat one more small piece of pie."

Frank waved off the offer with his hands. "Can't hold another bite." He glanced at his watch. "Time's getting on," he said. "Didn't know it was this late. I got to be going."

"So soon?" There was regret in her voice.

"I'm supposed to meet with Hugh in a little while," Frank said. "And then I got to go, ah, visit a cousin of mine over in South Carolina."

●   ●   ●

Frank did not like lying to Evelyn, even if part of the lie had been the truth. He did plan to meet with Hugh Joiner, though Hugh knew nothing of the meeting. He needed Hugh to do what Hugh did best: quietly investigate the history of Jed Carnes. Frank knew that if he started asking odd questions, or if Fletcher did it, there would be suspicion. Hugh had a way about him, an easy, casual manner that did not create curiosity. Hugh would be a good sheriff one day, Frank thought.

Also, there was the matter of Evelyn. He did not want her to believe he was using her. Smiling, he remembered her yellow dress glued to her body. He sighed, shifted his weight on the seat of the car. His palms began to sweat on the steering wheel. Maybe he should stick to what he told Evelyn, he reasoned. Maybe he should go to South Carolina after meeting with Hugh. Maybe he should look up Hilda Dewberry. *"Cousin"* Hilda.

Frank coughed a laugh from his throat. Compared to Evelyn Carnes, Hilda Dewberry ought to be conducting her business from Porter Clinton's pig farm, he thought.

He slowed to a stop at the highway leading into town. A John Deere tractor chattered along, followed by a half-dozen slow-moving cars. He could see the man on the tractor glance over his shoulder at his cruiser, then pull off the highway onto the shoulder of the road to let the cars pass.

It always amazed Frank that the sight of a sheriff's car had such power. He eased onto the highway and passed the tractor. The driver grinned sheepishly and wiggled his hand in greeting, and Frank nodded toward him.

He thought of Jed Carnes as he drove. Maybe he was wrong. Maybe it was all coincidence. But it needed to be checked. The news-story descriptions of Pegleg, confirmed by Fletcher, fit Jed—a small, wiry man. And Jed had walked with a limp, at least for a while, but a limp earned in the army would be remembered only as a wound of honor, not a calling card of fear.

But Reba and Remona and Cecily had insisted that Pegleg was a large man. And they had sounded so certain, Frank did not doubt them. Yet they had seen him only for a short time, during moments of hysteria. To them, Pegleg could have been a giant.

● ● ●

Hugh Joiner listened attentively to Frank's story of his lunch with Evelyn Carnes—a drop-by to talk about digging in the sawdust piles, Frank explained—and of what Frank had learned about Jed Carnes' wound and his use of a walking cane.

"You don't think he was Pegleg, do you?" Hugh asked.

"I got no idea," Frank told him, "but I don't want to overlook anything."

"I thought Pegleg was colored," Hugh said. "All the stories I've ever heard said he was colored."

"I could be barking up the wrong tree, but I want you to put some dates together," Frank suggested. "See if Jed would of been using the cane when that Conley boy was killed."

Hugh stood and bobbed his head. "I'll check it out." He adjusted the gun belt that fit level on his slender hips. His uniform was clean, pressed to a razor edge in the pant legs and shirt sleeves. A hint of his aftershave lotion drifted in the air of Frank's office. He looked comfortably cool in the gathered heat of the office.

Why don't he ever sweat? Frank wondered.

"You know to keep this quiet," Frank said.

"Sure," Hugh replied. A smile eased into his face. "That's a good-looking woman, Frank."

"Who you talking about?" Frank asked. He could feel a blush blooming over his forehead.

"That Carnes woman."

"Good Lord," Frank growled. "You beginning to sound like Fletcher."

"Just an observation," Hugh said. The smile stayed. "Where you going to be?"

"Thought I'd go out and talk to Irene Pilcher, Jed's sister," Frank answered. "I'll call you later."

•   •   •

Irene Pilcher looked old and frail. She had the appearance of a person who had withered inside, like dried fruit. Her ribs and shoulders caved in over the thinness of her body. Her arms were barely larger than the bones that moved them to gesture Frank inside the house.

"Won't take but a few minutes of your time, m'am," Frank said gently.

"I ain't got much more than a few minutes left," Irene told him. She snickered. "Come on in."

Frank followed her into the house. The curtains of the windows were closed against the sun, trapping the air in the house, and the house had a cool, musty odor, like mildew and live-in cats. It was an odor Frank despised, one that made him nauseous. No, he thought, this won't take long.

Irene directed him to a chair in the living room and he sat, waiting for her to settle into a worn spot on the sofa. She looked at him curiously.

"Uh, m'am, I just wanted to talk to you a little bit about your brother Jed," Frank said.

"Jed? He's dead," Irene replied.

"Yes, m'am, I know. I just wonder if you could tell me something about him."

Irene's head bobbed. She smacked her lips.

"Jed, he was a pretty little thing," she said in a loud voice, as though the distance across the room to Frank required shouting. "All blond-headed. Curly blond-headed, he was. Uh-huh." Her head bobbed faster.

"Sounds like he was a favorite of yours," Frank said.

"I was older," Irene answered. "Mama and daddy had me and they wadn't another one here for fifteen years, and then they was four boys.

And Jed was the youngest." She giggled. "I was almost thirty when he was borned. He was like my own baby. All the older boys didn't pay him much attention." A cat leapt suddenly from the floor to the sofa and curled beside her. The cat startled Frank. He had not seen it in the dim room. She stroked its head absently. She seemed to know what Frank wanted to ask, and she added sadly, "It was hard on the boys in them days."

"How's that?" asked Frank.

"They was always having to work, from the time they was little-bitty people," Irene told him. "It was hard. Hard on all of us. My mama used to say we got to the Depression before it got to us."

"But Jed did all right for himself," Frank said.

"Jed was smart," Irene confided. "Smarter than the other boys. Got out on his own when he was old enough and started up his own sawmill business over there in Crossover. Oh, it caused some bad blood too. The other boys was always trying to get Jed to give them something, bail them out of their troubles, but Jed wouldn't mix money and blood. Said he'd give them a job, but he wouldn't give them no money." She paused and sighed deeply. "They never did make things right with one another."

"That's too bad," Frank said. He shifted forward in his chair. The cat raised its head to gaze at him through the slits of its green eyes. "Mrs. Pilcher," he added hesitantly, "I wonder—I wonder if Jed ever had any, well, particular trouble with anybody."

Irene's head stopped bobbing. She fixed her eyes on the cat, and on her hand rubbing the cat's head. She said, in a soft, crackling voice, "He's dead now. No need to be bringing up things."

"Yes m'am," Frank mumbled. He rolled his hat in his hand, fingering the felt brim. "What I'm trying to do," he explained, "is to find out how it was after he got back from the army. Guess you don't know it, but we found a dead man's bones in one of the sawdust piles on Jed's place. I was thinking somebody might of got mad at him, or something, and buried that body over there to put the blame on him."

Irene lifted her face to his. "You better ask that wife of his," she advised.

"Well, m'am, I have talked to her. Not much she can tell me."

"That don't mean nothing," Irene said bitterly. "That woman just as soon tell you a bald-faced lie as to look at you. Always been that way. She come from that white-trash Welborn bunch down in Shiloh. Always wanting more'n she had. You find a Welborn, and you find a liar."

"Well, I don't know about that, m'am," Frank said. "I'm just checking up on things."

"Jed didn't like the colored," Irene said quickly. "His brothers was always calling him a little nigger when he was little. Make him fighting mad, but he was too little to fight. They was always aggravating him."

Frank knew that Irene Pilcher was ready to tell him something she had never told anyone. He also knew that his next question either would open the floodgates or would clamp her lips closed. He wished he had Hugh with him. Hugh would know how to ask the question.

"I always heard tell that Jed got mixed up in something a long time ago. Had to do with a colored man," Frank lied. He paused. The lie was bitter in his mouth. Lying to such a sick woman, baiting her, was wrong. But it wasn't exactly a lie. Not completely. It was a guess, a lure to hook the words in Irene Pilcher's mouth and pull them from her. "That's why I was wondering if there was something you might could tell me."

Irene did not speak for a long moment. Then she settled her small shoulders back on a cushion that was burrowed into the sofa, and she looked away toward the murky space of the room.

"They was talk—by the other boys," she said quietly. She paused again.

My God, Frank thought, I was right. "What kind of talk, Mrs. Pilcher?" he pried gently.

"About some colored boy," Irene answered. "Said that Jed killed him. Said the colored boy got in a ruckus with him over not being paid for the time he'd worked."

"When was that, Mrs. Pilcher?"

Irene did not answer the question. She sighed painfully and rubbed her hands together, massaging the arthritic knots of her knuckles. "He was so pretty when he was a baby," she said. "All that curly blond hair." She looked up at Frank. "The other boys said they'd help hide the body. That's why they was always mad at him for not helping out when they needed a little something."

"Well, that's over and done with," Frank told her. "If it's true, Jed got away with it."

"On this earth, maybe," Irene said. Her voice cracked. "But he took it to Judgment Day. He didn't get away with it then."

From across the room, in the shadowy light, Frank could see the dampness of anguish seeping into Irene Pilcher's eyes. Jed Carnes had been her baby, almost as much as he had been the birth baby of their mother. Irene could not see him killing another man. She could only see curly blond hair.

EIGHTEEN

Ada Winter took Tom and Elly with her to the late-afternoon feast of sorrow at Reba's house. It was a feast prepared after the funeral by members of Old Spirit Baptist Church, a feast of field vegetables cooked in heavy pots, seasoned with spoons of lard and fatback meat, a feast of fried chicken, of catfish seined from Sweetwater Creek, of sweet potato pie and marble cakes. Two small sugar-cured hams were on the table, a gift from Fuller Davis. The hams had been sliced thin, to last. The smell of biscuits was thick in the tiny house, where the women gathered to offer their comfort to Reba. The women moved politely, but uncomfortably, around Ada and Elly, many of them wearing the cast-off dresses of the white women they served as cooks and housekeepers. White people did not attend the sorrow feasts of black families, yet everyone knew that it had been Ada Winter who was behind the arrest of Harlan Davis, and that, too, puzzled them. What did Ada Winter want of them?

Outside, the men gathered under the chinaberry and oak and pecan trees, the older men clustered in a circle of chairs that had been dragged from the house and placed under the largest oak. The younger men were away from them, at the trees that fronted the barn. Both groups nibbled from plates of food served them by the women who drifted in and out of the house, and they talked in grave, ominous tones about the killing of Rody Martin by the man they called Pegleg. The image of Rody's dressed-up skeleton floated among them like a specter, leaving the impression of horror that Reba had predicted. None of them had ever seen a skeleton. Not of a man. The voice of Rody's skeleton was an echo. It said, *Look at me. . . .*

The men shook their heads, wagged them hopelessly. It had been years since Rody was killed, yet Rody's funeral had reminded them that Pegleg was still on the loose. Pegleg could show up again, anywhere, aiming his hammer at any of their heads.

"Keep my gun on me," one of the old men said.

"Get me some dogs," another old man vowed.

"God's gon' be looking after us," Dooley Witcher assured them pontifically, his whole body nodding, as he pushed the legs of his chair deeper into the sandy dirt, but there was a look of doubt on Dooley's face as well. The bones he had seen in the open coffin before the altar of Old Spirit Baptist Church did not seem ready to dance for joy at being dead.

Away from them, near the barn, the younger men smoked cigarettes finger-rolled from their Prince Albert tins, and they waved gnats away from their faces with their huge, powerful hands. They squatted under the shade of the trees and flicked pebbles across the yard with their thumbs. A quart jar of moonshine whiskey was slipped secretly among them, and they ducked their heads to swallow from it, keeping an eye on the house for faces that could be watching them from the windows.

"Sheriff ought to be doing something," they complained softly.

"Sheriff ain't gon' do nothing. It ain't white peoples Pegleg killed."

Jule was center stage.

"Colored man," he said, "he ain't gon' have no sheriff looking out for him."

"That's right."

"Colored man, he on his own."

"That's the truth."

"What you reckon they gon' do to that Mr. Harlan Davis for beating up on Reba's little girl? They ain't gon' do nothing. They done throwed him in jail, but he out now. They ain't gon' do nothing."

"Nothing." Their voices simmered with anger.

Tom sat with Son Jesus at the base of the chinaberry tree they had climbed hundreds of times, and he listened with amazement to the talk that rumbled from the gathering of men who were dressed in Sunday clothes worn thin by years of scrub-board washing. He had never heard black men complain, not with such openness, such bitterness. It was as though they did not know he was there among them, or as though he, somehow, was not like other white people. And maybe that was it, Tom thought. He was part of the legend of Conjure Woman, and that made him different. It was like being a half-breed from some of the western stories he had read by Zane Grey.

"My mama said they was gon' make Mr. Davis go back to jail," Tom said earnestly. "She said the sheriff was gon' find Pegleg."

The men stopped talking and turned to stare at Tom.

"Well, now, boy, your mama means good," Jule drawled in a voice that was more familiar to Tom, "but, child, she ain't the sheriff."

"What she said," Tom replied stubbornly.

"Uh-huh," Jule mumbled, nodding his head easily. "She was good to stick up for Remona."

The other men nodded agreement.

"No sir, wouldn't want your mama mad at me," Jule added. "She stand up to the old Devil, hisself, when she get mad."

"Mama said Harlan Davis ought to be horse-whipped for what he done to Remona," Tom declared. He spat on the ground like he had seen grown-ups do at Dodd's General Store.

"Well, your mama's a good woman," Claude Capes said seriously. "Yes sir, a good woman."

"Now, don't you go saying nothing to your mama about the talk going on out here," warned Jule. "You know I done told y'all boys about spreading loose talk."

"Shoot, Uncle Jule, I ain't gon' say nothing to Mama," Tom said. "I know women ain't supposed to know what men talk about."

"Don't you say nothing to Mr. Hack and Mr. Troy, neither," Jule added.

Tom was puzzled. His father and Troy were men, not women.

"Why not, Uncle Jule?"

"Well, because they ain't here to be listening, that's why," Jule replied. "Don't that make sense?"

Tom shrugged. "I guess so."

Jule laughed easily. He took the jar of moonshine and turned his head and swallowed quickly from it, then he wiped his mouth with the sleeve of his shirt and passed the jar on to Duck Heller.

"Them boys is a mess," Jule said. "I swear, they don't know nothing about nothing. Wadn't for me, they wouldn't know how to stand up and pee."

A soft, deep chuckle rolled around in the circle of men. Their somber mood seemed to fly away, and the broad smiles that Tom had always seen lodged in their faces began to grow out of the corners of their lips.

"Them boys used to think babies come from them long-legged

birds," Jule continued. He looked across the yard to Dooley Witcher and the old men fanning themselves with the brims of their hats, then he turned to Tom and Son Jesus. His face was playful. "Ain't that right, boys? Who was it told y'all how babies is made?"

"You did, Uncle Jule," Tom said proudly.

"Yes sir, you right. Yes sir, I did," Jule proclaimed.

"Who told you, Jule?" asked Duck.

The chuckle rolled again. Henry Hanover had the jar. He stepped behind Grady Sorrells' broad shoulders and tilted it to his mouth and drank.

"Don't you go starting with me, Duck," Jule countered. "I might be telling you things you ain't wanting to hear."

The chuckle became a laugh. Someone in the back of the circle said, "Look out, Duck." Someone else said, "Amen."

Tom saw Son Jesus lean forward from the chinaberry tree. He saw Son Jesus look up at his Uncle Jule, saw him wait for the laughter to die down.

"Mr. Harlan make a baby with Remona," Son Jesus said calmly.

The men fell silent. They turned to Son Jesus.

"What you say?" asked Jule.

"Mr. Harlan make a baby with Remona," Son Jesus repeated.

"How you know that?" demanded Jule.

Son Jesus' eyes blinked once at his Uncle Jule, then he turned his face away. "'Cause I know," he answered quietly. "He done what you said about babies with Remona."

None of the men spoke. They watched Jule kneel beside Son Jesus.

"Now, boy, why you saying that?" Jule asked.

Son Jesus lifted his face slowly to Jule's. His expression was serene. "My mama say I'm the man of the family now, since my daddy been found."

"Why, Lord be, boy, sure you are," Jule said gently. "But why you know that about Remona?"

"I know," Son Jesus said.

And the men knew he was not lying.

• • •

Frank realized there was a problem before Hugh crossed the Cornerstone Café to his table. It was in Hugh's face, in the deep furrow that cut over the bridge of his nose like a large comma when he was worried. Frank picked up his tea and drank slowly from it. Let it be a flat tire on the car, he thought. It had been a long day. His energy was gone for anything more taxing. His mind flashed over the day—a funeral with dressed-up bones, a woman ripe for taking, teasing him in a yellow dress that would have pulled away on touch, a sad story from a sick woman who wanted to hide the truth. It was enough for any man.

Hugh slipped into the booth across from Frank. "Trouble," he said quietly.

Frank sighed. "Tell me about it."

"Hack Winter's wife called—Ada. She said Reba's girl—the one that got beat up—was saying she's been raped by Harlan."

"Shit," Frank mumbled.

"Ada thinks there might be some trouble over there," Hugh added.

Frank flicked an incredulous look across the table. "You don't say?" he snarled. "I'd bet my ass on it." He shifted on the seat of the booth and reached into his pocket and pulled out a wad of bills and began to count out the change for his meal. "Ada say the girl was gon' testify?"

"I didn't ask," Hugh admitted. "She was at Reba's house when it came up, and then she went to her home to make the call, but she said she and Hack was going back over to Reba's house. She didn't seem in the mood for details."

Frank laughed wearily. "I guess not. That's a high-strung woman when she gets her dander up." He looked at Hugh. "You ever hear of a colored bringing up a rape charge against a white man in this county?"

Hugh shook his head. "Only thing I know about is that Bohan boy, fifteen or twenty years ago. Tried to get Logan to arrest some peckerwood sharecropper that he caught raping his sister. He didn't last twenty-four hours."

"Yeah, I remember that," Frank said. "I knew that boy. Elbert was his name. We called him Tadpole. I went fishing with him some when I was little." He pulled out of his seat and stood. "Tell you the truth, Hugh, we just about messed up this world, ain't we?"

• • •

Frank knew when he arrived at Reba's house that his interview with Remona would be intense. A number of men and women were still gathered outside in the fading light of day, and their stares were cold and somber. He suspected the men had been drinking, gathering courage for a vengeance of words, if not action.

"Let's go slow and easy," Frank said to Hugh. "Why don't you stay out here and try to calm things down, while I go in and talk to Reba's girl."

Hugh nodded. "It don't look much like a welcoming committee, does it?"

"Slow and easy," Frank said again.

"You ain't never seen slow and easy like you're about to see it," Hugh mumbled, opening the door of the car.

● ● ●

Frank's eyes swept the room as he stepped inside Reba's house. He saw Reba and Cecily sitting beside Remona on an old sofa. Ada Winter was sitting in a chair that had been pulled close to the sofa. She was squeezing a towel over a water basin and then applying it to Remona's face. Hack Winter and Jule and Dooley Witcher were standing in front of the fireplace. Son Jesus sat quietly in a chair near the window. The smell of food from the feast of sorrow was still thick in the room.

"Reba," Frank said softly in greeting.

"He's gone too far this time," Ada said angrily.

"Ada, you keep your temper," Hack said in a soft voice.

Ada jerked her head to glare at her husband. "I'm not close to being as mad as I'm going to get if something's not done about this," she snapped.

"Well, m'am, that's what I'm here to find out about," Frank told her. He moved to stand in front of Remona. "Why don't you tell me about it? Don't be scared. Just tell me."

● ● ●

Frank knew the story he heard was true, but also useless. A white jury would snicker about it, call it hearsay gossip, even if a written charge reached court. Such a charge would be wadded into a paper ball and dropped into a trash can like a candy wrapper. Still, he listened, and he believed.

Jule had stormed inside the house with Son Jesus' story of Harlan Davis, and Remona had finally admitted that Son Jesus was right: she had been raped by Harlan Davis. Many times, she had been raped. At first she had denied it, but then Son Jesus was taken to her and she had looked at him and the truth had spilled tearfully from her, and the small house had filled once again with wailing.

"Oh, sweet Jesus, why you let this happen to my girl?" Reba had cried loudly and painfully. "When you gon' stop hurting my babies?" She had cuddled Remona to her and rocked her, and she had let the bellowing of shame that roared out of Remona enter into her.

Frank said little during the telling of the rapes. He listened, but he also watched. Cecily looked away uncomfortably, pretending to console her younger sister. Frank knew that Cecily had her own story, but she would not tell it. None of them would. Harlan Davis could have raped every black woman in the county and none of them would admit it. The only reason Remona's story was being told was because of Son Jesus and Ada Winter.

"All right," Frank said. "I'll check into it." He added, to Reba, "You know she'll have to testify."

A look of confusion crossed Reba's face. She turned to Ada.

"She will," Ada said adamantly.

"Well, m'am, that'll have to be up to her and her mama," Frank replied.

"He's right, Ada," Hack said. "It's up to them."

"She done told you what happened," argued Jule.

"She did," Frank said. "That's true. But she'd have to tell it again before a jury."

"Ain't no white jury gon' put no white man in jail for having his way with a colored girl," Jule said sorrowfully.

"They will if I have anything to say about it," Ada snapped.

"But, Mrs. Ada, don't no womenfolks get on the jury," Jule moaned.

"Maybe it's time they did," Ada said. She glared at Frank.

"I can't argue that," Frank replied. "All I can do is check things out. Talk to some more people. Maybe it's happened before." He looked at Cecily. She turned her eyes quickly to Remona.

"I can only tell you that I'll do what I can," Frank continued. "But unless she testifies, it won't mean anything."

"Somebody gon' kill her, she does," Reba said.

"I'll do all I can to keep that from happening," promised Frank. "But I'm not gon' lie to you. It could be nasty." He turned to Jule and Dooley Witcher. "I know there's some upset people here, and I don't blame nobody for being that way, but I hope nobody does nothing that's gon' cause more trouble. Tell everybody to leave it to me, and to give me some time."

"We gon' be praying," Dooley said earnestly. "God's gon' take care of everything."

"I hope so," Frank said. "I hope so."

• • •

Frank did not believe that Harlan would openly confess to rape, though there was an arrogance about him that was unpredictable and dangerous, and there was a chance—remote but possible—that the man would want to brag about taking black women in sex. One name was all Frank needed, someone to corroborate what Remona had told him, and maybe he could unravel Harlan like a pull-string on a fertilizer sack.

"What next?" Hugh asked in the car as they pulled away from Reba's house.

"A little talk with Harlan," answered Frank. "You find out anything?"

Hugh laughed lightly. "Not a thing, but I was going slow and easy, like you said. Didn't nobody say a word about Harlan. They were worried about Pegleg. How'd you make out?"

"I listened."

"He do it?"

"Yeah, but short of him signing a confession, it ain't gon' be easy to prove."

"You don't expect that, I guess."

"Not hardly."

"He's gon' be pissed," Hugh said.

"I don't doubt it," agreed Frank. "When we get back, you better set it up with Fletcher to keep check on things over here. Have somebody riding around, so everybody can see them."

Hugh nodded. "How was Ada Winter?"

Frank shrugged in answer. Ada Winter was an angry woman, a fighter. "I think I'm beginning to understand why Hack never talks a lot," he said. "But to tell you the truth, she's probably the best thing that girl's got going for her."

"You think Harlan's liable to do something against her?" asked Hugh.

"Not unless he's completely crazy," Frank said. "Hack may be quiet, but I wouldn't want to mess with him. Or Troy. I suspect Harlan feels the same way."

It was early evening, more dark than light. Frank eased the car into Harlan Davis's yard and switched off the motor. He sat, calmly watching the door leading into the kitchen.

"You expecting trouble?" asked Hugh.

Frank shook his head. "Naw. I just wonder how long it's gon' take him to come out from behind that door, where he's watching us."

"You see him?"

"Don't have to. He's there."

The door opened, and Harlan stepped out onto the porch and stood staring at the sheriff's car.

Frank chuckled softly. "That didn't take long. He's tighter'n I thought he was. Let's go talk to him."

Harlan said nothing as Frank and Hugh approached the porch. He stood above them, glaring down.

"Harlan," Frank said pleasantly.

"What you want?" Harlan demanded.

Frank continued up the steps to the porch. He glanced through the window and saw Alice Davis slip out of the kitchen to another room inside the house, then he turned to face Harlan.

"You ever had your way with Reba's girl? The youngest one? Either one of them, for that matter?" Frank asked.

Harlan's face furrowed in suspicion. "Where'd you get that idea?"

"Let's just say I got a reason to ask."

"Bullshit," snapped Harlan. "What they been saying?"

"They been saying you the sorriest kind of man alive," Frank answered. "They been saying you raped that little girl."

Harlan spat off the porch. "Niggers," he hissed. "Goddamn them, they'll say anything."

"Why do I get the feeling they're telling me the truth?" Frank said.

"You gon' arrest me again?" Harlan asked arrogantly.

"Not yet," Frank told him. "No, not yet. You can call this a friendly little visit, or you can call it a warning. I just want you to know that I'm gon' check it out every way I can, and if I find out something, I'm gon' drag your ass before the judge, and if he lets you go, you're gon' be thinking I've moved in with you." He paused. His eyes narrowed on

Harlan's face. "I can't stand men like you, Harlan," he whispered. "It makes me sick that I went to war so men like you could walk around free as a breeze."

A slight, smug smile eased into Harlan's face. "That all you got to say, General?"

"No," Frank answered. "If I hear you've done a thing against Reba or her family, or anybody else—white or colored—I'm coming back over here, and God himself couldn't keep me off your ass. Do you hear me?"

Harlan laughed. He spat again off the porch and turned and walked inside his house, slamming the door behind him.

◈ ◈ ◈

Tom pretended to be sleeping. He wasn't. He was listening to the house. The house spoke to him in a familiar language of squeaks and moans. He knew each room by its own voice—the long, tired whine of the floorboards in the kitchen, sagging with age; the sharp complaint of the doorjamb in the bedroom of his mother and father; the scratching of a loose nail against a two-by-four in the wall of Elly's bedroom; the echo of popping—like finger knuckles—from Troy's heavy step in his room, far back, almost hidden. The voices told Tom where people were in the house, tattled on them like a gossipmonger with a loose tongue.

He heard the screen door open to the front porch near his bedroom. It was a squeal of pain from the rust of metal hinges. The flooring of the porch spoke of two people walking softly. A rocker creaked, then another. A sigh drifted across the porch, curled in the night air, then swept through the screened window of his room. The sigh was from his mother.

Tom waited for a long moment, listening. He could hear nothing from Troy's and Elly's rooms except tuned-down music from a radio. Both would be in bed—Elly reading, Troy drifting to sleep to the twanging sound of love songs. Tom pulled the cover back and put his feet gently on the floor. He did not worry about the voices of his own room. He knew the voices, knew where they were, knew how to avoid them. In his own room, Tom was as silent as an Indian stalking a deer.

At the window, Tom listened to the whispered conversation of his parents.

"He'll get away with it, sure as I'm sitting here."

"It's not in your hands anymore, Ada."

"I can't just sit around with that kind of attitude. That little girl's telling the truth, and you know it."

"I don't doubt it, but it ain't gon' be easy to prove."

"She'll testify. I can get her to do that."

"All you gon' do is cause her more trouble than she's already got."

"How can she be in any more trouble than she already is? Harlan Davis already knows about it. You can bet on that."

"Maybe it'll make him leave her alone."

"Maybe it'll make him feel like he can do whatever he wants to, whenever he wants to do it. You saw Remona. She's scared to death. So is Reba. And you know what's going to happen. In two or three days, Alice Davis is going to show up and tell them to get back to work. And then what are they going to do?"

There was a pause, a moment that stretched across the distance from the porch to Tom's window. He could hear the slow monotony of the two rockers.

"Well," his father said, "best thing for Reba to do is find another place to live."

Tom heard his mother sigh again, a restless, irritated sigh, a sigh of exasperation. It was a sigh he had heard many times, and he knew her reply would be sharp and bitter.

"I'll tell her that in the morning. Ask her why she's waited so long to build that mansion on all that land she's got."

"Ada..."

"Well, don't go saying things that are just plain ridiculous."

"I was thinking somebody might have a house that's empty," his father countered. "There's a few around. William King's got a place. So has Doyle Allgood."

One of the rockers paused. His mother's, Tom guessed.

"She's talked about Doyle's place," he heard his mother admit.

"I'll talk to him tomorrow at church," his father assured her.

Tom heard his mother sniff. She was on the verge of tears. The rocker started again.

"We got to do something," his mother said.

"We will."

"I just keep thinking how I'd feel if it was Elly or Miriam that he'd raped."

"Yeah. Me too," his father replied.

"What would you do?" asked his mother. "If Elly came to you and said Harlan Davis had pulled her in his barn and raped her, what would you do?"

There was another pause. Tom could hear his father's rocker slow to a stop.

"I don't know. I guess I'd want to kill him," his father said simply.

"Yes, I guess you would," his mother replied. "And wouldn't nobody say anything about it if you did. Now, tell me something else: How can I tell that little boy of ours—asleep in there—that his daddy could kill a man for raping his sister, but it's different for Sonny's sister? How can I make him understand anything about right and wrong, when the world he lives in changes the rules every ten minutes?"

NINETEEN

Frank liked hearing the steeple bell of the First Methodist Church of Overton. The sound of the bell was steady, rhythmic, strong, dependable. Except for his years in the army, Frank had listened to the bell each Sunday of his life, for the bell could be heard—faintly—even on the farm in the Oakland community where he had lived as a child. The bell meant what it meant, without confusion or contradiction. The bell was a calling.

He stood at the sink of his kitchen and rinsed the plate he had used for breakfast, then dried it and placed it in the cabinet. The kitchen smelled of reheated coffee and overcooked sausage that was either turning bad or had been seasoned too heavily with sage. Cooking his own breakfast was one of the things that often reminded Frank of his loneliness, and one of the things he truly missed from his marriage. The good breakfast. The good smells of the good breakfast. Biscuits. Bacon that had not been burned. Eggs fried in bubbles of butter, the yolk punched. Grits steaming. Coffee freshly percolated.

He dried his hands on the dish towel and looked out the half-window that was positioned directly over the sink. He wondered if Sharon had cooked the good breakfast with the good smells for her new husband in Atlanta. God knows, he was a lucky son of a bitch if she had. She could cook, for sure. She could damn well cook. And when she was in the mood, she could love. But oddly, it was not the cooking and the loving that Frank missed the most. It was the talking. Sharon had rejoiced in talking. And in the end, that had been the reason for their divorce. He had been away too much, being in law enforcement. Too much. She had needed someone to talk to, someone who would talk to her, and she had found him in the high school music teacher who came twice a week to hear her painful attempts at playing the piano.

Frank had never understood that he, too, needed the talking. Not until it was too late.

The bell of the First Methodist Church stopped ringing.

I should be in church, Frank thought. Got to start going again. Got to.

He took his cup of coffee and walked through the house to the screened-in back porch, and he sat in the rocker that Sharon had given him on their first anniversary. He put his cup on the small end table beside the chair and picked up the stack of papers he had taken on Saturday night from his office. The papers were the reports of the Pegleg murders. He began to thumb through them again, looking for something he might have missed in his earlier readings.

No one had ever seen the face of the man called Pegleg. When he appeared, during his rampages, he wore a brown full-face mask, like the bottom corner of a seed sack that had two holes cut in it for the eyes. It was not a Klan mask, but it was like one. Those who had looked through the eye slits, and lived, vowed his face was black. He wore gloves and old clothing that smelled of oil and rot. He walked with a curious limp, the stories insisted, like a man with a wooden leg, and so he was called Pegleg.

Blue Conley had been killed almost four months after Jed's return from the army, a time when Jed would still have been limping from his wound. Blue Conley was the husband of Amos Whitley's daughter, the same daughter that Amos had warned Jed to leave alone. It was reasonable to believe that Jed would have blamed Blue for Amos's threat, Frank thought. Not a good excuse to kill a man, but Jed—or Pegleg—did not seem to need an excuse.

The same was true of the second man—Compton Mays. Compton had worked for Jed only a short time, according to the report that someone in Logan Doolittle's office had filed, a report that Logan knew nothing about, Frank suspected. Compton was probably the man Irene Pilcher had told him about, the one who had argued with Jed about money, and if so, he was also the man that Jed's brothers had helped to bury.

And then there was Rody Martin. Rody had worked for both Jed and Harlan, yet there was nothing Frank had read, or had ever heard, that suggested a quarrel between Rody and Jed, or Rody and Harlan, for that matter. Unless, of course, Jed or Harlan had forced himself on Reba or Cecily. No, not Reba, Frank thought. Reba was too old. Nor would Reba have kept quiet while watching Remona suffer. Not Reba, then. Cecily was more likely.

Frank balanced the papers on his lap and leaned his head against the backrest of the chair. He remembered the look on Cecily's face when he questioned Remona. It was the look of fear. Cecily knew things she would not talk about.

There was another thing that bothered Frank: the limp. If Jed was Pegleg, did he fake the limp after the murder of Blue Conley to keep the myth of Pegleg alive? Or had the limp, the image of Pegleg, become so powerful that people saw it, even if it was not there? It was possible, Frank knew. The mind played tricks, scared itself into believing what the eyes did not see or the ears did not hear. He had witnessed a lot of that in the war—men locked in a seizure of fear, firing wildly at ghosts.

Frank drained his cup. The coffee was cold and bitter. It was only ten-thirty in the morning, yet he was already tired. Maybe if he got away from the house, away from his office, he could relax, he thought. Maybe if he went fishing. Maybe if he took the morning off to visit the farm where he had lived as a boy, if he walked the fields he had plowed, following the slow-stepping mule named Fanny. Maybe if he drove back to Crossover and spent a few minutes sitting under the canopy of a shade tree, drinking iced tea with Evelyn Carnes. Maybe if he did any of these things, he would clear his thinking.

He chuckled to himself and rocked forward, out of the chair, and picked up his coffee cup. It was too humid to fish. And if he drove to Crossover and invited himself to sit under a shade tree with Evelyn Carnes, drinking iced tea, it would become too humid there also. What he really wanted to do was disappear for a day or so. Like Tom Winter and Sonny Martin had done. Lean back in a boat and drift. Just drift. Let the waters take him somewhere, anywhere. But he knew there were no rivers calm enough for drifting. Along the way, there would be rocks and waterfalls. There were always rocks and waterfalls.

What he *should* do was dress and go back to talk to Remona again, and maybe Cecily. They would tell him nothing he did not know, but it would give him a chance to be present in Crossover. By now, he thought, the word would be out that Remona had accused Harlan of rape. Give the fire of the story a little air, fan it a bit, and it could flame out of control. Anything could happen. Thank God it was Sunday. On Sunday, passions would at least be tempered. And maybe that was better for Harlan than for Remona. Frank had heard angry mumbling among whites about the beating of Remona. No call for it, people had said. Part of the mumbling would have come from Ada Winter's insistent demand that something should be done, and part of it was nothing more than Harlan himself. Disliked as he was by most people, a charge of rape would not win friends for him.

Frank strolled back through his house to the kitchen and put his empty cup in the sink. Hugh had warned him of the danger of the Klan when word got out about Remona's rape accusation, but he was not worried about the Klan. In other parts of the South, the Klan had been on a rampage since the war, but in Crossover there were few men who actually had ever pulled a sheet over their head for doing anything but sleeping late. It would be different if Reba lived in the Mossy Creek community. In Mossy Creek, membership in the Klan was almost a requirement for residency, which made the occasional demonstrations almost comical. Everyone knew everyone, even when disguised with hoods. They even called one another by name, for God's sake.

No, Frank thought, there was no reason to worry about the Klan.

What had bothered him most was the hard look of anger that he had seen on the faces of the black men who had gathered at Reba's house for the feast of sorrow following the burial of Rody, the men who first heard the story of the rape. There had been an aura about them, something Frank understood too well. He had seen it many times on the faces of men in war. It was a look of pain metabolizing to bravery. In the war, it had caused men to charge machine guns, not caring what happened to them. In Crossover, it had the scent of revolt.

He went to the telephone and dialed the sheriff's office. Hugh answered.

"Everything quiet down there?" Frank asked.

"Pretty much," Hugh told him. "We had to throw Joey Prichard in jail last night for being drunk, and he just woke up a few minutes ago, crying his ass off, saying how sorry he was about everything."

"Maybe he learned his lesson this time," Frank said.

"I wouldn't bet my house on it," Hugh replied. Then: "Fuller Davis called about thirty minutes ago. Wanted to know if it was true about Harlan being accused of raping Reba's girl."

"What did you tell him?"

"I told him it was. I said you'd talked to Harlan about it, and we'd be checking it, but all we knew is what the girl said."

"What did he say?" asked Frank.

"Nothing. Not a word, Frank. He just hung up."

"Those boys are gon' kill that old man," Frank said quietly. "We got anybody riding around in Crossover?"

"Fletcher," Hugh answered. "I told him just to be seen but not to start talking to everybody he runs into."

Frank chuckled softly. "Now, that's what I wouldn't bet my house on. Fletcher's got his mama's ways. Even if she is my aunt, I never met a woman who could outtalk her."

"I'll drive over there this afternoon and spell him," Hugh said.

"That's all right," Frank told him. "I'll do it. I might even go back to talk to Reba."

"You're sure? I can do it."

"That's all right. I'll do it," Frank said. "But I do want you to do me a favor."

"What's that?"

"I know you found out that Jed was using his cane when Blue Conley was killed, but I want you to take it a little further. Put together a report on the dates of the rest of the Pegleg killings, then see if you can find out what Jed was doing at the same time."

"You still got that bug about him being Pegleg, don't you?" Hugh said.

"I don't know. I wouldn't doubt it, but I don't know."

"I ran into Nelson last night," Hugh said. "He told me they were gon' start digging in Jed's sawdust pile tomorrow, since they'd finished up with the road scraping."

Frank thought of Evelyn Carnes. She had already given him permission to dig, but perhaps he should ask her again. It would be the friendly thing to do, and he did have the afternoon to spend. Riding around Crossover, being seen, could be boring.

"That's right," he said. "But keep it quiet. I don't want half the county over there. If Nelson comes in, tell him the same."

"If he comes in," Hugh said. "I ain't going looking for him. I'm telling you a fact, Frank, that's a scary son of a bitch."

● ● ●

Crossover Methodist Church had a membership of one hundred and two, with an average attendance of seventy-three. Weekly contributions amounted to less than a hundred dollars, not enough to cover maintenance of the church and also pay a full-time minister. Crossover Methodist belonged to the Crossover–Mount Sinai–Davenport–Cuttercane circuit, which meant a sermon every four weeks for each of the four churches of the circuit. The traveling minister was Reverend Harry Hinton. Harry was in his mid-fifties, a short, chubby man with long strings of shoe-polish-black hair that he finger-combed over the gleaming bald top of his head. Harry had been one of those the Lord called late in life to preach. The calling had happened, Harry proudly proclaimed, on his fortieth birthday. It came out of a dream, a vision as clear as a Norman Rockwell painting on the cover of the *Saturday Evening Post*. Until then, Harry had worked a debit route for an insurance company in Dallas, Texas.

Exercising wisdom, and kindness, the Methodist Church had issued Harry a local preacher's license and assigned him to the Crossover–Mount Sinai–Davenport–Cuttercane circuit, persuading him that a college education and a degree from a seminary would not be necessary. To Harry, it was an ordination as holy as being named Pope. His combined pay from the four churches was equal to his take from the insurance business. In addition, he got a parsonage, a car allowance, and a full Sunday dinner for his family, which included his wife and five beefy children. Ada Winter, who thought Harry was a fool, had quipped more than once that he had misunderstood the Lord's calling. "It was not to go forth and preach. It was to go forth and *leech*."

Harry did not prepare sermons. He willed them to fly from his mouth. It was his contention that the problem with preachers in the year of the Lord 1949 was having too little faith and too much seminary. All they had to do was stand there and let God put words on their tongues. If God couldn't do it, then anything they said was a waste of energy and most likely inspired by Satan, dressed to the gills in a forty-dollar preacher's suit.

Harry's technique was simple, and well understood by Deep South believers in Jesus, who often used the same technique to deliver themselves from personal hardship and depression. He would stand behind the pulpit, as majestically tall as being on tiptoe would permit a short man to be, and he would slowly, and with great show, open the Bible. Then he would close his eyes and circle his hand over the opened book. After a moment of dramatic tension, he would jab a finger down on the page like a divining rod finding water. Whichever verse his finger touched was the text of his sermon.

Harry could rave for an hour about any verse in the Bible, including "Jesus wept."

Though Ada did not like Reverend Harry Hinton, she faithfully attended church as the wife of the Sunday school superintendent, and even took her turn preparing Sunday lunch for Harry's clan of carnivores, an experience that Troy had once compared to a festive hog-slopping. Ada had not even corrected him.

And on the Sunday following Remona Martin's admission about being raped by Harlan Davis, Ada sat with her family in the third pew, left side, as Harry took his place behind the pulpit of the Crossover Methodist Church, wiggled his face into a holy frown, and opened the Bible. He closed his eyes, lifted his chin, raised his hand, uncurling the index finger of his right hand. His hand paused, then dropped.

The verse his finger touched was from Isaiah, chapter 63, verse 8, and Harry read it in his high-pitched, nasal voice: " 'For he said, Surely they *are* my people, children *that* will not lie: so he was their Saviour.' "

Ada's body jerked in surprise. She sat up in the pew, alert, and looked around her. She could see expressions of shock on the faces of the congregation. Maybe God did have something to do with Harry Hinton's finger, she thought. Before church service began, there had been frenzied bickering about Remona's charge of rape against Harlan Davis. Was it true? Or was it something the girl had lied about because Harlan had slapped her? The guessing had been divided, and a mood of unrest and divisiveness had settled over the churchyard. The only thing everyone agreed on was that something more than gossip was needed to settle the issue, and to Ada, Harry Hinton had just delivered that something. Under other circumstances, there may have been reason to suspect that Harry was deliberately influencing the argument by preselecting his text. But that was impossible. Harry had arrived only minutes before services were to begin, and had spoken only to Mary Hawkins, the pianist, asking her to change the first hymn from "Just as I Am" to "O for a Thousand Tongues to Sing." Harry knew nothing about Remona.

Harry was never comfortable when God led him to the Old Testament. The Old Testament was too full of names he could not pronounce, and the verses made no sense when randomly selected. Still, Harry always managed to find something inspiring in the mystery of the words. His sermon on the "children *that* will not lie" was filled with anecdotes about his own children, who squirmed with embarrassment in the front pew, under the watchful and threatening eye of Carlene Hinton, their mother.

"Raise them up right, fearing the Lord God Almighty, and they won't go lying," Harry proclaimed with red-faced fervor. "No matter how terrible the truth is, they ain't gon' lie about it."

Every member of the Crossover Methodist Church knew one thing about Reba Martin—even those who thought she was crazy: Reba Martin was as religious as any of Jesus' disciples had ever been, and if she had taught her children anything, it was to fear the Lord God Almighty. She even had a son named Son Jesus, who, like a prophet of old, had revealed the story of rape against his sister. And to deny that God was making a point about Remona through Harry Hinton's rambling sermon was to deny that you could get the attention of a Missouri mule with a two-by-four.

When the church service ended, at twelve-fifteen, the argument that Remona could have been lying about Harlan Davis was over.

"Wonderful sermon," Ada gushed to Harry at the front door of the church.

It was the first time Ada had ever commented on one of his sermons. "Why, God bless you, Sister Ada," Harry stammered in disbelief. "God bless you."

•   •   •

By the time he reached the Crossover community on Sunday afternoon, Frank had decided against visiting Evelyn Carnes. It would be too obvious. He would call her on Monday morning, informing her that a crew of convicts, under heavy guard, would begin digging in the sawdust piles where Rody Martin's bones had been found. Perhaps on Monday afternoon he would see her. An official visit, of course. A matter of courtesy. He could not let the image of Evelyn Carnes undressing in her bedroom interfere with his duty.

His duty—his immediate duty—Frank believed, had nothing to do with buried bones. It was to find someone else who would be brave enough to come forward and admit she had been raped by Harlan Davis. It would not be easy, and he knew it. He believed that Cecily was his most likely candidate for corroborating her sister's story, but she had said nothing during his questioning of Remona. If hearing her sister's troubling confession had not caused Cecily to talk, nothing would.

He had thought of asking Lucy Hix to make some inquiries. Lucy's fluttering tongue, which worked far harder and far more efficiently than her dustcloth, had led Frank to more than a few arrests for minor crimes. He had, in fact, earned a reputation for having an almost eerie sixth sense about such things as whiskey runs and break-ins, because of information generously and freely shared by Lucy. But rape was different from moonshining or stealing, and though he knew Lucy would return to him with tidbits of rumor, accented by arched eyebrows and facial tics and rolling shoulders and confidential whispers, he was not sure how he would conduct an investigation based on hearsay and the exaggerations of Lucy's body language.

It would be better to let someone else do the asking, Frank had decided—at least for the time being—and that someone was Ada Winter. She was already involved. Perhaps more than she realized. A white woman willing to risk being ostracized by her community by standing up for a black family was more than rare. It was unthinkable. Or it had been. Ada Winter had learned a lesson or two from Eleanor Roosevelt. Ada was not concerned with expected behavior, not when being right was on the line. She was not the kind of person to be intimidated.

Keeler Gaines and Arthur Dodd had been right, Frank thought, as he headed his car along the narrow road leading to the Winter home: Things were changing. In little ways, at least. The war had done it. The war had made people think different, even if they did not know it, and by thinking different, they were beginning to act different without realizing it. War had always done that, he guessed, and maybe that was the good of war. He remembered what Jabbo Lewkowicz had said: "Hell, if it wasn't for people getting their ass blown off, war would be the greatest thing that man ever invented." Frank had always believed there was more truth in Jabbo's statement than even Jabbo realized. War had taken Jabbo from a shoemaker's shop in Brooklyn to a sales job at Gimbel's department store. War had taken Frank from a forty-acre farm in the Oakland community to the sheriff's office of Overton County.

He saw Tom in the shadows of a large oak tree that grew near the corner of the barn, and he slowed his car to watch. Tom had his arms dangling at his sides, like a gunfighter in a western movie. He made a sudden move, his right hand flashing to his waist. He jerked a butcher knife from his belt and raised it, head high, and then twirled it toward the tree. The knife hit the tree and glanced off, and Tom shook his head in disgust. Frank laughed. Wonder who he thinks he is today, he mused. Jim Bowie, probably. Lord, that boy was something to behold.

Tom turned to the sound of the car rolling to a stop in the yard. He watched as the sheriff opened the door and got out.

"How's it going?" Frank asked, strolling toward him.

"Fine," Tom answered.

"Looks like you trying to kill that tree," Frank said easily.

Tom grinned. "Mama and Daddy's inside," he told Frank.

"Where's Sonny?" Frank said.

Tom shrugged. "At his home, I guess. Mama said he was feeling bad about all that's going on. His daddy being buried, and what's happened to Remona."

Frank nodded seriously. "Yeah. I guess so."

Tom mimicked Frank's nod. "When it rains, it pours," he said, trying to sound profound.

Frank stopped the smile before it struck his face. "Y'all get that fence up over at Reba's house?"

"Just about," Tom answered. "I guess we'll be working on it again tomorrow."

"Don't overdo it," Frank said.

"No sir."

"Well, I guess I'll go on up and talk to your mama and daddy a minute. Don't you cut yourself on that knife."

"Naw," Tom replied. "It ain't that sharp."

"Your mama know you got it?" asked Frank.

Tom looked away meekly. "I think so," he mumbled.

"Aw, don't worry. I'm not gon' say nothing about it," Frank assured him. "You just be careful, and get it back to the kitchen before she knows it's gone. You ought to try throwing it underhanded. That's how I used to do it."

Tom watched in awe as Frank walked away toward the house. Frank Rucker was exactly the kind of man he wanted to be when he grew up. Somebody who understood the simple joy of throwing a knife at a tree and keeping it a secret from the mamas of the world. And maybe that was what he would be, Tom thought: a sheriff. He wondered if Frank carried a knife. Probably, he decided. Strapped to his leg, maybe, covered over by his pants. Tom picked up the knife from the ground and took five long steps away from the tree. Then he balanced the blade in his hand, with the sharp edge away from his palm, and he took a half-step toward the tree and threw the blade underhanded, like he would throw a softball. The blade turned once, then stabbed hard into the tree trunk. Tom laughed gleefully.

● ● ●

Ada Winter was in a talkative mood, almost to the point of blithering. She poured tea left from the traditionally abundant Sunday lunch and insisted on giving Frank a large helping of banana pudding. Frank and Hack sat at opposite ends of the kitchen table and listened as Ada described a short visit to Reba's house before church.

"Reba's scared to death," Ada declared. "I guess nobody knows Harlan Davis better than she does, and she knows he's liable to show up and burn their place down, just for the meanness of it."

Frank asked about Remona and Cecily and Son Jesus.

"I didn't talk to either one of the girls," Ada admitted. "Reba said they were pretty much staying to themselves. Cecily needs to be back at work, but she wants to be with her mama too. I don't know what she's going to do, but they can't afford for her to quit her job." She sighed and sat at the table. "She helps out all she can."

"What about the boy?" asked Frank.

Ada shook her head sadly. "He's the one Reba's most worried about, I guess. She said he hadn't said much of anything. Just goes and sits down in the barn. I was going to take Tom over there this afternoon, but Reba said she thought it wouldn't do any good. She thinks he's got to work it out himself."

"She's probably right," Hack offered.

"I know she's scared of Harlan," Frank said, "but you don't think she's really expecting any trouble, do you?"

"When you've had as much trouble as Reba's had from that bunch, you grow to expect it," Ada answered. She added, "It's a shame that Fuller's boys had to take after their mama's daddy."

"What's that supposed to mean?" Hack asked with surprise.

Ada threw an annoyed glance at her husband. "Their granddaddy on their mama's side was Odell Kemper. He was about as worthless as they come."

"Where'd you hear that?" Hack said.

"I found out about him when I was looking into Wanda Crook's family history," Ada said irritably. "He was her great-uncle on her daddy's side."

"Good Lord, Ada," Hack said wearily.

Frank smiled.

"Don't 'Good Lord' me, Hack Winter," Ada said in a huff. "What you ought to be worried about is having your own good name spoiled by that little fact."

"My name?" Hack said.

"Whether you know it or not, mister, you're related to Odell Kemper too."

"Me?"

"You are by marriage," Ada said. "Your second cousin Billy Atkins married Odell's granddaughter."

"Good Lord," Hack muttered again. He shook his head in resignation.

"Well, maybe you don't think it means a thing, but for your information, every family in this community is related one way or the other, by blood or marriage—though, Lord knows, half of them don't claim the other half."

"I guess that's right," agreed Frank. "Same way where I grew up. Anyway, I'm trying to keep a lid on things over here. I've got a car just driving around, to let people know we're close by."

Ada wiped her hand across her forehead, pushing a stray curl of hair back into its wave. "I saw Fletcher earlier," she said bluntly. She looked at Frank. "I know he's your kin, but I wouldn't say he's the right man to have over here."

"Why's that?" Frank asked.

"People see Fletcher and they think Logan Doolittle," Ada answered, "especially anybody that's colored. Everybody remembers how Logan thought all those Pegleg killings were a big joke, and they just naturally think that's the way Fletcher was too. And everybody remembers how Logan and Harlan Davis and all that bunch were as thick as fleas."

Frank nodded and pushed the empty banana pudding bowl away from him. He did know, of course, that Logan and Harlan had been close friends. He remembered a barbecue that Harlan had sponsored for Logan when Logan was running for sheriff. Yet he had never thought of Fletcher being friends with either Logan or Harlan, but what he thought did not matter. If Ada Winter believed it, others believed it also.

"Well, I hadn't looked at it that way," Frank admitted. "I'll take care of it. But you said Logan and Harlan and that bunch. What bunch?"

"Oh, that whole group of them," Ada answered, ignoring a look of caution from Hack. "Jed Carnes, Coy Philpot, Harlan's brothers—all of them. Everybody around here knew they were always up to something, but you think Logan ever did a thing to stop it? Nothing. My guess is, he was making too much money off the moonshining and everything else."

Frank leaned forward in his chair, propped his elbows on the table, laced his fingers, brushed his chin against the knuckles of his forefingers. The expression on his face was one of interest. He said, "Coy Philpot? I thought he was a big church worker."

"He is now," Ada said quickly. "And, as far as I know, a good man. They go to the Baptist church; we're Methodists. But that's not the way he's always been. Coy Philpot used to be one of the sorriest men who ever took up space in this community."

"All that's just talk, now," Hack cautioned. "Not worth the breath it takes to say it."

"Call it what you want to," Ada snapped. "The truth's still the truth, no matter how you slice it. You know as well as I do that not too many people did a lot of mourning over here when Logan got killed, and as much as I hate to say it, the same was true for Jed when he died, though everybody felt bad for Evelyn, being left alone like she was, never having any babies."

"Ada, not everybody's gon' feel the same way you do," Hack said gently.

"I didn't say they did," Ada countered. "I'm just saying that was the way it was with a lot of people."

Frank glanced out the kitchen window. He could see Tom creeping along the side of the well house in a squat, keeping below the sight line of Hack and Ada. Frank wiped his face to hide the smile.

"A lot of people's not everybody," Hack said as a warning.

"I didn't say everybody," Ada shot back. "I said a lot of people."

"I don't doubt it," Frank said, turning his eyes away from the window. "Logan wadn't the easiest man to get along with, once he had his mind set about something." He swallowed from his tea, then added, "So you think everything's all right over here? Nobody looking to cause any trouble?"

"None that we see," Hack answered.

Ada thought of Harry Hinton's sermon and the after-church talk that marveled at the power of God to deliver a message even through the most unlikely source. "I think everybody's waiting to find out what you're going to do," she told Frank. "Most people I know think Remona told the truth."

"I'm going to keep looking and keep talking," Frank said. "What I need to find is somebody who can back up what Remona said. Maybe he did the same thing to somebody else." He looked at Ada. "If you hear of anything like that, I'd appreciate knowing it."

"I'll see what I can find out," Ada said. "Maybe somebody's said something to Reba by now."

"I'd appreciate it," Frank repeated. "I'll be back tomorrow sometime. We're going to dig around that sawdust pile where we found Rody, see what else might be there." He stood at the table and again glanced out the window. He did not see Tom, but he could hear a dog whimpering beneath the window, and he guessed that Tom was there, eavesdropping. "I saw Tom outside when I drove up," he said, raising his voice slightly. "Seems like he's doing fine these days."

Ada sighed wearily. "Knock on wood," she said. She tapped her knuckles on the table.

"Nothing wrong with him," Frank said. "He's just got spirit. He'd of been a good soldier."

Outside, a dog barked gleefully.

TWENTY

Nelson Doolittle had deliberately chosen his work gang of six men from the black inmates and had said nothing to them about the work they were to do. He wanted to see the look on their faces when they realized they would be digging for bones in a sawdust pile. He licked his lips, tasted the nectar of the smile waiting to bloom, drummed his fingers on the steering wheel of the truck. A few more miles, and they'd begin to wonder, and then they would become suspicious, and then afraid. He wanted to giggle.

The Reverend Asbury Echols, in a private meeting with the board of deacons of the Faith Baptist Church of Overton, had once called Nelson Doolittle an enigma. No one in the meeting knew what he meant, but it sounded right enough, like a disease happening to a good person. And though none of them would have called Nelson a good person, they had all wagged their heads gravely, with mumbling meant to be agreement. They were, after all, in the sanctuary of the church.

"Our prayers need to be with him," Reverend Echols had concluded.

"Amen," the deacons had replied. Praying for Nelson was far more acceptable than praying with him.

If anyone had researched the disease-sounding word used by Reverend Echols—though that in itself would have been difficult, since none could spell it—they would have discovered how accurately it described Nelson Doolittle. Nelson was a certifiable enigma, a strange and dangerous man. He carried with him always a black, leather-covered, red-lettered, gold-leafed version of the King James Bible, the cover worn smooth by his handling, the gold edging faded from his thumbing. No one in Overton County read the Bible as diligently or as habitually as Nelson, yet reading the Bible was merely his preoccupation. His occupation was running the chain gang for the Sheriff's Department.

Nelson had been given his job by Logan Doolittle, his first cousin, during Logan's reign as sheriff. It was an appointment that had shocked everyone. Nelson had never liked Logan and Logan had never liked Nelson, but hiring Nelson had not been a matter of nepotism with Logan; it was an act of desperation. None of the men of Overton County had wanted the job. The pay was less than sharecropping yielded, the hours were long and tense, and the men to be guarded were considered outcasts, lowest of the low, blights on humanity.

To Nelson, the job was a godsend. It had taken him out of the fields, away from the sizzling heat of the sun and the foul scent of mule sweat, and it had given him a truck to drive, a uniform to wear, a deputy sheriff's position of authority, and time to read from the Book. A godsend.

Three months after taking the job, in March of 1942, Nelson had earned a reputation for violence that was remembered at least once every day in Overton County. He had killed a white man named Gene Crawford for an attempted escape while digging a drain ditch through a swamp. The other prisoners had protested that Gene Crawford, who was skittish, was merely running from a rattlesnake.

"Run from one, killed by one," was the whisper that made its way out of the jail and into the county. "Shot Gene once from the truck. Shot him two more times, close up. Then spit a wad of tobacco juice on him."

It was a story that every prisoner knew well. Nelson made sure of it. "I got one eye on you and one eye on the Book," he would announce at the beginning of each workday. "You see a snake, you better let him bite you." And then he would spit, and a smile would worm into his brooding, hard face.

Retaining Nelson had been a bitter decision for Frank Rucker. In his way, Nelson was as sorry as Logan had been. No one liked Nelson. No one. Yet everyone knew that not a single prisoner had escaped from the chain gang under Nelson's watchful one-eye gaze—the eye not reading from the Book—and Frank had relented to Fletcher's serious advice: "He ain't worth a pinch of owl shit, Frank, but they ain't a man walking that ain't scared that sonbitch is gon' shoot them and then spit on them. Tell you the truth—and I ain't never said this to nobody—but the first thing I did when I saw Logan in his bed with a bullet hole through his head was look for some tobacco spit. You ain't got to like the asshole, but you better keep him on the payroll."

● ● ●

Nelson glanced into the rearview mirror as he pulled his truck onto the logging road that led along the back of Jed Carnes' property. He saw the look of wonder and worry running over the faces of his chained-together prisoners crowded in the body of the truck, saw them whisper low to one another. A shiver of delight shot through his chest. Behind the truck, he saw a sheriff's car, driven by Fletcher Wells. He knew that Fletcher was irritated over being around him. He coughed roughly to cover the laugh in his throat.

Jingles Marsh sat next to Nelson in the front seat. Jingles was old, small, his face leathered to a deep, wrinkled black from his years of working the chain gang as a trusty and a water runner, serving a thirty-year sentence for the robbery of two smokehouse hams from Reuben Redwine. Jingles had once worked for Jed Carnes, knew Jed's treatment of blacks. He knew also of the discovery of Rody Martin's skeleton in the sawdust piles of Jed Carnes' abandoned mill. Everyone on the gang knew. The story had drifted through the steel bars of the jail and the barbed wire of the work camp like the rancid scent of death.

"What we doing here, Mr. Nelson?" Jingles asked fretfully.

"We gon' do some digging," Nelson answered gruffly.

"What we digging for?"

Nelson let a moment pass before he answered. "Bones."

A sigh turning to a moan rose from Jingles. "What kind of bones?"

Nelson spat out of the open window of the truck. "Nigger bones," he answered.

Jingles sat back against the seat, pushed against the door. The moan was like a hum in his chest.

Nelson grinned. He said, "Jingles."

"Yes sir?"

"You got your hand touching the Book. You don't get it off, you gon' be picking your nose with your elbow."

"Yes—yes sir," Nelson stammered.

● ● ●

From her front porch, Evelyn watched for the truck, though she did not believe she would be able to see it from the distance and from the coverage of the trees. The call from Frank—early enough to wake her, though she had pretended to be awake and housecleaning—had predicted the truck would be arriving shortly after sunup.

"We want to get started early," Frank had explained. "Shouldn't take too long."

"Oh, Frank, take all the time you want," she had cooed in answer. She had paused, then added, "You coming over with them?"

"I'll be by later," Frank had answered. "Fletcher's with them."

"Oh . . ."

"Just wanted to let you know."

"Well, I'll have some tea and lemonade in the refrigerator, so you be sure and drop by," she had insisted.

"I'll try to," Frank had promised.

She sipped from the coffee cup that she held and stretched her shoulder muscles. The sun promised another day of heat and stillness, with humidity thick enough for swimming. She closed her eyes and imagined a bath. A long, cool tub bath in baking-soda water. Nothing was as relaxing. No, she thought. She could not take a long and cool bath. Frank could arrive anytime. Or maybe he wouldn't come at all. A pout soured in her mouth, and then a wave of embarrassment. She was thirty-five years old and behaving like a teenager.

From across the field, in the woods, she heard the low growling of a motor.

They're here, she thought.

● ● ●

Nelson Doolittle paced before the men standing near the truck, holding his Bible in a curled fist. A V of perspiration was imprinted front and back on his brown uniform shirt, running from his heavy shoulders. Two circles of perspiration were under his armpits. The men watched him, glancing warily to the sawdust mounds. They were dressed in black-and-white stripes, were shackled at the ankles by short lengths of the trace chain used for mules pulling plows. They held shovels and rakes. Fletcher Wells stood to one side, smoking a cigarette, a scowl on his face. He had had to help roll away the tree that had fallen across the logging road, blocking it, and he, too, was perspiring freely.

"Y'all dig easy," Nelson ordered. "You looking for bones. First time you see anything looking like a bone, you stop and holler out. Then we gon' hand-dig it out. Y'all hear me, now?"

The men nodded.

Nelson smiled and looked toward the mounds. He rolled the plug of chewing tobacco that clogged his cheek and stained the corners of his mouth. "I got one eye on you and one eye on the Book," he whispered menacingly. "You see a snake, you better let him bite you." He shifted the shotgun that he held to the crook of his elbow. Then he spat. Loud. Mean. A brown stream that landed at the feet of Jingles Marsh.

"Shit," Fletcher muttered to himself.

●   ●   ●

Frank was restless. He had dreamed a kaleidoscope's dream of dark, troubling images, the crystals of his mind spinning against an ethereal light with each thrashing turn in his bed. Remona being raped by Harlan Davis on a pallet of cotton spread across the ground, the white of the cotton gleaming under the sunfall. A field of bones in a sawdust graveyard, with stick crosses marking the skeletons, like the stick crosses he had left for dead soldiers in the woods of France and Germany. A hobbling, shadowy figure—filthy, his face covered in sackcloth of oil stains and red dust—swinging a club at the bones, shattering them in puffs of chalk dust. Evelyn, lounging on her bed in her tight yellow dress, a deck of playing cards—men and women having sex—fanned across the pillows. Tom Winter twirling his knife at a tree, the knife becoming a bayonet in the air, like a magician's wish, and the tree becoming a German soldier with twigs growing out of his steel helmet. And, suddenly, he was there again—not under the caul of a dream, webbed to his bed, but *there*, his back pushed against the cold wall of a bombed-out German farmhouse, his rifle tucked to his chest, its barrel inches from his face. He glanced across the room, saw Jabbo Lewkowicz huddled in a corner, rifle raised. Jabbo's eyes were blazing. Galen Pitts was near Jabbo, also huddled, also waiting. Frank knew that Jack Cason was somewhere in the room but could not see him. The room was twilight dark, twilight quiet. Frank could hear nothing in the room but his own breathing and the beating of his heart. Outside, there were footsteps, the cautious moving of men, and the low-bass sound of German voices. He picked out a word, understood it. *"Wo?"* the voice said. "Where?" Another voice answered. The footsteps stopped. He could hear the shucking click of metal. From the corner of his eye, he saw Jabbo's body uncurling in a leap, heard Jabbo's cry, heard the spit of gunfire and the startled shouting of men outside the farmhouse. And then he was on his feet, firing wildly into the twilight. Behind him, he heard the bellowing of Jack and Galen, the scream of their bullets shrieking past him. In front of him, he heard the terrible tearing of flesh, the cries of pain, the hissing of air bellowing from lungs. It was over in seconds, and he crept out of the farmhouse with Jabbo and Galen and Jack, crept to the bodies. Four dead, one still breathing. A boy. Fifteen, maybe. His pale-blue eyes gazing numbly toward the sky. His right arm had been shot away. His chest bubbled in blood. He rolled his eyes toward Frank. He whispered, *"Töten mich."* Frank could hear Jabbo swallow a cry. "What'd he say?" Frank asked. "He wants you to kill him," Jabbo said bitterly, kneeling over the boy. "Goddamn it, why they send out boys?" he added. He touched the boy's face. *"Nein,"* he whispered. The boy blinked once. *"Bitte,"* the boy said. It was a word Frank understood: "Please." Frank watched Jabbo stand, watched Galen and Jack turn away, watched Jabbo pull his service revolver from its holster, watched him aim it at the boy, saw the boy smile faintly, heard the boy again say, *"Bitte."*

The loud, fast-beating bell of his alarm clock had startled him, causing his body to jerk awake, and for a moment, in the puddle of night still gathered in his room, he had believed he was standing outside a bombed-out German farmhouse, over the body of a young German soldier—a boy—begging to be killed, and the alarm was the rapid firing of Jabbo Lewkowicz's pistol.

He had pulled himself from the bed, shutting off the alarm, and had sat breathing heavily, letting the jumbled dream fade into the gray mire of his brain, perspiration trickling down the center of his chest like blood from a soft wound. The dream of the young German boy, his child's voice whispering, *"Bitte,"* was the dream that Frank could not exorcise.

And then he had groped his way into the kitchen and made coffee, and he had sat at the kitchen table in his underwear and watched morning become a blush of light that was as purple as the hull of a fox grape. He had called Evelyn still dressed in his underwear, and from the sound of her voice—too perky, but with the edge of sleep—he had been certain his call woke her, and he had wondered what she was wearing, if anything.

Now he waited for Lucy Hix, and he was not sure why he was

waiting for her. Maybe he would tell her of his dreams and see if she could make sense of them. No, he would not do that. Lucy was not a dream-reader. Lucy was a gossip. If he wanted a reading of his dreams, he would go to Conjure Woman, and that fascinated him. What would she say of the dreams? Maybe he would go. Put down his two dollars and turn up his hand and let Conjure Woman make words of the cursive lines that filled his palm like an ancient language on the walls of caves. No. He couldn't do that. He was the sheriff. The sheriff was hired to find evidence, not to seek answers of riddles that teased him in sleep.

Still, something made him wait for Lucy. It was an intuitive thing, a nagging little self that seemed to sit on his shoulders like something out of the comic strips, a miniature, elfish caricature of his own body, tugging at his ear, saying, *"Wait for Lucy. Wait for Lucy."*

He wiped at his ear involuntarily.

Put things in order, he thought.

There were three issues. Digging for the skeletons in the sawdust mounds of Jed Carnes' abandoned sawmill was one. Pegleg was another. The rape of Remona Martin was the third.

He shook his head, suppressed an annoying shudder. No, there were only two issues. The skeletons in the sawdust pile and Pegleg were one and the same. Pegleg had put them there—if, in fact, they were there. The rape of Remona was not related to long-buried bones and Pegleg. The rape of Remona was its own ugly mess. It would be easier to juggle nitroglycerin than to handle the rape.

●   ●   ●

When she did arrive, a few minutes after eight, Frank understood why he had waited for Lucy Hix.

She said, in a jabbering command, "Mr. Frank, you got to do something about that Harlan Davis."

"What's he done now?" Frank asked.

Lucy stared at him incredulously. "What's he done?" she cried. She threw her purse across the kitchen table and yanked the hat pin out of the blue straw cup of a hat that was perched haphazardly on top of her oil-black hair.

"He's done took that little girl of Reba Martin's and ruined her, that's what," she said angrily. "And that ain't the first time. No sir, not by a long shot it ain't."

"All I've heard about," Frank said deliberately.

"Well, you ain't heard much," Lucy snapped. She put her hat on top of the refrigerator and picked up the coffee cup that Frank had been drinking from and carried it to the sink and began rinsing it. "No sir," she muttered, "you ain't heard much at all."

"Sounds like you know more'n I do," Frank said.

Lucy huffed a laugh. "I know plenty."

"Uh-huh," Frank muttered. He buckled his gun belt to his waist and picked up his hat. He knew that if he pretended to be uninterested, Lucy would flood him with her stories. If he pressured her with questions, she would become obstinate.

"What you ought to be doing is talking to people in your own backyard," Lucy said.

Frank looked at her curiously. "My own backyard?"

"Ivy Garner and Lonnie Beecher, that's who I'm talking about, like you don't know who," Lucy countered irritably.

Frank knew Ivy Garner and Lonnie Beecher well. Both lived in tenant houses on the farm that Frank had inherited from his father and mother. Their husbands—Caleb Garner and Luther Beecher—operated the farm on a fifty-fifty arrangement, which was far more generous than any landowner in Overton County permitted. The arrangement was secret. Or was supposed to be. Both Caleb and Luther had worked for Harlan Davis before moving across the county, from Crossover to Oakland.

"My daddy always say, 'When the cow gets out, look in your own backyard first,'" Lucy quoted, in a voice that was meant to sound wise.

"Your daddy was a smart man," Frank said. He started toward the door, then turned back to Lucy. "Ivy and Lonnie, both?"

Lucy rolled her eyes and sighed. "Lord, Mr. Frank, you ain't that dumb. Ain't you seen them babies they got? Both of them's got a light-skinned one, ain't they? Where you think that comes from?"

Frank could feel the tickle of embarrassment. There were many light-skinned blacks in Overton County. Pale-caramel color. Hues and tints that had flowed out of Africa and Europe and mixed with Indian. Black, white, red. More than a hundred years of mixing by dots and dabs. Genetic throwbacks that popped up like a game of dodgeball between generations. And not all of it from rape. Some of it had been love given, love taken. In secret, maybe, but still honest. In his own family, there were whispers of his grandfather being in love with a light-skinned black woman in South Carolina. Had even built a home for her, the rumors had suggested. Maybe there were children. Frank did not know. The rumors had been careful, select.

"You think they'll talk to me?" he asked.

"What you ask me for?" Lucy said. "I ain't them. All I know is you got some colored folks fit to be tied over what Harlan Davis done."

Frank pulled his hat on his head and glanced at the clock on the kitchen counter. It was eight twenty-two. He knew that Nelson Doolittle would already have his chain gang crew digging.

"I got to go over to Crossover," he said. "But I sure wish you'd do me a favor."

"What you want?" Lucy asked suspiciously.

"I wish you'd go out to the homeplace and talk to Ivy and Lonnie. Tell them it'd be all right to talk to me. I won't use their names, or anything they say. I just got to get some idea of what's been going on."

Lucy shook her head. "Mr. Frank, they be saying I come running to you."

"Tell them I heard about it somewhere else and asked you about it. Act like you warning them that I may come around."

Lucy moaned, "Lord, Mr. Frank."

"Lucy, let me ask you something," Frank said. "Do you think there's twelve white men in Overton County that's gon' put Harlan Davis in jail for raping some little colored girl, when all they got is one word against another? Not in a hundred years. What I've got to have is more'n one person to stand up and point a finger. Now, here's what you tell Ivy and Lonnie, and anybody else you know that's had to deal with Harlan Davis: You tell them I'm gon' walk away from it if somebody don't decide to help me out. You tell them I'm not afraid of Harlan, or all the talk, or anything else, but I'm not a fool, either. You tell them that."

Lucy stared at Frank with surprise. She had never heard him speak so bluntly. She wiggled her head in a nod.

"Lucy, there ain't no way on God's green earth that I'm gon' be able to put Harlan Davis in jail unless somebody helps me out," Frank said gently. "You been around me long enough to know that. I expect it'd be a lot easier if you'd pave the way a little bit."

"I ain't got no way out there," Lucy said timidly.

"You take my car," Frank told her. "You know where the keys are. I got the sheriff's car."

"What's people gon' think, me driving around in that brand-new car?"

Frank smiled. His personal car was a 1947 Ford.

"They're gon' think you looking good, Lucy."

Lucy laughed nervously.

TWENTY-ONE

The call on his two-way radio came from Fletcher at nine-twenty, just as Frank was crossing the bridge on Sweetwater Creek.

"We found one." Fletcher's voice crackled in static.

"The whole body?" Frank asked.

"Looks like it. They just started uncovering it," Fletcher answered.

"I'm almost there," Frank replied.

"Want them to keep digging?" Fletcher asked.

"It's what they're there for," Frank said.

"Ten-four," Fletcher said.

"Yeah. Ten-four," Frank mumbled. He slipped the hand-held microphone back onto the V-neck of its holder. He disliked using the two-way radio. Especially talking to Fletcher. Fletcher changed his voice on the two-way, pitched it higher, dragged out the words until, mixed with static, they sounded like fingernails raked over a chalkboard.

At least he had guessed right, Frank thought. A second body had been buried under the sawdust and shavings piles of Jed Carnes' mill. They would find the third one before the day was over. He was sure of it. And then there would be the haggling over which bones belonged to which name and, after that, two more woeful funerals. He wondered if the families of Blue Conley and Compton Mays would dress their skeletons in new blue suits for the burials.

He reached the turnoff of the logging road leading to the sawdust piles and slowed his car to a stop. Evelyn Carnes was a half mile up the road, waiting, tea cooling in her refrigerator. Maybe he should drive on to her house, tell her that a body had been found, spend a few minutes calming her. He wondered if she was wearing the yellow dress. No, he thought. I can't go there now. Not now. He had work to do. Evelyn Carnes could wait. Later, the tea would taste better, the sight of the yellow dress, or green dress, or blue dress, or whatever dress she had chosen to drape over her body, would be even more pleasing.

●   ●   ●

By ten-thirty, the skeleton, buried deep, its leg bones up near the chest cavity, had been removed from its sawdust grave.

"Looks like he was dumped in facedown," Frank judged.

"Look at the size of them bones," Fletcher said. "He must have been a big sonbitch."

"Blue Conley," Frank said.

"How you know that?" Fletcher asked.

"He was buried a lot deeper than Rody, which means he must have been put in earlier. And from what I hear, he was a big man."

"You right about that," Fletcher replied. "I remember him. Built like a bull."

"You remember where he was killed?" Frank asked.

"Best I can remember, it was out in his barn. He lived pretty close to here, unless I'm turned around," Fletcher said.

"Didn't have to take him far, then," Frank said. "I'd guess the way they did it was to dig a hole just big enough to hold him, right where they were piling the shavings and sawdust, and then they dumped him in it and covered him up enough to keep him hid. When the mill was cranked up the next day, it didn't take long to finish the job." He looked at Fletcher. "I don't imagine Logan ever had any of y'all poke around in any of these piles, did he?"

Fletcher sucked smoke from his cigarette, dropped it, toed the tip into the ground. He shook his head.

"Well, what's done is done," Frank said. "Unless I miss my guess, they'll find the other one pretty soon, but I'd almost bet a week's pay he ain't close to this hole."

"What you want us to do with them?" Fletcher asked.

"You bring the blankets with you?"

Fletcher nodded.

"Wrap them up, one to a blanket. You find any scraps of clothing, keep it all together. Then carry them over to Pug Holly."

"I give you ten to one that Jed was mixed up in this some way and Logan knew all about it," Fletcher said. "May of been what got him killed."

"What makes you say that?" asked Frank.

Fletcher shrugged. "Aw, hell, Frank, things was different back then. I guess everybody but you knew Jed was slipping Logan money here and there. Logan's Law, Frank. Logan's Law. It's just the way things were back then. I even heard Logan say one time that Jed was getting too cheap for his own good. Way things are looking right now, I'd lay odds it was Jed that pulled the trigger on Logan."

Frank nodded. He said, "I better watch my step, Fletch, or you'll be wearing my badge."

Fletcher grinned awkwardly. "Where you going?"

"To talk to some people," Frank said.

A smile cut across Fletcher's face, then dropped under Frank's hard gaze.

● ● ●

Evelyn Carnes was sitting in a rocker on her front porch, fanning herself with a fan advertising the Anderson Flour Mill, when Frank rolled his car to a stop beside a water oak and got out. The heat of the day had gathered quickly, even under the oak's shade. A skim of perspiration soaked into his shirt. He could smell the sweet odor of talcum powder that he had dusted on his chest that morning.

"Well, there you are," Evelyn called. "You must be melting."

"Just about," Frank said wearily, crossing the yard.

Evelyn stood and walked to the edge of the porch. "It's so hot I keep expecting to find a hard-boiled egg every time I crack one open," she said giddily.

Frank smiled. He liked humor in a woman. He said, "I hope it's all right to stop by."

"Don't be silly," Evelyn told him. "I been expecting you to show up. I've got tea and lemonade in the refrigerator. You must be thirsty."

"I could use something cool," Frank said.

"Come on up and sit down. You hungry?"

Frank took the steps slowly. "Just a little thirsty," he answered.

"You want tea or lemonade? Or both? I mix them, myself. Makes it taste cooler."

"Sounds good," Frank said.

Evelyn handed him the fan. "Well, you just sit down and fan yourself. I'll be right back." She turned and went into the house.

Frank sat in one of the rocking chairs and removed his hat and placed it on the porch beside the chair. He rolled the Anderson Flour Mill fan over in his hand and looked at the advertisement, a drawing of a lush field of wheat with the sun spraying down over it. The words *Food for Life* bled out of the bottom of the drawing, like roots from the wheat. He remembered brightly patterned flour sacks that his mother had unraveled at the seams to make skirts and blouses for his sister and shirts for him, even as adults. After the war, he had watched farm children dressed in flour-sack clothing, faded from washing, and he had ached over their poverty.

Evelyn returned to the porch, carrying two glasses filled with ice cubes and the mix of tea and lemonade, a pale straw coloring.

"I hope you like it," she said, handing a glass to Frank.

Frank swallowed from the glass. The taste was surprisingly good. "Sure do," he said. "Never thought about it, putting tea and lemonade together."

"I did it one day when I had just a little bit of both in the refrigerator," Evelyn said, sitting in the other rocking chair. "I loved it. I call it tea ade." She smiled. "Have they started digging?" she asked.

"They been at it for two or three hours now," Frank answered.

"Have they found anything?"

Frank pushed forward in his chair. "They found another one, like I thought they might. And I expect there'll be another one before too long." He looked at Evelyn. She was wearing a pale-blue summer dress that was pulled tight under her breasts. A look of shock bloomed in her face. She drew her hands slowly, involuntarily, to her mouth. A small cry rose in her throat.

"It's nothing to worry about," Frank assured her. "We'll take them away when they finish. But I need to talk to you about it."

"Did—did Jed have anything to do with it?" Evelyn asked in a frightened voice.

Frank did not answer for a moment. He watched her eyes welling with tears. "I don't know. He may have."

"Oh, my God," Evelyn whimpered. "Oh, my God..."

"What Jed did is not your fault," Frank said. "But I've got to be honest. There's a chance he was involved some way. Might have paid somebody."

Evelyn stood suddenly. She put her glass of tea on the small table between the two rocking chairs and walked to the edge of the porch and crossed her arms in front of her, hugging herself. Then she leaned her shoulder in a sag against one of the porch columns. Frank stood, watching her carefully.

"I don't like asking you this," Frank said softly, "but you told me you looked in that trunk one time. Did you see anything . . . unusual in it?"

Evelyn turned back to him. The tears were seeping from her eyes. "No," she whispered. "I just saw them—them cards, like I told you. They were on top of everything, with his cane and some of the army stuff. Soon as I saw them, I closed the trunk back. I was scared Jed would come up and find me."

"It's all right," Frank said. "We don't have to talk about it anymore." He put his glass on the table and stepped close to her. "I'm sorry to make you feel so bad."

Evelyn tucked her head. Her body trembled, then she opened her arms and threw herself against Frank, clasping him. He circled his arms around her. My God, he thought, she did it. Wilted into him. It felt good. Not like sex, but good.

"Oh, God, I'm so scared," she sobbed.

"Nothing to be afraid of," Frank said.

"What'll people think?"

"Nobody's gon' blame you for what Jed did," Frank told her. "Nobody."

She turned her head on his chest and closed her eyes. Frank could feel her gulp in breathing. He stroked her back easily.

"It's all right," he said. "It's all right."

"Will—will you stay with me a little while?" Evelyn whispered.

"Yes," Frank said.

◐   ◉   ◐

Frank had stayed with Evelyn for almost an hour, listening to her rambling anguish over having been the wife of Jed Carnes. Nothing she said had triggered Frank to interrupt her. He had simply let the words rain around him until they began to echo in repetition, and Evelyn had finally paused and laughed and said, "I sound like a parrot, don't I? 'Polly want a cracker, Polly want a cracker.' I'm sorry. I just haven't been able to talk to anybody about all of that." She had looked at him softly.

"I don't know why it's so easy to talk to you, Frank. Gracious, I've told you things I've never told anybody. It must be the sheriff in you— getting people to rattle off every little dark secret they've got."

"Wish it was that easy," Frank had replied.

He had left, promising to call her in the afternoon to tell her if the digging was finished and what had been found, and he had driven toward Dodd's General Store. He was not nearly as worried about the bones and Pegleg as he was about Harlan Davis, or, more specifically, what people were saying about Harlan. His two-way radio crackled with Fletcher's voice as he pulled to a stop in front of the store.

"We found the other one," Fletcher said.

"Where at?" Frank asked.

"Just like you thought; on the other side of that hill where they was digging," Fletcher told him.

"All right," Frank replied. "Bundle them up and take them to Pug. Tell Nelson to make sure they don't leave a mess over there."

"Where you at?" Fletcher asked.

"Over at Dodd's store."

"You coming back soon?"

"Later. I don't know when."

"That's a ten-four."

"Yeah. Ten-four."

Arthur Dodd was alone in his store. He was standing in front of a small mirror hanging from the wall behind the cash register, rubbing Noxzema into the bright-red skin of his forehead.

"Got a little burn, I see," Frank said.

"I look like a damned lobster," Arthur grumbled. "Went out to rake around the store without my hat on." He twisted the top on the Noxzema jar, shook it hard, and slipped it back onto the shelf.

"You gon' sell that?" Frank asked.

"Well, shit, Frank, I just took out a little dab."

Frank smiled. "I think I'll start checking the level in my Co-Colas."

"Yeah, Frank, you ought to do that. I pop them open and pour out what I want and fill them back up with moonshine and then pry the top back on. Why you think I stay overrun with customers?" Arthur said dryly. Then: "What's going on with Harlan?"

"What I thought I'd ask you," Frank said. "You hear any talk?"

"Not much," Arthur replied. "It's the kind of thing people don't talk about too much. Lot of head-shaking, not much else. Don't nobody put it past him, but don't nobody want to get caught up in it. What you ought to be worrying about is the way the colored are acting."

"How's that?" asked Frank.

Arthur played a cigarette out of its package and dug a kitchen match across the top of the counter. The match popped fire and Arthur lit the cigarette. He said seriously, "Duck Heller was in a little earlier this morning to buy some snuff for his mama—you know that old woman's almost a hundred, Frank?"

"That right?" Frank said.

"Anyhow, Duck had this worried look on his face, and I just come out and asked him about it. He said he was worried about Jule."

"What for?" Frank asked.

"Said Jule was mad as a hornet about what happened to Reba's girl. Said a lot of other colored folks was feeling the same way." Arthur drew from his cigarette and spit the smoke across the counter. "I tell you, Frank, the colored have changed a lot since the war. I don't know if anybody else sees it, but I do."

"I think everything's changed," Frank said.

"That's the truth," Arthur muttered. He ran a hand across the glass top of the display case on his counter, looked at the dust rolled into his palm, then wiped it on the leg of his pants. "By the way, y'all find anything over at that old sawmill Jed had?" he asked.

Frank ticked in surprise. "How'd you know we were over there?"

"You told us you were gon' do some more digging around," Arthur said, "and I saw Fletcher over here yesterday afternoon. Stopped in to get me a pack of cigarettes, and he drove up, wanting to know when I'd started opening up on Sunday." He laughed. "I got to tell you, Frank, sometimes I wonder how smart Fletcher is. Took me ten minutes to convince the son of a bitch that I was just getting some cigarettes."

Frank smiled an accommodating smile. He thought: You ought to work with him.

Arthur flicked ashes from his cigarette toward an ashtray, missed, raked the ashes on the floor with his finger. "Anyway, we was talking about Rody's funeral. I still think that's the strangest damn thing I ever heard of, burying a skeleton dressed in a blue suit. Tell you the truth, I'd like to of had some pictures of that. I could probably sell them for a dollar apiece."

"Wouldn't doubt it," Frank said.

"Y'all find anything?" Arthur asked again.

"Two more sets of bones," Frank told him.

The expression on Arthur Dodd's face was sudden shock, then excitement. "I'll be damned," he whispered. He shook his head, squashed his cigarette dead in the ashtray. "Well, you better tighten your belt and grab your balls. That gets out, you gon' have your hands full."

"How's that?" asked Frank.

"The colored, Frank. The colored. They gon' be up in arms. They already pissed off about Harlan. Now they gon' want to know what you doing about Pegleg. So's everybody else."

"What I'm doing is trying to find out all I can about everything that's going on," Frank said. "You hear anything, I'd appreciate it if you'd let me know."

"What kind of things?" Arthur asked.

"Anything," Frank said.

• • •

Arthur Dodd did not know it, but he had answered the question that had plagued Frank subconsciously since Remona's admission that she had been raped by Harlan Davis. He did not need to keep quiet about the bodies—the bones of the bodies—that Nelson Doolittle's chain gang had scratched out of the sawdust piles on Jed Carnes' property. He needed to bring it out in the open, to make an issue of it. He had been in the war with a sergeant from Kansas, a man named Bobby Angel, who made the same simple declaration before every battle: "Let's go stir the pot, boys. Let's go stir the pot."

He would stir the pot, let it boil until the bubbles of trouble simmered to the top. If the blacks of Overton County became skittish over the finding of the bones and remembered the fear of Pegleg, they might begin to talk and let things slip. Trouble heaped upon trouble. Killings and rapings. And out of the fluttering of angry, restless tongues, there might be stories that mattered.

He drove quickly back to Overton and made two visits—to Avery Marshall and to Ben Biggers.

Avery Marshall III was the district attorney of Overton County, a Harvard University Law School graduate who had returned to Overton to follow the natural order of his calling, but also with ambitions for

Congress. Friends called him Avery Three, and it was a compliment. His father, Avery, Jr., or Avery Two, and his grandfather, Avery, or Avery One, had also served the office of district attorney and had gained reputations as fair and compassionate men.

Frank asked Avery Three one question: "If I get enough to put Harlan Davis in jail, are you going to be afraid of prosecuting him on a charge of rape against a colored girl?"

Avery's smile—a lopsided grin, a boyish, impish look of delight—answered the question before the words left his mouth: "I'll do it in a heartbeat, Frank, but my God, I hope you know what you're doing. Didn't Logan teach you anything?"

"What does that mean?" asked Frank.

"Swimming upstream is one thing," Avery said. "Salmon do it all the time. But did you ever hear of one jumping up Niagara Falls? That's about the odds you'll have. Maybe you had a little difficulty with geography in school, Frank. This, my friend, is the South. Logan's Law."

Frank glared at Avery. He said, "You're right. I wadn't too good in geography, but I was damn good in history. Straight As. And unless a lot of books and a lot of people lied to me, the Confederate Army waved the white flag, which means we abide by the Constitution. Believe it or not, Avery, that means something to me. I saw some good boys die feeling the same way."

Avery arched his eyebrows. The grin became a laugh. He snapped his fingers in applause.

"And another thing," Frank said. "I ain't Logan."

"No, you're not," Avery said. He added, "And I, for one, am eternally grateful. All right, I'm with you. But get me something to work with. Don't leave my drawers flapping in the wind."

"I won't," Frank told him. "But don't go saying anything about this right now."

"Lord, Frank, that's asking a lot," Avery said in mock seriousness. "I'm a lawyer, for Christ's sake."

• • •

Ben Biggers, the publisher of the *Overton Weekly News*, was an overweight, complaining, conceited man who waddled the streets of Overton like an irritated hippopotamus. He was also one of the county's most boastful bigots. "Niggers," Ben Biggers contended, "are gon' bring the good white people of this world to their knees."

Frank told Ben about the discovery of the two skeletons in their sawdust graves.

"So?" Ben said.

"Thought you'd want to know," Frank said.

"This got to do with that Pegleg fellow?" Ben asked.

"It does," Frank answered.

Ben snorted, rocked his heavy body in his swivel chair. "Logan couldn't find out nothing about all that," he said. "Niggers killing niggers. Ain't worth the ink to print it. Besides, that was a long time ago. I expect that bunch of niggers over in Crossover found out who it was and buried his ass with the rest of them."

"Just thought you'd want to know," Frank said again.

"Talking about niggers, I hear you trying to make a case out of Harlan Davis raping some little colored girl," Ben said roughly.

"Just doing what I'm paid for," Frank replied.

"You better go careful there," Ben advised. "You know damn well ain't nothing gon' come of that. You like your job, you better go careful."

●   ●   ●

The meeting with Ben Biggers went as Frank had expected, yet he knew that Ben would scatter the story of the discovery of the two bodies over the pages of the *Overton Weekly News* like confetti, and he knew there would be a cynical editorial about the waste of county funds in trying to solve unsolvable crimes. Probably have mention of Logan and Logan's death. Probably ask why more wasn't being done to find the killer of one of Overton County's unselfish, tireless public servants.

Ben would not write of Harlan, however. Not yet. He would save the story of Harlan Davis for a follow-up, if, and when, Harlan was arrested. It would be a word-bullet assault on the Sheriff's Department, demanding to know why the sheriff was so interested in prosecuting one of the county's most successful farmers, from one of the county's most honored families.

There was one other person he needed to see, but Frank could not force himself to bicker with Pug Holly face-to-face. Instead, he called Pug from his office.

"For Christ's sake, Frank, what the hell you think I'm running over here," Pug growled, "a goddamn nigger museum?"

"Pug, I want to tell you something," Frank said in an even, firm voice. "I am in one more nasty mood. You give me any shit—any shit at all—and I'm gon' come over there and slap a set of handcuffs on you and drag your fat ass across town and throw you in jail, and I'm personally gon' bring a case against you for dereliction of duty, and as God is my witness, I'll make it stick. I got a file on you a half-inch thick. You hear me?"

There was a pause. Frank imagined Pug scrubbing the perspiration from his forehead.

"What the hell's eating you?" Pug said after a moment, his voice wavering.

"I'm tired of your bullshit, that's all," Frank told him. "We both got a job to do. I don't bitch to you about mine, and I don't expect you to bitch to me about yours."

"Aw, shit, Frank, calm down," Pug whined. "You know I don't mean nothing against you."

"You damn well better not," Frank warned. He added, "Now, here's what's going to happen: I'm sending Hugh over there to take care of everything—and that's from making sure every bone goes with the right body to letting the families know what's gone on. We ought to have them out of there in a day or so."

"Fine with me," Pug mumbled.

"Good," Frank said.

• • •

There was only one other call to make: Evelyn Carnes. He glanced at his watch. It was twenty minutes after three. In the last seven hours, he had already dealt with three of the most annoying people he knew— Nelson Doolittle, Ben Biggers, and Pug Holly. If a man's pay was based on the people he had to encounter, he had earned his day's wages and was due for an extended vacation.

He leaned back in his chair, stretching the muscles in his lower back. Then he lifted his feet to the corner of his desk. Maybe he needed some help, he thought, and he remembered a pledge that he and Jabbo Lewkowicz and Galen Pitts and Jack Cason had made during a night of too much wine and cognac in Paris. It had been Jabbo's idea: "Boys, you ever need me, you get on the horn. And I don't give a shit what it's for. You want to rob a bank, I'll be riding shotgun. You want to kick somebody's ass, I'll get him from the blind side. You want me to teach

your wife what sex is all about, I'll be there with my drawers down."
Under the umbrella of lifted cognac glasses, with music and laughter and
the poetry of the French language ringing them, they had all promised
loyalty and availability.

Frank laced his hands behind his head, smiled easily. Jabbo and
Galen and Jack in Overton. That would be a sight. He could deputize
them. Put them on the roads of Overton County. Have them dog people
like Nelson Doolittle and Pug Holly and Ben Biggers. Nobody would
want to mess with Jabbo and Galen and Jack.

He unlaced his hands, rubbed his face with his fingers. It was a good
daydream—Jabbo and Galen and Jack.

He reached for the phone and dialed Evelyn Carnes' number. She
answered on the first ring.

"Evelyn, it's me, Frank," Frank said. "Sorry I'm so late getting back
to you."

"Oh, fiddle, Frank, don't worry about it." She forced her voice to
sound light. "They find anything else? I heard them leaving about an
hour ago."

"Yeah, they found one more body. That ought to be all of them."

Evelyn sighed heavily, dramatically. "It just scares me to death, knowing there's been dead people on my property all these years."

"Nothing to worry about," Frank told her. "They're gone now."

"Scares me, anyway," she said pitifully.

"You gon' be all right?" asked Frank.

"A little jumpy, but I'm all right," Evelyn answered. "Maybe I should
have you drive over here and teach me to shoot a gun. A girl's got to
protect herself."

"Well, we'll do that soon," Frank said softly. "Right now, I've kind
of got my hands full."

"Of course you do, but you are coming back over this way, aren't
you? We haven't seen the last of our sheriff, have we?"

Frank smiled. "I'll be back soon. Maybe tomorrow."

"I'll have the tea and lemonade ready," Evelyn said.

●　●　●

It was four o'clock when Frank left his office. Tired. Heat-drained.
He would go home to shower, he decided. Stand under the cool of the
water. Nap, maybe. Aim the fan at the bed and sleep the secret afternoon

sleep. And then he would dress and go to the Cornerstone Café and have an early supper, before the vegetables got soggy and limp.

Northwest, in the distance, he saw a range of thunderclouds. Huge mountains of thunderclouds. Maybe some rain would come out of them, he thought. The skin of the ground was so dry it was cracking open, turning to dust. Cotton and corn, blistered, shriveled in the fields. Rain would be a blessing. He thought of his own farm, of the worried head-shaking from Caleb Garner and Luther Beecher as they watched the crops they had planted hanging limp in neatly plowed rows. Both had mumbled the same sharecropper's lamentation to Frank: "Don't know. Don't look good. No sir, it don't."

He wondered if Lucy had talked to Ivy and Lonnie. If she had, they must have refused to say anything about Harlan Davis. Lucy would have crowed the news over the telephone, unless it was the sort of news that burned the ears of anyone who heard it.

Lucy was waiting for him when he pulled his car to a stop under the shade of the pecan tree that loomed over his sideyard. She was pretending to sweep the front porch.

"You still here?" Frank said.

"Been waiting for you," Lucy answered in a low voice. Her eyes scanned the yard suspiciously.

"What's up?" Frank asked.

"Come on in the house," Lucy ordered.

He followed her inside, through the living room and into the kitchen.

"Place looks good," Frank said.

"I been working myself to the bone," Lucy said wearily. She sat at the kitchen table and wiped her face with a handkerchief. Frank couldn't remember ever seeing her perspire before.

"You talk to Ivy and Lonnie?" Frank asked.

Lucy nodded vigorously. "They scared to death," she said.

Frank sat at the table across from Lucy. "They're not gon' say nothing, are they?" he asked.

"You know that old pair of mules your daddy used to have?" Lucy said. "Well, you could hitch them up to they tongues and couldn't pull a word out of them. No sir."

Frank leaned back against the chair and looked past Lucy to the window above the sink. He could see the thunderheads bowing at their peaks. "I guess I don't blame them," he said.

"Uh-huh," Lucy whispered gravely. She pulled her chair close to the table, leaned over it to face Frank. "*They* ain't gon' say nothing, but it don't mean I ain't," she added. "I knowed Reba all my life. She's a good woman. They done picked on the wrong family this time."

"So you've got something to tell me?" Frank asked.

Lucy lifted her hand and wiggled her finger at Frank. "Now, I ain't gon' say this to nobody but you. Anybody says I said it, I'm gon' swear on a stack of Bibles high as my head it ain't so. You could point that pistol gun you got at my head, and it wouldn't do no good. No sir, it wouldn't."

"You got my word on it," Frank told her.

"Uh-huh," Lucy mumbled again, her eyes squinted in a dare.

"You know I wouldn't go against my word, Lucy," Frank assured her.

"Better not," Lucy said. She licked her lips, looked around the room as though it hid invisible spies. "They was three men over there in Crossover who was doing all that stuff to them colored women. Having a big old time, seeing who it was that could have they way with the most colored women."

"How do you know that?" Frank asked.

Lucy glared at him in disbelief. "Ivy and Lonnie done say so," she said. "They was both done by all three of them men one time down in Mr. Harlan's barn. Said them men kept bragging about how many colored girls they done had. Said they had them some cut marks in one of them stall gates, keeping count. Had a board apiece."

Frank wiggled his head wearily. He rubbed his face with his fingers, stroking his top lip. "Who were they?"

Lucy sat back, again looked around the room for invisible spies. "Mr. Harlan, he was one. Mr. Jed Carnes, he another. Mr. Coy Philpot, he the other one."

Frank looked up. "Coy Philpot?"

Lucy exaggerated a nod. "Him and Mr. Harlan and Mr. Jed."

"All right," Frank said softly. "I appreciate you telling me, Lucy."

"I ain't told you nothing. You remember that."

"I will," Frank promised. He pushed away from the table and stood.

"You ain't going out there to Ivy and Lonnie, are you?" Lucy asked anxiously.

"No. Not out there," Frank said.

TWENTY-TWO

It was late afternoon when Jule drove into the front yard of Reba's home and got out of his car and crossed the yard in a strong stride. He opened the screened door without knocking and closed it hard behind him. Reba and Son Jesus were inside, reweaving the bottom of a chair with strips of dried cane.

"What you pestered about?" asked Reba.

"They done found the rest of them boys that Pegleg killed," Jule announced in an angry voice.

Reba began to wring her hands in anguish. "Where at?"

"Over there at the sawmill, where they found Rody," Jule told her. "I run into Claude. He was over at the store when that Mr. Fletcher come in, saying he was out there when they dug them up."

"Oh, sweet Jesus," Reba moaned.

"They all been found now," Jule said bitterly. "But that don't mean nothing."

"It means they gon' be buried the right way," Reba replied in a sigh.

"What's gon' happen then?" demanded Jule. "Ain't nobody gon' do nothing about finding out who killed them." He leaned toward Reba, his body bowed at the waist as if in pain. His eyes were bloodshot, the eyes of a man who had been drinking, but Reba knew it was not drink; it was anger. He said in a hiss, "That Pegleg man's out there, walking around, feeling high and mighty. He gon' be coming after anybody he wants to. Ain't nobody gon' do nothing about it." He turned and stalked to the window and looked outside. He added, "Gon' keep my gun with me. He come at me like he come at Rody, I'm gon' shoot him."

"You ain't bringing no gun around here," Reba said stubbornly.

Jule did not turn away from the window. "Gon' keep my gun with me," he said again.

"You go walking around with a gun, somebody gon' shoot you," warned Reba.

Jule shook his head defiantly. "Gon' keep my gun," he vowed.

Reba turned to Son Jesus. "Honey, why don't you go on down and help out Remona."

"Where's she at?" Jule asked. It was a question with command.

"Down to the garden, hoeing the grass out of the beans," Reba answered. To Son Jesus: "You help her out, honey; it won't take long."

"Don't like her being far off from the house," Jule said. "Ain't no telling what can happen, her being off from the house."

"She ain't far," Reba said.

"I'll go help her," Son Jesus said.

"You call out if she ain't there," Jule told him.

"Yes sir," Son Jesus said. He left the house through the kitchen door.

"You scaring that boy," Reba said to Jule. "Ain't no call to scare him."

Jule pivoted back from the window. He looked at Reba with a harsh gaze. "He better be scared. He better be. You wait. Won't be long to Mr. Harlan has him out in them fields, bossing him around like he was a mule. He better be scared. He gon' have Mr. Harlan out in front of him and that Pegleg man behind him."

"Jesus gon' watch over him. Jesus got work for him to do," Reba said softly.

Jule stepped back and shook his head. "Jesus?" he said. "We talking about the same Jesus that was taking a nap when Rody was killed? The same Jesus that had his head turned when Mr. Harlan do what he want to with that girl out yonder hoeing beans? That the Jesus you talking about?"

"Don't be going on about Jesus like that in my house," Reba snapped. "You gon' talk about Jesus like that, you leave this house."

Jule shrugged, walked to the door. He paused, looking back at Reba. "Gon' keep my gun," he said.

● ● ●

Outside, a breeze whipped across the tips of grass. The thunder-heads—miles high, they seemed—that had been gathering since early morning had drifted closer, their whipped-cream tips swirling in a high wind. Son Jesus knew that his mother did not want him to hear their talk of bones being dug up from sawdust mounds, or Uncle Jule's outbursts about what he would do to Pegleg, or anyone else, if he had to. Uncle Jule was already mad. Madder than Son Jesus could remember. Had been talking mean about Harlan Davis and what Harlan Davis had done to Remona. Saying Harlan Davis was not fit to live. It was better to be with Remona.

He had helped his mother and Remona and Uncle Jule plant the bean garden in a cleared-out patch of new ground off the ridge that sloped into the swamp. The ground was rich in the deep, moist woods dirt of decayed leaves, and the beans had sprouted quickly. Even in the drought and heat, they had grown into a lush tangle of vines. The grass, too, was lush.

He saw Remona from the top of the knoll that shielded his home from the field. She was bending over, holding the hoe low, near the blade, and she was hacking furiously at a clump of grass. She was not digging the grass. She was killing it.

"Mama told me to come help out," Son Jesus said as he crossed the field.

Remona did not stop digging. "Where's your hoe?" she said harshly.

Son Jesus stopped. "I ain't got one," he answered quietly.

"Well, you ain't gon' do much digging, are you?" Remona grumbled.

"I can use yours," Son Jesus said after a moment. "You can rest some."

Remona stopped her attack on the ground, pushed herself up on the handle of the hoe, and turned to look at him. Stings of perspiration cut across her face. One eye was still puffed from Harlan Davis's fist. She was breathing heavily.

"I ain't mad at you," she said.

"You sound like it," Son Jesus told her.

Remona wiped her face with her hand. "I ain't," she said. She lifted the hoe and handed it to Son Jesus.

"They found the rest of them men that Pegleg killed," Son Jesus said.

"Where at?" Remona asked.

"Over in them sawdust piles, where they found Daddy."

Remona looked away, toward the knoll. "It don't make no difference," she whispered.

"Thomas say they gon' find Pegleg," Son Jesus said.

Remona looked at her brother wearily. "What he know about finding anybody? They ain't gon' find no Pegleg. They ain't even gon' look."

"Thomas say his mama say the sheriff was gon' find him."

"Son Jesus, you got to quit hanging around that boy," Remona said sharply. "He ain't nothing but a talker, that's all. You hear his mama say anything? No, you ain't. It's just him talking. You hang around him, you gon' wind up in trouble, that's what. Anyhow, that Pegleg man ain't nowhere around here. He been gone. Thomas don't know nothing he talking about. What he say about Mr. Harlan? They gon' take Mr. Harlan off for what he done to me? Mr. Harlan, he white. What color you think I got on me? What color you got on you? You think Mr. Harlan gon' stop what he's been doing, you don't know nothing about white people."

Son Jesus slapped the hoe against a sprig of grass growing near a bean stalk. He heard the blade strike a buried rock, felt the sting of it run up his arms.

"Uncle Jule say Mr. Harlan ain't gon' hurt you no more," Son Jesus muttered.

Remona laughed. Short. Bitter. "Uncle Jule just talking. Acting like he's mad. What's he gon' do? He ain't gon' do nothing."

Son Jesus could feel the swelling of a presence he did not understand. "Ain't nobody gon' hurt you no more," he said quietly.

●   ●   ●

Frank sat in his sheriff's car in front of Holly's Funeral Home, which was three blocks off the Overton square and the last building constructed in the city before the war. Its architecture was something between a church and a plantation house, a too elegant look for most of the citizens of Overton County, especially those in good health. When Pug Holly had announced that he would have a grand opening of his new facility, the event was immediately hailed as a macabre social occasion, and the comments had ranged predictably from "I wouldn't be caught dead in there" to "What do you have to do to get an invitation? Die?" Drugstore humor. At the hardware store and in the barbershop, the humor had been more direct: "I wouldn't let Pug Holly embalm my goober, much less my whole body, and personally I don't give a damn if that place looks like a new Ford Motor plant."

If Holly's Funeral Home was new-slab modern, as Pug had proclaimed, no one knew it. Not a single person attending the grand opening had accepted his offer to visit the preparation room, with its slabs and drainage system, its needles and knives and bottles and chemicals. Those who had summoned the nerve to go to the opening were content to eat cookies and peanuts and trimmed-and-quartered egg salad sandwiches and to drink punch in the receiving rooms and the chapel, and to wander the grounds, inspecting the truckload of azaleas that Pug had imported from Anderson, South Carolina, and had planted like ground cover.

Now, eight years later, Holly's Funeral Home was almost a tourist attraction, especially during the season of the azaleas, and the gentle jesting about Pug's grand opening had been tempered by whispers of awe and by silent wishes to die during the season of the azaleas.

It was, to Frank, a contradiction that a man like Pug Holly would own, and care for, such a place. It was like Harlan Davis's yard. Too spectacular for the person who owned it. If personalities were flowers, Pug would have been a bitter weed. But maybe it wasn't all Pug's fault that he was one of the absolute assholes of Overton County, Frank thought. Pug had been ridiculed enough. Growing up in a funeral home, always smelling slightly of formaldehyde. Always shorter than everyone else. Always flabby. Always picking fights. Always getting his ass kicked. There was a belief that Pug became a mortician not out of loyalty to his father but in order to get even with the tormentors of his childhood. Someday, he would have them stretched out on a slab before him, death by death, and he would gouge their bodies like a matador spearing a bull. And maybe it was true, Frank decided. He had seen the remains of some of Pug's tormentors after Pug had worked them over. No one said of them, "He looks natural, don't he? Looks like he just went to sleep and didn't wake up." People gasped when they saw the remains of Pug's tormentors.

The front door to the funeral home opened, and Frank saw Deborah Holly, as plump and red-faced as Pug, escorting three older people to a car parked under the dark-green awning that extended from the front porch. He recognized George Willoughby and Ouida Cash and Geraldine Lamont, and remembered hearing the announcement over the *Obit-*

uary Column of the Air of the death of Howard Willoughby, their brother. The Willoughby name was well-known in Overton and Overton County. The first dry goods store had been established by Caesar Willoughby in the early 1800s and had been operated in succeeding generations by Willoughby descendants. George and Ouida and Geraldine and Howard were from a family of eight. Now only the three remained. One of them, one day, would stand alone beside a grave, and his or her loneliness would be very great, Frank thought. He shuddered. He would not want to be the last of such a family.

Two boys on bicycles sped down the sidewalk, going too fast, saw the sheriff's car, slowed, stopped, ducked their heads, turned back and pedaled quickly away.

They've done something, Frank reasoned. It was easy to tell. Boys wore guilt like makeup on a Paris or New York whore. Guilt over something. Pestering girls. Stealing a watermelon from some backyard city garden. Being chased from the movie theater for talking too loud. Something.

He watched the car driven by Ouida Cash ease away from the funeral home, saw Deborah Holly walk up the steps and open the door. As she did, Hugh stepped out. Frank watched them react, speak polite words of momentary awkwardness, watched Deborah go inside, watched Hugh stand for a moment, looking back at the door. Frank tapped the horn of his car lightly. Hugh turned, saw him, walked to him.

"Get in," Frank said.

Hugh said nothing. He got into the car, and Frank backed into the street and pulled away.

"You walk over?" Frank said after a moment, knowing the answer. Hugh walked everywhere, especially in Overton. Hugh believed that law enforcement officers should be seen.

"Yeah," Hugh said. "It's just a few blocks."

"You get everything straight with Pug?"

"Uh-huh," Hugh mumbled. "Wadn't much he could do but declare them dead and do up a report. Reeder Higginbottom's coming over tomorrow to pick them up. Pug's raising hell about having colored bones in his place, but I suspect you know that."

"You get a look at them?" asked Frank.

"Yeah," Hugh answered. "Both of them's got a caved-in skull. That's a mean son of a bitch that'd do that, Frank."

"He ain't pleasant," Frank said. "You want to ride out to Benny's and get a cup of coffee and some barbecue?"

"Suits me," Hugh answered.

Frank turned the car onto Stonebreaker Street and headed south.

"What's the problem?" Hugh asked after a moment.

"I got some information on the rape of Reba's girl," Frank told him.

"What?"

"Been going on for a long time, it looks like," Frank said. "Hell, they even kept score."

"Who?"

"Harlan and Jed and Coy Philpot."

Hugh turned in his seat and looked quizzically at Frank.

"Yeah, what I thought too. I guess Coy's one of the newest pillars of the church," Frank said dryly.

"They kept score? What's that mean?" asked Hugh.

"Cut notches on a stall gate in Harlan's barn. I guess they had a game going."

"How'd they do that? That barn's right next to his house. You'd think his wife would've known something."

Frank shrugged, rolled his hands over the steering wheel. "Maybe she did," he said softly. "Or maybe she was gone off somewhere when all that was going on."

"What do you want to do?" Hugh asked.

"Tomorrow morning, I want you to go over to Crossover," Frank said, "and I want you to let it slip at Dodd's store that there may be somebody—some white person—who's about to say something about the carrying-on with colored girls."

"You trying to spook Harlan?"

"Not Harlan. Coy, maybe. If it gets back to him."

"Why me?" Hugh asked. "I don't mind doing it, but you know those people a lot better'n I do."

"That's why," Frank said. "They know I wouldn't say anything, and if I sent Fletcher over there, nobody'd pay him any attention, anyhow." He paused, pushed back in his seat. "Besides, you pretty good at that kind of thing."

Hugh could feel the coloring of a blush. Frank was not a man free with compliments. "What about this Pegleg thing?" he asked.

"Just talk it up, that's all," Frank told him. "Let's see if we can't pry loose some tongues on everything that's going on over there."

"You don't think Pegleg's around anymore, do you?" Hugh said.

"Don't look like he is," Frank admitted. "It's been six years since Rody was killed. I expect he's either dead or gone."

"I hope you're right," Hugh replied uneasily. "I hope you're right."

●   ●   ●

The rain began at sunset. Heavy drops at first, splattering with the noisy popping of small firecrackers, and then the cement-dark underbelly of the thunderclouds broke like a fragile shell and the water poured out in sheets, mixed with a swirling wind, and beat hard against the earth.

Harlan Davis stood at the window of his living room and gazed outside, holding a beer. He was annoyed. He knew the rain was coming, and was needed, but he knew also that the rain would wash out the card game he had planned that night for his barn. No one would drive through the fury of such a storm. Already, Curly Sharpe had called. Curly was a mechanic who lived near Athens, where the storm had hit early. "It's a goddamn gully-washer," Curly had complained. "It run over the road and flooded up in my garage."

A spit of lightning, like a rip in the dark cloth of the cloud, flashed suddenly, the thunder exploding not far away. Harlan stepped back instinctively.

"You better get away from that window," Alice said fretfully. She sat in a chair, her legs curled beneath her, a large white shawl wrapped around her shoulders and pulled to her chin by her hands. She was afraid of storms, afraid of the electric snakes leaping across the skies with thin, licking tongues, afraid of the thunder booms and the lashing rain that made floods.

Harlan raised the bottle of beer to his mouth and swallowed three times in long gulps.

"How many of those things have you had?" Alice asked.

"None of your damn business," Harlan growled. He counted quickly in his memory. Five. Five beers since midafternoon. "How many little nips of vodka have you put away today when my back's been turned?" he said cynically.

"I don't know what you're talking about," Alice said. "I don't even know where you keep that stuff."

A low, mean laugh, barely audible, rolled in Harlan's chest. "You stupid bitch," he sneered. "You think I don't know how much drinking you doing? In the first damn place, I can count and subtract, and I know damn good and well that I ain't got near as many bottles left as I buy."

"You must be drinking them yourself," Alice said defensively. "Or that sorry lot of friends you hang around with."

Harlan turned his shoulders to look at her. "Goda'mighty. You worse than your daddy was. I ain't had a drink of vodka in a year."

"Well, don't think I been taking it," Alice said. "Maybe Mason or George got it."

Harlan laughed again. Again low, mean. He turned back to the window.

Another burst of lightning, like stick figures in a frenzied dance, spewed across the sky, hit earth, crackled. The house lights dimmed, went off, popped on. From her chair, Alice could see the silhouette of trees outside the window blink white, like the negative of a photograph.

"Harlan, please get away from the window," Alice whined.

Harlan turned to her. A hard glare was in his face. "Yeah, and why don't you get your lazy ass out of that chair and go fix me some supper?"

Alice pulled the shawl closer to her face. The storm that she feared was in the room with her. "I don't feel good," she whispered.

"Shit," Harlan mumbled. "You don't never feel good."

"It's not my fault you run off my help," Alice protested.

Harlan's eyes did not move from her. "She better have her black ass back to work in the morning, or they gon' be living in the goddamn woods," he snarled.

Alice shifted in her chair. She could hear the rain drumming against the roof, could smell the water.

"You think I'm letting a bunch of niggers run over me, you got another think coming," Harlan said. He drained the beer from the bottle and began walking toward the kitchen.

"I wouldn't make Reba too mad if I was you," Alice said quickly.

Harlan stopped, turned back. "What's that supposed to mean?"

"I just wouldn't, that's all," Alice answered. "You already stirred up a hornet's nest."

"Goddamn it, woman, don't you talk to me like that," Harlan ordered.

"You better talk to your daddy before you go off doing something," Alice said.

Harlan took a step toward her. "What's my daddy got to do with it?"

"He was by here today, when you was out."

"What was he doing here?"

"Come to see you."

"What'd he say? He say something?"

Alice watched the eyes of her husband. His eyes were small and dark, and when he became angry, they turned dull and cold. His eyes told her that he was angry.

"He said it was being talked all over that you'd done something to Remona, and the colored people were fit to be tied."

His eyes burned into her. Heat from the cold. He did not speak for a long, brittle moment, and then he whispered, "That nigger's gon' pay for that. By God, I mean it."

"Did you, Harlan? Did you do something to her? Did you rape her?"

Harlan stepped to her, knelt suddenly at her chair, and caught her shawl in his hand, binding it tight against her throat. "You listen to me, goddamn it," he hissed. "What I do with nigger girls is my business, and don't you never say a word to me about it again, and if my daddy ever asks you anything about it, you damn well better keep your mouth shut about anything that goes on around here, you hear me?"

Alice inhaled, held her breath. The hot scent of beer from Harlan's mouth was on her face. She said, in a gasp, "Let go of me, Harlan."

Harlan released his grip and stood and stared back down at her, then he turned and started toward the kitchen.

"Harlan," Alice said quietly.

He stopped, looked back. Cold eyes.

"Don't ever touch me again," she whispered. "If you do, I'll kill you."

TWENTY-THREE

The rain fell throughout the night, changing from storm to steady, stopped at sunrise, and when people stepped from their homes and looked around, they declared, almost in a single voice, "It was a washing rain."

There was much said in the expression. The rain had washed in gullies across fields of cotton and corn and grain, and the wind had snapped giant limbs like so many small twigs, and the sight was one of destruction—rain and wind battering the earth into submission. Sheet tin, rusting, curled up on barn tops like fried bacon. Two-inch-deep lakes shimmered in pastures. The confetti of newspaper and magazines, left outside by the habit of readers lazy-rocking on porches, clogged shrubbery and trees.

"A washing rain, sure enough," the people said.

A washing rain also meant a new vigor, a baptism, something that fed the marrow of bones, caused muscles to twitch with energy. Cleanup to be done. Things to be repaired. Axes and crosscut saws and hammers playing the music of work. Yesterday's parched ground now soggy, with musty underground springs refilled and water spurting out of nozzle holes that ran along the troughs of roots. There would be gatherings in shops and stores, and people would be speaking of colossal gusts of wind and the eerie sounds of silence between gusts and how they had had their ears fine-tuned for the train sound of tornadoes chewing up ground like a sausage grinder. The storm that had crackled throughout the night would crackle throughout the day, in declarations that had the splendor of lightning.

For a few hours at least, the earth of Overton County and the people of Overton County would be revived.

Frank Rucker shook his head over the fallen pecan-tree limb that had missed his sheriff's car by two feet. Half a tree, it seemed. He would saw it later, he decided. Maybe split it and dry it in his garage, to be used later for barbecuing. Better than hickory, he thought, though he was sure there would be plenty of hickory for the taking. A man with a truck or a wagon could put in his firewood for the winter with a day's work of cutting up fallen limbs in the yards of neighbors.

He backed his car out of his yard and began a slow-paced drive toward Crossover. The sun was remarkably bright, glittering on all that it touched as it always did after a summer rain. He had already called his office at the Sheriff's Department. "Half the damn county got blown away last night," Fletcher had reported. "Nelson's already got people out cleaning off roads. Jail's empty." And he had said to Fletcher, "You hold it down. I'll check in later. Right now, I'm gon' do some riding around."

Surprisingly, Fletcher had not questioned him about where he was going, or why he was going there.

It would be a slow, long day. He was sure of that. Could sense it. It was like a lull in the fighting of war, when men stood up from foxholes and stretched their muscles and yawned from deep, pleasant yearnings for sleep. A slow day. Exactly what he wanted. Slow days had ways of causing things to happen.

He had thought of calling Evelyn Carnes but had changed his mind. A drop-by would be better. A drop-by was more like official business than a telephone call, and he had played it carefully to this point. No reason to risk embarrassment. Better to have business as a fallback.

Still, he wouldn't mind having the seesaw tilt in favor of the personal over business. Rain nights always left him lonely, always made him wish for someone warm beside him. On rain nights, he missed Sharon more than any other time. Curled against her, his shoulder cradling her head, one hand cupping her breast, the tickling moisture of her breathing falling gently over the inside of his arm. He wondered if the piano player felt the same to her, or if Sharon missed him on rain nights. They had been a fit. Yes, they had. Body-to-body, they had been. The piano player was a smaller man. His chest would not cover her back with the fit that she had liked.

He shuddered, had a flash of Evelyn against him in bed, her back heat-fused to his chest, his one hand on her breast.

"Oh, Lord," he said aloud, rubbing the palm of his hand over his pant leg.

● ● ●

"Oh, Lord," Frank repeated as he pulled his car to a stop in the front yard of Evelyn Carnes' home. He licked his lips, swallowed, sighed. The muscles of his abdomen closed like a fist grip. He could feel his palms fill with perspiration.

Evelyn Carnes was in her front yard, wearing a tight red blouse and red shorts that stopped high on her thighs. Her legs were as slender-muscled and tan as a teenager's on a Florida beach. He had never noticed that she was so tan. She was tugging at limbs that had fallen from the oak.

"I think I see help," she trilled as Frank got out of the car.

"Looks like you need it," Frank replied.

She dropped a limb on a small pile and flicked her hands to clear the rubbish from them. "I thought I was going to be blown all the way into town," she said.

"Anything fall on the house?" Frank asked.

"Just some twigs," Evelyn told him. "But I've got a chinaberry down in the backyard, by the barn, and it seems like half the tin blew off the barn roof. Thank God I got rid of all the animals."

"I'll tell Caleb and Luther about it, if you want me to," Frank said. "They do some roofing once in a while, when they got the time."

"Who're they?"

"They sharecrop my farm," Frank said. "Used to live over here. Thought you might know them."

Evelyn's eyes flashed in recognition. "Oh, Ivy and Lonnie's husbands. They used to help me out some, until Jed got mad over their husbands' not wanting to work for him. Then he wouldn't let me hire them anymore."

"They're good people," Frank said. He picked up a limb and dropped it on the pile, forcing his eyes not to look at her.

"Well, I'd like that," Evelyn chirped. She laughed lightly. "Tell them Jed's gone and I don't know the first thing about a sawmill." Then: "I've been out here since sunup, trying to beat the heat. It's going to be sweltering before the day's out, with all that rain."

"You're right about that," Frank said.

"I was about to take a break," Evelyn said. "I already feel clammy. Come on in. I'll get us some tea."

"Tell you what," Frank said. "I'll go take a look at that chinaberry tree and the barn. Why don't you go on in and turn on the fan and stand in front of it a few minutes, and I'll be in shortly."

Evelyn mugged an exaggerated expression of surprise. "Why, Frank Rucker, you sound just like a knight in shining armor. But I can't turn on my fan. All the lines are down. I don't have a spark of electricity. Even worse, I can't make a phone call, and it's a mortal sin to take away a woman's lifeline to the world."

"I guess so," Frank said.

"But you're sweet to think about my well-being," Evelyn cooed. "No doubt about it: you're a knight in shining armor. All you need is a white horse."

Frank grinned sheepishly. If that's what it takes, he thought, I'll have a herd of them out here by sundown.

"I won't be but a minute," he said.

The chinaberry was not large but was leaf-heavy. The wind had twisted it, splitting it as the blow of an ax would. One side had fallen against an old mule-drawn cotton-stalk cutter. The other side lay on open ground. It would not need to be cut up in pieces. When the ground could bear the weight of a tractor, it could be dragged away and dumped into a ravine.

Frank went to the barn and glanced inside. Good, he thought. Still got a John Deere. Maybe it needed a battery charge, but he could get it running and then drag off the tree. Give him a reason—more personal than business—to come back.

He glanced toward the house. Inside was a woman wearing a red blouse and red shorts who was playing him like a cat toying with a mouse. Damn it, he knew it. Knew the game. It was worse than being a teenager trying to curb the artesian well of hormones that turned boys into puddles of stupidity. He thought of being in New York with Jabbo Lewkowicz and of listening to Jabbo boast about women waiting for him on every street corner in Brooklyn. "I'm not going to miss a one, by God," Jabbo had vowed. "Not a one." Jabbo had lasted only a year on the streets of New York before winding up dazed in front of a justice of the peace. "Damned if I know what happened," he had admitted on his Florida-bound stopover visit with Frank. "One day I was whacking half the women in Brooklyn, and the next day she had my nuts in her hand and she was dragging me off to get a marriage license. And you know what, Frank? I was happy to be dragged."

Frank wondered if Jabbo was still married. Probably. Jabbo was a talker. Jabbo's wife would not have needed conversation from another man.

He heard a sound at the house and turned to it. Evelyn stood at the screened door of the kitchen, waving to him.

"Tea's ready," she called.

"Be right there," Frank answered. "Just want to check out the barn."

"It's getting too steamy to stay out," Evelyn said. She had the top of her blouse pinched with her fingers and was shaking it to circulate air over her breasts. The screened door was held open between her legs.

Goda'mighty, Frank thought. He could feel the seesaw tilting. He stepped inside the barn, out of view of the house, quickly opened his belt and unbuttoned and unzipped his trousers, and retucked his uniform shirt. If it was a game worth playing, he needed to look the part.

• • •

Of all the things that Hugh Joiner had learned about Frank Rucker, nothing had been more impressive than the wisdom of his instincts. If Frank had ordered the deputies of Overton County to load the Civil War cannons on Courthouse Square against an impending invasion of communists from Russia, Hugh would have been outside, trying to cram bowling balls down the barrels. Instinct was Frank's great gift, the blessing that had been bestowed upon him in some mystic ceremony from another world. Hugh was certain that Frank was better than bloodhounds at finding invisible scents and better than Ouija boards at spelling out answers to baffling questions. Maybe as good as Conjure Woman. Hugh believed that Frank's instincts had saved his life dozens of times in the war, which was probably why he always acted embarrassed about the ribbons and medals that had decorated his chest in the postwar parade that welcomed him home. How could you pin a medal on something you could not see or explain?

It was Frank's instinct, more than a reason or a plan, that had sent Hugh to Dodd's General Store on a let-slip mission on the day after the washing rain. Hugh did not want to seem smug about it, but Frank had been right: He was good at dropping hints, at prying without seeming to pry. It was not a particularly difficult task, not for a man who had been reared in a home with five sisters. His sisters were always dropping hints, letting things slip with the appearance of innocence but with messages that were deliberate and deadly serious. An art, it was. Word pictures with soft brush strokes and delicate shadings of color. It had been easy enough to learn, watching his sisters.

He did not have to wait long to deliver the message Frank wanted delivered.

"What's all this talk about Harlan?" J. D. Epps asked.

"What talk?" Hugh replied easily.

"About him and that little colored girl," J. D. said. "Reba's girl."

Hugh looked away, rolled the Coca-Cola he held in his hands. He sniffed once as though suppressing a sneeze, then shook it away. He knew that J. D. and Arthur Dodd and Keeler Gaines and Charlie Hazelgrove and three or four other men were watching him with interest.

"Well, we don't know much more'n any of y'all do, I guess," Hugh said. "We're still looking into it, still poking around." He faked a sneeze, sniffed again. "We been kind of busy with finding the rest of them bones over in that sawdust pile."

J. D. settled back against his chair, smiled his broken-tooth smile. "I wouldn't be worrying about no bones," he advised. "What y'all better be worrying about is Harlan. You got a bunch of niggers running on at the mouth about what's happened to Reba's girl and what they gon' do about it. That's what I'd be keeping on top of. Harlan ain't gon' put up with that."

"Aw, shit, J. D., it ain't nothing but talk," Charlie drawled. He looked at Hugh. "I reckon y'all hear a lot of that, don't you?"

Hugh forced a frown across his forehead, a trick often used by his oldest sister, Martha. "We hear some," he said in a guarded voice.

The men leaned forward in their chairs.

"What kind?" asked Keeler.

"Just talk," Hugh answered.

"Goddang it, Hugh, what does that mean?" J. D. demanded.

Hugh shifted his weight, took a drink from his Coca-Cola. "Well, it means just that: talk. Same stuff y'all been hearing, I guess."

J. D. wagged his head. "You better take what a nigger says with a grain of salt."

Hugh inhaled, held the breath, slowly released it. Then he said, "We just listening to what anybody says, white as well as colored."

No one spoke.

Hugh laughed nervously. "Hey, I didn't mean nothing by that." He looked at J.D. "You're right. It'd be hard to bring a man to trial just on a colored man's word."

J.D. mumbled something Hugh could not understand, fumbled his tobacco pouch out of the bib pocket of his overalls.

"Well, I got to go," Hugh said cheerfully. "We riding around trying to see what kind of damage was done last night. I tell you one thing, it ain't a good time to be on the chain-gang after a storm like that."

"It tore things up," Charlie Hazelgrove said.

"It was a washing rain, all right," Arthur added.

• • •

Hugh did not have to look in the rearview mirror of his car. He knew the men at Dodd's General Store were watching, waiting for the car to be out of sight. Only then would they begin to talk. Slowly at first. Tentatively. Mumbled questions.

"What you suppose he was talking about—'white as well as colored'?"

"You reckon some white person's been saying something?"

"Sounded that way, you ask me."

"Harlan better watch out. You get the right white man talking, Harlan could be ass deep in trouble."

"Tell you the truth, I'd hate to see a man spend jail time just because he can't keep his pecker in his pants, but Harlan takes things too far sometimes."

"Ain't that a fact."

"Hugh was talking about somebody, I guarantee it. You see how quick he tried to cover his tracks?"

"Frank finds out he let it slip, there's gon' be some ass-kicking going on over there at the jail."

• • •

The washing rain also forced worms from their underground burrows, and they wiggled freely over the ground and the grass, easy enough to pick up and drop into a can half filled with mud. To Tom Winter, worms on the top of the ground was a command from God to go fishing, but his mother was firm in her refusal.

"The creek's out of the bank," she said. "And it's too slippery. You could slide in and we'd never find you. Maybe tomorrow, when the water goes down some. You go help Troy and your daddy clean up the yard."

Tom knew it was an argument he would not win.

"I been helping," he protested. "Anyway, they just about through. Daddy said it was too wet to drag anything down in the woods."

"Well, get out from under my feet," his mother complained. "I've got work to do."

"Can Elly take me to town?" Tom asked.

"No. Elly's got to help me. Besides, what do you want to go to town for?"

"I heard Troy talking to Daddy," Tom said. "Troy said he bet there were a lot of people in town that'd pay a pretty penny to get some help cleaning up their yards. Maybe I could hire out to some of them."

His mother looked at him, trying to hide the smile that wanted to fit on her face. It would be laughable, she thought. Tom conning people into paying him to pick up one twig at a time and walk it a half mile away, yammering nonstop about the storm. He'd have them believing a tornado ripped his own house apart, or that he had seen an oak tree with wheat straw driven all the way through the trunk by the force of the wind. Having Tom in Overton would be a cruel trick to play.

"Well, I don't know about that," his mother said after a moment, "but if you want to help out, why don't you go over to Mrs. Carnes' house and see if she needs you? I expect she's got trash all over her yard."

Tom blinked. His eyes blazed with possibility. "You think she'll pay me something?"

"I'm sure she would, but you should be willing to help out just because she's a neighbor, living alone. Maybe she'll give you some cookies, or something."

"Oh," Tom said, dejected.

"Neighbors don't charge for being neighbors," his mother preached.

"Yes m'am."

"Tell her to give me a call when the phone line gets put back up if she needs Troy or your daddy."

Tom nodded weakly. He began to drag himself toward the door.

"Tom."

Tom turned back.

"Let's see a little more spirit out of you."

Tom ducked his head and continued to the door. His feet were barely moving.

"Tom."

Tom stopped.

"Don't take Micky with you. I don't want her covered in mud."

"Uh-huh," Tom muttered.

• • •

Walking the road, it took Tom almost an hour to reach the turnoff leading to Evelyn Carnes' home. He had thrown enough rocks at utility poles to feel an aching in his arm. And he had rested often under tree shades to avoid the danger of sunburn or, worse, sunstroke. Twice he had turned back, reasoning that Evelyn Carnes would already have the trash in her yard raked up and removed, and it would be a senseless trip. He had changed his mind both times because there was always the possibility that Evelyn Carnes would, indeed, offer to pay for his help. He would protest, tell her that his mother would not like it if he accepted money for doing what a neighbor should do, and she would insist and he would finally be forced to take a dollar or two. Not for his own gain, of course, but to keep Evelyn Carnes from feeling bad about all his labor going unrewarded. Maybe she would throw in a few cookies too. She always had cookies.

At the turnoff he saw the sheriff's car and ducked behind a ridge of sumac that grew on the roadside.

Wonder what the sheriff's doing here? he thought.

Maybe they had found some more bones. New ones. Maybe he was there questioning Evelyn Carnes about what she knew but was not telling. Maybe Evelyn Carnes had seen Pegleg and was too scared to admit it.

Tom could feel his blood surging in him. He squatted, waited for a few seconds, craned his head up and gazed through the limbs of the sumac. He could not see anyone. Sheriff's inside, he reasoned. He stood in a half-crouch and studied the roadside. It was lined in sumac and scrub pine and scattered chinaberry trees, leaving pools of shadows from the sun. Oak and pecan trees clustered in the front and back yards.

Nothing to it, Tom thought. He could be as quiet as a deer if he wanted to be. Could crawl up to the house, even under it, and nobody would ever know he had been there. No dogs around since Mrs. Carnes got rid of the beagles that Mr. Carnes kept.

Still, though, it was risky, he decided. If the sheriff caught him, he could be arrested—or turned over to his parents. It was not worth the chance. Maybe he would learn as much simply by walking up the middle of the road to the house and listening at the front door before knocking. At least nobody could accuse him of being sneaky.

He stepped back into the road and began a lazy stroll toward the house, whistling softly. He stooped, picked up a rock, tossed it aimlessly at a small pine, shook his head over the miss. If anyone was watching from the window, everything would seem normal.

He reached the yard, stopped at the sheriff's car, looked inside. No guns or handcuffs. He turned to the house, cocked his head. A faint strain of music seemed to float out of the clapboards and drift up into the trees. He crossed the yard to the front porch, took the steps, and moved to the door. The music was clear. Slow music. He crept to the window, peered cautiously inside. Through the gauze curtain, he could see Evelyn Carnes and the sheriff sitting together on the sofa. Close. Side by side. Arms touching. They were bending forward over the coffee table, looking at something. He jerked his head back, swallowed a laugh.

Got to get off the porch, he thought. The music stopped. He stood frozen. Voices from inside, too soft to understand. A giggle. An awkward cough. Another giggle. Footsteps across the room. Silence. Music. Tom recognized the song: "Tenderly." It was one of Elly's favorites. He crept slowly, noiselessly, down the steps, back into the yard, behind the sheriff's car. He could barely hear the music.

He squatted. A sudden tremor struck him. He could never tell anyone what he had seen. Of all the men he knew, he did not want the sheriff mad at him. The sheriff had killed men in Germany. Best to wait until the music's over, he decided. Then he would go up to the porch and call out.

He leaned against the bumper of the car, imagining Evelyn Carnes and the sheriff dancing to the music. Like the time he spied on Elly and Fender McConnell through the keyhole in the front door. Elly and Fender dancing so close they looked like they were trying to walk through each other. He giggled softly. Maybe he would tell Son Jesus. Son Jesus would keep it to himself.

The music stopped and Tom stood. He could not keep the smile from his face. He walked toward the house.

"Mrs. Carnes."

He stopped walking, waited.

"Mrs. Carnes, you there?"

He thought he heard footsteps inside the house.

"It's me. Tom Winter," he called.

The door cracked open and Evelyn Carnes pushed her head out of the opening. Her face was as red as the blouse she wore.

"Why, Tom, what're you doing here?" she said in a gay, nervous voice.

"Mama sent me over to see if I could help out cleaning up your yard," Tom told her.

Evelyn glanced back over her shoulder, then back to Tom. "Well, that's real sweet of your mama," she said. "But I've just about got it all done." She paused. "Sheriff Rucker stopped by a little bit ago and helped me out some. We just came in for some tea." She paused again, smiled sweetly.

"Uh, yes m'am," Tom said. He bit a smile.

"He was just about to leave," Evelyn added. Then: "You want some tea?"

"No m'am," Tom told her.

"Well, you just wait right there. We'll be out in a minute."

"Yes m'am," Tom said.

He stood waiting, trying to look nonchalant, knowing he was being watched. He bent over, picked up a twig, twirled it in his hand, pretended to whistle.

The door opened and Frank Rucker stepped onto the porch. His face was flushed. Evelyn stepped out behind him.

"I wouldn't worry none about that tree," he said to Evelyn in a serious voice. "Soon as it gets dry enough, it'll be easy to drag off."

"It'll be fine," Evelyn said lightly. "I sure do appreciate your help, Sheriff."

Frank nodded, pulled his hat on his head. "Glad to do it."

"You'll remember to ask Caleb and Luther about working on the barn roof?"

"I'll try to mention it this afternoon," Frank said. He touched his fingers to the brim of his hat and turned to Tom. "Tom," he mumbled.

Tom grinned.

"Y'all get hit hard last night?" Frank asked.

"Broke some limbs," Tom told him. "But it wadn't too bad."

Frank nodded, pulled at the knot in his tie, looked away. "Well, I got to be going."

"Yes sir," Tom said.

"Thanks again for dropping by, Sheriff," Evelyn said.

Frank looked at her, then quickly looked away. "Glad to."

"I'll see you soon," Evelyn added. To Tom, it sounded like a question.

Frank cleared his throat, nodded again. "Yes m'am. I'll speak to you in a few days." He walked to his car, got in, and drove away.

"You sure you don't need some help?" Tom asked.

Evelyn did not move her eyes from the car disappearing down the road. "No," she said after a moment, a sigh of sadness in her voice. She turned and went back into her house and closed the door.

TWENTY-FOUR

Frank had mixed feelings. Either he needed to put Tom Winter in jail for the safety of the community, or he needed to pin one of his war medals on the chest of the little irritant. A medal for saving a life. Frank's life.

God, it was close.

Too close.

Sitting there beside Evelyn Carnes, her bare leg touching him, her hands flitting over his arm casual-like, pointing out pictures in a family photo album, Frank had felt the hot breath of temptation curling around his neck.

She had unbuttoned the top button of her red blouse, and when she bent forward over the album he could see the flesh of her breasts, tan to the nipple. Tan off her shoulders. Tan down her chest. Tan disappearing under the low-cut brassiere. She could get tan that way only by sunbathing in the nude.

Wearing perfume that smelled like the sweetness of lovemaking on a bed of crushed honeysuckle blooms.

And that drop of water from the sweating bottom of her tea glass. It was aimed deliberately at her thigh. Had to be.

"Oh, my goodness, I'm taking a tea-glass shower." She had giggled, extending her leg, the thigh muscle popping up in a tan ribbon that ran beneath her red shorts. Then rubbing the water off with her fingertip, rubbing it sensuously in a circle. Moaning playfully. "Ooooh, that feels soooo cool." Across the room, "Tenderly" playing on the record player.

If Tom Winter had not appeared when he did, no telling what might have happened.

Whatever it might have been, it was not the right time. Not with all that was going on. All he needed was to get caught with Evelyn

Carnes when he should have been out asking questions about Pegleg or Harlan Davis. His badge would be ripped from his shirt.

There would be time for Evelyn Carnes.

Soon, he hoped. Soon.

When it did happen, he would need to put a cow bell around Tom Winter's neck. The little shit. Had a grin on his face that cut from ear to ear.

Frank thumbed his fingers across the top of the steering wheel.

God, don't let it rain again tonight, he thought.

● ● ●

By the time he walked into the Sheriff's Department, the only reminder of the presence of Evelyn Carnes was the faint scent of her perfume lingering on Frank's right shoulder. It was enough to cause Fletcher to look up, wrinkle his nose in a question.

"Bug spray," Frank said. He went into his office and closed the door, then opened a drawer at his desk and took out a bottle of Old Spice aftershave and rubbed a few drops over his face and shirt. He glanced at himself in the small wall mirror. His face was still flushed, like the face of an annoyed man with high blood pressure.

He sat at his desk and began to thumb through a stack of letters that Mildred Lewis had left for him. Mildred was the wife of Arlo Lewis, who had been a deputy in Overton County for thirty-two years before retiring to his farm and the fishing lake he had built—probably with convict help, though Frank had never asked. Mildred ran the Sheriff's Department. It did not matter that her title was clerk and her official duties were limited to recording arrests and filing. It did not matter that Frank was the sheriff. Mildred had her own rules, and everyone honored them.

There was nothing important in the letters, and Frank pushed them aside, knowing that Mildred would answer them, or had already answered them, scrawling an imitation of his signature across the correspondence.

He turned in his chair and gazed out the window. The streets of Overton were more crowded than usual, but the streets were always crowded after a storm. Farmers and wives of farmers and children of farmers, with fields too wet for work, using the time to shop or to visit at the benches that lined the courthouse square. It had been the same when he was a boy. He remembered the haughty, slightly offended look of shopkeepers. Country-come-to-town glares. Sometimes he still got that look. Or thought he got it. Maybe that was why he enjoyed driving around the county, spending time in the seven communities that were under his jurisdiction, stopping in the small country stores, such as Dodd's, where he had spent so much time lately. No one had haughty looks in small country stores.

Wonder what the townspeople would say about Evelyn Carnes picking up tree trash in her red blouse and red shorts? he thought.

He smiled at the image floating easily across his mind: Evelyn walking the streets of Overton in her red blouse and red shorts, her tan legs on parade. There would be heart attacks. Women would faint. It would be more than country-come-to-town news. The whispering would be sweeter than a sun-split peach dripping with juice.

He chuckled softly, wagged his head to clear the image. A gnawing, like hunger, shivered across his abdomen.

The ringing of the phone jarred him. He answered before the second ring.

"Frank, it's me: Hugh."

"You do it?" Frank asked.

"Yeah," Hugh told him.

"Good."

"What now?" Hugh asked.

"Nothing. Now we wait," Frank said. He hung up, opened his desk drawer, and pulled out a small black notebook. And then he made three long-distance telephone calls. Not to the three men he wanted to call— not to Jabbo and Galen and Jack—but to three men who would serve his purpose. Their names were Zane Crider, Bert James, and Hollis Benefield. He had been to war with Jabbo and Galen and Jack. He had only been fishing with Zane and Bert and Hollis.

• • •

The waiting would drag into the night, and through the next day, and the next. Frank left his office only to go home, returning each morning before sunrise. He sat at his desk, closed off from the comings and goings of the outer office, patiently gazing out of the window that overlooked the north side of Courthouse Square, watching the slow shuffling of people on sidewalks, cars circling the square like turtles, the storefront conversations. Yet nothing interested him as much as the congregation of men, with their checkerboards and their talk, who occupied the bench on the courthouse lawn in view of his window. As Frank watched the men, the men watched the courthouse and the window that hid Frank behind the glare of the sun. It was a good sign, Frank thought. The let-slip gossip that Hugh Joiner had left among the men at Dodd's General Store had wiggled its way across Overton County.

Each day, the gathering at the bench increased, and Frank made notes of the new faces that appeared from the communities surrounding Overton.

Keeler Gaines from Crossover.

Doug Mabry from Mossy Creek.

Artie Cromer from Oakland.

Will Cook from Mars Shoals.

None of the names meant anything serious. Word was out. That was all. And they had come to hear the latest and to take up watch of his window, as though the window would suddenly fly open and answers would pour out of it like water through a pipe. There was no reason to have Hugh or Fletcher check privately on any of them. Doug Mabry, maybe, Frank thought. Doug belonged to the Klan, but the Klan had nothing to do with Doug's being at the courthouse bench. Doug was nosy. Liked showing off. Liked snickering over nigger jokes. Liked the talk about women's tits that was always a topic of the courthouse bench crowd.

The other members of the Sheriff's Department seemed to sense that Frank wanted to be left alone. It was in his mood, in his silence, in the signal of the closed door leading into his office—a clear signal, since he seldom closed it. They interrupted his waiting only for an occasional report, some tidbit of news they believed would interest him: Burial plans for the skeletons of Blue Conley and Compton Mays. A complaint from Zeke Castleberry of Cane Creek about Luke Austin's cows tearing down his corn crop. The arrest of Willie Garber for fighting with his brother, Moss, over the affections of Bertha Kingsley—Willie's second arrest in three months on the same charge. A suspicious car fire, with the suspicion being on Donny Fulbright for burning his own cracked-block Chevrolet. Gaines Hughley found passed-out drunk in the backyard of the First Baptist Church of Overton.

Frank's answer to each report had been the same: "Handle it."

•   •   •

Early on the morning of the third day, on Friday, the waiting ended. Mason Davis, Harlan's brother, sat among the men on the courthouse bench in view of Frank's window. Frank smiled. He picked up the telephone and made one call. "This morning," he said to Zane Crider. "Soon as you can get here. How about calling Bert and Hollis for me."

"You got it," Zane told him.

"Remember what I told you," Frank said.

"Shit, Frank, it's too damn crazy to forget."

Frank hung up and called Hugh into his office. "Tell Fletcher I want him driving around over in Crossover today," he said. "All over it. Every road they got. Every pig path. Tell him I want to make sure everybody over there gets a good look at his car."

"Okay," Hugh said. "Anything else?"

Frank leaned back in his chair and again looked out the window. He could see Mason Davis staring at the courthouse. "Yeah," he said after a moment. "Paper comes out today, don't it?"

"Unless Ben's run out of ink," Hugh answered.

Frank swiveled back to Hugh. "A little later this morning, there's gon' be three men show up here. When they do, I want you to go down to Ben's office and get me a copy of the paper. Tell Ben we may have some more information for him soon."

"What men?" Hugh asked.

"I'll tell you later," Frank said.

"You know Ben's gon' hotfoot it over here soon as he hears you may have something else going on," Hugh said.

A half-smile crossed Frank's lips. He did not reply.

•   •   •

At eleven o'clock, three middle-aged men dressed in business suits, each carrying a briefcase and a shoe box, entered the Sheriff's Department and asked to see Frank.

"What for?" Mildred Lewis asked suspiciously.

"Business," one of the men said curtly.

"In there," Mildred said, gesturing with her head. She watched the men enter the office, heard Frank greeting them. The office door closed.

"Well, I never," Mildred muttered in an offended voice.

"Looks official to me," Hugh told her. Then: "Frank wanted me to get him a paper. I'll be back in a few minutes."

"Don't drag your feet," Mildred ordered. "I'm going to lunch early."

"Be right back," he promised.

• • •

Inside his office, Frank said, "I appreciate this. I really do."

"What's this about, anyhow?" one of the men asked.

"Just dangling a carrot, Zane. Just dangling a carrot," Frank answered.

"Shit, Frank, what kind of answer's that?" Hollis Benefield demanded. "Jesus, I don't mind doing a fellow a favor, but I hate putting on a goddamn tie just to be called a carrot, and I had to borrow this damn briefcase from my brother, the one that sells insurance. He thinks I'm fixing to knock over a bank or maybe even get a job."

Frank smiled. He walked to the window. "You see that bunch of men sitting out there on that bench?"

Hollis moved close to the window, looked out. The men on the bench were staring at the courthouse.

"Christ, that's scary," Hollis said, stepping back. "I feel like I'm in a goddamn fish bowl. What're they doing?"

"Trying to figure out who you are, I expect," Frank said.

"When they find out, I hope to God they tell me," Bert James mumbled. He lit a cigarette and sat in a straight chair in front of Frank's desk. "By the way, what'd you want these shoe boxes for?"

"Curiosity," Frank replied.

Zane laughed. He was a tall man with a red face and a red shock of hair. "Where'd you come up with this crazy stunt, anyway?"

Frank smiled, shrugged. It was an old war trick. Dressing young American soldiers in German uniforms and treating them like kings in front of old prisoners, making the Germans believe they were being sold down the river. He had seen it work. It had unpried jaws shut as tight as steel traps.

"Who gives a shit," Bert said. "We're here." He reached for one of the shoe boxes and opened it. "We brought you some of Poss's barbecue." He took out a sandwich and handed it to Frank, then passed the box to Hollis and Zane. Hollis opened another box and took out four beers. "You mind?" he said to Frank. "We'll take the bottles with us."

"All right with me," Frank said. "But I'll pass. I got a Coke over here."

Hollis pried the tops off the beers with a church key, handed them to Bert and Zane.

"When you coming back over to go fishing?" Zane asked.

"Soon as I take care of a couple of things here," Frank said.

"They running on the Oconee," Hollis said, chewing on his sandwich.

"We gon' put out some trotlines this weekend," Bert added. "You ought to shake free."

Frank glanced out the window. The gathering at the bench had grown. "I got one I'm running over here right now," he said.

● ● ●

Twenty minutes after they had entered the courthouse, Zane Crider and Bert James and Hollis Benefield walked out of Frank's office, carrying their briefcases and shoe boxes. Ben Biggers was sitting in the waiting room, puffing from the hurried waddle from his office. The men walked past him without looking, each wearing a silent, brooding look, and then they disappeared down the corridor of the courthouse.

"Who the hell were they?" Ben asked Hugh.

"You got me," Hugh answered. "They were here to see Frank."

"What'd they have in them shoe boxes?"

"Ben, I don't have the foggiest idea," Hugh said. "Shoes, for all I know."

"Shit," Ben mumbled. He pulled himself from his chair and hobbled painfully to Frank's office. He opened the door without knocking.

"Well, Ben, I guess I ought to say 'Come in,' " Frank said.

"I'm already in," Ben snapped. "What the hell's going on over here, Frank?"

Frank sat in the chair behind his desk. "Work," he said dryly.

"Kiss my ass," Ben snarled. "Who were those men?"

Frank did not answer immediately. He sat, gazing at Ben, as though searching for an answer, and then he said, "Friends. Old fishing buddies."

Ben spat a sarcastic, bitter laugh. "Looked like the federal government to me."

Frank picked up a pencil from his desk, began to drum the eraser on the desktop.

"You not gon' tell me, are you?" Ben said.

"I've got nothing to tell you," Frank answered.

"Well, you ought to kick your deputy's ass. He said you had some more information about this Pegleg thing."

"Pegleg?" Frank said, forcing surprise.

Ben's eyes narrowed. He bent over Frank's desk, leaned on the knuckles of both hands. "It ain't Pegleg, is it? It's Harlan. Is that what you're telling me? Word's out you been talking to some white man, getting stuff on Harlan."

"I've been talking to a lot of white men about a lot of things," Frank said patiently. "White men, white women. White boys, white girls. Black men, black women, black boys, black girls. That's how you do this job."

Ben lifted his hands from the desk. He glared down at Frank. "You know, you really ain't worth a shit at this job, and I don't give a damn how many medals they pinned on you. You ain't nothing but a redneck, asshole farmer." He paused, then added, "And I got a strong feeling I know who it was that put that bullet in Logan's head."

Frank rose slowly from his chair. His fist closed over the pencil that he held, and the pencil snapped. "Ben," he said quietly, "I'm gon' forget you said that. I'm gon' wipe it out of my mind. I'm gon' lay it off to high blood pressure, or too much sun. But I'm gon' tell you straight out that I better never hear it again. You understand me?"

Ben did not speak. He glared at Frank. A mustache of perspiration beaded over his top lip.

"Hugh told you what I told him to say," Frank continued. "I hope we'll have something soon, but we ain't got it now. Soon as we do, you'll know it. Now get out of my office."

"You can't order me around, goddamn it!"

Frank smiled wearily. "Ben, I'm in a shitty mood. Can't you tell that?"

Ben held his gaze for a moment, then wheeled and stalked out of the office.

● ● ●

The first man to break from the wildfire gossip leaving Courthouse Square in dented pickup trucks and well-used cars was the man Frank most wanted to break: Coy Philpot.

Coy's wife, Mazie, called Frank at the Sheriff's Department at four-thirty. Coy would like to speak with him, she told Frank. Privately. In the cemetery of the Life of Christ Baptist Church in Crossover.

"Tell him I'll be there at six o'clock," Frank said.

"Please," Mazie pleaded, "don't tell nobody it was me that called. And don't tell nobody Coy wants to see you."

"I won't," promised Frank. He dropped the phone onto its cradle, yanked his hat from the corner of his desk, and walked out of his office.

"You leaving?" asked Hugh.

"I'll be back later," Frank said. "Where's Fletcher?"

"He just called in a few minutes ago," Hugh answered. "Said to tell you everybody he saw was jittery as a whore in church, wanting to know why you called in the feds."

"He say anything about Harlan?"

"Said he was pissed. Said he was over at Dodd's, spouting off about you taking up for the colored instead of going house to house trying to find Pegleg after them bones were dug up."

Frank shook his head. He muttered, "Jesus." Then: "Anything else?"

"Yeah," Hugh replied after a moment. "Said to tell you to stay out from over there, or keep your gun handy. Said Harlan and Mason had started drinking and talking crazy."

"What about George?" Frank asked.

"Didn't mention George," Fletcher told him. "From what I hear, George don't hang around them when they been drinking. I guess he's got more of his daddy and mama in him than them other two."

Frank did not reply. He pulled his hat on his head and started for the door.

"Where you going?" asked Hugh.

"Out," Frank said. "Get in touch with Fletcher and tell him to come on in."

"Want me to go with you?"

"No. You stay here."

"You be careful," Hugh said.

"I'm planning on it," Frank told him.

● ● ◉

It was not surprising to Frank that Coy Philpot wanted to meet at the Life of Christ Baptist Church. The church was small, well-concealed by a grove of cedar and pine, impossible to see from the Sweetwater Creek road. Coy would feel safe there. Safe from the eyes of passersby and safe from the wasted existence of his past. It was in the Life of Christ church that Coy had experienced his conversion, and Frank did not believe in belittling such a great miracle. He had never snickered at Coy, as he had heard the men of Dodd's General Store do in their carrying-on. Maybe he would have if he had not been in war, where he had heard men begging for God in the last horrible seconds of their living. Blood filling their throats and their lungs. Wild, surprised eyes watching their own souls spinning loose from their bodies. Lips quivering as if to say, "Who is that? Who?" The last frantic look around, as though someone near them would touch their forehead and magically absolve them, bring them instantly into perfect reconciliation with their first clean moment of life, their first splendid baby-gasp of air. Men who had damned God for putting them on killing fields seemed always to fling their last cry for help to him. And maybe that was what their dying meant, Frank thought. Maybe their dying was God's help.

He would not insult Coy Philpot, yet he would not let Coy wiggle off the hook.

He had tried to make it easier for Coy to talk. Had changed from his sheriff's uniform to work clothes. Had driven his own car to keep down attention. Had made certain that no one saw him turn off the road to the church. He had done his part; Coy had to do his.

He saw Coy's pickup behind the church, and Coy in the cemetery, standing beside a tombstone. Coy was tall and once had been a thick, powerful man. Now he had the look of someone recovering from a long illness. Slender. Skin-wrinkled. Pale. A man who had aged fast. He was in his mid-fifties, Frank guessed, but looked ten years older. Frank stopped beside the truck, got out of his car, walked through the cemetery, and stood across the grave from Coy. He waited for Coy to speak.

"My mama's and daddy's graves," Coy said softly after a moment, with a nod toward the tombstone. "I put up a new stone a few months ago."

"Looks good," Frank said.

"Got it from old man Makepeace down in Elberton," Coy said. "Him and Daddy knowed one another. He give me a good price on it."

"Don't think I know him," Frank said.

Coy looked up at Frank. "Guess not. Him and his folks always worked the quarries. My daddy used to help drag out them slabs when they wadn't nothing to do on the farm."

Frank nodded, crossed his arms, shifted his weight, read the names on the tombstone—Abel and Inez Philpot. A single, simple declaration proclaimed their death: *Gone to God.*

"Appreciate you coming out, Sheriff."

"Glad to do it, Coy."

Coy cleared his throat, turned away from the tombstone of his parents. "I ain't got much to say." He paused. "I spent most of my life in sin, the sorriest kind of man you ever seen, and I'm gon' spend the rest of my days in shame." He paused again, looked at Frank, held Frank in his gaze. "But where I'm going when I die, it'll be all right. I'm going to God, Frank. Be with my mama and daddy again. That's when I can tell them how bad I feel about the shame I brought on them."

"I'd say they already know that," Frank told him gently.

Coy began to rock his body. "Word is you know some things," he said.

"Some," Frank replied.

"You watch out for Harlan," Coy warned. "Harlan's been caught by Satan."

"I won't argue that," Frank said. Then: "What about the girl, Coy? Harlan do it?"

"Didn't ask him," Coy replied. He pulled a cigarette out of his shirt pocket, lit it with a kitchen match that he popped to fire on his thumbnail. His hands were shaking. "Wouldn't put it past him," he added.

"Want to tell me about the gate in Harlan's barn?" Frank said.

Coy's head jerked toward Frank. Terror danced in his eyes.

"I know about it," Frank said calmly.

The terror in Coy's eyes glazed to water. He blinked rapidly. "I hope you forgive me, Sheriff, but I done talked to God about all that. I can't give you no help there."

Frank did not speak for a moment. Waited for Coy to continue, but Coy, too, was waiting. A hawk cried from the top of a dead limb in an oak, and Frank looked up. The hawk sprang into the air, was chased by sparrows. Fighter planes after a bomber.

"You been talking to Harlan?" Frank asked.

"He come to see me earlier this afternoon," Coy answered. "Said you was siding with the colored. Said you'd called in some federal boys, and he guessed they was after him." He paused, looked at Frank. "He ain't never had nobody push him."

"Anything else?" Frank said.

Coy sucked on his cigarette, pulled the smoke deep inside his chest, then blew it out slowly. He picked a thread of tobacco from his lip. "He thinks you been asking around about him. Said he'd seen your car up at Jed's house and over at Dodd's store. Said that was why he thought you'd called in the federal boys, to check on something you might of found out."

"He threaten you?" Frank asked.

A sad smile edged into Coy's face. The smile was his answer. Still, he said, "Ain't nobody but God can scare me now."

"You know I got to take this all the way," Frank said softly.

Coy bobbed his head, drew on his cigarette. After a moment, he said in a whisper, "You know something, Sheriff? I ain't never killed nothing. Not even a rabbit. Always been scared to death of killing anything." He paused, sniffed, drew again on his cigarette. "Guess maybe the only thing I ever killed, now that I think about it, was me." He shook his head again. A quiet rasp rolled in his chest. "But I know I'm a soldier in God's army now, and that makes me feel good. God's army don't kill, but I used to do things bad as any killing. After Jed come back from the army, they was a bunch of us—me'n Jed and Harlan and Harlan's brother Mason and one or two others—that was wild. We didn't care about nobody or nothing. My daddy kept telling me I was gon' wind up in hell, and he was pretty near right. But God wouldn't let me. He put me in his army."

Frank could see the trembling in Coy's hand relax. There was a strange, beatific look in his face. Serene. Soothing.

"Well, I better be going on," Frank said. "I appreciate you talking to me."

Coy nodded. He dropped his cigarette and stepped on it. "You watch out for Harlan. Harlan's mean. You crowd him, he's gon' fight you. He's like a rattlesnake. He don't care what happens to you, or me, or nobody else."

"I'll remember that," Frank said. "You do the same. You watch out."

"Uh-huh," Coy mumbled.

TWENTY-FIVE

Evelyn Carnes lay on her bed, her shoulders wiggled into a hump of three feather pillows covered with new pillowcases from Belk's department store, the pillowcases fresh washed and sun dried and hand pressed. A book was open on her lap. The book was Lloyd C. Douglas's *The Big Fisherman*, a gift from her Sunday school class following the death of Jed. She had tried to read it for months but was still on Chapter Six. Light from the table lamp on the night table beside her bed cupped over her right shoulder. She knew it was only her imagination, but the light seemed to give off a blistering heat. Sun heat. The same sun heat of the unbearable day. Not a breeze from sunup to sundown. Even the air from her fan had been warm—was still warm as it hummed from the dresser, oscillating in its slow, hypnotic swivel. She touched her throat. It was sticky, a thin glue of perspiration.

Evelyn sighed and slid the book from her lap to the bed, closing it.

Oh, Lord, she thought. I've lost my place.

It didn't matter.

Chapter Six was easy to remember.

She slipped from her bed and picked up the damp hand towel she had folded and placed in the enamel water basin on the night table. She dabbed it against her throat and face and ran it under her hair at the back of her neck. The air from the fan blew across her neck, and for a moment it seemed cool and tickling. She crossed the room to stand in front of the fan, pulled her nightgown away from her body to let the air filter through. The nightgown was light cotton, white with a pink bordering at the neck and shoulders.

She thought of the lemonade and tea in the refrigerator. Every day since Tuesday, since the day after the storm and the finding of all those bones, she had made lemonade and tea for Frank Rucker, but Frank Rucker had not returned and he had not called. Probably scared off by

Tom Winter. Probably worried that Tom had said something totally untrue to his mother and that people would be thinking the worst. Maybe tomorrow she should have a Sunday-afternoon visit with Ada. Let the subject come up. Then she could laugh it off. Tell Ada that they were doing nothing but looking at her family photo album while they took a tea break from working in the yard. The yard-working part was not entirely true, of course—only she had picked up limbs—but Ada would not know the difference. Frank was the kind of man who would help a lady after a storm, and that was almost as good as doing the work itself.

She had watched for Frank's car since early morning. Had put off her Saturday shopping in Overton and sat on her front porch watching the road, choking in the heat on a day when the sun was baking the earth like a biscuit. All she had seen were slow-crawling cars traveling to and from Overton in little funnels of red dust.

No matter. It was his loss. The lemonade. The tea. The chance to sit on the screened-in back porch, with the fan oscillating between them, from one face to the other, like blown kisses, and spend a few pleasant moments of harmless chatter.

Frank Rucker was not worth such bother. No man was.

She went from her bedroom to the kitchen and poured a mixture of lemonade and tea over a glass filled with ice cubes.

Outside, cicadas made music—violins, she thought—and Evelyn drifted from the kitchen to the living room window facing the front yard. A lopsided, less-than-half moon lay in the sky, like a deflated yellowish balloon. She could see the lacework of leaves waving gently on the bottom limbs of the white oak at the corner of the house. She thought: Thank God, a breeze. She unlocked the door and opened it and stepped outside. The breeze swept across her face. She closed her eyes and inhaled deeply. She could smell the biscuit of the cooked earth, the perfume of the small red roses that crawled the trellis at the end of the front porch, the faraway scent of hay that had been cut in some neighbor's field—Hack Winter's field, she guessed.

And then she paused. There was another odor. Oil.

She heard a noise, like the movement of cloth against cloth, near the rose trellis, and she turned to look.

The man was a silhouette, a darkly shadowed figure outlined against the trellis. She could see the cloth covering his face.

A small, startled gasp flew into her throat, and then a scream.

She threw the glass of lemonade and tea at the figure, watched him dodge, sweep away at the glass with his hands, stumble backward. In one hand, he held something—a gun, or an ax, or a heavy stick.

She turned quickly, instinctively, to the door and threw herself inside the living room. Her hands jerked at the lock, and she heard it click. The scream still poured from her lungs, high-pitched, like the song of the cicadas. She heard the heavy thumping of steps across the porch.

She pushed away from the door and began to run, a tripping, blind run, toward her bedroom. Her mind was exploding with flashes of brilliant, intense light, and from somewhere, in some cranial darkroom of memory, she saw the shotgun.

She heard the wood of the front door crack open. It had the sound of lightning splintering across the earth.

The shotgun was under the bed, where Jed had always kept it. She had never moved it, even after Jed's death, had been afraid of it, as afraid of the shotgun as she had been of Jed. She knew it was loaded. It had to be. Jed had kept it loaded, half wishing someone would be foolish enough to invade them. Jed had had an itch for killing.

She dropped beside the bed and reached and touched the gun's barrel. It was cold.

Footsteps—thundersteps—boomed from the hallway, one foot seeming to fall heavier than the other.

Evelyn yanked the gun from beneath the bed and twisted to a sitting position. She glanced at the mirror that had been angled to see the kitchen—the same mirror that Frank Rucker had stared into as she dressed, she knowing that he was watching—and she saw the man stumbling toward the door, his sack-covered face bobbing against the wall. She raised the gun, thumbed back the hammer of one of the two barrels, yanked at the trigger. The shell exploded in the room, and the kick from the explosion slammed the gun stock against her cheek, cutting it. She could hear the glass of framed pictures shattering, the splintering of wood as pellets rained through wallpaper and wallboard.

There was no cry from the man, only the hurried retreating of footsteps, a noise of banging at the front door, two heavy, running steps across the porch, then silence.

Evelyn waited, crouched behind the bed, the barrel of the gun resting across the mattress, the echo of the shot still vibrating in the room. She could feel a sharp pain, like a bee's sting, on her cheek, and she instinctively raised her shoulder to wipe against it. She saw the blood from the cut on her nightgown. She began to cry and to tremble.

She did not know how long she stayed behind the bed, crying, trembling, touching the edge of the bedsheet against her cheek, listening for the sound of footsteps outside. She heard only the cicadas, or the memory of her scream, or the ringing of the shot. The cicadas and the memory of her scream and the ringing of the shot were the same high pitch.

When she did move, she crept, cat quiet, bent over, holding the shotgun before her. Out of her bedroom, down the hallway, into the kitchen. She sat in a chair near the telephone, nestling the shotgun across her lap, and she lifted the receiver and began to dial. Her fingers were jerking uncontrollably. The only sound in the room was the sliding click of the dialing.

● ● ●

Frank had been home only an hour when the phone rang. He knew it was after ten without looking at his watch, or at the small clock with glow-in-the-dark numbers he had purchased after his divorce. The day had been easily timed by an internal rhythm that was almost mystical to him. He had spent the morning in his office, watching the courthouse bench and the larger-than-usual gathering of men, talking their animated talk, making bold, jabbing gestures toward his window with rolled-up copies of the *Overton Weekly News* wrapped in their fists. The *News* carried Ben Biggers' story of the discovery of two more bodies in Jed Carnes' sawmill, with Ben's editorial—as Frank had predicted—on the waste of county funds in searching for a man who was probably as mythical as a Martian. The killing of three colored men in 1943 was easy to explain, according to Ben. Just a feud. Something the colored had been doing since the first shipload arrived from Africa. "What most Americans fail to understand," Ben had written, "is that African tribes were always at war with one another. Those tribal wars are still going on, and that, most likely, is what the mysterious Pegleg is all about, since nobody but Negroes have been attacked." In late afternoon—lingering past sundown—Frank had spent an hour working at the grave site of his parents, both dead within the past year; another hour at Benny Whiteside's diner, having barbecue and talking to Benny about a deep-sea fishing trip Benny was planning to the Florida Keys; and then, back at his home, at night, thirty minutes writing a letter to his sister Florence, who lived with her husband, Jarrell, in Richmond, Virginia. The phone rang as he was licking the envelope to seal it.

Evelyn Carnes' voice was a whisper: "Frank?"

"What's wrong?" asked Frank.

"Peg—" Evelyn said. She began to sob.

Frank could feel the chill at his throat. He had felt it in the war before battles. "Evelyn, what is it? What's happened?"

She answered through the sobs. "Pegleg. He—tried—to kill me."

"My God," Frank muttered. "You all right?"

She could not answer for crying, but he knew she was nodding.

"You stay where you are," Frank said. "I'll be right there."

He pushed the phone dead with his thumb, released it, and began to dial quickly. Hugh answered on the third ring.

"Get Fletcher and get over to Jed Carnes' place," Frank ordered.

"What's going on?" asked Hugh.

"Pegleg," Frank answered. He hung up without explaining, then yanked the telephone directory from the dresser drawer and thumbed to the page containing Hack Winter's name. He dialed the number, waited. Four rings. Five. It was Ada Winter who answered, worry in her voice.

"It's Frank Rucker," Frank said. "Could I speak to Hack?"

"Just a minute," Ada said. Frank could hear her calling for Hack, telling him, "It's Frank Rucker." He could hear movement through the house, Hack coming from another room, could hear Hack's deep breathing as he tucked the telephone to his ear.

"Anything wrong, Frank?" Hack said.

"Something's going on over at Jed Carnes' place," Frank said. "I think somebody's tried to break in. I'm on my way, but it's gon' take some time. You and Troy mind checking on it?"

"Be glad to," Hack told him.

"You be careful," Frank said.

•   •   •

Hack saw the front door immediately. It was open, hanging on the top hinge, the wood paneling smashed.

"Daddy," Troy said anxiously.

"I see it," Hack said. He glanced toward his son sitting beside him. Troy's thumb played over the hammer of the shotgun he held. "Don't do that," he added.

He stopped the car with the light beams on the dangling door.

"Let's take it easy," Hack whispered. He opened the car door and stepped outside, then reached back inside and motioned with his hand for the shotgun. Troy handed it to him and got out of the car on the passenger side.

"You going in?" Troy asked.

Hack nodded.

"I'm going with you."

"You stay close," Hack said.

"Yes sir."

They crossed the yard slowly, paused at the porch.

"Evelyn," Hack called in a strong voice.

There was no answer. He called again. Again, no answer.

Hack stepped onto the porch. He raised the barrel of the shotgun, thumbed back the hammer.

"Daddy—"

Hack waved away his son's worry. He stepped to the door, peered inside.

"Evelyn," he said quietly. "It's me: Hack Wilson. Me and Troy. You in there?"

He did not hear a voice. He heard a whimper. A child's whimper. He pushed the dangling door aside and stepped inside in a motion so quick it startled Troy.

"Evelyn, where are you?"

The whimper became a cry.

"In the kitchen," Troy said.

"You stay here," Hack commanded.

"Daddy—"

"Stay here."

Hack stepped cautiously across the living room. He stopped at the kitchen door, glanced down the hallway, and saw the mangled wall outside Evelyn's bedroom, then turned back to the whimpering that came from the kitchen. He stepped inside, scanned the room. In one corner, huddled behind a chair, her arms wrapping her knees, he saw her. Her hair was matted over her face. Dried blood covered her cheek. A shotgun was on the floor beside her.

"Troy, get in here," Hack called.

•   •   •

He had driven wildly, dangerously, from Overton, over highway and snaking dirt roads, his car straining to be airborne, and when he braked it to a stop in the front yard of Evelyn Carnes' home, Frank could smell the scorched-water heat from the radiator. He glanced at his watch. He had made the drive in twenty minutes. It was impossible, but he had done it.

He scanned the yard, followed the light beams from Hack Winter's car to the front door. He muttered, "Son of a bitch."

Out of reflex, he yanked his revolver from its holster and crossed the yard in a long, quick stride, stepped onto the porch and to the front door.

"Hack," he called.

"In the kitchen," Hack Winter answered.

Evelyn was sitting at the kitchen table, holding a bath cloth to her cheek. Frank could see the blood on the cloth and on the gown she was wearing.

"How bad's she hurt?" Frank asked.

"A little cut on the cheek," Hack told him. "It'll be sore, but it's not bad."

Evelyn looked up. Her eyes bubbled with tears.

"Let me take a look," Frank said. He slipped his revolver back into its holster and knelt before her, took her hand holding the bath cloth, and pulled it away. The cut was small, under the corner of the eye, more a bruise than a cut.

"It'll be all right," Frank said softly. "Hack's right. We'll get some medicine on it."

"He—tried—" Evelyn stammered.

Frank touched her face gently. "It's all right. You don't have to say nothing. Not now. We'll talk later, when you're feeling better." He looked up at Hack.

"Troy's called Ada," Hack said. "She's on her way in Troy's truck."

Frank nodded. "You see anything?"

Hack shook his head. "Troy's looking around out back, but whoever it was is long gone, I reckon. Front door's beat up. You saw that. Some damage back in the bedroom and the hallway. She shot at him."

Frank turned back to Evelyn, surprise in his face. "You did?"

She turned her head, nodded once.

"You hit him?"

"I don't know," she whispered.

"Don't think so," Hack said. "I didn't look good, but I didn't see no blood, except what Evelyn's got on her."

"We'll check it out," Frank said. To Evelyn: "You need anything?"

She answered in a timid, small voice. "My robe. Could somebody get it?"

He had not realized that she was in her nightgown. His eyes scanned her. He could see the flesh of her breasts protruding against the thin, almost transparent cotton. The heat of a blush swept his face. He glanced at Hack. Hack was looking away, uncomfortable.

"Be happy to," Frank said.

"It's in the bedroom," Evelyn told him.

"Down the hall?" Frank asked. It was a ridiculous question, and he realized immediately that he had asked it because Hack was there.

She nodded again. "I had it laying at the foot of my bed," she said quietly. "It's yellow."

● ● ●

An hour and a half later, Frank walked out of the woods below Jed Carnes' barn with Fletcher Wells following close, the beam of their flashlights bobbing over the ground with each step they took. Frank's uniform was soaked with perspiration. He was breathing deeply.

"He damn well ain't hanging around," Fletcher grumbled. He added, "Slow down, Frank. I stepped in the swamp down there. I'm wearing my foot raw."

Frank slowed his gait. "Maybe Hugh and them saw something."

"They didn't see diddly-shit," Fletcher said. "What you got is some crazy nigger on the loose, somebody that knows these woods like the back of his own hand. I guarantee it. Just like it was when Logan was sheriff. You got Pegleg."

"Maybe it wadn't," Frank said. "Maybe it was just somebody with rape on his mind."

"Didn't she say he had a sack on his face?" Fletcher said.

"Said she thought so," Frank mumbled. "She didn't get a good look. It was dark."

"Pegleg," Fletcher said firmly. "And Pegleg's a nigger."

Frank did not reply. Fletcher was as dumb as a stick. He could hear the squish of water in Fletcher's shoe.

"That them?" Fletcher asked. He tilted his flashlight toward the house.

Frank looked up. He could see the silhouette of three men under the outside light of the kitchen door—Hugh, Hack, and Troy. He grunted. "Yeah."

"See anything?" Hugh called as Frank and Fletcher neared the house.

"Nothing," Frank told him.

"Too dark," Hugh said. "Anyhow, whoever it was had a jump on us. He probably wadn't nowhere around by the time we got here."

"Yeah, I guess," Frank said in a grumbling voice. He stopped under the umbrella of the light, took his handkerchief from a pocket, and wiped the perspiration from his face.

"I just called the house," Hack said. "Ada said Evelyn was feeling better. She'll be staying over with us."

Frank nodded solemnly. "Appreciate you getting over quick as you and Troy did," he said. "I'm not gon' bother her anymore tonight, but tell her I'll come by in the morning and talk to her."

"We gon' keep somebody over here tonight?" asked Hugh.

"Yeah," Frank answered. "I want you to stay around." He looked at Fletcher. "I want you to call Arlo and Buddy. Tell them I'm gon' need them in the morning."

"Buddy?" Fletcher said. "Shit, Frank, Buddy Crump's pushing seventy. He ain't had a badge on in five years."

"I ain't asking him to dig ditches," Frank said sourly. "I just want some people over here, taking turns watching out."

"What for?"

Frank glared at Fletcher, at the question. "I'd like to make damn sure this place is still standing after we get to the bottom of this."

"You think somebody's gon' burn it?" Fletcher asked.

"I don't want to give nobody the chance," Frank said. He turned to Hack. "You don't remember your dog barking, or anything, do you, Hack?"

Hack shook his head, looked at Troy.

"I didn't hear nothing," Troy said. "But I was playing my radio."

"All right," Frank said. "Well, I guess that's all we can do for now. Be better to look around in the morning."

"You need us, you call," Hack said. "We usually go to church on Sunday morning, but we don't have to."

"Appreciate it," Frank told him. He added, "I guess people will be talking about this. Might as well tell everybody at the church that we'll be doing everything we can to find out who's behind it, but tell them I'd be grateful if they'd stay away from over here."

"Sure will," Hack said. He looked at Troy. "Come on, son, let's go home."

"How about sticking around a minute, Frank?" Hugh said. "Got a couple of things to ask you." There was a message in the soft, too casual sound of his voice.

● ● ●

Frank watched the taillights of the cars driven by Fletcher and by Hack disappear before he turned back to Hugh.

"Come on inside," Hugh said.

Frank followed him without speaking.

In the hallway leading to Evelyn's bedroom, Hugh stopped. "I think she hit him," he said.

"Why's that?" Frank asked.

Hugh touched a tiny hole in the patterned wallpaper. "Look at that. Unless I miss my guess, that little speck on the wallpaper is blood. That didn't come from her. Looks like a single pellet that hit flesh before it stuck in there."

Frank leaned close to the wall, examining it. There was a speck, a dot, almost invisible, blotting the edges of the tear where a pellet had entered the wall.

"This the only one?" Frank asked.

"No. I saw two or three other places," Frank said. "Maybe it's nothing. If she did hit him, she didn't get much. A few strays."

Frank stepped back, looked toward the bedroom. "She said she was behind the bed. If that's so, and she did hit him, she got him up high."

"What I'd think," Hugh said. "Shoulder, maybe. And it's away from where the main wad hit the wall. But you gon' get that with a shotgun."

"If he dropped any blood going out the door, I didn't see it," Frank muttered.

"Like I said, I think she must of just nicked him. Wouldn't of been a lot of blood. Not with shotgun pellets. He may have some buried in him, but that ain't likely to do much more'n sting like hell."

"Let's get some pictures in the morning, and then cut it out, see if we can find the pellets," Frank said. "I'll have Mildred check the hospitals in the morning."

"I can do it," Hugh offered.

Frank took a step into the bedroom, looked at the bed, then the wall. "No," he said after a moment. "You keep an eye on things here. We'll take care of that."

◉ ◉ ◉

Ada Winter had not bothered to advise Tom to go to sleep. She had simply led him to Troy's room and to the floor pallet that Elly had hurriedly prepared. Elly's room would be surrendered to Evelyn Carnes, and Elly would move into Tom's room.

"Don't go asking Troy a million questions when he comes in," Ada instructed, "and don't go roaming around all over the house. We've got a guest, and I'm sure she doesn't want to see you walking around in your underwear."

"Yes m'am," Tom mumbled, and then he pretended to yawn. "I'll probably be asleep before my head hits the pillow."

He watched his mother roll her eyes in exasperation before he closed the door to the bedroom that was Troy's private domain, a room that Tom seldom entered. His mother's footsteps faded down the corridor, and the dark silence of Troy's room rolled around him. He turned his head slowly, taking in things. A soft moonlight oozed through the window, falling across Troy's closet and Troy's dresser. The closet door seemed to whisper, "Open me." The drawers of the dresser teased him. On top of the dresser, the cocked face of a stuffed donkey—a gift from a girl Troy refused to identify—gazed comically at Tom with glass button eyes.

Tom dropped to the pallet beside Troy's bed, sliding into the fold of the sheet. It would be wrong to go through Troy's closet and dresser. Troy would kill him.

He turned on his side, facing the bed. Under the bedcovers skimming the floor he saw a magazine and pulled it out. It was an *Esquire*. The magazine fell open to a picture of a beautiful, skimpily clad woman. Tom giggled.

Suddenly, the light of a car threw a spear into the room, and Tom closed the magazine and shoved it back under the bed, rolled on his pallet, and tucked his head into the pillow.

He lay quiet, listening. He could hear voices, but not the words. His father's voice. Troy's voice. His mother's voice, or maybe Mrs. Carnes or Elly. And then he heard footsteps in the hallway, and the door opened.

"You asleep, squirt?" Troy asked.

Tom squirmed, opened his eyes, looked up at Troy with his best impression of being groggy. "Huh?"

"Aw, bullshit, Tom, don't go playing games with me," Troy mumbled. "I know you ain't asleep."

"Was too," Tom said.

"You ain't touched nothing in here, have you?"

"No," Tom answered in a hurt voice. "I been trying to sleep."

Troy began to undress. "You touched anything, I'm gon' know it. I know where everything in this room is."

Tom sat up. "Y'all find out who it was trying to kill Mrs. Carnes?"

"We didn't find nothing," Troy said, grumbling. He dropped his pants to the floor and stepped over Tom and fell into his bed.

"Mama was saying it was Pegleg."

"I don't know."

"Mrs. Carnes said he had a mask on his face."

"Then you know as much as I do. Now go to sleep. I'm tired."

Tom dropped back to his pillow and lay quietly for a moment, gazing at the stuffed donkey on the dresser. The light from the moon shimmered on the donkey's eyes. "Troy."

"Go to sleep, Tom."

"What would you have done if you'd seen him?"

"Seen who?"

"Pegleg."

"I'd have shot him, like I'm gon' do you if you don't shut up, turdface."

"Mama said Mrs. Carnes ought not be living over there by herself. Said there were too many crazy people around."

"Mama's right. Now shut up."

"She needs some dogs," Tom said.

"I said shut up," Troy warned.

"I wonder what he looks like," Tom said.

"Well, you keep your eye on the window," Troy told him. "Word is, he looks in windows before he decides who he's gon' kill."

Tom sensed a chill crawling over him. His mind flashed. He remembered listening to the music coming from Evelyn Carnes' home— a walled-in sound, like something heavy had been draped over it. And he remembered peeking through the window, seeing the sheriff and Evelyn Carnes sitting close together, looking at a book, or something. He wondered if Pegleg had watched Evelyn Carnes the same way, or if Pegleg was there when he had been there. Maybe hiding under the house, waiting for him to leave, waiting to kill the sheriff and Evelyn Carnes at the same time. Maybe I scared Pegleg off, he thought. Maybe saved the sheriff's life and Evelyn Carnes' life.

He lifted his head from his pillow, looked at the window. He could see the fuzzy edge of a juniper growing near the house, with a dangling limb that had the shape of a head. "You better quit trying to scare me, Troy," he said.

"You see him, you wake me up," Troy said.

Tom eased his head back onto his pillow, keeping his eyes on the window. "Can you smell him, like Mrs. Carnes said?" he whispered.

"Yeah. Smells like dead fish," Troy mumbled.

"Mrs. Carnes said he smelled like oil."

"Dead fish and oil, both," Troy said. He sniffed the air.

"What're you doing?" Tom asked.

"What's that smell like to you?" Troy said, in a hushed voice.

"What?"

Troy sniffed again. "That."

Tom sniffed. He could smell oil. Was sure of it.

"Aw, it ain't nothing but you," Troy said. "I thought it was dead fish. You must of pooted."

"Shut up, Troy," Tom said, his voice quaking.

TWENTY-SIX

It was an off day for preaching at the Crossover Methodist Church, and of the Winter family, only Hack attended church. Church services on off days for preaching began early, at eight o'clock, and included only devotion and singing in the sanctuary and then Sunday school. It was during the period for devotion that Hack stood and said, "I need to talk about some disturbing news."

The congregation sat motionless, their eyes fixed on Hack, their faces lined in sudden worry. Hack Winter would not use the word "disturbing" to describe something unless it was, without question, disturbing.

"Last night, somebody broke in on Evelyn Carnes," Hack continued, "and from the way it looks, it might have been the man that we been calling Pegleg."

A gasp flew from the throats of the women. A few men coughed.

"She managed to get a shot off at him when he got in the house," Hack said, "but it don't look like she hit him."

"Frank, how is she?" Corrine Gaines asked fretfully. She was holding Keeler's hand in a vise grip.

"She's fine. She's over at our house. She got a little cut when the gun kicked back on her and hit her on the face, but it's nothing bad."

"The sheriff know about it?" Arthur Dodd asked in a concerned voice.

Hack bobbed his head. "He got a call from Evelyn, and then he called me, and me and Troy went over there and found her before the sheriff and his deputies got there. He's looking into it today."

"Is there anything we can do?" asked Corrine.

"Nothing I can think of," Hack answered. "Just wanted everybody to know. Just want everybody to be careful."

"Can we come over and visit Evelyn this afternoon?" Corrine asked.

Hack paused a moment. He knew his wife would object, but he also knew he could not refuse Corrine Gaines or anyone else. "I expect that'd be fine," he said softly. "Evelyn just wanted everybody to know she'd be grateful for their thoughts."

The congregation spilled from the church in shock, asking the same question: "Why Evelyn?" No one had an answer.

"Everybody better keep an eye out," the people said, warning themselves as well as their neighbors. Standing in the churchyard, they divided the names of the elderly and volunteered to check on them.

•   •   •

When he returned home from church, Hack found Ada and Elly in the kitchen, preparing lunch.

"Where's Evelyn?" Hack asked.

"Frank came over to ask her some more questions, then he drove her to her house to pick up some more clothes," Ada answered. "Troy followed them over to drive her back. I don't think she slept a wink last night."

"I don't doubt it," Hack said. "I missed a few hours myself."

"What'd the people at church say, Daddy?" asked Elly.

"I guess you could say they're in shock," Hack replied. "Scared. Some of the women said they'd be by later."

"Oh, Lord," Ada fumed. "They'll have this house full of food by sundown. Stuff I'll just have to throw away. I wish you'd told them not to, Hack. It's not a funeral we're having here."

"You can't stop some things," Hack said. Then: "How'd Frank look?"

"Like he'd been up all night," Ada answered.

"I expect he has," Hack said. "Where's Tom?"

"He went with Troy. He had to see that knocked-down front door on Evelyn's house, or die on the spot. He told me he had dreams about Pegleg all night. Said he kept seeing him at the window."

"Well, if Tom started talking to him, he's left the county for good by now," Hack said dryly. He sat in a chair at the kitchen table. "Frank better get to the bottom of this thing pretty soon, or he's gon' have more trouble than he can handle," he added.

Ada dropped pieces of chicken into an iron skillet. The hot grease sizzled. "What's that supposed to mean?" she asked.

"Some of the men were talking hotheaded," Hack said, "saying

Frank's done nothing but lock himself up in his office the whole week. Said word was out that he'd called in some people from the federal government, the FBI probably, and he was just sitting there. And that's not good. Leads to a lot of grumbling."

"Well, they ought to let him do his job," Ada said. She pointed her fork to a pot on the back of the stove. "Elly, honey, you better take those potatoes off and drain them and put some butter and milk in them and start mashing them."

Elly nodded, took a pad, and moved the potatoes off the stovetop.

"Most of them think Frank ought to lay off Harlan and start finding out who this Pegleg fellow is," Hack said.

Ada laughed sarcastically. "Harlan must have been out politicking this week."

"Guess so," Hack said. "But they got a point. You can't have somebody almost killed and not do something about it."

Ada rolled the chicken in the skillet. "Well, he's not locked up in his office now."

"Mama, did you put some fatback in the beans?" asked Elly.

"No, honey, I thought you'd done that."

"I will," Elly said.

Hack stood. "I better go change out of my church clothes."

"You better talk to your youngest son when he comes back," Ada warned.

"What for?"

"You know how he gets. We turn our back on him, he'll be off with a stick gun, trying to find Pegleg."

"Maybe I just ought to tie a leash around him," Hack said wearily.

"Well, you can't let him go running around loose right now, that's for sure," Ada insisted.

Hack shook his head and left the kitchen. It would be easier to stop the wind with a fishnet than to keep Tom from wandering off.

● ● ●

Harlan Davis had taken his first drink of bourbon at seven-thirty. A straight shot, measured by one full swallow from the neck of the bottle. He had chased it with coffee that he had brewed an hour earlier.

By noon, the bottle of bourbon was half empty and Harlan had changed from coffee to beer as chasers. An under-skin tickling, like a gentle fingernail stroking from a beautiful woman, covered his body, made him giddy, and he sat at the kitchen table with a silly grin lodged in his face. His eyes were bleary. He needed the whiskey. He was sore and tired, but he felt good. All-over good. Men who could not drink and feel good, feel happy, were men who did not know how to drink. Drinking was a slow thing: keeping the taste on the tongue, letting the alcohol seep into the throat and stomach.

He had tried to fry bacon, had burned it, but he had eaten it, anyway. Bacon and three eggs that he had scrambled in the bacon grease.

If he had a wife worth a pinch of owl shit, she would have been out of bed, cooking for him.

He laughed softly. Stupid bitch, he thought. She'd be in bed half the afternoon, hiding under the covers, swearing to some sickness. She'd started it early that morning, before sunrise, when he'd tried to strip her.

"I don't feel good," she'd told him.

She had pushed at him, rolled her body away from him, pinched her gown to her body with her legs, wrapping herself in it.

"Leave me alone," she'd whined.

But he had shown her, by God. She'd turned away from him for the last goddamn time.

He took another slow swallow from the bourbon, let the taste hold on his tongue, let the whiskey slide down his throat.

His grin dug deeper in his face.

The gown had ripped away like paper. He had unpried her legs as easily as bending a green stick.

Through the kitchen window, looking toward the sideroad, he saw a car, an old 1939 Ford, headed toward Reba Martin's house.

Niggers, he thought.

Behind the first car was another car. A 1940 Chevrolet.

More niggers.

He turned to look at the clock on the kitchen wall. It was twelve forty-five.

The niggers were going to Reba's to eat Sunday lunch.

He pushed up from the table, stood for a moment to let the dizziness of his sudden move leave his stomach. He staggered to a cabinet under the kitchen counter and opened it and removed a bottle of vodka, and then he stalked through the house to the bedroom.

"You hungry?" he said to Alice.

The covers were pulled up to her closed eyes. She shook her head.

"Well, I damn well am," Harlan snarled. "So roll your ass out of bed."

"Go away, Harlan," Alice said weakly.

Harlan laughed boyishly. "Why, shoot, honey, did I say anything about you cooking? I ain't gon' make you do no cooking if you don't feel up to it. You already fed me. I just want you up and dressed." He put the bottle of vodka on the night table beside the bed. "Here, I got you some medicine for what ails you."

Alice looked at the bottle, then looked away.

"Looks good, don't it?" Harlan said in a teasing voice.

"Go to hell, Harlan," Alice whispered.

"Oh, honey, I am," Harlan chortled. "Me 'n' you both. Now get up and put you on some clothes and some makeup. I want you looking pretty as a picture, like one of them church women prissing around in the choir loft. I'll be back in a little while."

Alice pulled the covers down to her chin. "Where're you going?"

Harlan's drunk-grin flashed. "I'm going down to Reba's and find me a nigger woman to come up here and cook us some Sunday food."

"Leave them alone," Alice said. "You already in enough trouble over them."

Harlan's laughter filled the room. He said, "Shit."

●　　●　　●

Reba's home was crowded. Reba, Cecily, Remona, Son Jesus, Jule, Duck and Mary Heller, Grady and Pretty Sorrells. The smell of frying chicken billowed in the kitchen and living room, drifted outside through cracks in windows and doors. Turnip greens bubbled in a large pot. Corn bread with crackling sat steaming in three iron skillets. A large bowl of mashed potatoes was in the warmer of the wood-burning stove.

The women were gathered in the kitchen, sliding around one another as they cooked, the singsong of their voices high and merry. The men and Son Jesus were sitting in the living room, and the men were speaking in low, muttering tones about Pegleg's break-in on Evelyn Carnes. It was a story that had thundered across the county since midmorning, told in bits and pieces, heavily coated in hearsay and half-truths that ranged from murder to rape.

"He done gone crazy," Grady pronounced heavily. "Gone to breaking in on white peoples."

"White folks ain't gon' put up with that," Duck said. "They gon' be after every colored man they see."

"That's the truth," agreed Grady.

"I got my gun with me, out in the car," Jule said. "Pegleg, he come after me or Reba, or one of these babies in this house, I'm gon' shoot him dead."

"You just talking," Duck said.

"I ain't talking," Jule vowed. "Ain't nobody hitting me in the head with no hammer. Ain't gon' hit nobody here, neither. I'm gon' be staying right here to Pegleg's in the jail or dead."

"You just talking," Duck said again.

"I ain't talking," Jule vowed again.

"Got my gun too," Grady said.

"You better," advised Jule. He licked the roll on his cigarette and lit it.

They were still trading opinion and disagreement when they heard a door slam in the front yard. Jule looked up toward the window. He said to Son Jesus, "See who that is."

Son Jesus slipped out of his chair and went to the window. He stepped back. "Mr. Harlan," he said.

Jule pushed up, hobbled to the window. "He drunk," he moaned in a sinking voice.

Duck and Grady did not move.

Jule watched Harlan wander away from his truck, stand for a moment, scanning the yard, then begin his stagger toward the door. "Lord, he coming in," Jule sighed.

There was no knock. The door opened and Harlan stepped inside. His head swiveled to the unmoving men. A grin cracked over his face.

"Goddamn," Harlan exclaimed. "What's going on, Jule? Looks like a goddamn nigger convention."

In the kitchen, the singsong of voices stopped.

"I asked you a question, Jule," Harlan said. "You gon' answer me?"

A shudder ran through Jule. He said, his voice subdued, "Just having Sunday dinner, Mr. Harlan."

"Where you been, Duck?" Harlan boomed. "You look like you been to preaching, or you been doing the preaching."

"Yes sir," Duck answered softly. He touched the tie knotted at his throat.

"Praise the Lord and pass the gravy," Harlan crooned. He laughed, turned to the kitchen. Reba was standing in the kitchen door, holding a long fork. He could see Cecily and Remona standing behind her.

"What you want, Mr. Harlan?" Reba asked sharply.

Harlan glanced back at the men. The grin returned. He rolled his body toward Reba. "Right now, a piece of that chicken wouldn't be bad."

"It ain't done," Reba said.

Harlan took a step toward her. "Well, it's as done as it's gon' get for you. I want your ass in the car," he said in a low, threatening voice. "Or your girl's ass. Or both your girls' asses. Miss Alice ain't feeling good. We ain't got nothing cooking up at our house, and we need somebody up there doing it."

Reba shook her head. "No sir," she said defiantly. "We about to have our own dinner. You just go on back home. Tell Miss Alice I'll bring her something up there later on."

"We hungry now," Harlan said.

"Well, I can't go right now, and my girls can't, neither," Reba said.

"One of you is," Harlan hissed.

Jule took a nervous step toward Harlan. "Mr. Harlan, why don't you go on home now. You been drinking a little too much."

Harlan whirled back to Jule. "You sass me, and I'm gon' put my shoe about a half-mile up your black ass."

Jule stepped back. He turned to the door, opened it, and rushed outside.

Harlan laughed. His eyes covered Duck and Grady, daring them, then he turned to Reba.

"We ain't wanting no trouble, Mr. Harlan," Reba said, her voice quaking.

"Ain't gon' be none," Harlan said arrogantly. "I come to get me a nigger cook woman and I'm walking out of here with one."

"No sir," Reba said, shaking her head vigorously. She waved her arms to push Cecily and Remona back into the kitchen, then she stepped into the living room, holding the fork in front of her. "It ain't right, you coming in here like this. Your daddy ain't gon' like this."

Harlan threw up his hands comically, like a man avoiding a blow, then he peeked through his hands and looked around, rolling his eyes in pretended fear. "Well, damn," he said, "my daddy ain't here, unless he's hiding somewhere."

"Mr. Harlan, he ain't gon' like this," Reba insisted. "You go on home."

Harlan's fist whipped up. He took a long, menacing step toward Reba, and Reba closed her eyes.

Son Jesus cried, "Mama." He sprang from the corner of the room, where he had been standing, and jumped in front of his mother. "Don't you hit my mama," he growled, in a voice Reba had never heard. Deep. Bold. Unafraid.

Harlan wobbled one step back. His fist stayed curled. "Why, you little shit," he said. A sneer unrolled across his face. He waved his fist in front of Son Jesus. "You want to know what this feels like?" he added in a slurring whisper. "You ask your sister."

"Ain't gon' hit my mama," Son Jesus said evenly.

From behind Harlan, Grady and Duck eased up from their chairs.

"Mr. Harlan," Grady said, his voice trembling.

Harlan did not move or look back. "You put your black asses back in them chairs," he snapped.

The door opened suddenly and Jule stepped inside. He was holding an old shotgun.

"Mr. Harlan, you leave them alone now," Jule said harshly. He thumbed back the hammer on the gun.

Harlan pivoted slowly at the sound of the click. A look of surprise blinked in his eyes, then the grin crawled back into his face. He lowered his fist slowly.

"I'll be a son of a bitch," Harlan said easily. "You gon' shoot me?"

"I got to, I am," Jule warned nervously. "You go on home now."

Harlan laughed. He looked at the gun in Jule's hands. "That that old gun I traded you for pulling corn?"

Jule nodded. He motioned with the gun toward the door. "You go on home now," he said.

"That old gun ain't worth a shit," Harlan said. "Probably blow up on you."

"Go on home, Mr. Harlan," Jule pleaded. "I ain't wanting to shoot you."

"You ain't going to," Harlan said. There was merriment in his voice.

"Will if you make me," Jule said. He nodded vigorously. He could feel his blood thundering in his chest. A strange, surging courage filled his arms. "Yes sir, will if you make me."

Harlan rolled his shoulders, looking at Duck and Grady and Son Jesus. Then he raised his hands, palms out. "Well, shit," he said lightly. "I don't guess a piece of fried chicken's worth getting shot over." He stepped toward the door. Jule backed away, keeping the barrel of the gun pointed toward Harlan. At the door, Harlan stopped. He began to giggle. "Damn," he muttered. "You a sassy little nigger, you know that, Jule?" He twisted his head to look toward the kitchen. "Re-monnn-a," he sang. "I'll be baaa-ack. Me and you, we'll cook a stew." He laughed. Hard. Thunderous. "Me and you, we'll cook a stew," he sang again. Then he turned and stumbled through the door.

No one in the house moved until the sound of Harlan's truck leaving the yard died away.

Inside the kitchen, Remona began to wail, and the wail was covered by Son Jesus' pulling her into his shoulder.

Reba moved in three quick steps to Jule. She grabbed the shotgun from him. "What you doing with this gun in here?" she snapped. "You gon' get us killed with this gun."

For a moment, Jule did not speak. He stood, his hands out in front of him, as though the gun were still in his hands. An incredulous look was pasted on his face. Then he said, "You gon' get killed you ain't got one."

"You take this gun right now and you put it back where you got it," Reba commanded. "Ain't no guns gon' be in this house. Ain't gon' have no more killing here. Not here. You hear me, Jule?" Her voice quivered with fury.

Jule shook his head sadly. He reached for the gun. "You gon' get killed," he said softly. "You ain't got no gun, you gon' get killed."

"I got God," Reba said proudly. "God's better'n any gun they ever was. God ain't gon' let me and my babies get killed."

Jule shook his head again.

"You take that gun back to your place, right now," Reba ordered.

"Com'on, Jule. Me 'n' Grady'll go with you," Duck said softly.

"Uh-huh," Grady said.

Jule's body sagged in surrender. He crossed to the door, holding the gun by his side, then he walked outside. Grady and Duck followed, closing the door quietly behind them. Son Jesus stood by the window, watching.

• • •

He was only pretending to look for evidence, still Frank needed the time in the woods. Alone time. Time to think. Time away from the yammering of Arlo and Buddy, who were remembering—or misremembering—the Pegleg murders of 1943.

In the daylight, with a magnifying glass, he was certain that Hugh's finding of blood specks in the wallpaper of Evelyn's hallway was correct, and Hugh had taken photographs and had gently peeled off the paper and gouged out three pellets for the state crime lab. Yet there had been no reports of a gunshot wound at any of the hospitals in a five-county area. That meant that whoever had tried to attack Evelyn had only been nicked, or had gone off to Atlanta or to Anderson, South Carolina, to be tended. Nicked, most likely. There would have been more blood if he had been hit directly.

Frank had learned nothing new in talking with Evelyn at Hack Winter's home, or on the drive back to her house, but he did not trust himself to ask the right questions. If needed, he would have Hugh talk to her later. Hugh would be more clearheaded about things. Frank was too involved, too cautious, too protective. Was still jittery from thinking about her almost being killed. His fault too. Or could be. He had wanted to stir things up with the story of finding the bones of the men that Pegleg had killed, but it had never occurred to him that Pegleg himself would be part of the stirring up. Besides, Pegleg had never attacked a white person. And why Evelyn? Did Pegleg think that Evelyn knew things about the dead men? It could be, he reasoned. If Pegleg had been hired by Jed, it was possible that Jed could have bragged to his wife about it. Maybe let a name slip. And maybe Pegleg had seen Frank's car parked at her house and wondered what she was telling him.

At least he could cross off one suspicion: Jed was not Pegleg. Or if he was, he had learned some kind of carnival trick for snaking up through the dirt over his coffin.

From off in the woods, near the swamp, he heard the braying of a dog, and he stopped walking and listened. The braying grew more frantic, then stopped. A rabbit chase, he thought.

He leaned against a tree, breathing heavily, feeling the tickle of perspiration between his shoulders. Then he pressed his ear against the tree trunk and closed his eyes. Once, when he was a child, his father had told him that if he could hear the heartbeat of a tree, he could hear secrets that no one had ever heard. He needed a secret now. Needed the tree to whisper to him.

He stepped out of the woods onto the logging road leading to the sawdust piles, and an eerie sensation swept through him. It was as though he was being watched. Not by a person, but by spirits. By the men whose bones had been pulled out of sawdust, piece by piece. He stood, letting the shudder leave him, and then he continued up the road.

A crow cawed. Then another. A blue jay fussed.

He had talked twice with Fletcher in the office. Calls were flooding the place, Fletcher had warned. Mostly blacks working up courage. "They gon' be shooting at shadows," Fletcher had predicted. "Doodlebug's got a meeting planned over at his church this afternoon to talk about what they gon' do."

"Well, I guess I don't blame him," Frank had said. "Better tell Hugh to go over there and see what he can find out. Tell him to try and calm those people down."

Above him, the crow cawed again, and the blue jay fussed. A bird quarrel, Frank thought. Jabbering across treetops. Birds were a lot like people. Or people were a lot like birds.

● ● ●

It was one-thirty when Frank returned to Evelyn's home and to the argument occurring between Arlo Lewis and Ben Biggers. Ben was red-faced, soaked with perspiration, panting from anger. Arlo was struggling to keep from laughing.

"What's the trouble?" Frank demanded.

"This sawed-off piece of shit won't let me in the house to take pictures," Ben snapped.

"Watch your language, Ben," Frank warned. "This man's a deputy."

"*Was* a deputy," Ben hissed.

"He still is," Frank said. "I swore him back in this morning. Him and Buddy, both."

"What the hell for?" Ben asked. "This county ain't got the money to go hiring every Tom, Dick, and Harry every time somebody breaks in a house."

Frank smiled. "This ain't exactly a break-in, Ben. There's a little more to it than that."

Ben thrust his face close to Frank's. Frank could see the blood pumping in his neck. "No, I reckon it ain't," he said in a mean voice. "You got some nigger that thinks he can go around killing white people, and you ain't doing nothing but taking a Sunday-afternoon stroll around the woods."

"Be careful, Ben."

"You better know what the white people of this county think," Ben said. "They think it's time you did a nigger roundup and started kicking ass until you find out which one's doing this."

"Go on in the house, Ben. Take your pictures," Frank said calmly. He nodded to Arlo. "Let him in, but go with him. Don't let him take anything out of there."

Ben turned away, spat, then turned back to Frank. "You think you're king of the heap, don't you? You in your last term, boy, and you better get used to it. You think the niggers are gon' reelect you? You better go check the rolls, boy."

Frank did not answer. He turned and started toward his car.

"The governor's gon' get a call about this," Ben vowed. "I'm gon' fly your ass like a flag over the courthouse, if it's the last thing I do."

TWENTY-SEVEN

The loft of the barn was hot and thick with the smell of hay, but the heat and the hay scent did not bother Harlan. He could feel nothing but the dullness of the whiskey, the numbing sensation of floating, and in his mind a breeze swept through the opened loft door. He sat slouched in his chair, one elbow leaning on the cardplaying table, his fingers stroking the neck of the opened bottle. His shirt was unbuttoned halfway. A string of perspiration seeped off his shoulders and streamed down the furrow of his chest, puddling over the roll of flesh covering his stomach. He stared at the puddle, mesmerized by the matting of hair coating his skin.

I'm a hairy sonbitch, he thought.

He grinned foolishly, remembered getting in a fight with Harry Glanville when he was twelve, Harry picking at him because he did not have hair around his pecker. Beat the shit out of Harry, too. Him and Mason. Got Harry when he was walking home from school one day. Held the asshole down and pulled out all the pubic hair he had with a goddamn pair of needlenose pliers. Screamed his ass off.

He touched a finger to the puddle of perspiration, lifted his finger, focused his eyes on a bubble, then tipped it to his tongue. Be damned, he thought. Tastes like bourbon.

He lifted the bottle, swallowed from it.

It was his second bottle of the day.

Shit, he needed it, he reasoned.

Between the niggers and the bitch he was married to, he needed every drop he could pour down him.

Wonder what she's telling her old lady? he thought.

Maybe she'd stay gone. Sneak back in when he was off somewhere, and take her stuff and leave. Said she would. Said she would when she drove off. Said she'd had enough.

Stupid, whimpering bitch.

He could still smell her in the house. A sick, flower smell.

Not in the barn.

He dropped his head back, inhaled slowly, deeply. Hell, no. Not in the barn. The barn was a man's place.

He swallowed again from the bottle, put it down, stretched, easing the ache that ran from his neck down his shoulders, into the pit of his back. He picked up a screwdriver from the table, tapped it lightly against the bottle. The *ping* amused him. Tap. Tap. Tap. Ping. Ping. Ping. He grunted a laugh. I'm a damn musician, he thought. Ought to be on the goddamn Grand Ole Opry.

A dog barked from the yard of the house.

Shit, he thought. She's back. He tilted his head to the opened door of the loft, listened, heard nothing but the dog's bark. Then nothing. Parked out front, maybe.

He'd never had a dog as worthless. Her dog. Not his. Ought to blow its damn head off. All it did was squat under the porch and sleep. You could throw a rabbit on top of its nose, and it wouldn't move a hair.

Kill it tonight, he decided.

He twisted his body to look through the opening of the loft where the hay had been hoisted and stored. The sky was fading to a rose color, the color before sundown. Either it was late in the afternoon or he was drunker than he thought and the whole damn world was rose-colored.

A sound drifted up from below him, a small sound, and he leaned forward in his chair and looked down the opening holding the ladder.

Probably a chicken.

He leaned back. The sound rustled again.

"Barrrrk, barrrrk, barrrrk," he crowed, mimicking a quarreling chicken. He laughed. "Barrrk, barrrrk, barrrrk." He tapped the screwdriver against the neck of the bottle. It pinged dully.

Something snapped below him. A click. Sharp. Clean. He leaned forward again, tipping the chair, craned to look down the opening.

His eyes blinked in recognition. He grinned.

"Well, damn," he said, almost pleasantly. "Now, what the hell you gon' do with that thing?"

It was the last sound Harlan Davis would ever utter.

The wad of pellets hit him below the ribs on his right side.

And in the barn, the sound of the gun echoed like a bomb that would not stop exploding.

●　●　●

Frank stood under the stream of the shower, under the heated water, letting the water wash the day off his skin. Wash away the sun and the red-dust grime, the perspiration that wrapped him like thin waxed paper. Wash away Ben Biggers. Wash away the frightened face of Evelyn. Wash away the annoying sensation that he held two pieces of a rope of answers in his hands but he could not pull them together—not with Samson's strength or his own wit.

The water spilled off his hair, curled over his face, and he inhaled the clean-air scent the water left on him.

"You got trouble brewing," Fletcher had advised seriously.

And Fletcher—dumb-as-a-stick Cousin Fletcher—had been brilliantly perceptive for once in his life.

Damn right, trouble was brewing.

White men of Crossover—of Overton County—were sitting on porches, waiting for Pegleg with rifles and shotguns balanced across their laps, like old men he had seen in France and Germany, and black men were simmering in the kind of silence that became a rage of fear with a careless word or a quick movement.

He had sent Hugh to the afternoon meeting of blacks at Doodlebug Witcher's church to try and calm the situation, and Hugh had returned with a worried expression.

"Jesus, Frank, that was scary," Hugh had said. "They didn't say a word. Not one of them. Not even Doodlebug Witcher. Not to I got ready to leave."

"What'd they say then?" Frank had asked.

"Wadn't *they*," Hugh had answered. "It was Amos Whitley. He stood up just as I was walking down the aisle to leave, and he said, 'Whoever it was that broke in on Mrs. Carnes, it wadn't nobody here. Ain't no man here that's gon' mess with no white woman.' That's what he said, word for word. Exactly." He had added, "Goda'mighty, Frank, you ever hear that old man talk? He's got a voice like God. Made my skin crawl."

"You tell them I wanted them to give me some time?"

"I did," Hugh had replied, "but I wouldn't put a dime against a doughnut that anybody was listening."

Frank turned off the shower, stood for a moment, letting the water slither down his body. Then he reached for the towel and stepped out of his tub.

"...nobody *here*," Amos Whitley had said. "Ain't no man *here*..."

Did that mean something? Frank wondered, slowly rubbing the towel over his shoulders. Did Amos Whitley and the rest of the men gathered at Old Spirit Baptist Church know something about Pegleg? Who he was, or might be? And was that why they were at the church—to have their own trial, conduct their own justice by customs that were more ancient than the laws of Georgia?

A lot could be said in a few words. Or in silence.

The telephone began to ring. Frank wrapped the towel around him and moved quickly from the bathroom to the kitchen.

The call was from Fletcher.

"Frank, we just got a call from Fuller Davis. Harlan's dead," he said anxiously.

● ● ●

There were two cars and a truck at Harlan Davis's house when Frank arrived. Frank knew the truck and one of the cars belonged to Harlan. The other car belonged to Fuller Davis, who was sitting quietly on the steps leading to the back porch. Lights burned in every room of the house, like a bright puddle in the buried earth of night.

The call from Fletcher lingered in Frank's hearing, a buzzing of words.

"What happened?" he had asked Fletcher.

"Damned if I know," Fletcher had answered. "Fuller said Alice found him in the barn. Said he'd been shot. If you ask me, I'd say Pegleg. I'm telling you, Frank, when this gets out, we gon' be up to our ass in alligators."

He had given Fletcher instructions to call Pug Holly and Dr. Jake Arlington, and to find Hugh Joiner and Buddy Crump and Arlo Lewis. "You get everybody together and come on over, and don't waste time doing it," he had ordered.

"We'll be right behind you," Fletcher had vowed.

Frank stepped from his car and exhaled in relief. At least George and Mason were not there. George and Mason would be trouble. Especially Mason. He walked across the yard to Fuller. A dog pulled up on its front paws at the side of the porch and growled.

"Hush," Fuller said. The dog settled back to the ground.

"Is it true?" Frank asked gently.

Fuller nodded. He looked very old, very tired.

"Where's Alice?"

"In the house," Fuller answered.

"How's she holding up?"

"Ain't saying much," Fuller said. "Like she's numb. I told her to lie down and rest some."

"I got a doctor coming over," Frank said. "He'll tend to her. Where're the boys?"

Fuller looked up and held his gaze for a long moment on Frank. "I ain't called them yet. I will now that you got here. I thought you'd want to look things over."

"I appreciate that," Frank said. "Might be best if you wait a few more minutes. Hugh and Fletcher are on the way."

Fuller nodded his understanding.

"Where's he at?" Frank asked.

"In the barn," Fuller told him. "Up in the loft. The lantern's burning. I lit it to look him over."

"Why don't you wait here. I'll go take a look."

Fuller dipped his head and stared at the ground. "I knowed it was bound to come to this," he whispered.

"I'm sorry it did," Frank said. He shifted awkwardly and glanced toward the barn. He could see the dull glow of a light coming from the opened hay door of the loft. He turned back to Fuller. Fuller had called his sons sorry. It was a truth that ate at him like a cancer feeding from his blood.

"I'll be back in a minute," Frank added.

● ● ●

Frank had never been inside Harlan Davis's barn, but he knew what it was like. Every barn he had ever entered was basically the same, as though built from the same blueprint and then filled with the same goods giving off the same scents. Cotton seed hulls and cotton meal. Dried corn in the shuck. Oats and wheat. Mule and cow manure from the stalls. The powdery smell of poisons for boll weevils. Old oil and grease. Fertilizer, damp-caked by a leak from a nail hole in the tin roof. Frank had known farmers who had preferred to spend time in their barns than in their homes, because their homes did not have the odor of work. His own father had been such a man.

He did not believe that whoever killed Harlan was in the barn, but still he pulled his revolver from its holster and waved the beam of his flashlight over the main floor. He saw the ladder leading to the loft— exactly where he knew it would be—and he moved cautiously toward it. The lantern light that he had seen from the yard spilled out of the opening, coating the steps in faint yellow-orange streaks.

He took the steps slowly, pausing at each step to listen. He could hear nothing. At the ladder's top, he peered into the loft. The burning lantern was hanging from a rusty trace chain that had been nailed to a rafter, and its soft canopy of light fell over a worktable. Frank stepped into the loft. He saw Harlan's body immediately, sprawled across the floor, lying in the blurred shadows of the light. A dark coating of blood had oozed from his abdomen and trickled across the floor, puddling at his side. The smell of blood and bile was warm in the warm air.

"Jesus," Frank whispered. He aimed the beam of his flashlight at the wound. It was large and ugly. A shotgun, he thought. Close range. He moved to the body, turning the flashlight to Harlan's face. A hiss of anger seemed frozen on the still, hard features. He rotated his flashlight over the body. Near the right hand, he saw a screwdriver. It looked as though Harlan had been holding it, then released it when he hit the floor.

He knelt next to the body and leaned close to Harlan's face and sniffed. He could smell the strong odor of whiskey. Probably drunk when he died.

He stood and did a slow turn to study the loft. A small pile of hay was stacked near the front. Curiously, there was an old mahogany desk, a writing table that once had been elegant, and three cane-bottom chairs standing close to the worktable. A bottle of whiskey was on the desk, uncapped, almost empty, but Frank did not see a glass. A half-empty pack of Chesterfields was beside the bottle. He switched off his flashlight and crossed to the worktable and examined it under the glow of the lantern. It was littered with tools and glass jars filled with nails and nuts and bolts. And then he saw it. At the foot of the worktable, shoved slightly underneath, he saw a trunk, its lid standing open. Jed's trunk, he thought. The trunk Evelyn had described to him.

He turned on his flashlight again and knelt and aimed the light into the trunk. The first thing he saw, hanging on the side of the trunk, was a coarse brown seed sack with eyeholes cut into it.

"Goda'mighty," he whispered. "Pegleg."

He moved back to Harlan's body and carefully pulled Harlan's shirt open at the shoulders. On the right shoulder, he saw five puncture marks high off the arm and three deep scratches torn through the skin and flesh. The puncture marks and scratches had been rubbed with iodine.

He dropped the shirt, leaned back from the body. A chill snaked over his neck. Son of a bitch, he thought. She hit him.

He stood, waved the flashlight around the loft. A row of dirt-dauber nests was plastered to the ridgeline, like brown upside-down mud huts. A bird's nest was on a crossbeam, with one gray feather hanging off the lip. He stepped over Harlan's body and climbed down the ladder.

On the main floor of the barn, he turned the beam of the flashlight to the stall gates. On the second gate, he saw the notches. Three boards. Saw cuts. Five notches on the top board, four on the second, three on the third.

"You worthless bastard," Frank said aloud. Too loud. He could hear his voice echoing in the barn.

● ● ●

The news of the killing of Harlan Davis hissed over the party-line telephones of Crossover with the speed of a serpent's tongue. Each telling grew like yeast in bread dough, puffing up until whatever small grain of truth may have existed in the telling had been buried in the swell. An hour after Frank arrived at Harlan Davis's house, the roads in front and to the side of the house were crowded with cars, and pools of men and women and children stood about, gravely staring at the barn where Harlan's body had been found, gravely whispering among themselves.

"You reckon he shot himself? Somebody was saying they'd bet on it."

"Harlan? Ain't no way. From what I hear, they didn't nobody find a gun. I guarantee you it was some nigger that done it, with all that talk going on."

"Could of been. From what I been hearing, a bunch of colored men got together today down at Doodlebug's church to talk about what happened to Reba's girl."

"I'll give you ten to one it was Pegleg. Missed killing Evelyn Carnes, but by God, he didn't miss old Harlan."

"You right about that."

"You reckon the talk got back to Alice, and she got mad and shot him?"

"That ain't a bad guess. Harlan treated her like shit. Somebody was saying she was beside herself, like people get when they come to their senses after they done something they can't help, and she's got a temper. Harlan was always saying she could go crazy at the drop of a hat."

"Sheriff called in the doctor to give her something to dope her up."

"That right? I heard she was just sitting there at the kitchen table, not saying a word, while they was looking over Harlan."

"She looked kind of dazed to me. I seen her leaving with Mason's wife. I guess that's where she'll be staying tonight, if she don't go to her mama's house."

"Sheriff better keep his eye peeled. He'll have Mason and George to deal with, and Mason's mean as Harlan ever was."

"They was here a little while ago, with their daddy. They seemed quiet enough to me, but you can't never tell about them boys."

"I feel sorry for Fuller. He's a good man. Got the sorriest boys I ever heard tell of, but he's a good man. Good as they come."

"Somebody was saying whoever done it left a note telling who it was, and the sheriff's going after him tonight."

"Yeah, well, you can't believe everything you hear."

Frank did not try to break up the crowd. It would have been useless. The crowd would dissolve when the talking was finished, when the stories had circulated and were in their second or third telling. He knew the stories were mostly harmless. He also knew the crowd had not learned of Alice Davis's confused blithering over finding Harlan. Harlan had been drinking hard since early morning, she had admitted, and he had gone to Reba's house and had come back a half hour later, spewing about Jule pulling a gun on him. She had called his father, had called Fuller, while he was at Reba's. Fuller had advised her to get away, to let Harlan pass out on his own. They had argued, and then he had disappeared into the barn. "He was like that when he got to drinking," Alice had said listlessly. "Sometimes he'd stay out there two or three days."

She had taken Fuller's advice, had left in midafternoon to visit her mother, she told Frank in a shivering, frightened voice, and had returned around eight-thirty, bringing leftover food from her mother's table. When Harlan did not answer her calls, she went into the barn, believing he must have fallen asleep from the drinking, and she had found him, blood-soaked, in the loft.

She had not seen anyone, or heard anything. No running. Nothing.

Frank had not asked Alice, or Fuller, about the trunk. He did not think they had seen it. He had rifled through it quickly, removing those items that would have belonged to Pegleg—the mask, the oil-dirty clothing, gloves, a jar filled with a black paste that might have been made from soot and grease, and a hammer. He had shoved all of it into an empty fertilizer sack that he found on the worktable, and then he had taken the sack to his car while Fuller was inside the house, calling George and Mason. He would deal with Pegleg later. Now it was important to keep it quiet. He had enough on his mind. The news of Pegleg could wait.

◦   ◦   ◦

By eleven o'clock, Harlan's body had been removed to Holly's Funeral Home. Pug Holly's report from his brief examination had been exactly what Frank had guessed—shot at close range by a shotgun. Dead before he hit the floor, Pug had suggested to Frank, and Dr. Jake Arlington had confirmed it. No way to pinpoint how long. Anywhere from four o'clock on, Pug believed. Probably closer to eight than four, though, as fresh as the blood was on the flooring. Pug had added, "I'd be looking for some nigger, if I was you."

"Pug," Frank had said in a quiet, but threatening, voice, "I'd appreciate it if you'd keep your goddamn mouth shut. I got enough trouble."

Frank moved through the crowd, toward his car. He moved slowly, deliberately. If there was temper to deal with, he wanted to do it immediately.

"You reckon it was Pegleg, Frank?" Keeler Gaines asked.

"No, it wadn't," Frank told him sternly.

"You sure?"

"I'm sure."

"Don't go worrying about nothing over here," Keeler assured him. "We gon' keep the lid on things."

Frank nodded. Keeler's reaction was as good as a blessing. A murmur of voices, repeating Keeler in one way or another, followed Frank. Good, he thought.

At the edge of the crowd, he saw Hack and Ada Winter. They stood silently, solemnly, watching him approach. Troy and Tom stood nearby. Frank could see Tom's eyes flaming with imagination, and for a moment he wanted to laugh. He wondered what Tom was thinking, or scheming.

Ada stopped him.

"I'm sorry about what happened, Frank," she said. "For Fuller's sake, and Alice's sake, I'm sorry about it. Hope my call about Remona didn't have anything to do with it."

"No m'am. It just happened," Frank told her.

"Evelyn's at the house with Elly," Ada said quietly, privately. "She wanted to come over, but I thought it was best she didn't, after what she's been through."

"Yes m'am," Frank mumbled. He bobbed his head once and walked on toward his car. He was glad Evelyn was not there. He did not need distractions.

"You want somebody staying over here tonight?" Fletcher asked.

"Yeah," Frank said. "Set up some shifts. Keep a close look on the road going down to Reba's house."

"What for?"

"Fletcher, just do it, damn it," Frank said irritably.

"You think Reba had something to do with it?" Fletcher asked.

Frank turned to stare at Fletcher. He shook his head in despair. "Not the first damn thing," he said. "But I ain't worried about what I think. I'm worried about what may be running through the minds of other people, and to tell you the truth, Fletcher, that includes you. Just do what I tell you."

Fletcher wagged his head. "You want Hugh to stay with me?"

"No. He's going back with me," Frank said. "Use Buddy and Arlo. Tell them not to let nobody in the barn or anywhere around it. I'll be back in the morning."

"What about the Carnes place?" Fletcher asked.

"It's a chance we take," Frank said. "Right now, we better be here."

"Where you going?" Fletcher said.

"I got some things to do," Frank answered. He motioned to Hugh and pointed toward the driver's side of his car. He opened the passenger-side door and slipped inside and leaned his head against the seat and closed his eyes. He could feel the car rock with the weight of Hugh sitting beside him. A queasy, slight taste of bile caked in his mouth. It had been a long time since he had seen a man's guts blown away.

"Where to?" Hugh said.

"The office," Frank told him.

Hugh eased the car onto the road and drove away. After a moment, he said, "You find something back there?"

"Yeah," Frank said. "Pegleg."

Hugh looked at him incredulously. "You're kidding."

"It's in that sack in the back seat," Frank said, gesturing with his head. "Got the mask, the gloves, clothes, the hammer. Even got a little jar of black stuff for coating the face. I guess Jed passed on a few tricks he learned in the army."

"Where'd you find it?" Hugh asked.

"In a trunk in the loft, a trunk that Jed gave to Harlan. Evelyn told me about it."

Hugh smiled. "Well, it might of been in Jed's trunk, but Jed wadn't Pegleg. Couldn't've been. He was in the hospital when Rody was killed."

"I know."

"It was Harlan, then?" Hugh said.

"It was both of them," Frank answered.

"What do you mean?"

"I thought it was somebody Jed had hired, at first," Frank said. "Some colored man he had something on. Or maybe more'n one person. Everything fit but the size, and Lord only knows, that ranged from a midget to an elephant. But it wadn't anybody he'd hired. It was him and Harlan. Jed probably killed the first two and probably had Harlan help him carry off the Conley boy, but it was Harlan that killed Rody."

"You got all that stuff in the back seat you took from Harlan's place, but have you got any hard proof about Jed Carnes?" Hugh said.

Frank shook his head. "No," he admitted. "I just know it. It's the only way to figure the difference in the size, but no, I can't prove it. I'm just telling you. I don't want nothing said about it—not now, and maybe never. Shouldn't of said anything myself. No good in talking about it unless I can prove it, and I can't."

Hugh knew that Frank was thinking of Evelyn Carnes. "It stays right here with me, Frank, and you know that," he said. Then he asked, "Why'd Harlan break in on Evelyn?"

"He had to take some heat off himself," Frank said. "If he got people talking about Pegleg, they'd quit talking about him and maybe make us go off on a wild-goose chase."

"What're you gon' do about it?" Hugh asked.

"Right now, nothing," Frank told him. "We got to find out about this other thing first. We got a dead man on our hands. A sorry sack of shit, but he's dead."

"You got any ideas?"

"Not the first one," Frank admitted. "I want to look around in the morning, to see if we can find anything else. Then I think I'll go talk to Jule. Alice was saying Harlan had had a run-in with him in the afternoon. I hope to God it wadn't him, or some other colored man. If it was, we got more trouble than we ever want."

"You don't think it was Alice, do you? There was some talk going on back there about her temper."

Frank shook his head. "I doubt it. She was too scared of him."

"I can't think of anybody else," Hugh said. "You?"

Frank shrugged and leaned heavily against the car door. He thought of Coy Philpot, whose notches were on a stall gate in Harlan's barn. Coy, who had never killed anything, not even a rabbit. Coy, who had become a soldier in God's army. But soldiers killed, Frank thought. For God and country and to save their own hides, soldiers killed, and maybe Coy had, at last, taken up the gun. He had a reason. A lot of people had a reason.

"Well, I hate to say it, but whoever it was did the world a favor," Hugh said.

"I can't say that I disagree," Frank mumbled. "I just hope it ends right there in that barn. But something tells me it won't. Something tells me it's gon' be hanging over our heads for a long time. I don't know that me and you will ever know the truth."

TWENTY-EIGHT

Tom had never seen Jule work as diligently. He did not loiter with nonsense talk or funny stories. He did not rest to slow-roll a cigarette and slow-smoke it down to a pinch of paper that he could hold between his thick fingernails.

Jule fussed over the fence, ripping down the old boards that he and Tom had half nailed, and putting them up again, gruffly commanding Tom and Son Jesus to hold the boards still as he leveled them by sight and then pounded them securely to the posts. He had a worried, irritated look, a headache look.

"Got to get this job done, boys," Jule grumbled. "Y'all ain't done nothing right. Look at them boards. They a sight. Them boards gon' drop off them old posts in the first good wind."

"Uncle Jule, you put them boards there," argued Tom.

"Don't you go sassing me, boy," Jule mumbled. "You go on back home, you start sassing me. Your mama'll hear about all that sass."

Tom sighed and squatted and held the board against the post. At the other post, Son Jesus knelt silently, holding the board. He had barely spoken all morning.

"It's hot, Uncle Jule," Tom complained, believing that Jule suddenly would feel the imaginary heat and agree and amble off to find the shade of a tree.

Jule glared at Tom. "You the laziest white boy I ever seen," he said. "Can't see how it happened. You got a brother that's the hardest-working white man in this county. Can't see how y'all any kin at all."

"I stayed up half the night, Uncle Jule," Tom whined. "Up there at Mr. Davis's house."

He saw Jule freeze.

"You should of seen it," Tom added quickly. "They was blood all over the place, where they took the body out of the barn. Troy said it looked like a pig had been stuck."

Jule placed a nail on the board that Tom held against the post and swung his hammer once. The hammer glanced off the head of the nail, sending it spinning to the ground.

"Don't want to hear nothing about no blood," Jule said in a low voice. He picked up the nail.

"Troy said Mr. Davis got what he deserved," Tom continued. "Said he was just a sorry piece of trash for doing what he done to Remona."

Jule did not reply. The hammer flicked in his wrist, striking the nail. Three, four, five blows. The nail disappeared. The head of the hammer left an indention, a ring the size of a half-dollar, in the board.

Tom kept his hand on the board, holding it needlessly. He gazed off across the pasture, and a story, or a fragment of a story, began to seep from the library of stories he had read, or maybe from a movie Troy had taken him to see. A gunfight in a street. Men facing off, their arms hanging loose at their sides, their eyes locked in the narrow slit of a stare, their fingers twitching inches away from their holstered guns.

"What you doing?" Jule said irritably. "I done nailed that board."

Tom released his hand and settled from a squat to a sitting position on the ground.

"They was saying last night it was a showdown," Tom said. "Said Mr. Davis and whoever it was that killed him was up in the loft, and the first dog bark they heard, they was supposed to draw guns and shoot. Mr. Davis was too slow." He glanced at Son Jesus, still holding the board at the other post. Son Jesus was staring at the ground. He seemed lost in thought.

"What they said." Tom sighed. "Wish I could of seen it."

Jule turned and glared down at Tom. "Don't want to hear no more about that," he said harshly. "We got work to do."

Tom shrugged and stood and dusted the seat of his pants. He could not understand why Uncle Jule and Son Jesus had no interest in the killing of Harlan Davis. He had wanted to stop at the Davis house that morning when Troy drove him over to work on the fence, but Troy would not stop. "Quit pestering me," Troy had snapped. "A man's been killed. Goda'mighty, leave it alone, Tom."

Tom watched Jule bending over, nailing Son Jesus' end of the board into the post. The sound of the hammer cracked like rifle shots. Tom

299 • THE RUNAWAY

turned and stretched and looked longingly up the road, toward Harlan Davis's house. He wondered if the barn and the ground were still stained with blood, wondered if there would always be a stain.

A wisp of dust crawled along the road, and Tom saw a black car moving slowly toward them. It was the sheriff's car.

"Yonder comes the sheriff," Tom announced.

The hammering stopped. Jule turned and stared down the road. A frown of worry wormed into his face. Son Jesus stood from his squat and moved away to the shade of the chinaberry tree.

"Wonder what he's coming down here for?" Tom mumbled.

● ● ●

Frank rolled his shoulders against the seat of the car. His muscles felt as broken and scattered as the puzzle pieces of Harlan Davis's murder. At least he knew who Pegleg was—both Peglegs. Or who they had been. Even if he could not prove it about Jed Carnes, he knew.

He saw Jule standing with Son Jesus and Tom at the fence, watching him approach. He shook his head. No telling what Tom had been saying. Whatever it was, it clouded the truth, but it was probably a better tale than the truth. He touched his shirt pocket and felt the shotgun shell he had found early that morning in the broom straw of a field behind Harlan's barn. The sulfur smell of gunpowder was still strong on the shell, and the cut of the firing pin still bright on the brass casing. He did not know if it was the shell that had killed Harlan, but it was likely—highly likely. And whoever fired it would have disappeared south of the barn, where he had found the shell. Reba's house was south. And Jule's.

Frank wanted the outline of the shell in his pocket to be seen by Jule. He wanted to watch Jule's eyes, to see if they made a confession his tongue would not make. And of course, he could be wrong, he reasoned. The shell could have been fired by Harlan, shooting at birds.

He pulled the car to a stop in the yard and opened the door and got out. I'll know soon enough, he thought.

"Morning, Jule," Frank said easily. He looked at Tom and Son Jesus. "Boys."

Jule mumbled, "Morning." His eyes locked on the outline of the shotgun shell in Frank's shirt pocket. He swallowed hard, then looked away.

"I was telling Uncle Jule and Son Jesus about last night," Tom said brightly.

"That right?" Frank said. His gaze stayed on Jule. It was not easy to read Jule's reaction.

"Yes sir," Tom answered. "I was telling them they ought to go up there and see where Mr. Davis was bleeding on the ground."

Frank shook his head slowly. "Don't think that'd be a good idea right now," he suggested. "We trying to keep people away from there for a little while."

"I saw the cars up there this morning, when Troy brought me over," Tom added. "Troy said y'all was still working on things."

"That's right," Frank replied. He paused, looked away to the fence. "About got the fence up, I see."

"Yes sir," Jule muttered. He took his handkerchief from his pocket and swabbed it across his forehead. "Yes sir, we working at it."

"Looks good," Frank said. Then: "Say, Jule, I just been asking about, seeing if anybody knew anything about last night."

"No sir, ain't heard nothing," Jule replied quickly. He tried a lopsided grin, which fell quickly from his mouth. He ducked his head, pawed at the ground with his shoe.

"Didn't hear no shooting?" Frank asked. "Thought you might have, living between here and there. What you think it is, a mile or so from your place to Harlan Davis's place?"

Jule stroked his chin with his hand. He waved at a gnat. "Don't know, sir. No sir, I don't. Ain't too far."

"And you didn't hear anything?"

"No sir. Didn't hear nothing. Don't hear like I used to, nohow."

"Uh-huh," Frank said. "Say, Jule, you got a shotgun?"

Jule's foot froze in mid-paw, and then he put it down for balance. He stuck his hands into his pockets and bobbed his head slowly. "Got a old thing," he drawled.

Frank let the answer dangle. He watched Jule continue to bob his head and look away. Then he said, "Thought you did. Thought you had one when we was looking for the boys."

Jule's head stopped bobbing. He cocked it. "No sir, didn't have no gun with me that time. Some of the others did, but it wadn't me. That old gun of mine ain't worth nothing. Ain't never shot it."

"You think I could take a look at it?" Frank said.

Jule licked his lips. A crown of perspiration coated his forehead. He wiped it again with his handkerchief. After a moment, he nodded. "Yes sir," he said. He added, "I got it up there at my place."

"Well, it don't really mean much," Frank said. "I was just curious. Why don't we get in the car and ride up there. Won't take but a minute."

"Can me and Son Jesus come?" Tom asked enthusiastically.

Frank turned to Tom. Tom's face was beaming. He glanced at Son Jesus, still standing in the shadows of the chinaberry. It wouldn't hurt to take them, he thought. Maybe it would even relax Jule.

"Don't matter to me," Frank said. "All right with you, Jule?"

Jule nodded. He looked away, toward the house.

"Why don't you run up there and tell your mama you're going with me," Frank said to Son Jesus.

"She ain't here," Tom answered quickly. "Troy took Reba and Remona back over to my house. My mama's gon' take Remona back over to the doctor."

Frank nodded. "I see. That's nice of your mama. Well, we won't be gone long."

● ● ●

Jule had never been in a sheriff's car. He sat in the front passenger's seat, jammed against the door, his body stiff as a plank, a greasy, sick feeling in his stomach. The door handle was close to his hand, and he thought of yanking the door open and rolling out and then running across the field. But one man had already been killed, and when killing was in the air, nothing could stop it. Besides, he couldn't run, not with one leg shorter than the other.

Tom leaned forward from the back of the car, his head poked over the seat between Jule and the sheriff. He yammered to Jule about the ambulance that had collected Harlan Davis's body and how he could see blood seeping through the sheet used to cover Harlan, and Jule nodded absently and muttered, "That right?" He glanced at Frank. His eyes flicked to the revolver belted to Frank's hip. His heart was pounding, his head ached. The sheriff was putting guns and killings together, and the first colored man he found with a gun was the colored man he was going to haul off to jail. He rolled his head to look out the window. In the distance, he saw a single huge oak, and he suddenly imagined himself in jail, with a mob outside, twirling ropes.

"You know where Uncle Jule lives?" Tom asked Frank.

"Sure do," Frank answered. He nodded with his head to a house tucked off in the middle of pecan trees. "Right up there."

"Yes sir," Jule mumbled. He swallowed a moan that rose in his throat.

"A sheriff's car's better than my daddy's car," Tom announced. "Ain't it, Son Jesus?"

Son Jesus did not reply. In the back seat, he sat, like Jule, against the door, cuddled into himself.

"Here we are," Frank said. He stopped the car in the yard of Jule's house and got out. Tom bolted from the back seat. Jule and Son Jesus crawled out of the car cautiously, silently.

"This Merle Whitfield's place?" Frank asked casually.

"Yes sir," Jule said in a low, trembling voice. "Mr. Whitfield, he lives over in Athens. He got all this land from Mr. Fuller, then he up and quit farming."

"Seems like I heard that," Frank replied. He looked around. He had seen a hundred houses like the one Jule lived in—clapboard, covered with tar paper, rusting tin roof, drooping porch, so much dry rot a good wind would blow it into the next county. He turned to Jule. "Let's have a look at that gun, Jule."

Jule nodded solemnly and trudged across the yard to the house. He opened the door and stepped inside. Frank followed him, and Tom followed Frank. Son Jesus lingered in the yard.

Tom paused at the door. "Com'on, Son Jesus," he urged.

Son Jesus shook his head and turned away.

"Well, stay out there, then," Tom groused. He stepped inside, near Frank.

The house was little more than a toolshed. It had one large room with a fireplace, a small kitchen with a woodstove, and a back room that Jule used for storing his junk. His bed was in the large room, in a corner. The house smelled of fatback and corn bread, the only two things Jule knew how to cook, or cared about eating if he could not mooch a meal from Reba. Merle Whitfield had been promising to repair the leaking roof for three years but had not yet done it. The barn on the property was in better condition. "Got to keep his cows dry," was the way Jule had assessed Merle's failure to fix his house.

Jule stood in the middle of the room. He rubbed his face nervously with his hand. His eyes settled on the bed. The gun was under the bed. It was an old gun, a single-shot twelve-gauge. The stock had been splintered on top and tacked back together with headless nails, then wrapped in black tape.

Might as well give it up, Jule thought. He sagged and crossed the room.

"I keep it under the bed, here," he said.

"Makes sense," Frank told him. He thought of the gun under Evelyn's bed. It had saved her life.

"Uh-huh, where I keep it," Jule mumbled. He leaned over and pulled back the covers that had spilled off the unmade bed. "Right under here," he added. He reached, but his hand did not touch the gun, and a wave of surprise swept over him. He dropped to his knees and hands and lowered his head and looked. The gun was not there.

"Oh, Lord," Jule sighed. He jerked back from the bed, like a man struck by a coiled snake, and looked up at Frank fearfully. "It ain't there," he said.

Frank did not speak for a moment. Then he said, "Where you suppose it is?"

Jule scrambled to his feet and began to pace the room, searching frantically. "Lord, Mr. Frank, I don't know," he moaned. "Where it was yesterday. Where I put it. You can ask Duck and Grady. They was with me."

"You think maybe somebody stole it?" Frank asked.

"Yes sir. Had to. Right there's where I put it yesterday. Yes sir. Right before we had Sunday dinner down at Reba's. Somebody done broke in and stole it."

"Maybe Duck or Grady stopped by and borrowed it later on," Frank said.

"No sir," Jule said urgently. "They was with me all afternoon. Didn't go home to about sunset, then I come on home."

Frank nodded slowly. He looked at Tom. "Why don't you run on outside and let me talk to Jule a minute," he said.

"You want me to look for the gun?" Tom asked eagerly.

"Not in here," Frank told him. "Poke around outside, if you want to. Maybe somebody leaned it up against the house or the barn and forgot about it. We'll be out in a minute."

"Yeah," Tom said. He raced from the house.

Jule backed away to his bed and sat on the edge of it. "I ain't lying,

Mr. Frank," he said. "No sir, I ain't lying. I ain't got no notion where that gun is."

Frank touched his shirt pocket, fingered the outline of the shell. "What gauge was that shotgun, Jule?" he asked.

"Uh—seems to me it was a twelve-gauge," Jule mumbled.

"You sure?"

"Uh—seems to me that's what it was," Jule said. "I ain't never shot it."

"Not even at birds, or rabbits?" Frank asked.

"No sir. It wadn't much of a gun. Mr. Harlan give it to me for pulling corn."

"Alice Davis told me Harlan came down to Reba's house yesterday and you might have had some kind of run-in with him," Frank said in a soft voice. "That right?"

Jule tucked his head. A tremor ran down his arms into his hands, and he caught the sheet on the bed and began to twist it. He nodded once.

"Why don't you tell me about it," Frank said.

"He come up to the house, acting drunk, cussing up a storm," Jule said. "Told Reba he come to drag Remona back up to his house. Say he was gon' get her black ass back to working." He looked up at Frank. His eyes were wet. "Mr. Frank, I couldn't just stand there and let him scare them womenfolks. No sir, I couldn't do it. I told him he'd have to go on."

"You have the gun with you?" Frank asked.

Jule nodded sadly.

"You pull it on him?"

"Yes sir," Jule confessed in a whisper. He looked up at Frank. "I wadn't gon' shoot him. Just wanted him to leave us be."

"He didn't come back, did he?" Frank asked.

"No sir. He was drunk. I reckoned he done passed out. But I was watching out. Why Grady and Duck stayed the afternoon. Reba, she make me take the gun back up here. Say she don't want no guns in her house."

Frank frowned. "Harlan ever done that before? Ever scare Reba like that?"

"Yes sir," Jule answered, wagging his head vigorously. "Mr. Harlan, he a mean man when he get to drinking. Colored man better watch out for Mr. Harlan."

Frank walked to the window and looked out. He could see Tom near the barn, looking in a wagon for the missing shotgun.

"Yes sir," Jule moaned. "Colored man better watch out for Mr. Harlan."

Frank turned back to Jule. "We got a little problem here, Jule," he said.

Fear stroked in Jule's face.

"Alice Davis is bound to tell Mason and George what Harlan said, that you talked back to him, pulled a gun on him, and Mason and George won't take that lightly," Frank said. "They gon' be looking for somebody, and I don't expect they'll be looking much farther than you."

"Lord, Mr. Frank," Jule cried.

"It's all right," Frank said gently.

Jule nodded, waited.

"But I'm gon' have to take you to jail," Frank said.

Jule rocked on the bed. He began to tap his chest with his hand.

"Wish I didn't have to," Frank said. "But right now, way things are, you gon' be better off in jail."

"I didn't kill nobody, Mr. Frank," Jule wailed.

"I ain't saying you did," Frank said. "But I don't want no more killing in this county. We had enough."

"Who's gon' watch over Reba and them babies?" Jule said. "Pegleg's on the loose."

"No," Frank said after a long pause. "No, he ain't. Pegleg's dead."

Jule looked at him, puzzled.

"I'm gon' tell you something you can't tell nobody right now," Frank said. "Harlan Davis was Pegleg."

"Oooooh," Jule sighed. He beat again on his chest. "How you know that?"

"I found everything in his barn. The mask, the clothes, everything."

"Why ain't you telling people?" Jule asked.

"I don't want to muddy the water. Not right now," Frank answered. "It'll come out soon enough."

Jule leaned off the side of the bed. He shook his head sadly. "He kill Rody."

"That's right," Frank said.

Jule gazed at the floor, then he buried his head in his hands.

TWENTY-NINE

Avery Marshall III's walk down the corridor of the Overton County Courthouse was a leisurely stroll, a politician's walk. Pausing to speak to passersby, ducking his head into offices to exchange greetings, waving glad salutes. He was tall, merry-faced, and handsome in the way of a band singer or a movie actor, a friendly, outgoing man. And yet he also had the look, or the nature, of someone distinguished from birth. The look of a professor with grand thoughts showering in his brain like the fireworks of a celebration. He could have been a professor. Had the credentials for it. The only man in the history of Overton County to attend Harvard. There were times when Harvard slipped into his conversation, and the people who were listening to him reeled in awe, or smirked in disdain. They did not understand him, but they were impressed by him, even if some of them—the smirkers—would never admit it. Ada Jo Pendleton, a secretary in the Permits Department, called him Pretty Words. Ada Jo had a crush on Avery, an affection that might have caused embarrassment for other men, because Ada Jo was short and heavy. Avery handled it with charm.

When he opened the door to the Sheriff's Department, he paused, grinned a closed-mouth grin, and winked at Mildred. Mildred blushed.

"He in?" Avery asked.

"Yes sir," Mildred answered sweetly.

Avery winked again, strolled to Frank's office, opened the door, and stepped inside.

"Well, Frank," he said casually, "I think it's time you let me in on what's going on."

Frank leaned back in his chair, swept a hand toward a seat in front of his desk. "Fact is, I was about to call you."

Avery folded himself into the chair. "You made an arrest today, I understand. At least that's the word on the street. Jule Martin, is that right?"

"Well, it's sort of an arrest," Frank said.

Avery cocked his head curiously. "I like your style, Frank. You're the only law enforcement officer I've ever heard of who 'sort of' makes an arrest. You got enough on him for me to 'sort of' prosecute him?"

"What I've got is a dead man, a shotgun shell I picked up in a field, a story about Jule pulling a gun on Harlan early yesterday afternoon, and now that gun's missing," Frank told him.

Avery braced his hands together in front of him, fingertip to fingertip. "Ummm," he mused. "I could make a Whereas or two out of that, but that's not a lot for a murder conviction."

"Well, it's not quite that," Frank told him. "I'm holding him on suspicion of murder."

"Your Honor, what we've got here is *suspicion* of murder," Avery intoned. A playful smirk turned on his lips. "That ought to be good enough for an old-fashioned lynching."

Frank rocked back in his chair. "I don't know if Jule killed him or not," he said. "But he had a run-in with him yesterday afternoon, and that'll get out."

"Already is," Avery said. "Word is, Harlan's brothers are slightly annoyed. At least Mason is."

"Right now, I figured it'd be safer for Jule in here than being target practice. I'm just buying a little time, and I need you to help me make a down payment on it."

"Speak to me," Avery said.

"Let's begin with this one: Harlan Davis was Pegleg."

Avery sat up. "Whoooa," he said. "You sure?"

"I am," Frank said. "I found the sack mask and some old clothes and some blackface makeup and a few other things in a trunk in the barn."

"Maybe somebody put them there to throw you off," Avery suggested. "After they interrupted Harlan's breathing."

Frank shook his head. "No chance. The night Pegleg broke in on Evelyn Carnes, she took a shot at him. Hugh found some holes in the wall that had blood spots on them, and we figured he'd been hit a little bit. I found pellet marks on Harlan's right shoulder, and I expect Pug'll find some pellets when he starts digging around."

"Damn," Avery said. He blew a soft whistle from his lips. "I think I'm going to have to reconsider nominating Harlan for Man of the Year posthumously." He bobbed his head in astonishment. "I assume you're keeping the Pegleg thing quiet for a reason."

"Nothing particular," Frank replied. "I just didn't want to fan the fires over at Harlan's house last night, and I thought I'd wait until Pug did his examination."

"Good move," Avery said. The veneer of amusement that seemed permanently fixed to his face faded. His eyes narrowed in a gaze on Frank. "Did you ever think you'd really kill a man when you went to war, Frank?"

"I figured there was a good chance of it," Frank said.

"Well, old war buddy to old war buddy, it used to terrify me, just thinking about it," Avery said. A smile flickered back into his face. "Of course, there was a little difference between us. I was pushing papers in the Pentagon while you were crawling through the mud in France, but don't let anybody tell you that a paper cut on the pinkie can't ruin a man's day." The smile grew. "You saw Paris, didn't you?"

"I did," Frank said.

Avery sighed. "Me too. In 1937. I went over for the summer. Hell of a place. Beautiful women. I still have fantasies of them." He paused. The smile faded again from his face, and he had a sudden look of being old, more the features of his father than himself. "We're a lot alike, Frank. Do you know that?"

Frank chuckled. "We both liked Paris," he said, "but I think we'd be stretching it if we took it any further than that."

"No, I mean it," Avery insisted. "We both *left*, Frank. Got away from here."

"A lot of other people did too," Frank said.

Avery bobbed his head in agreement. "Yep. They did. But that's not what I'm talking about. They *went away* and came home when it was over. They picked up a few Purple Hearts and some stories, but they didn't change. Not really. Not much. Or if they did, they don't know it yet. We *left*. There's a difference, Frank. We left and came back with something we don't quite understand. We're not the same people we were growing up here." He paused again. The grin flashed. "Other than the fact that you despised Harlan Davis—like everybody else in their right mind—that's why you're doing what you're doing for Jule, and that's why I'm going to help you do it."

Frank frowned quizzically.

"Don't ask me to explain it," Avery said cheerfully. "I can't. I don't give a hoot in hell what the answer is, but I know there is one, and it doesn't have a lot to do with that poor, deceased man that Pug's got stretched out on his slab and has probably mutilated by now." He lowered his voice. "But it's got everything to do with leaving Overton County and then coming back." He shook his head slowly, let the smile crease deep into his face. Then he added, "Now, what are we going to do about Jule?"

"We've got to hold him as long as we can and hope I can find out who killed Harlan," Frank answered. "In the long run, that man may be Jule."

"Well, that gives you about twenty or thirty minutes," Avery said. "The good Judge Teasley is already getting an earful, I'd guess. He'll want some charges on the table, or he's going to order you to turn Jule loose. And as soon as we file the charges, he's going to convene the grand jury and he'll have an indictment before his breakfast settles, and, Frank, he's a light eater."

Frank shifted uncomfortably in his chair. Avery was only half kidding. Kendall Teasley had occupied the judge's bench for the Superior Court of Overton County for more than twenty years. He was a sour, impatient man who well understood the power of political windstorms, and a black man accused of killing a white man was a windstorm of savage force. He would slather the case in axle grease to get it on the court calendar.

"How long can we stall on suspicion?" Frank asked.

"I doubt if you'll get through the day," Avery answered honestly. "It all depends on how much pressure Teasley gets." He paused again, leaned forward in his chair. "I think you should know that he's agitated with you right now."

"Why?" Frank said.

"He's big buddies with Ben Biggers, and Ben's on a Frank Rucker crusade."

"Yeah," Frank mumbled. "I know."

Avery stood and began pacing, his thumbs jammed into his belt. It was the same pose he used before a jury. Frank suspected he had learned it in an acting class.

"Well, you know how a smart-ass college boy can be, don't you, Frank?" Avery said after a few moments of pondering. "Fact is, you just haven't convinced me that you've got enough evidence to charge Jule with murder. Now, what I suggest is this: We bicker a couple of days, unless the judge puts us in a corner." He paused, let his grin wiggle across his face. "Pull a Frank Rucker trick and create a little diversion," he added. "By the way, just who the hell were those guys who showed up here a few days ago? I know they weren't feds. I checked it out."

Frank could feel a blush filling his face. He did not answer.

"You're a sly old fox, Frank," Avery said. "You don't have any idea how many asses got puckered over that little sideshow you staged. The moonshine business went dry overnight." He laughed. "But you got what you wanted, didn't you? You got them talking. Loose lips sink ships, right?"

Frank flicked away the comment with a wave of his hand. "I was in the army," he said. "Never learned much about sinking ships."

Avery slipped from the desk and strolled to the door, opened it, then closed it again. He turned back. The grin was almost a laugh. "You know what the rest of the word on the street is?" he said.

"What?" Frank asked.

"The word is that Frank Rucker is a nigger-lover."

Frank said nothing.

"It's a hell of a thing, isn't it, Frank? You took over for the sorriest asshole who ever pinned on a badge, and you've got people out there daydreaming about Logan being resurrected."

Avery clucked his tongue, sighed a laugh. "It sounds real shitty, doesn't it? Being called a nigger-lover." A softness, like a sad memory, clouded his eyes. He said, "Aw, hell, that's not even what it is; it's just what it's called." He opened the door and walked out, whistling.

●   ●   ●

Duck Heller did not want to be where he was, but he could not refuse Reba. She had assaulted him with puddles of tears and with anger, with wringing hands, with cries to Jesus, with agony that had the sound of a ghost in ghostly pain, and he had reluctantly agreed to drive her to Softwind, to the house of Conjure Woman.

"I ain't going in there," he had vowed to Reba. "Gon' drive you over there, but I ain't going in."

He stood beside the car in the purple-dark night, smoking his finger-rolled cigarettes, his body tense, his heart sputtering. Son Jesus sat in the back seat, tucked against the door, and gazed at the single lightbulb that glowed in a weak dot from the window of the house.

In the house, Reba sat before Conjure Woman, watching the great round face that was lifted, eyes closed. Conjure Woman seemed to be listening to something—to someone—from planets of air. She did not move. Only the slow pulsing of blood in her neck made her seem human. Without the blood pulse, she could have been a statue sculpted from black stone, polished with an oil rag.

Reba had come to beg.

"Why they take away Jule? Jule ain't done nothing."

"Why they keep on hurting my babies?"

"Who gon' help us out?"

"Where the food gon' come from?"

"Tell Jesus to talk to Reba. Tell him I done everything he say to do."

Conjure Woman had listened without speaking, listened until the sobbing became quiet and still. And then she had placed her hands on Reba's face, kneading it softly, and a peace had settled over Reba.

"Hush, now," Conjure Woman had whispered. "Hush, now." She had pulled her hands away from Reba's face and placed them in her lap, and she had closed her eyes and lifted her face.

And Reba sat and waited. Felt herself floating in time, as if time had become a liquid, a deep sea with an ink bottom and shards of light splintering across the surface, dancing dots of the sun encased in silver bubbles.

And then Conjure Woman's lips parted slightly and she began to blow gently across Reba's face, and the air was cool, like frost.

And from behind Conjure Woman, Reba saw Rody. Rody in his new blue suit. Full-fleshed. Smiling. She did not see his mouth move, but she heard his voice: "You gon' be all right. All right." And then Rody pivoted slowly, like a man in a slick dance step, and he walked off into the air. Reba tried to speak his name. Could not.

Conjure Woman's eyes opened. She dipped her face and gazed at Reba.

"Go bring me the boy," she commanded.

"My baby?" asked Reba.

"Go bring me the boy," Conjure Woman repeated.

Reba moved quickly from the chair and rushed to the door. "Son Jesus, come here," she called in a squeal. "Come on."

Duck stepped away from the car. He glanced at Son Jesus. "Your mama wants you, boy," he said, quaking.

Son Jesus did not speak. He opened the car door and slipped from the seat and crossed the yard and went into the house.

Inside, Reba caught him by the arm and tugged him toward Conjure Woman, then she stepped back.

"Don't be afraid, honey," Reba whispered.

"No m'am," Son Jesus said calmly.

Conjure Woman's eyes narrowed on Son Jesus' face. Looked into him. She stood slowly, reached to touch his face with her fingertips. Then she lifted her hands over his head, cupping it. A silky caul of light, like a bright pewter, seemed to glow from her palms. A short, startled cry flew from Reba.

"The sign be coming," Conjure Woman said in a low, rumbling voice.

Son Jesus did not move. He watched the burning in Conjure Woman's eyes. Saw a glaze fall over them. Saw her close them.

"What—what sign?" Reba asked.

"Sign when he know who he is," Conjure Woman whispered. "When he know what's over and what's waiting." She moved her hands slowly to his face, pushing the caul of light into him. "He see the white face, he know," she said. Her hands trembled. "My hand be on him."

And then Conjure Woman dropped her hands, and Son Jesus turned and walked past his mother and out of the house.

"There be a day when he be leaving. Let him go. He be back," Conjure Woman whispered.

"Leaving? Where to?" Reba asked fretfully.

"To what's waiting on him," Conjure Woman answered. She looked at Reba. "You come get me when Jule go to the court," she said.

"He going to court?" Reba asked fearfully.

"You come get me," Conjure Woman said again.

• • •

Frank glanced at his watch. It was ten minutes past six and he was already bed-tired, having just left Fuller Davis. An ache was in his chest, in his throat, his mouth. Telling Fuller that Harlan was Pegleg had been the hardest task he had yet faced as the sheriff of Overton County. He would see the old man's face in his dreams. The great sadness of the face. Damp eyes closing over a hurt that burrowed deep into his flesh and soul. Hurt so unbearable that it paralyzed him. To move would have caused him to shatter like a delicate crystal glass dropped on a rock. He had simply waved one hand—or the fingers of one hand—in a weak flipping motion that said to Frank: Leave me. And Frank had mumbled, "I'm sorry, Mr. Davis. I truly am."

And now, in the presence of Hack and Ada Winter, he would have to tell Evelyn about Harlan being Pegleg, and that would not be easy, either. But he would say nothing about Jed, not about Jed also being Pegleg. She could take it the wrong way if he started talking about his two-Pegleg theory. The news of Harlan would be enough. She would be shocked, maybe hysterical. Maybe she would wilt into his arms, seeking comfort, as she had done after the discovery of the skeletons in the sawdust piles. And he was willing to give comfort, but not in the presence of other people. Maybe he should tell them separately—tell Hack and Ada and then ask Evelyn to go for a drive with him. Back to her home. Tell her there were a couple of things he wanted to clear up. And when he got her there, he would tell her the truth. Wilting would be all right in her own home. Maybe he would suggest that she take a trip when everything was over and done with, get away for a week or two. And maybe he would offer to go along with her, or let her go along with him. Maybe it was time to drive up to New York City and see his old friend Jabbo Lewkowicz. Evelyn would look fine on Times Square in her jonquil-yellow dress.

Yes, she would.

He pulled his car to a stop in Hack Winter's yard, saw Tom under the shade of a pecan tree, turning the crank on an ice cream freezer. Remembered the ear-to-ear grin on Tom's face at Evelyn's house.

Better tell them all at once, he thought. Everybody but Tom. Let his mother explain it. He'd already had his share of Tom Winter's questions for one day. And there had been plenty. Still, not as many as Tom had surely asked his mother about Jule being taken away. And it had been awkward. He had had to wait at Reba's house for Ada Winter to return with Reba and Remona, and then he'd had to explain to Ada and Reba what he was doing. Not easy. Not with either of them. Ada fuming with anger. Reba wailing in despair. And Tom and Son Jesus: Tom outside the house, pacing and peeking through the window like a cat; Son Jesus gazing off toward the woods, standing as quietly as someone posing for a painting.

At least Ada had calmed down, Frank thought. She had called his office shortly after his meeting with Avery Marshall and had apologized for her outburst. "It just didn't seem right," she had said, "dragging Jule off to jail, but I know you got to keep him safe."

Now he would have to tell her that Judge Teasley was convening a grand jury on Thursday to consider the charge of murder against Jule. It was something that Avery Three could not stop. "Did my best," he had explained to Frank, "but it didn't work. Jule's going to be charged, and it'll stick, Frank. He's going to trial."

Ada Winter would not take the news of the grand jury calmly, he thought. The telephone lines would be blistering with her complaints.

He got out of his car and walked over to Tom. "Looks like it's cranking a little slow," he said.

"Just about done," Tom replied, pushing hard on the handle. "It's strawberry."

"Sounds good," Frank told him. "Where's your mama and daddy?"

"Mama's in the house with Mrs. Carnes. Daddy and Troy went over to put a new door on her house."

"That's nice," Frank said.

Tom stopped the cranking, shook his arm, puffed in exaggerated exhaustion. "They'll be back pretty soon. Troy just called. Said they was about finished."

"Well, I think I'll step inside and speak to your mama and Mrs. Carnes while I wait for your daddy."

Tom grinned. "Mama said I could have what comes off the dasher. That's the best ice cream in the churn."

"Sure is," Frank said. He started toward the house.

"Is Uncle Jule all right?" Tom asked.

"He's fine," Frank told him.

"I sure hope you find that shotgun," Tom said. "It's old. Oldest one I ever saw."

Frank turned back to Tom. "You saw it?"

"Yes sir," Tom said eagerly. "Yes sir. Uncle Jule had it one day. Said he was going squirrel hunting. It had black tape all over the stock."

"When was that?" Frank asked.

"A long time ago," Tom answered. "I was pretty little. Last year, maybe. Maybe longer'n that."

"You ever see Jule shoot it?"

Tom turned the handle once, squinted his eyes in thought. "Yes sir," he said. "Pretty sure I did. Don't remember where, but I'm pretty sure he shot it. Maybe at a squirrel or something. Son Jesus was with me. Maybe he'd know."

Frank studied Tom. What Tom had said sounded like a story. Likely was. But maybe he was telling the truth, and if so, Jule had lied about never firing the missing shotgun. And one lie could lead to another and another and another. "You better start cranking that freezer before it starts melting," he advised.

THIRTY

He had spent the day, the Wednesday after the death of Harlan Davis, in a zigzag drive through Crossover, in search of the men who best knew Jule Martin, yet Hugh had heard nothing that he did not expect to hear or could not have predicted. Had warned Frank that nothing would come of the questions, and he knew that Frank agreed with him. "I guess you're right," Frank had said, "but we got to ask, anyhow. Somebody's got to know something about that gun."

Duck Heller and Claude Capes and Grady Sorrells and Henry Hanover had all given him the same answer in the same intonation, with the same lowered-head hesitation: They knew about Jule's shotgun. All had seen it. Duck and Grady had even admitted going with him on Sunday to return it to his home. "Yes sir," Duck and Grady had said. "Seen him put it under the bed, then we went on back down to Reba's."

"Naw sir," had been their answer to his question about remembering any time that Jule might have vowed to get even with Harlan for what had happened to Remona.

And though they had answered his questions, they had volunteered nothing, and he did not blame them. They knew the odds. The odds were not in favor of Jule. No reason to get caught up in the squabble. Jule would understand. Come visiting day at the county jail, they would mumble their apologies, and Jule would mumble back his forgiveness. It was an old rite of manhood if you were colored.

The only thing that had made them look up, show shock, was when he told them that Harlan had been Pegleg. It was hard to tell, but after the exhibit of shock, Hugh believed he could see each of them smile. Not in their faces, but in their eyes.

It had been Frank's decision to tell them about Pegleg. Not about Jed Carnes, but about Harlan Davis.

"I'll be telling Ben Biggers about it this afternoon," Frank had said. "Might as well let them know. Maybe they'll get some sleep tonight."

It was late afternoon, and Hugh had one more stop to make. Not one that he wanted to make, either: Fuller Davis's house. The funeral for Harlan had been earlier in the day, a graveside service attended only by family members. A decision of kindness by Fuller. Harlan had not lived the kind of life to draw a crowd of mourners.

"Better go by and check on him," Frank had instructed. "He took it hard when I told him about Harlan being Pegleg."

It was not easy understanding people, Hugh thought. Fuller Davis and his late wife had always been two of the county's finest citizens. Fair in every way. Givers. And their three sons had been a blight on humanity, like a disease that crippled and left mangled bodies and coated everyone and everything it touched with fear.

Hugh turned his car onto Railroad Road, past Dodd's General Store. He saw J. D. Epps at the gas pump, pumping gas into his truck. J. D. lifted a hand in greeting, and Hugh waved back but did not stop.

Railroad Road followed the tracks into Overton, crossing over and back at sideroads leading to the farms of Crossover. As a boy, Hugh had once walked one of the rails for two miles before slipping off, but he would not have slipped if Barton Maxey had not made him laugh by cutting the fool. Crazy damn Barton Maxey. He was a doctor now, somewhere near Atlanta. He wouldn't let Barton Maxey give him an aspirin. Crazy damn fool.

He turned right onto Sweetwater Creek Road, glanced at his odometer. It was one of his private habits to check the distance between locations. Two and two-tenths miles later, he pulled to a stop in front of Fuller Davis's home. He saw Fuller working in a small flower garden at the side of his house, kneeling in a carpet of color, in the jubilant brightness of daisies and zinnias and marigolds and roses. Getting out of his car, Hugh walked over to Fuller.

"Mr. Davis," Hugh said quietly in greeting.

Fuller nodded and continued his work.

"Flowers look nice," Hugh said. "I remember seeing Mrs. Davis out here all the time when I was little."

"She liked daisies," Fuller replied softly. "Used to have them all over the yard, when she was able to get outside and work them. I never had the touch for keeping them growing like she did."

"My mama likes daisies too," Hugh said.

Fuller pushed himself up from the ground and dusted his hands. "I know your mama. She's a good lady."

"Yes sir," Hugh mumbled. He cleared his throat, looked away. Once, Fuller Davis's farm had been the finest in Overton County, the kind of farm that made other farmers slow down in their drive-bys and shake their head in admiration and say to their wives or children, "He's got him a showplace." In the past few years, the farm had aged, as Fuller had aged. Only the flower garden seemed bright and young.

Fuller turned his face to Hugh. A stubble of white beard covered his cheeks and chin and throat. His eyes were damp. He was very old, Hugh thought.

"I guess you come to tell me something," Fuller said.

"No sir," Hugh replied quickly. "I was just passing by and saw you in the garden. Just thought I'd stop and tell you I'm sorry about what you're going through, especially this morning."

"What Harlan done was wrong," Fuller said. "Ain't easy to bury a boy you raised and know he's in hell."

"No sir, I guess not," Hugh said.

"Sheriff find out anything else?"

"No sir," Hugh answered. "I guess you know he's got Jule Martin in jail. Grand jury's gon' meet tomorrow."

Fuller bobbed his head. "Don't know why. Jule wouldn't of done it. I knowed Jule and his people all my life. His daddy helped me out on the farm a long time. Best man I ever knew, white or colored."

"Well, sir, we're still checking on it. Talking to people."

"Wadn't Jule," Fuller said again.

"I hope you're right," Hugh told him. "I like him. He don't seem the sort to do anything like that."

"You tell the sheriff for me, tell him it wadn't Jule. Tell him I'll stand bail if they'll let him have it."

"Yes sir. I'll tell him."

Fuller leaned over and broke a single daisy and held it in his hand, gazing at it. "They's been enough killing," he whispered. "More'n enough."

• • •

It was Avery Marshall III's habit—as it had been the habit of his father and his grandfather—to stop each morning in the Cornerstone Café for coffee. His father had called it mixing. A good word, Avery had learned. Mixing meant belonging, and belonging was the very soul of the job that he had and the job that he wanted. He had never known of a United States senator who did not mix with some circle of men or did not belong, or at least give the appearance of belonging.

Some mornings it was not so bad, stopping at the Cornerstone Café. Cool mornings. Feel-good mornings. Thursday morning was cool, feel-good. He opened the door to the café, stepped inside, waved to Beatrice Haymore, who was working behind the counter.

"Coffee?" Beatrice asked.

"Usual," Avery told her.

"Bourbon on the side?" Beatrice kidded.

"Two fingers deep," Avery said.

Beatrice laughed her familiar laugh.

There were only four other people in the café, and Avery knew all of them—Champ Fergis, Tommy Longley, Bud Richardson, and Ansel Spearman. They were sitting together at a table in the center of the café, where they sat each morning for their breakfast of gravy and biscuits and coffee before retiring to the courthouse benches to waste the day.

"Look what the cat drug in," Ansel said, as he said every morning.

"How's it going?" Avery said pleasantly, as he said every morning.

"Fair to middling," Ansel replied, as he replied every morning.

"Grab a seat and take a load off," Tommy boomed, as he boomed every morning.

Avery pulled a chair from another table and sat. He knew by the sparkle in the eyes of the men that they were eager to speak to him. Or to tease him. He was the college boy, a fact they both admired and resented, and he had spent long hours mitigating their distrust by joining in their storytelling, or by being deliberately, and selectively, dumb.

The story that the Men of the Center Table—as Avery had named them—liked best was the one he had invented about Jacques Nightpisser, an aide to Napoleon. Avery had explained that it was Napoleon who had begun the practice of people using last names—which, in itself, had drawn suspicious looks. "It's true," Avery had vowed. "You boys know the Bible. Did Adam or Eve have a last name? Nobody did until

Napoleon came along. He had so many soldiers, he had to come up with a way of keeping up with them, so he gave them last names, and those names most often related to what they did. Blacksmiths were called Smith. Cooks were called Cook. Ansel's people would have fought with spears, or made them. That's where the name Spearman came from." Bud Richardson had tilted his head in disbelief and said, "So where'd this Nightpisser fellow come from?" And Avery had answered in his most pretentious voice, "He was a bedwetter. Not a bad fellow, but he had a weak bladder. Napoleon finally had him shot."

The story had earned howls of laughter, and Avery had been forced to retell it many times, as a parent retells the same story to a child. And, like a parent, each time he told it, he embellished it. None of the Men of the Center Table knew it, but in less than a year, they had learned more about Napoleon's campaigns than the history teachers of Overton High School knew.

"What's been going on, guys?" Avery asked lightly, as Beatrice placed his coffee in front of him.

"Nothing much," Bud said.

"Why you asking these old fools a question like that?" Beatrice said. "Lord, they couldn't find their butt with a road map and a Seeing Eye dog. Four old fools, that's all they are."

The men laughed. Beatrice swished away from the table.

"When you gon' bring that nigger to trial?" Ansel said.

It was the kind of question Avery hated. Hated the arrogance of it. Hated the slur. Yet it was the kind of question he had learned to tolerate in Overton. It was at the heart of Logan's Law. "You're never going to change that kind of attitude," his father had advised on his return from Harvard and the army. "Just let it slide over you. Only an ignorant man quarrels with ignorance."

"You mean Jule Martin?" Avery said pleasantly.

"I mean that *nigger*," Ansel answered. He laughed, looked around the table. The other men laughed also.

"Grand jury's going to meet this afternoon," Avery said. "I guess we'll find out something then. Sheriff's still doing some investigation."

"Wasting taxpayers' money," Bud sniffed, through a blue cloud of cigarette smoke. "I guarantee you, if Logan Doolittle was still the sheriff, that nigger'd already be toes-up."

Avery forced a smile. "Well, there's still a few questions to answer."

"What's this Ben Biggers was saying last night about Harlan being that fellow the niggers called Pegleg?" Tommy asked.

"What'd he say?" Avery asked.

"Said you and the sheriff come to see him yesterday with some horseshit story about Harlan being Pegleg."

"That's right," Avery replied.

"Well, shit, Avery, they ought to of pinned a medal on his chest before they lowered him in the ground," Tommy said in a flat, mean voice that he meant to be comical. "Seems to me he didn't kill no white people."

Avery turned to face Tommy. He could feel rage. He wanted to shout, "Does that matter, asshole? Does that really matter? Do you want somebody in your community who kills when he wants to?" He did not. He said, instead, "Well, Tommy, you got to remember that was the same man who broke in on Jed Carnes' widow. And she's white."

Tommy grinned an old-face, stupid grin. He glanced at Ansel, then toward Beatrice. He leaned in at the table, whispered, "Maybe he was just trying to get him a little piece on the side. That's a good-looking woman. Maybe she was teasing him."

Avery could feel the red coloring of anger in his face. He swallowed. Pushed a weak smile across his lips. "Maybe so."

"Come to think of it," Champ said, "maybe what Mason was saying makes some sense."

Ansel rubbed the tip of his chin. "Yeah. Could be."

Avery was curious. "What's that?"

Champ tilted his head to look at Avery. "Mason was saying that Harlan had told him and George that Alice said she was gon' kill him. Maybe she caught on that he had his eye on that Carnes woman."

Tommy coughed a laugh. "You rile a woman, by God, she's liable to do anything."

"When did Mason say this?" asked Avery.

"Yesterday," Champ answered. "We was on the bench when he come by with that oldest boy of his. Said he'd been by the funeral home to settle up with Pug. Old Mason was pretty tore up."

"Pissed off too," Ansel added. "He said the sheriff wadn't doing nothing but hiding that nigger. Way he was talking, him and George ain't gon' sit around with their thumbs up their butt waiting for the sheriff to do something. I guarantee you if I was a nigger, I'd stay clear of them two."

"How'd it come up?" Avery asked. "About Alice, I mean."

The men looked at one another, as if pondering an answer.

"I think maybe I asked him how Alice was doing," Ansel said.

"Yeah, seems like that was it," Tommy agreed.

"Mason said she wadn't saying much," Champ remembered. "Said she didn't seem too tore up about Harlan being dead. Never did come over to the funeral home, and I ain't sure she even went to the funeral."

Avery drank from his coffee, shook his head in the ancient ritual of men in cafés considering a perplexing problem. He knew not to push the question that filled his mouth.

"I guaran-damn-tee you one thing," Bud offered in a heavy voice. "She took some grief off Harlan. Won't surprise me none if she blowed him away."

"I wonder what made Harlan say such a thing to Mason and George?" Avery said.

"I'd guess they was drinking," Bud answered. "Them boys always been bad to drink, especially Harlan and Mason. I don't think I ever seen George when he was glass-eyed, but them other two could pour it down a funnel. You could smell it on Mason yesterday. Made me feel bad for his boy. He looked like he didn't want nothing to do with Mason."

Beatrice appeared at the table with the coffeepot, refilled cups. She said to Avery, "You sitting with a bunch of fools. You don't watch out, you gon' catch fool fever."

The men laughed good-naturedly.

Thank God for fools, Avery thought. Even those who needed road maps and Seeing Eye dogs to find their ass. Fools never knew when to keep quiet.

●   ●   ●

By eleven o'clock, Avery had scan-read every arrest record in Overton County for the past ten years. He was stunned at the number of times Harlan Davis had been arrested—fifteen, but never with more than a single night spent in jail. Each time, his father had bailed him out. Each time, the charges had been dropped or reduced to a fine. Among the arrests, two had been on complaints from Alice Davis for abusive behavior. Charges dropped, both reports read.

He replaced the files and went into his office and reread Frank's report on Harlan's death. Alice had stated that she left in midafternoon to visit her mother and, upon returning, discovered Harlan's body in the loft of the barn. Pug Holly had guessed the death to be between the hours of four and eight—closer to eight—and Jake Arlington had agreed. Unquestionably, Alice could have returned, shot her husband, waited before calling Fuller.

The only thing that Frank had against Jule was a possible motive— the issue of holding a gun on Harlan—but even that was lukewarm. Every white man in the county would have done the same thing as Jule if Harlan had threatened a member of his family. But the gun was missing, and that made it important. Jule had contended that someone had stolen it, and that was certainly a possibility. There was always petty theft among blacks, most of it items taken out of need or passion. Besides, he had talked to Jule, and like Frank, he had believed Jule's story. He could not say it openly, not as the district attorney, but he also did not want to see a man sentenced to the electric chair because it would be easy to convince twelve white men that finding Jule guilty would solve all their problems.

Alice Davis had more reason to kill her husband than anyone, Avery thought. It was in her history. But proving it would take time, and it would be a delicate, touchy issue. Time. He needed more time. He reached for the telephone on his desk, quickly dialed his father's number. His father answered.

"Hey, Pop," Avery Three said to Avery Two. "You busy these days?"

"I was thinking about washing the car tomorrow," Avery Two answered lazily. "What have you got in mind? I thought you had the grand jury this afternoon."

"I do. That's why I'm calling. I thought maybe you'd like to have a little fun, if you're up to it," Avery Three told him.

"Suits me," Avery Two said. "I assume you're talking something legal."

Avery Three laughed.

THIRTY-ONE

Kendall Teasley, an abnormally small man with a small, pinched face and a large gourd-shaped head, resembled an artist's rendering of an alien from Mars. He perched behind his large desk, mahogany with a clean, rich shine, and glared over his wire-rimmed glasses at the men sitting before him. It was, to the judge, a suspicious gathering—the sheriff, the district attorney, and the district attorney's father. He was not particularly fond of Frank Rucker, did not totally trust Avery Three, and had always been inexplicably intimidated by Avery Two.

"This had better be good," he said. "I'm not in the mood to be entertained by shenanigans, and I can tell you before you start that I've spent more than my fair share of time over the last forty-eight hours listening to bickering about this colored man you've been coddling over in the jail, Frank. You just heard the grand jury. They indicted him, and I plan to hear the case in two weeks, so if you're here to stall, you're going to lose that argument."

Frank sat quietly, remembering the grand jury hearing. It had taken fifteen minutes to indict Jule Martin, causing Avery Three to lean to him in the courtroom and whisper, "I think we just made the goddamn *Guinness Book of World Records*." Joe Harvey, the foreman of the jury, had said, "Let's get this over with. I got a shipment of cars coming in this afternoon." Joe Harvey owned the Ford dealership in Overton.

"Now tell me what this is all about," Kendall Teasley said.

Both Averys smiled. In unison. The same smile.

"Well, Judge, we just wanted to talk a little bit," Avery Three said in a pronounced drawl.

"What about?"

"First thing, I'd like to recommend that we keep Mr. Martin secured in the jail and not put him on the chain gang."

"What for?" the judge snapped.

"I believe, sir, you would agree that there's some pretty hot-tempered people spending a lot of time talking about this case," Avery Three answered. "It's my assumption that you wouldn't want to put Mr. Martin in harm's way prior to the trial. Out in the open, he'd be a pretty easy target."

The judge frowned, touched the rim of his glasses. He said, after a moment, "Keep him in jail. Don't matter to me."

"I'd ask you to sign an order on that matter," Avery Three told him. "Just to keep everything proper."

"Draw it up," the judge said.

"Yes sir."

"What else?" the judge asked.

Avery Two cleared his throat. He said in a pleasant voice, "I've talked it over with my son. We thought it would be best to tell you that I'm going to act as Mr. Martin's defense counsel."

The judge's head jerked up. He pulled his glasses from his face, squinted his small eyes. "You're going to do what?"

"Defend him," Avery Two said. "We just thought we'd run it by you to see if you have any objections."

"Objections? You're goddamn right I do," Kendall Teasley snapped. "What the hell's wrong with you, Avery?"

"Well, Kendall, I've always wanted to take on my boy in court," Avery Two said. He paused, glanced at his son, smiled again. "I think this is the time."

The judge slapped his hand on his desktop. "You are not going to make a mockery of justice in my courtroom," he roared.

The two Averys shifted in their chairs. In unison.

"That's not what we're trying to do, Your Honor," Avery Three said calmly. "We're trying to be up front with you. I discussed the case with my father earlier today, seeking his advice as the former district attorney, because the evidence we've got at the moment against Mr. Martin is a little weak, to say the least. He advised against bringing the charge." He paused, wiggled in his chair, leaned toward the judge, and added in a voice that sounded confidential, "But knowing the mood of the community, and your own regard in this matter, I decided against tendering that advice to you, or to the grand jury. This afternoon, my father called to inform me that he would offer his services to Mr. Martin." He paused again, spoke softly. "I must tell you, sir, it came as a

shock to me, but I believe there's no prohibition against retired prose-
cutors appearing for the defense."

"Denied!" The judge, struck the desktop again with his hand.

The two Averys looked at each other, frowned the same frown.

"Sir, we're not in court," Avery Three said.

Kendall Teasley rose from his seat, leaned over the desk, balancing
on the knuckles of his hands. "You're in *my* goddamn court, and I'm
telling you that you're trying my patience. Both of you. You want to
play games, play games. Far as I'm concerned, you can flip a coin to see
who does what. Now get out of here. The next time I want to see you
is in court." He whipped his head toward Frank. "And there's something
I want to say to you, Sheriff. I'm tired of all this bullshit bickering I
have to listen to. As far as I'm concerned, you've violated the dignity of
this office by going to the press about the evidence you have on Harlan
Davis being that Pegleg fellow. From now on, I'd damn well better know
about anything like that before I read about it in the county paper. You
understand me?"

"Yes sir," Frank mumbled. He stood. The two Averys stood.

The judge shook his head in disgust. His eyes were blazing. He said
in a low voice, "I want to know how the niggers of this county got all
of y'all eating out of their hands. It's going to be people like y'all that
tear this country down."

Both Averys smiled. In unison.

●　●　●

"We've been through this before, Tom," Ada said impatiently. "Just
give him some time. A few days. You got to remember, honey, Sonny's
been through a lot, with his daddy being buried, and what happened to
Remona, and Jule being arrested. Sometimes people just have to catch
their breath. I swear, you're like a horsefly sometimes. You just don't
know when to go light somewhere and let people catch their breath."

"Yes m'am," Tom muttered woefully. He leaned back in his chair
at the kitchen table and sighed dramatically.

"Don't start that with me, Tom," his mother warned. "Where's
Troy?"

"He's working on the tractor," Tom said.

"Well, you can help him, can't you?"

"He run me off. Said I was aggravating him."

"Then go find your daddy and see what he's doing."

"He'll make me shuck corn."

"That's not gon' hurt you," Ada said.

"What about that king snake in the corncrib?" Tom argued.

"That king snake's not gon' bother you."

"It bit Troy."

"Oh, good heavens, Tom—Troy was trying to pick it up."

"What if it's hungry? What if it couldn't find a rat, and it decided I looked like one?"

Ada turned to her son, bracing her hands on her hips. "Tom, you either get out from under my feet and find something to do, or I'm gon' make you sweep every floor in this house."

Tom pulled himself painfully from the chair and dragged across the floor to the door. It had been four days since the sheriff had appeared at Reba's house in search of Jule and Jule's shotgun, and he had not seen Son Jesus since that day, but his pleading had not worked with his mother. "Leave them alone," she had said repeatedly. "Anyhow, it's too wet to get out." And she was right about it being wet. For two of the four days, it had rained—sweeping afternoon summer storms that rolled across the land. Not like the storm they had had the day before Tom caught the sheriff at Evelyn Carnes' home, but still wet enough. He had spent the time reading a collection of Bobbsey Twins books that had been given to Miriam by one of their older cousins, named Brenda. Brenda had eyes so narrow they looked like one eye and Tom had once called her Cyclops, which earned him one of the few swattings ever administered by his mother. Tom hated the Bobbsey Twins. The Bobbsey Twins wouldn't have lasted five minutes with Huckleberry Finn—two minutes with Tom Sawyer.

Outside, the day was clear, the sun glittering off the still-damp leaves of the pecan trees and the chinaberry and the oaks, leaving them looking waxed. A clean smell drifted in the air, an earth-bath smell. Tom watched a robin dive to a rain puddle in the yard, saw the robin peck at the ground and draw out a worm. The bird sprang up on a flutter of wings and disappeared into a pecan tree. The day was too good for work. Below the house, in the pasture, the trees seemed to suck in a breeze from the fields like the drawing of bellows. It was two miles through the woods from his house to Son Jesus' house—a pine needle path that had been worn to a shine by the boys' feet. It was like a rabbit's path that curled among the trees, and Tom knew his scent was on it and Son Jesus' scent was on it.

Maybe I ought to go fishing, Tom thought. Maybe that's what Son Jesus was doing—fishing.

A sudden flutter of pity struck him. Son Jesus had seen his father buried—or the bones of his father. He had listened to the crying of his sister because a man had beaten her and had tried to make a baby with her. Tom thought of his own father, how sad it would be to see his father in a coffin and to see that coffin lowered into the ground for men to cover with dirt. He thought of Elly. What if Harlan Davis had beaten Elly and had forced Elly to go with him into the barn? His daddy would have killed Harlan Davis. Or Troy would have killed him. Maybe that was what Troy was thinking when he said that Harlan Davis got what he deserved. Maybe Troy was thinking about Elly, or Miriam.

Tom looked toward the barn.

Maybe I'll let Troy teach me how to drive his tractor, he thought.

● ● ●

To Troy, Tom was hopeless. He would either wreck the tractor or kill himself and anyone in his path. The tractor might as well have been an airplane or a tank.

"Great Goda'mighty, Tom," Troy exclaimed, dragging him from the seat of the John Deere. "This ain't no damn toy. You about to jerk its guts out."

"It shakes too much," Tom complained. "I can't hold on."

"A tractor's like a mule," Troy said. "It knows when it's got a fool trying to drive it." He cut the switch to the tractor and listened to the motor sputter dead. "Sounds like you blew a valve," he growled, "and I just got it running good."

"Don't sound no different to me," Tom observed seriously.

"Well, good God, you little poot, how would you know how it sounds? You ain't never paid the first bit of attention to it."

Tom shrugged.

"What's the matter with you, anyhow?" Troy asked. "Why don't you go help Sonny put up that fence?"

"We finished it," Tom answered.

Troy swiped the sleeve of his shirt over his face. "Well, maybe it fell down in the rain, the kind of work y'all must of done on it."

"I don't know," Tom mumbled. Then: "Troy, if Harlan Davis had done to Elly what he done to Remona, would you have killed him?"

Troy kicked his shoe against the tractor wheel. "I don't know," he said after a moment. "Maybe. I'd of wanted to. Look, why don't you go fishing, or something. I got to see if I can get this tractor going again."

"I don't like going fishing by myself," Tom told him.

"Go read a book, then."

"Don't feel like reading."

"Well, go to the house and find Mama. She'll put you to doing something. It's gon' dry out in a couple of days, and you gon' have your little butt back in the cotton field with a hoe."

"Yeah," Tom said weakly. He was suddenly tired. Driving a tractor, even for a few feet, was hard work. Work was the last thing he wanted to do. "I think I'm gon' find me some places to put my rabbit boxes this year."

"Don't you get down near that creek," Troy warned. "I ain't gon' drag you out of the water again."

"I won't," Tom promised.

"Go tell Mama where you're going," Troy ordered.

"All right."

● ● ◗

He had wandered farther from his home than he had promised his mother, but it was not like a runaway, and he was not near the creek. Still, he was wet from the leavings of the rain, and he found a path from the woods to the road leading to Evelyn Carnes' home. Maybe the sheriff's back, he thought. And he grinned. Maybe nobody else could see it, but he could. The sheriff was sweet on Evelyn Carnes. Wouldn't be if he had to live around her, Tom thought. Of all the things to be happy about, it was Evelyn Carnes returning to her own home. It was bad what had happened to her, and she was nice, but she talked enough for twenty people. And everywhere she walked, she left a trail of cologne that would have gagged hummingbirds or made them swear off sipping the juice of flowers for food. No wonder his daddy and Troy had taken the time to put up another front door and fix the hallway in her house. He had watched both of them roll their eyes behind Evelyn Carnes' back.

He paused at the turnoff to her house. No sheriff's car. Maybe the sheriff was busy.

A hawk floated high above him, and he watched its easy glide. The hawk flapped its wings once, caught another current of air, pointed a feathered finger toward the sun, tilted, circled lazily. Nothing would be better than flying, Tom thought. It was a dream he had had hundreds of times. Flying like a hawk. Flapping his arms. Closing his eyes against the wind. Sleeping on the air.

The hawk disappeared into the woods behind Evelyn Carnes' home, the same woods that led to the sawdust pile.

That's where he ought to put some rabbit boxes, Tom thought suddenly. He had seen rabbit droppings littering the woods around the sawdust piles. Big droppings. Canecutter probably. Canecutters would sell for fifty cents. He looked in the direction of his house. It was a long way off. Too long. If he caught canecutters, he would have to drag them two miles, maybe longer. Two or three canecutters could be as heavy as a deer.

Still, he would look. Maybe he would learn to drive Troy's tractor and check on his rabbit boxes from the seat of the John Deere.

It took only a few minutes to reach the logging road heading to the abandoned sawmill. The road grass had been smashed by trucks and cars that had removed the bones of dead men from the sawdust pile, and the walking was easy for Tom. He saw deer tracks in the soft top mud. Deep tracks. Shallow tracks. A family of deer, he guessed. Nothing could crawl up his chest in wonder as quickly as seeing a family of deer. He could not understand why anyone would kill a deer.

He walked the road in a languid fashion, a stroll, watching for the family of deer and the hawk. He saw nothing but the rain-wet gloss of tree leaves.

Near the canopied opening of the woods at the lip of the sawdust piles, Tom paused and let his imagination breathe. He was in a place of ghosts. Could feel them. Ghosts could pin themselves to trees like the cobwebs of spiders. Sticky strings of bones puffed by the wind. Almost invisible.

He inhaled slowly, bravely, like the heroes of books going into battle. He would not run. No matter if the ghosts whirled up off the trees and threw a cobweb net over him. He would stand his ground. Would fight them with his bare hands, wrapping their glue into his fist. And he would listen for their shrieks of madness. Ghost voices were like night bugs.

He moved forward slowly in the road, his hands waving before him, like an air swimmer. And then, at the edge of the woods, he stopped. He could see the top of a head at the sawdust piles. He jumped into the woods, behind a sourwood tree and peeked around the trunk. The head came up. It was Son Jesus.

What's he doing here? Tom wondered.

He saw Son Jesus stand and brush sawdust from his hands. Son Jesus looked around slowly, then started walking toward the road, toward Tom.

Probably looking for his daddy's missing foot bone, Tom thought. Maybe thinks his whole daddy couldn't be in heaven without his foot bone. Even if he found it, it wouldn't do much good. You couldn't put a foot bone in a coffin that was already covered with dirt.

Tom squatted. A giggle rippled through him. Son Jesus would jump out of his pants if he started moaning. The giggle left him. He couldn't do that. They were at the sawdust pile where Son Jesus' daddy's bones had been uncovered. If there were ghosts around, he would be one of them.

Tom stepped out from behind the tree, whistling.

Son Jesus stopped abruptly. Froze.

"Hey, Son Jesus, what you doing over here?" Tom called, walking toward him.

Son Jesus glanced back over his shoulder at the sawdust pile. He did not answer.

"I been looking for places to put out rabbit boxes," Tom said. "Lots of rabbit droppings all over around here. Big ones. Canecutters, probably."

Son Jesus ducked his head and slipped his hands inside his pockets. For a moment, Tom thought he looked like Uncle Jule. It was the way Uncle Jule had stood talking to the sheriff. Head down, rolling the side of his shoe in the dirt.

"Why you here?" Tom asked again. "I thought you was scared of this place."

Son Jesus wagged his head. "Uh-huh."

"Then why you over here? You looking for your daddy's foot bone? Your mama told me at the funeral that you wanted your whole daddy buried."

Son Jesus looked toward the woods. There was a vacant, almost numb look on his face. No smile, and Son Jesus was always smiling. Always. His head dipped slowly in a nod.

"What I guessed," Tom said, with a comforting sigh. "Want me to help you dig around for it? I ain't doing nothing else."

Son Jesus shook his head. He turned toward the logging road.

"I expect something drug it off, but shoot, Son Jesus, your daddy don't need that bone," Tom said sympathetically. "He's a spirit. Spirits don't need bones. They all put back together when they get to heaven, and you don't need bones to walk on clouds. That's in the Bible. Anyhow, all bones look alike. Them bones y'all buried wadn't your whole daddy, Son Jesus. That was just his skeleton. Your daddy was made out of flesh. That's why all bones look alike. You got to put flesh on bones to make a person who he is. That's why you ain't got to be afraid of bones."

"Uh-huh," Son Jesus said.

"Why didn't you come by and get me?" Tom asked. "I'd of helped you look."

Son Jesus started walking slowly past Tom.

"Where you going?" Tom said.

"Got to go on home," Son Jesus answered.

"What's the matter with you?" Tom demanded. "You acting crazy."

Son Jesus stopped but did not turn back to him. He said in a soft voice, "My mama say I got to quit spending so much time with you. She say we growing up, and it ain't right for whites and colored to be together all the time."

Tom was stunned. "Why'd she say that?"

"She just say it."

"Well, what about next week? We gon' be hoeing cotton together."

Son Jesus shook his head. "We gon' start working for Mr. Fuller."

"Mr. Davis?" Tom said in shock.

Son Jesus did not reply.

"That don't make no sense," Tom said.

"Mama say Mr. Fuller ain't like Mr. Harlan."

"You ain't gon' be working all the time," Tom argued. "Maybe we can go fishing on the weekend."

"Uh-huh," Son Jesus mumbled.

"I'll get Mama or Elly to bring me over, or you can just walk over to my house through the woods," Tom said. "Shoot, I can meet you halfway."

"I got to go," Son Jesus whispered.

"Well, go on," Tom said bitterly. "See if I care."

Son Jesus started walking away.

"I don't care one bit," Tom said.

Son Jesus stopped walking. Paused. Started walking again.

"I don't," Tom said. His voice was small, weak.

• • •

He could not sleep. He lay in his bed and stared out the window at the dark silk of the night, moon-lit, star-misty. He rested his hand on his chest, as though feeling the scar of a wound. And there could have been a wound. Something had been taken out of him. His mother had tried to explain it. "It's just the way things are, Tom," his mother had said. "You're getting older. Things change. You'll be all right. You've got lots of friends. Why, I saw Rachel Jarrett this afternoon with her mama. She's cute as a button. Turned red as a beet when I mentioned your name. Seems to me you might have a little girlfriend when you get back to school."

He had tried the argument of pity with his mother. "What's Son Jesus gon' do? You just gon' let him go to work with somebody that don't know him, somebody that don't care nothing about him?"

"Sonny'll be all right," his mother had said quietly. "He'll be working with Mr. Davis. Mr. Davis is a fine man."

He knew that his objections had stung her in some way. Could see it in her eyes. "But, Mama, me'n Son Jesus have been together since we was babies. It's the way it's supposed to be. Conjure Woman said so."

"Sometimes what people say and what happens are two different things," his mother had said in a melancholy voice.

Later, at night, Tom had listened through the wall of his room as his mother talked to Elly. "He looked like his heart would break when I talked to him about Sonny working for Mr. Davis. Sonny's been his little friend since they were babies."

"Mama," Elly had said softly, "they're growing up. They can't be babies all their lives."

His mother had sniffed back tears. She had said, "I stopped by Reba's house yesterday. She wanted to know where Mister Tom was.

Mister. She called him *Mister* Tom. Made me want to cry, hearing her say that. I guess it's come to that."

"Mama, that's Reba's doing, not yours," Elly had replied.

"I can't help it," his mother had blurted in answer. "It *feels* like it's my doing."

It was Fuller Davis's doing, Tom thought. He was the one who had talked Reba and Remona and Son Jesus into working for him. His mother had explained that Fuller Davis was helping Reba by giving them work. "He feels bad about what happened to Remona, and to Sonny's daddy, and to Jule," his mother had said. "He's just trying to make up for it."

"Why can't I see Son Jesus when we ain't working?" Tom had asked.

His mother had not spoken for a long time. Then she said, "Well, we'll see. We'll see."

Tom moved his hand. The aching in his chest was too tender to touch.

THIRTY-TWO

Every seat in the courtroom had been claimed by eight-forty, ten minutes after Neal Jenkins, the bailiff, unlocked the doors simply to unclog the courthouse corridors. The whites gathered downstairs, the blacks upstairs in the balcony, the same system of segregation used at the Overton Theater. There the comparison ended. No movie in the history of Overton had ever attracted a crowd as large as the crowd attending the trial of Jule Martin, not even *Gone With the Wind*. The doors Neal Jenkins finally closed were closed on a two-abreast line that streamed down the corridor and spilled outside, covering the courthouse lawn.

"Goda'mighty," Ansel Spearman drawled from the window of the Cornerstone Café. "What they expecting to happen over there? A lynching?"

Bud Richardson stood beside Ansel, pushed up on the toes of his feet, craning his neck as though he were lodged in the crowd. "I'll be glad when it's over with. All I been hearing about for two weeks."

Ansel snorted. "All you been talking about, you mean. Goda'mighty, Bud, you worse than some old woman."

"Well, listen to the pot calling the kettle black," Bud grumbled. He added, "Talking of pots, I wish I'd of boiled me some peanuts this morning," he said. "I could of made me a small fortune today."

"Aw, shit, Bud, you'd have to work," Ansel said.

"That's a point," Bud admitted.

"Still can't figure why Avery Two's going against his boy," Ansel said, shaking his head.

"I'll give you two to one Avery Three had that all set up," Bud suggested. "Shoot, Avery Two ain't gon' do nothing but sit there. They'll have this thing wrapped up before high noon."

"Well, good God, Bud, they ain't much to it, you ask me," Ansel declared. "It's all cut and dried."

*   *   *

For the first thirty minutes of the trial of Jule Martin, Ansel Spearman was as prophetic as Moses. In the first thirty minutes, the case was read and the jury selected. Neither Avery Three nor Avery Two entered a single objection to the first twelve men called. Judge Kendall Teasley said nothing about the selections. He glared over his glasses at both Averys, but he said nothing. He would have challenged at least eight of the jurors, especially if he had been Avery Two. Among the jurors selected were five members of the Ku Klux Klan. Five that he knew. Probably more. Avery Two had either lost his fighting spirit in a courtroom or had turned dumb as a stick. Or he had a trick up his sleeve. Likely a trick. According to the list of witnesses, Avery Two planned to call only one name: Jule Martin.

The judge adjusted himself in the elevated chair behind the bench, balanced the tips of his toes on the riser that kept his feet from dangling, leaned his elbows on the flat surface of the desk, and let his eyes rove over the audience. He had learned through the years that, more than defendants and witnesses and bickering lawyers, the most interesting cast of characters at any trial were the onlookers. The onlookers could be as spellbound as children hearing a ghost story or like sharks with blood in their mouth.

He saw Fuller Davis sitting between his sons, Mason and George. It was interesting to him, because of his own diminutive size, that Mason and George were small, wiry men, unlike Harlan. Harlan must have seemed a giant to them, probably the reason they followed after him, did what he ordered them to do. They both had dark, suspicious faces. Especially Mason. Lips curled down at the corners in a sneer, a dare in his eyes. George simply looked dumb, but somewhere in his eyes there was a gentleness—he was like someone trapped in the wrong body. Fuller seemed subdued, Mason irritated. Trouble, the judge suspected. He looked, but he did not see Alice Davis.

He moved his eyes to the right of the center aisle of the courtroom, saw Evelyn Carnes. Dressed in yellow, with a matching yellow hat. She looked like a goddamn canary, but Lord, she looked better than she had looked when Jed was alive. Rumor had it that she was seeing Frank Rucker. If so, he was a lucky son of a bitch.

Ada Winter sat on the row in front of Evelyn. A shiver clawed at the judge's neck. Behind her back, people called her Eleanor Roosevelt, and she deserved it. Goddamn meddler, siding with the niggers, stirring up trouble. Hack was seated beside her, and beside Hack were his two boys, one bull-strong, the other a pissant troublemaker who would con his way through life on a smile and a line of bullshit a mile long. Nothing wrong with Hack, he reasoned, but damned if he didn't have his hands full.

The judge lifted his head and studied the back of the room. More trouble. A group of men who he knew had been friends of Harlan's were sitting in the back row. He'd talked to the sheriff about them, hoped the sheriff had enough men to handle them, if they needed handling. He touched his gavel. His gavel was like a weapon to him.

He glanced to the balcony. A tapestry of black faces with white eye-dots were staring down at him. All there to watch the show, huddled shoulder-close, thinking they were demonstrating bravery by their presence. Probably the work of Ada Winter, getting them there. Whoever or whatever had caused it, they were there. Reeder Higginbottom, the undertaker, and Harper King, the doctor, and Dooley Witcher, the preacher, and a half-dozen more men who carried weight among the blacks. A young woman sat close to Reeder. Reba Martin's girl, probably, the one who worked for Reeder. And there was a boy there, sunk back in his seat. Reba's boy, the one they called Son Jesus. He'd laughed when he read the name in the case records. Just like the colored. They'd do anything to be different.

He hunched forward, let his eyes gaze into the balcony. Wanted the blacks to know he was aware of them.

And then he saw her. Sitting in the exact center. Huge. Dressed in white. Her white turban perched like a crown on her head. Conjure Woman. Her eyes were riveted on him. A clammy, heavy sensation seemed to crowd him. He reached for the glass of water on the desk, drank from it. What's she doing here? he wondered. He looked down at the papers in front of him.

"We'll hear opening statements," the judge said. He nodded toward Avery Three.

Avery Three unfolded himself from his chair. He strolled leisurely in front of Jule, glanced down at him, smiled. Jule's face was twisted in agony. Perspiration rolled from his temples.

"Your Honor, members of the jury," Avery Three said casually, "there's not really much to say about this. Harlan Davis of the Crossover community is dead, killed by a shotgun blast in the loft of his own barn. Everybody here has heard the details—the when and the how and all of that—so I see no reason to rehash what everybody already knows.

"It is the state's contention that Harlan Davis was killed by one Jule Martin, represented here as the defendant." He motioned toward Jule, then continued. "Mr. Martin has entered a plea of not guilty on the advice of his able counsel, and I will tell you the state expected as much. There's nothing unusual about that. In fact, just about everybody does it. If he had confessed to the murder, if he had pleaded guilty, there wouldn't be much need for us to do anything but turn that confession over to the jury and sit back and let the jury do its duty.

"But to tell you the truth, it's about that simple, anyway."

Avery Three turned to face his father. He nodded respectfully. His father returned the nod.

"You need only to know three things," Avery Three said. He raised the index finger of his right hand. "One, you need to know that Harlan Davis is dead." He raised a second finger. "Two, you need to know that on the day of his death, Jule Martin threatened the deceased with a shotgun—a fact that will be repeated several times today by the testimony of subpoenaed witnesses." He raised a third finger. "And three, you need to know that the gun Mr. Martin used to threaten the deceased, and the gun we believe was used to commit murder on the deceased, is strangely missing. Further, we have a shotgun shell found the morning following Mr. Davis's death in a field behind the barn. We also believe that was the shell used in the act of murder."

He folded his fingers down. "One, two, three," he said. "A, B, C. It's that simple." He did a slow pivot to face the jury, smiled. "It's that simple," he said again. He did a slight bow toward the judge, then to his father, and returned to his seat.

"That's it?" Kendall Teasley asked.

"That's it, Your Honor," Avery Three answered.

The judge fingered some papers in front of him. A deep-pink coloring of temper splotched his face. He looked toward Avery Two. "Counselor," he said.

Avery Two stood. He touched Jule on the shoulder, stepped from behind the defendant's table. He cleared his throat, looked at the jury, smiled.

"If I might make a personal observation, Your Honor," Avery Two began, "I'd like to compliment the district attorney on his mastery of the alphabet. His mother and I are understandably proud of all his scholarly achievements."

A giggle swam throughout the courtroom. Kendall Teasley's eyes shot up, squinted at the audience. The giggling subsided.

"However, I am a bit dismayed, as his parent and as a member of the Georgia bar, that he chooses to address this distinguished court with an attitude that borders on irresponsibility as well as disrespect."

Avery Three smiled.

"It is, I suspect, the result of prolonged exposure to Harvard University, which, as we all know, promotes the spirit of superiority," Avery Two added in a triumphant voice. "Personally, I would have preferred the University of Georgia for him, but his mother—"

"Counselor," the judge warned, "we are not here to discuss family matters. As you well know, I have not been in favor of this arrangement, so let's skip the sermons and get on with the case."

Avery Three dipped a bow toward Kendall Teasley.

"Your Honor, gentlemen of the jury," Avery Two said in a kind voice, "I am here today to represent a man accused of murder, but the case you are about to hear is not as simple as the district attorney would suggest. Honesty compels me to acknowledge that another, very significant issue is inherent in this proceeding: a white man was killed and a colored man is accused of killing him. My esteemed opponent, your district attorney, seems to believe this case is alphabet simple. I suggest to you he may well have used any number of clichés. He might have said this case, to the state, is as simple to understand as the difference between night and day, or hot and cold, or right and wrong." He paused. "Or black and white."

From the audience, Mason Davis snorted disgust.

Avery Two glanced toward him, glared at him with contempt.

"But I am not here to argue this case as black and white," Avery

Two said softly. "I am here to argue the facts, and the facts do not justify this trial's even being conducted. The district attorney is plowing a furrow of nerve and verb. He has the nerve to tell you this proceeding has a foregone conclusion, but he has twice used the verb 'believe.' There's a world of difference between *believing* and *knowing*. And knowing is what is necessary in any trial that holds a man's life in the balance.

"What we have is a murder. What we do not have is a weapon. We do not have a witness. We have an alleged argument between the deceased and the defendant. The state will try to persuade you that that alleged argument was motive. The defense will tell you that no such argument existed. The incident was merely the action of a man attempting to protect his family from harm, an action that any worthy man in this courtroom would have taken under the same circumstance."

Avery Two ranged close to the jury.

"Regrettably," he said, "the defense will find it necessary to examine the character of the deceased, and in that regard, I will offer my apology to his family at the outset. Still, it should come as no surprise to anyone. Harlan Davis was, simply put, an evil man."

Mason shot up from his seat. "You got no right to say that," he boomed.

Kendall Teasley's gavel cracked on his desktop. "Sit down, Mr. Davis," he ordered in a hiss.

Mason sat slowly, his eyes fixed on Avery Two.

"I will warn this court that I will not permit such outbursts," the judge growled. "The next such demonstration will earn a fine that'd choke a hungry horse, and if that's not enough, I will gladly add some bad jail time to it. Do I make myself clear?"

No one spoke.

"Good," the judge said. "Now, Counselor, are you about finished?"

"One more statement, Your Honor," Avery Two said.

"Get on with it," the judge instructed impatiently.

"It is the absolute rule of law in a civilized society that innocence or guilt may not be decided by hearsay or gossip," Avery Two said calmly. "It is not enough to say a man is guilty because he cannot *prove his innocence*. We must say a man is innocent unless we can *prove him guilty*. None of us would want less than that on our own behalf, and none of us should expect less for any other man, regardless of his culture, or his color, or what he believes or doesn't believe."

Avery Two scanned the jurors. "If you are here for the sole purpose of imposing a burden on Jule Martin, then you must have the decency to do it on a *burden of proof*, not because it may be the popular, or the historic, thing to do." He paused, fixed his eyes on a juror named Coleman Hannah, a man he knew to be a high-ranking member of the Klan, a farmer who had quit farming to work in the Overton textile mill. "Things are not like they used to be, no matter how much we want to pull in the reins," he said quietly. "The world's on top of us. We can't just tuck ourselves away here in Overton County, no matter how much we like being here. We can't just shut the door and say, 'We like it just like it is, just like it's always been.' We can't do that because it's not true. We just came out of a war that changed all of that forever. We won that war because being free meant too much to us. Now we've got to start acting like the men we're supposed to be, and that means being fair." He turned and walked back to the defense table.

The judge turned to Avery Three. "Counselor, if the lecture's over, call your first witness."

● ● ●

It did not take long for Kendall Teasley to understand why Avery Two had submitted only one name on his list of defense witnesses: the power of cross-examination. It was probably a shrewd move, the judge thought. Anyone who had been in a courtroom long enough learned that it was often easier to baffle a witness than to coach one.

The first witness Avery Three called was Frank Rucker.

The questioning lasted twenty minutes. The questions and the answers were rehash. His finding of Harlan Davis's body, his interview with Alice Davis, revealing the argument between Harlan and Jule, the discovery of a shotgun shell behind the barn the following morning, his interrogation of Jule, and Jule's failure to produce the shotgun he had used to remove Harlan from Reba's home.

And though everyone in the courtroom had heard the story many times, in many versions, with many exaggerations, they sat mesmerized by Frank Rucker's voice, which was surprisingly low and soft.

A blush, like the rose coloring of rouge, caked Evelyn Carnes' face. She leaned forward in her seat. She did not seem to be breathing.

"Your witness," Avery Three said to Avery Two in a cheerful voice.

Avery Two shifted in his seat at the defendant's table. He did not stand. "Mr. Rucker," he said, "you had an occasion to arrest Harlan Davis recently, did you not?"

"Objection, Your Honor," Avery Three said.

"On what grounds?" the judge asked.

"Relevancy," Avery Three replied. "Mr. Davis's arrest record is not on trial here."

"I am not submitting his record for review," Avery Two said. "I am inquiring about one occasion."

The judge pinched his lips, squinted at Avery Two. He knew exactly what the questions would be. "I'll allow it," he said after a moment.

"Mr. Rucker, would you answer?" Avery Two said.

"Yes sir," Frank said. "I did arrest him."

"On what charge?"

"Battery."

"Battery on who?"

"One Remona Martin."

"Is she related to Jule Martin, the defendant in this case?"

"Yes sir. She's his niece."

"Is this the same Remona Martin who had accused Harlan Davis of rape?"

"Objection," Avery Three said again, lifting his hand like a schoolboy answering a question. "There's been no case filed related to such an issue."

"Sustained," the judge said. He looked at Avery Two. "Stick to this trial," he advised.

"Of course, Your Honor," Avery Two said pleasantly. "Let me phrase it this way: In the aftermath of your arrest of Harlan Davis, did you have occasion to initiate an investigation—without charges being filed, of course—into an alleged accusation by the defendant's niece that Harlan Davis had forced himself on her for sexual purposes?"

"Objection," Avery Three said casually.

"Sustained," Kendall Teasley snapped. He glared at Avery Two. "Counselor, I've asked you to stay on course here. Now it's a warning."

"Sorry, Your Honor," Avery Two said. "We'll let that one drop for the moment." He picked up a pencil on his desk, played with it between his fingers. "One other question, Sheriff. Is there any real reason to assume the shotgun shell you reported finding in the field behind Harlan

Davis's barn is the shell used to assault Mr. Davis, or are you going on gut feeling as much as scientific evidence?"

Frank blushed. It was all gut feeling.

"I have no evidence, since we've been unable to find the shotgun that fired it," he said.

"Ummm," Avery Two mused. "Have you checked it against any other shotguns, say from Harlan Davis's own gun collection?"

Frank felt trapped. "No sir, we haven't," he said in a whisper.

"I find that a little odd, seeing as how the fields and woods around Mr. Davis's home must be littered with shotgun shells from hunting," Avery Two suggested.

Frank did not answer. It was a damn good point. He had asked Avery Three about the other guns. Avery Three had shrugged off the question. "Not enough time," Avery Three had said. "Don't worry. We'll handle it."

"Anything else?" the judge asked.

"Not at the moment," Avery Three said.

"Next witness," the judge ordered.

"I call Williard Heller, known as Duck Heller," Avery Three said.

And there began the parade of witnesses that the citizens of Overton County had crowded into the courtroom to hear.

Duck Heller.

Grady Sorrells.

Reba Martin.

Of each, Avery Three asked the same questions.

Did you know the deceased, Harlan Davis?

Do you know the defendant, Jule Martin?

Were you present during an alleged encounter between Harlan Davis and Jule Martin on the Sunday that Harlan Davis was killed?

Did you see Jule Martin with a shotgun aimed at Harlan Davis?

Did you hear Jule Martin threaten to shoot Harlan Davis?

Do you know what happened to that shotgun?

At what hour did you last see Jule Martin on that Sunday?

The questions were asked in a breezy, casual manner by Avery Three. Chatty. Friendly. Patient. His broad grin beamed in the courtroom.

"It's real easy," Avery Three emphasized to the witnesses. "Just answer yes or no, or tell to the best of your knowledge what I ask about. There's no tricks at all in these questions."

The answers were mumbled, especially by Duck and Grady.

Yes sir, they knew Harlan Davis.

Yes sir, they knew Jule Martin.

Yes sir, they were present during the encounter between Harlan and Jule.

Yes sir, they had heard Jule say he would shoot Harlan Davis. "If he had to," Duck added.

No sir, they had no idea what happened to the shotgun. Duck and Grady both volunteered that they had gone with Jule to his home, had seen him put the gun under his bed that afternoon, soon after Harlan Davis had left Reba's home.

The last time Duck and Grady saw Jule was around seven o'clock, when they left Reba's home. The last time Reba saw Jule was around seven-thirty, when he left for his own home.

Avery Two did not cross-examine Duck and Grady. "No questions at this time," he said. He sat, relaxed, leaning back in his chair, his legs stretched out under the table, his feet crossed at the ankles. He appeared to be more interested in his son's performance as the district attorney than in the case.

At the offer to cross-examine Reba, he shot to his feet.

"You had this house full of company," he said. "Was there any special occasion?"

"No sir," Reba said. "Just Sunday dinner."

"What'd you talk about?"

Reba glanced quizzically at Avery Three. He nodded calmly.

"Well, sir, I don't remember exactly what it was," Reba said. "Womenfolks was in the kitchen. I guess we was talking about what we was cooking."

"What about the men?"

"They was in the living room."

"You remember them talking about Pegleg?"

Reba frowned. "Didn't hear them, but Jule said they was. Later on, he said it."

"Why'd Harlan Davis show up at your place?"

"Said he was wanting somebody to come up to his place and cook for Miss Alice."

"Were you supposed to be up there? Is that why he came for you?"

Reba wagged her head. "No sir," she said in a strong voice. "Wadn't supposed to be working. It was Sunday. I go to church on Sunday."

"Had Mr. Davis been drinking?" Avery Two asked.

"Yes sir."

"You could tell that?"

"Yes sir. Could smell it."

"Was he acting funny?"

Avery Three raised his hand again. "Objection," he said. "What's that supposed to mean? Was he being comical?"

"I'll rephrase," Avery Two said. He turned back to Reba, moved closer to her. "Was Harlan Davis behaving in a threatening manner? Did he use foul language?"

"Yes sir," Reba answered. Her whole body nodded.

"Did he threaten anybody in particular?"

"He tell Duck and Grady to shut up and set down. He tell Jule he gon' kick him," Reba answered.

"Anything else?"

Tears welled in Reba's eyes, flashed in the light of the courtroom. "He tell Remona he gon' be back for her."

"Remona? Is that your younger daughter?"

"Yes sir."

"Is that the same Remona who was struck by Mr. Davis, resulting in his arrest?"

"Objection," Avery Three said. "Not relevant."

Avery Two whirled to face his son. "Of course it's relevant. And it's on the record. It goes to the heart of character, which directly addresses the question of threat versus the question of protection."

"Overruled," Kendall Teasley said sharply.

Avery Two turned back to Reba. He said, in a kind voice, "We all know the answer anyway. I just wonder: Had you ever seen Harlan Davis behave that way before?"

"Yes sir," Reba said strongly. She was fighting tears. "He bad to show up when he been drinking, saying what he gon' do to us, we don't do what he wants."

"Were you afraid of him?"

Reba nodded. She dabbed at her eyes with the handkerchief she held clenched in her hand.

"You know that the sheriff has proof that Harlan Davis was the man they called Pegleg, the same man who killed your husband, don't you?" Avery Two asked softly.

Reba nodded again.

"You're not saying these things to get even with Harlan Davis, are you?"

"No sir," Reba answered. She looked up into the balcony, saw Conjure Woman. Conjure Woman was gazing regally at her. Reba could feel a power growing in her chest. "No sir," she repeated.

"You were there," Avery Two said. "You heard what was said. Did Jule ever say he was going to kill Harlan Davis?"

"No sir."

"What did he say?"

"He say he gon' shoot Mr. Harlan, if he have to. Say he don't want to, but if he have to, he would."

"In other words, he was protecting you and your family?"

"Yes sir," Reba answered in a strong voice.

"Why did Jule take his shotgun home right after that?" Avery Two asked.

"I made him do it. Don't like no guns in my house."

"I see. And Jule did as you asked? He took the gun to his house?"

"Yes sir. Duck and Grady went with him."

"Were they gone long?"

"No sir. Just a little while. They drive up there and come right back."

"And then you had dinner and you sat around the rest of the afternoon, visiting. Is that right?"

"Yes sir. The menfolk was going to go to the church for a meeting, but they stayed home because of what happened."

"Did you talk about what had happened?"

"No sir. I wouldn't have none of that. It was over and done with."

"Was everybody there?"

"Everybody but Remona and Cecily and Son Jesus."

"Where were they?"

"Cecily and Remona gone over to Overton, to where Cecily live. Son Jesus gone off fishing. Duck give him a new cane pole he'd cut."

"He went fishing?" Avery Two said. "By himself?"

"Yes sir."

"Didn't that bother you a little bit, that he went off fishing right after this Pegleg fellow had shown up again only a few miles away and tried to kill somebody?"

"No sir." Reba's voice was firm. It was as though she had been expecting the question.

"Why not?" Avery Two asked pleasantly.

"Ain't nothing bad gon' happen to Son Jesus."

"What makes you so sure?"

"He special. Jesus look after him," Reba said.

There was a snicker in the courtroom, then silence. Kendall Teasley turned his face to Avery Three, ready for the objection. Avery Three said nothing.

"What does that mean: he's special?" Avery Two asked.

"Just a minute," Kendall Teasley said. He cleared his throat, drummed his fingers across his desk. He peered at Avery Three. "Counselor, am I going to have to start an auction here to sell an objection? Maybe I'm wrong, but it seems to me we're as far from relevancy as you get without a compass or a lifeline."

Avery Three grinned. He shifted in his chair, studied his father for a moment. He could see a smile sealed behind his father's lips. "Well, Your Honor," he said, "I can't disagree, but honestly, this is interesting. Would you tolerate one or two more questions?"

The judge sat back in disgust. He flicked his fingers in the air, giving permission.

"Let me ask again," Avery Two said to Reba. "Why is Son Jesus special?"

"Conjure Woman say so," Reba answered proudly.

No one laughed, as the judge expected. No one whispered. The courtroom was empty-silent. He looked up at Conjure Woman. Her eyes were aimed toward him. He could feel his heart racing.

"Is that right?" Avery Two said easily, after a moment.

"Yes sir. Day he was borned. She come to my house, say he was special."

Avery Two paced for a moment, nodding. Then he said, "I guess I'm a little dense, Reba, but special can mean a lot of things. Do you think she meant he was like—well, one of the prophets out of the Bible, or something like that?"

"Yes sir."

Avery Two stopped pacing. He did a full body turn, looked up in the balcony, gazed at Conjure Woman. She had not moved her eyes from the judge.

"Well, that's a high compliment," Avery Two said. "A high compliment. I hope she's right. This world needs special people." He turned back to Reba. "Did he catch anything when he went fishing?"

A small smile eased into Reba's face. "Yes sir. Caught him some catfish. We cooked them for supper."

"Sounds like you had a good day, except for a few minutes there," Avery Two suggested.

The smile on Reba's face grew. "Yes sir," she said.

"No more questions," Avery Two said. He started back to his desk, then turned. "I would like to recall Duck Heller at this time, Your Honor."

Kendall Teasley frowned. "You had your shot at him earlier. Why do you want to put him back on the stand now?"

"A question just occurred to me," Avery Two answered.

"Recall Duck Heller," the judge grumbled. He glanced at his watch. It was getting close to lunchtime.

There was a pause as Neal Jenkins left the courtroom for Duck Heller. A drone of whispers floated over the crowd, like the exhaling of air. Teasley leaned forward, his elbows resting on the desktop. The robe he wore was heavy, hot. He could feel the dampness of perspiration coating his forehead. He glanced toward Fuller Davis. Fuller's head was down. Mason was glaring toward the bench, red-faced with anger. An aura of killing surrounded him, like an offensive odor. Damn fool. The judge looked up. Conjure Woman had not moved. Her eyes were still on him, unblinking. She seemed to be alone in the balcony. He remembered the story of the Klan trying to burn her out, and how she had raised her hand and the cross had begun to burn. She was scary. He'd read about the Haiti people and their magic. Never believed the stories until he first saw Conjure Woman. It was during his time as a lawyer, defending a man named Joe Henley, who had been accused of stealing a Model T Ford from Julius Price and selling it. Joe had insisted on going to Conjure Woman, and he had reluctantly agreed, simply to keep Joe from going off half cocked and beating the truth, or the shit, out of Julius Price. Conjure Woman had told them where the car could be found, and it was there, at the home of a man who lived in Commerce.

The man in Commerce said he had never heard of Joe Henley. Said he had bought the car from a man named Gary Price, who turned out to be Julius's son. After that, Kendall Teasley never doubted the power of Conjure Woman. She could work her will, and he knew it. Knew by the look on her face. He wondered if she was working her will in his court.

Neal Jenkins led Duck Heller back into the courtroom. Duck was directed to the witness chair, reminded that he was still under oath. He looked confused and frightened.

"A thought just occurred to me a few minutes ago," Avery Two said gently. "You remember telling this court that you and Grady Sorrells went with Jule Martin to return the gun to his house?"

"Yes—yes sir," Duck stammered.

"On the way there, or on the way back, did you see anything out of the ordinary?"

Duck frowned. He looked at Avery Three. Avery Three shrugged.

"Uh, no sir, don't remember nothing."

"Not at all?"

Duck tilted his head in thought. After a moment, he said, "Well, sir, they was a car up the road when we was coming back."

"A car?"

"Yes sir."

"Whose car was it? Do you know?"

"I believe it was Miss Alice's car. Looked like it."

"What was it doing?"

"Seems to me like it was sort of just parked on the road."

"Which way was it headed? In the direction of the main road, or down toward Reba's house?"

"Down toward Reba's," Duck said, nodding his head. "Yes sir, that's what it was."

"And you think it was parked?"

"Yes sir, or it was going real slow."

"Did you say anything about it to Jule or Grady?"

Duck looked at Jule. Jule nodded vigorously. "Yes sir, we talked about it. Said Miss Alice must be coming back down to get some help, or she was out looking for Mr. Harlan."

"But she didn't show up?"

"No sir."

"You didn't see the car after that?"

"No sir."

Avery Two paused. He strolled slowly toward the jury box, his head down, his arms behind his back. He seemed deep in thought. Then he said, "No more questions."

"All right," Kendall Teasley said roughly. "The witness can step down." He looked at his watch. "It's eleven forty-five," he added. "You've got one more witness to call before you rest, is that right?" he asked Avery Three.

"That's correct, Your Honor."

"We'll hear that after lunch," the judge said. "This court will recess until two o'clock." He hammered his gavel once.

THIRTY-THREE

Avery Two waited beside Jule until Neal Jenkins led him away. "Don't worry," he said in a whisper to Jule. "I'll be in to talk to you in a few minutes."

Jule dropped his head. His face was empty, dazed, resigned. He began to follow Neal.

From near the railing that separated the crowd from the well of the court, Mason Davis sprang to his feet. He snarled, "You're a dead nigger, you hear me?"

Jule's head jerked up. He stumbled back.

Avery Two stepped in front of Jule. "Be quiet, Mr. Davis," he snapped.

"You nigger-loving son of a bitch," Mason sputtered angrily. "You better damn well sleep with one eye open."

Fuller Davis reached up and caught Mason by his arm and jerked at him. "Sit down," he ordered.

Avery Two took one step toward Mason, then felt someone's hand on his arm. It was his son.

"Leave it alone, Dad," Avery Three said. He motioned with a nod toward the aisle. Frank Rucker was rushing toward them.

"What's going on?" Frank asked. He turned to face Mason.

"Nothing, Frank. Just a little heated moment," Avery Three said easily. "That right, Dad?"

Avery Two pushed his son's arm away, inhaled, composed himself. He said nothing.

"Come on," Avery Three said. "I'm hungry, and I'm buying."

Avery Two glared at Mason, then began to walk up the aisle, followed by his son.

Frank waited until they were out of the courtroom, then he stepped close to Mason. He said in a quiet voice, "You want back in here this afternoon, you'd better pull yourself together, and I mean it."

"He will," Fuller promised.

"He better," Frank said. He turned and walked away, and the crowd that had watched the encounter, frozen in surprise and shock, followed him.

In the balcony, Conjure Woman peered down at Fuller and Mason and George. She did not move, even when Reeder Higginbottom asked if she wanted to go to his home for lunch. She did not reply. A trancelike look covered her face. Reeder Higginbottom backed away.

● ● ●

The two Averys, father and son, sat behind the closed door of Avery Three's office, nibbling at the baked chicken that Beatrice Haymore had personally delivered from the Cornerstone Café. Avery Three knew that Avery Two was still angry over Mason Davis's outburst.

"You know, you were smooth in there," he said to his father. " 'Nerve and verb.' A little cute, but good."

"It's old. I used it twenty years ago, when I was on your side of the table."

"I think you like the change," Avery Three suggested.

"You don't have to lather me with all that sweet butter," his father said. "I'm all right."

"Never saw you lose it," Avery Three told him.

"Never been around an asshole that bad," Avery Two answered.

Avery Three laughed. "Hey, that was a good move, bringing Duck back. What made you think of that?"

"I know Kendall," his father replied.

"What does that mean?"

"He's annoyed that I didn't cross-examine, and he's wondering why neither one of us didn't challenge the jury selection. He was looking at his watch. I thought I'd give him something else to ponder over lunch."

"Where'd the question come from?" Avery Three wanted to know.

His father shrugged. "Out of the air." He looked at his son and smiled. "But I liked the answer. What do you propose to do about it?"

Avery Three chewed thoughtfully. "Well, we could chase it, but it might upset the apple cart."

"Drop it?" Avery Two said.

"Why don't we put it on the back burner," Avery Three said. "We've still got Remona."

Avery Two smiled. "Yes, we do, don't we?"

"You ready for it?" asked Avery Three.

His father peeled a strip of chicken from the breastbone. "I am, indeed," he said. "In fact, I think I've got a twist for it."

●　●　●

Almost everyone attending the trial of Jule Martin had assumed that it would be impossible to get into the Cornerstone Café at lunchtime, or to find an empty seat at the fountain in the Mayfair Drug Store, and being wise, they had prepared picnics of fried chicken and sandwiches and had gathered under the oaks of Courthouse Square to eat and to talk openly about what they had heard in the courtroom.

The few who did not bring food chewed on snacks purchased from service stations.

Keeler Gaines was one of those who made his lunch from peanuts poured into a Coca-Cola. "What we need," he grumbled, "is a loaf of Merita bread, a can of sardines, and Jesus."

"What you need is some sense," Arthur Dodd told him, biting into the ham sandwich he had prepared that morning.

"Yeah, well, who's got sense and who ain't?" Keeler shot back. "Look at all the money you losing by closing down the store to come over here."

"I ain't losing a penny," Arthur argued. "Everybody I know is over here."

Keeler guzzled his drink. The salt from the peanuts tasted good. "I'm gon' go find Hack and Ada," he said. "Tom told me they had chicken. Maybe I'll give him a dime for a leg." He wandered off.

●　●　●

Evelyn Carnes stood with Hack and Ada Winter near the shaded steps of the courthouse, her picnic basket yawning open at her feet. She had prepared enough food for a half-dozen people, with the hope that she would share the lunch with Frank. In his office, maybe. With the door closed. But Frank had not come out of the courthouse, and he had barely looked at her during the trial. It was not easy joining in the chatter that careered across the lawn of the courthouse, knowing that Frank was inside, maybe thirty feet from her. He had warned her, of course. "I'll be busy," he had said. He had added, "No need causing any more talk than there already is." He was right, and she knew it. The talk about them was giddy and teasing, the kind of talk that teenage girls engaged in, and she had blushed it away, as teenage girls blushed away the rumor of romance. It was not uncomfortable for her, but it was for Frank. He had his hands full. Maybe after the trial.

"You got another egg salad sandwich, Mrs. Carnes?" Tom asked quietly, keeping an eye on his mother. He had already begged one from Evelyn.

"Sure do," she said. She reached into her picnic basket and handed the sandwich to Tom. It was extra full. Meant for Frank. She sighed as she watched Tom bite into it.

"Tom, what're you doing?" Ada asked sharply.

"Oh, Ada, they're just going to waste," Evelyn said. "I forced it on him."

Ada frowned. "Just so he's not pestering you."

"Oh, he's not."

Tom grinned. He eased away to the side of the steps. Ada moved close to Evelyn. She was fanning her face with a copy of the *Overton Weekly News*, which was full of Ben Biggers' propaganda about the African heritage of blacks and how that heritage twisted like a never-ending mountain river to Jule Martin's trail. In his judgment of guilt for Jule, Ben had written: *"It is not commonly known, but the Negro people have a gene not found in white people. It is a flawed gene usually associated with wildness and temper unbecoming in a civilized society."*

"I know Frank's going to be glad when this day's over," Ada said. "That little shouting match between Mason and Avery Two has got to have him worried."

"I'm sure he'll handle it," Evelyn said confidently. "Where'd they take Jule?"

"Probably keeping him inside somewhere," Ada said. "I doubt if they'd take him through this crowd back to the jail."

"Maybe that's where Frank is," Evelyn cooed. "With Jule."

Ada smiled. Evelyn's voice turned silly when she spoke of Frank. High-pitched and silly. "Probably," she replied.

"Wadn't that something about Alice's car being on the road?" Evelyn said. "Wonder if that means anything."

"I'd guess it means Harlan went back empty-handed and Alice got mad and said she'd go get Reba herself," Ada said. "She probably changed her mind when she saw Jule's car."

"Funny how it came up, though," Evelyn suggested. "Just out of the blue like that. I'd say Mr. Marshall knew about it all the time."

"Could be," Ada agreed.

"I haven't seen Alice at all," Evelyn said. "Wonder where she is."

"I heard she said she wadn't coming," Ada told her. "Said she was putting all that behind her."

Evelyn sighed. "I sure hope so." She added, "Lord, all that yelling that Mason was doing scared me. He looks meaner than Harlan."

"If he is, he'd have a forked tail and hooves on his feet," Ada said. She looked across the street and saw Reba moving slowly toward the courthouse, followed by Cecily and Remona and Son Jesus. Reeder Higginbottom and Doodlebug Witcher were with them. Reba looked tired, worried.

"I thought Conjure Woman was with Reba," Ada mumbled.

"She was," Evelyn said. "Did you see her sitting up there in the balcony? Scares me to death to look at her."

"I didn't see her come out," Ada said quietly, talking to herself as much as she was talking to Evelyn.

• • •

Inside the courtroom, Kendall Teasley peeked from behind the door leading to the judge's chambers. The courtroom was empty except for Conjure Woman. She sat unmoving in the center of the balcony, her eyes closed, a huge, white-shrouded woman mountain. The judge slipped the door closed quietly. "Damn," he whispered to himself.

• • •

Remona was nervous. She tried to keep her hands folded in her lap, but her hands were shaking. She looked down. She could hear the murmuring of voices from the courtroom, could feel the heat of the glaring eyes of Mason Davis. "Don't you go being scared," her mother had warned her. "Ain't nobody gon' do nothing to you." It was not easy believing her mother. Harlan Davis had already done things to her and it did not matter that he was dead. She could still hear him, could still smell the thick liquor scent of his breathing, could still feel his weight on her.

"Now, Remona, I've just got a few questions for you," Avery Three said gently, standing near her, his hands resting on the railing surrounding the witness chair. "All you have to do is answer me as honestly as you can. Say yes and no when that's all you need to say. When I finish asking my questions, Mr. Marshall over there may want to ask you some questions also." He smiled easily. "You don't have to be afraid of him. He's my father and I know him pretty well. I've never seen him get upset in the least little bit with a pretty girl."

"Get on with it, Counselor," Kendall Teasley said gruffly.

"All right, here's the first question," Avery Three said. "Did you know the deceased, Harlan Davis?"

Remona nodded hesitantly.

"I'd sure appreciate it, Remona, if you'd answer yes or no, just for the record," Avery Three said, without harshness.

"Yes—sir," Remona whispered.

"That's good. Now, the defendant in this trial is your uncle, Jule Martin, is that right?"

"Yes sir."

"And you care a great deal for him, don't you?"

Remona glanced at Jule. "Yes sir."

"From the testimony we've heard this morning, you were present on the day that Harlan Davis came to your mother's house and your Uncle Jule threatened him with a shotgun."

"Objection," Avery Two said sharply. "The threat is alleged."

"Alleged," Avery Three corrected. He bowed to his father, pivoted gracefully back to Remona. "Were you there when Harlan Davis showed up? I'm talking about the day he was murdered."

"Yes sir," Remona said, almost inaudibly.

"Tell your witness to speak up," the judge growled.

"Speak up a little louder," Avery Three said to Remona. "My ears are getting as old as I am. They need all the help they can get."

A little laugh rippled in the courtroom.

"Now, did you see the shotgun your Uncle Jule had?"

"Yes sir."

"Do you know where he got it from?"

"His car," Remona answered.

"So, it wasn't in the house?"

"No sir. My mama don't like guns in the house."

"Had Harlan Davis been drinking, do you know?"

"Yes sir, he was drinking."

"Are you sure? Did you see him take a drink?"

Remona paused. She looked at Jule, then looked down again. "No sir, I didn't see him take a drink."

"But you're sure he was drinking. Is that because of the way he was acting?"

"Yes sir."

"And you'd seen him act that way before, when you were at his house, working. Is that right?"

"Yes sir."

"According to records that we keep at the courthouse, Remona, Harlan Davis was arrested a few weeks ago for hitting you. Is that right?"

Remona nodded slowly, remembered the warning about answering the question. "Yes sir," she said.

"Was he drinking that day?"

"No sir."

"He just hit you?"

"Yes sir."

"Do you know why?"

Remona swallowed. Her mouth was dust dry. "He say I was talking to the sheriff, wasting time. Miss Alice say I stop the sheriff when he was driving by."

"Did you?"

"No sir."

"Now, Remona, I have a very hard question I need to ask you, and I don't want you to get mad at me for asking it," Avery Three said quietly. "You and your mama used to work for Harlan Davis and his wife. Is that right?"

"Yes sir."

"And now you work for Mr. Fuller Davis. Is that also true?"

"Yes sir."

"You didn't get hit by somebody else—like maybe your mama or your Uncle Jule—and make all that up about Harlan Davis just so you and your mama could quit working for him, did you?"

Remona's face jerked up. Her eyes blinked in surprise. A surge of anger tightened around her heart. "No sir," she said boldly. "Mr. Harlan hit me."

Avery Three did not speak for a moment. Then he leaned close to her and said, "I know he did. I just heard some talk along those other lines at lunchtime, and I wanted to put it in the record, because talk can muddy the waters. Now, here's my last question: Did you hear your Uncle Jule say he was going to kill Harlan Davis?"

Remona shook her head. "No sir. He try to get Mr. Harlan to leave. He say he don't want to shoot him, but he would if he got to."

"But he did have the gun?"

"Yes sir."

"Thank you, Remona," Avery Three said. He turned to his father. "Your witness."

Avery Two pushed back in his chair, stood. He poked his thumbs into the belt of his trousers and gazed at Remona, his body rocking like a high-wire walker taking his first cautious step.

"Remona, were you raped by Harlan Davis?" he asked.

Kendall Teasley cut his eyes to Avery Three, waiting for the objection. Avery Three said nothing.

"Counselor, do you have an objection here?" the judge asked.

"None, sir."

"Why not?" the judge demanded.

"Because I think that question has already clouded this issue and hangs in this courtroom," Avery Three replied. "The state is perfectly at ease in having it explored, since it is totally unrelated to the charge that exists, and I'm satisfied the honorable gentlemen of the jury understand that. Maybe if we hear it out, that will be abundantly clear, and we'll be done with it."

"Proceed," the judge said sourly.

"Were you, Remona?" Avery Two said. "Were you raped by Harlan Davis?"

"Yes sir," Remona answered quietly, shamefully.

"More than once?"

"Yes sir."

"Did you hate him for that?"

Remona dipped her head. "Yes sir," she mumbled.

"Enough to kill him?"

Remona's face shot up. She looked wildly to the balcony for her mother, but her mother was not there. Her mother was being held in the witness room. She saw Conjure Woman. Conjure Woman lifted her palm, and Remona could feel a calmness falling over her, a calmness like sleep.

"Did you hate him enough to kill him?" Avery Two asked again.

"When he was—doing that to me, I did," Remona admitted.

"But you didn't kill him, did you?"

"No sir."

"On the day in question, did Harlan Davis say anything to you? Directly, I mean. Just to you."

Remona bobbed her head. "He say he coming back for me."

"What do you think he meant by that?" Avery Two asked.

"I—don't know."

"But it scared you?"

"Yes sir."

"Were you in this courtroom this morning?" Avery Two said.

Remona looked at him quizzically.

"I mean in this room," Avery Two emphasized.

"No sir."

"You were not in this courtroom during testimony, or at the time court was recessed for lunch?"

"No sir."

"You didn't hear the threat made against your uncle?"

A muttering rolled over the courtroom.

"Counselor," the judge warned harshly.

Avery Two ignored the warning. "You didn't hear Mason Davis, the brother of Harlan Davis, tell your uncle that he was going to be a dead nigger?"

Kendall Teasley slapped his gavel on the desktop. "Counselor, that's enough," he boomed.

"I'm asking that question," Avery Two rushed, "because I wonder if that was what it was like being raped by Harlan Davis."

"Goddamn you," Mason screamed. He jumped from his seat and sprinted down the aisle toward Avery Two. "You nigger-loving son of a bitch."

Frank was sitting at the prosecutor's table. He rolled from his chair and tackled Mason, wrestling him to the floor. A babble of voices, of squeals, echoed in the courtroom. The pounding of Kendall Teasley's gavel was like a drum.

"Order! Order in this court!" the judge bellowed.

The talking, the squealing, stopped abruptly.

The judge was standing, leaning over the desktop. His face blazed red. "Sheriff, you take that man and you get him out of my sight," he ordered. "The next time I see him will be in the morning, before this court resumes, and he had better be carrying the mortgage to his farm, because this outburst has just cost him an arm and a leg. Now, this court is adjourned until nine-thirty in the morning. Counselors, I want to see both of you in my office, right now."

In the balcony, Conjure Woman smiled.

•   •   •

Kendall Teasley was pacing, dressed in his robe. He looked clownish. His face was still red. His eyes flickered fire when he blinked. He was breathing heavily.

Avery Three and Avery Two stood politely, not speaking, waiting for Kendall to gather his thoughts and his breath.

"I'm tempted to report both of you to the Georgia bar," the judge said at last, "and pull in every favor I've got out there to see that neither one of you ever steps foot inside a courtroom again, except to be prosecuted yourself."

"I apologize for my behavior," Avery Two said. He sounded sincere.

"Your behavior was reprehensible," the judge snapped. "You've been practicing law in front of my bench for more years than either of us care to remember, but what you just did in there was inexcusable, even in friendship."

"I agree," Avery Two said. "I lost my composure, but, Your Honor, you were not in the courtroom when Mason Davis verbally attacked me and my client. That's never happened to me, and I find it hard to accept."

"I heard what happened," the judge growled, "but that still doesn't give you privilege, not in my court."

Avery Two did not speak.

"But that's not the only thing that's pissed me off," the judge continued. "From the very outset of this trial, the two of you have been tap-dancing so damn much it's nauseating. I swear to God, I've been watching for hand signals about who's supposed to do what. You let a bunch of sheet-wearing idiots sit on the jury without dismissing so much as a fart in a windstorm. You don't object over the most objectionable issues. You ask questions that a first-year law student would know not to ask. Half the time I don't know which one of you is the prosecutor and which is the defender, and I know damn well both of you are smarter than that. So tell me what the hell's going on. Are you trying to confuse the jury as much as you are me?"

Avery Three cleared his throat. "It's a difficult case, Your Honor."

"How?"

"We don't have any evidence," Avery Three said honestly.

"You've got motive up your ass," the judge shot back.

"With all due respect, sir, we don't. We've got the *appearance* of motive, and frankly, if any of us had been put in the same situation as Jule Martin, we would have done the same thing—or worse."

"Then you tell me why we're prosecuting this case," the judge demanded.

Avery Three looked incredulously at Avery Two, furrowed his eyebrows, turned back to Kendall Teasley. "Sir, you advised me to bring the case before you for indictment. You were rather forceful about it."

"It was my understanding that you were going to find the shotgun," the judge said defensively.

"I—never suggested that," Avery Three replied.

"Somebody goddamn well did," the judge snapped.

"I don't know, sir. Maybe it was street talk," Avery Three suggested. "I know you have to listen to a lot of that. I don't envy you."

The judge huffed a wordless reply. He unzipped his robe and skinned it over his head and dropped it on top of his desk. He looked dwarfish in his shirt.

"All right, goddamn it, tell me what we're going to do about it," he snarled.

"You've only got two choices," Avery Two said calmly. "Finish the trial or dismiss it."

"On what grounds?" the judge asked belligerently.

Avery Two smiled. "On the grounds that you have ascertained—after a thorough examination of the documents—that your district attorney does not have enough hard evidence to convict."

Kendall Teasley turned his glare to Avery Three.

"That's stepping on the toes a little bit, but I guess I can survive it," Avery Three said.

The judge slipped into the chair behind his desk. He drummed his fingers on the chair arm. "I'll give it some thought," he said at last. "But if this trial continues, the two of you will begin behaving like lawyers, or I'm going to charge you both with contempt, and by God, I'll make it stick."

"Yes sir," Avery Three said.

"Now get out of my sight," the judge ordered. "I may want to get drunk—alone."

The two Averys left Kendall Teasley's office. Outside, they looked at each other. Avery Two winked. Avery Three laughed.

THIRTY-FOUR

Frank had never liked being at the jail. It was a cold place, with everything—inside and out—painted a lifeless gray, like a dull, cloud-heavy day. An odor of urine, covered by disinfectant, seeped through the walls separating the office from the cells. The sound of steel on steel seemed to ring from every movement—walking, the opening and closing of file drawers, the clicking on of lights and window fans. If the environment of the jail was intended to leave the impression of dread, it succeeded. Only Nelson Doolittle seemed to like it. Nelson and Goodboy Poole. Goodboy—his real name—was the jailer. He was in his mid-sixties, a bachelor with thin, orange-blond hair and a pink face, who had often been accused of being queer. Frank did not think he was, or if he was, he was discreet. He was at least friendly, which was more than anyone could say of Nelson.

The jail was located two blocks east of Courthouse Square. It was surrounded on three sides by a high chain-link fence with two strands of barbed wire running across the top. A grove of pecan trees grew inside the fence, showering the ground with pecans each fall. Prisoners fought with crows over the nuts. The crows usually won.

And though it was only two blocks away from his office, Frank did not visit the jail unless it was necessary.

Sometimes it was.

It had been that afternoon, after the angry adjournment of the trial of Jule Martin by Judge Kendall Teasley.

Getting Jule out of the courthouse, into a sheriff's car, and transported two blocks had been tense. Mason Davis was part of it. Most of it, in fact. And maybe he should have taken Mason to his office and held him until the crowd grew tired of standing around exchanging gossip like recipes. He had pushed Mason out of the courtroom and down the corridor to the south exit of the building. Had warned him about more trouble. Might as well have been advising the wind to blow bubbles. Mason had railed about the coddling of niggers, about the smart-ass attitude of Avery Two, about the need to teach Jule a lesson that every nigger in the county would remember. Should have locked Mason up, but that would have caused a bigger row, because of the men who had rallied to meet him outside, cheering him on. But George had promised to take him home to let him cool off, and that was good enough. George had seemed nervous, maybe embarrassed, at the way his brother had behaved. And maybe Frank had let Mason go because of Fuller. The look on Fuller's face as Frank pushed Mason out of the courtroom had been one of bewilderment, one of surrender.

It was curious, also, how the crowd had lingered. Was still there. At least most of them. He had seen Evelyn leaving in a car with Hack and Ada, followed by Troy and Tom in Troy's truck. He had nodded and Evelyn had waved. So had Tom. Tom grinning like someone who had been to a circus.

Standing at the front window, he could see cars still parked on the sidestreets leading into Courthouse Square, and people milling around them, talking. For an hour they had lingered, as though expecting something else to happen—something that was gathering in the air, taking shape, something built of words stacked upon words, with the mortar of anger holding them together.

One thing was for sure, Frank thought: Jule Martin was terrified.

"They gon' kill me, Mr. Frank," he had wailed, bent down in the back seat of the sheriff's car. "They gon' kill me."

He had tried to reassure Jule but had failed. And God knew, he didn't blame Jule. It damn well had been touch and go for a few minutes, with the car surrounded and men spitting threats, their eyes and their mouths foaming, like mad dogs.

Fletcher had read the group well, though, and it was good that Fletcher had been driving. He had turned on the red lights and the siren and had bowled through the men, bumping some gently away from the car.

"The bastards have got to believe you mean business," Fletcher had said, "and I, by God, do."

But it was also Fletcher who had persuaded him to stay at the jail, and persuaded him to call in Hugh and Buddy and Arlo.

"Frank, you don't know these assholes like I do," Fletcher had urged.

"Hell, I'm pretty much one of them. They ain't got a lick of sense when they get all juiced up and start listening to one another. They gon' be down here. Sooner or later, they gon' be down here. They see you leave, it's gon' be like a bunch of buzzards landing on a dead cow. You better stay here and wait it out. If they get drunk enough, they'll go on home."

Frank turned from the window. Hugh and Fletcher and Buddy and Arlo were all watching him. Goodboy Poole was at his desk, pretending to process papers. He had never had the entire Sheriff's Department of Overton County in his office at one time.

"They still there?" asked Hugh.

"Still there," Frank said.

"Maybe one of us ought to go up there and hang around," Hugh suggested. "See what the mood is."

"I know what the mood is," Fletcher said flatly. "I was talking to some of them boys from Mossy Creek. They're pissed. Told me if Jule got off, they were gon' go to their robes."

"Why don't I call Mildred up at the office," Arlo said. "See if she can tell us anything."

Frank nodded permission, and Arlo went to the telephone and dialed. He said, "How's it going up there?" And then he listened. "All right," he said after a few moments. He hung up, turned to Frank. "She said nobody had left. Nobody. Said she just saw Mason and a bunch of men come out of the café, and it looked like they was headed this way."

"Shit," Fletcher muttered. "I told you." He pulled his revolver from its holster and began to check it.

Frank moved back to the window, looked outside. He could see a trickle of people marching toward the jail. "We got any shotguns here?" he asked.

"Three or four," Goodboy Poole answered quickly. "They're in the cabinet."

"Break them out," Frank ordered.

"I can't," Goodboy told him. "Nelson's got the key."

Frank turned to Fletcher. "Break the lock," he said.

Fletcher crossed quickly to the gun cabinet and began hammering on the lock with the butt of his revolver. The lock snapped open, and Fletcher pulled the guns out and passed them around.

"Arlo, you and Buddy take a couple of them guns and lock yourself back there with Jule," Frank said. "Hugh, you take that side door over there. Fletcher, you stay with me."

"What you gon' do, Frank?" Hugh asked.

"Try to talk to them," Frank said. "Only thing I know. I don't want nobody shooting unless it comes down to it, and you let me be the first one to do it."

•   •   •

It was slightly downhill from Courthouse Square to the jail. Downhill enough to make a ball roll faster the longer it rolled, and that was how the crowd of men following Mason and George Davis moved— faster with each step. Frank watched them from the window and he remembered a small town in France, a nameless town to him, that had been liberated by an advance team, and the word had come to them that the Germans were gone, or dead, and they had begun a hurried march toward it. On the outskirts of the town, the inhabitants who had survived began to come out from behind doors and from under the cavelike rubble of destroyed buildings. Old men. Women. Children. Cautiously at first, creeping out. Suspicious. Uncertain. And then someone had shouted, *"Vive la France!"* and the stragglers had become a crowd and the crowd had begun to move toward them, their arms fanning the air. Faster and faster, until they were racing and their voices were ringing like bells with gladness. The crowd had overwhelmed them.

The crowd following Mason and George were almost in a trot by the time they reached the walkway leading to the jail.

"Call Fuller," Frank said to Fletcher. "See if he's home. If he is, tell him what's going on."

"What for?" Fletcher asked.

"Just do it, Fletcher," Frank said wearily. He opened the door and stepped out onto the landing leading to the yard. The crowd stopped.

"You got that nigger in there?" Mason snarled.

"Go home, Mason," Frank said calmly.

"I will, when you bring that nigger out," Mason said.

For a moment, Frank did not speak. His eyes scanned the crowd knotting close behind Mason. George was there, not up front, but back, almost hiding. He saw men he had known since childhood, two or three who had been teammates on the football team. Harley Cagney was one.

Harley Cagney had lifted Frank to his shoulders after a touchdown that beat Lavonia.

"You know I'm not going to do that, Mason," Frank said. "And you're not coming in here."

"Goddamn it, Frank, get out of the way," Harley Cagney shouted. "Ain't no need to get yourself hurt over some colored man. You ain't got enough men in there to stop us, and you know it."

"Maybe not, Harley, but it don't make much sense to find out, does it?" Frank said.

Mason took a short step forward. No one followed him. "What you gon' do? Shoot us?" he sneered.

"Well, Mason, that depends a lot on how stupid you get," Frank told him.

Mason leaned forward at the waist. A livid red colored his face. A dribble of saliva glistened at the corner of his lips. "I'm gon' give you thirty minutes to think about it," he said in a low, growling voice. "In thirty minutes, if you and them boys in there ain't gone, we gon' have us a reelection right here."

Frank's gaze did not move from Mason's face. He said, "You been seeing too many cowboy pictures, Mason. You're acting like a damn fool. But if it's thirty minutes you want, that's fine. If you're still out here in thirty minutes, I'm gon' arrest you, and I'm gon' put you back there in that cell, right across from Jule Martin. And I promise you, you won't like it." He looked up, let his eyes skim the crowd. "That goes for every last one of you." He turned and walked back inside.

Inside, Fletcher slipped close to Frank and bolted the door. "Jesus," he said. "They gon' tear this place apart."

"You want to leave?" Frank snapped.

"Hell, no, Frank, but you done the wrong damn thing."

"What the hell would you have done?" Frank demanded. "Turned Jule over to them?"

"You'd of been better off walking straight up to Mason and slapping the slop out of him," Fletcher said. "That's the only thing that little asshole understands."

Frank could not help it: a smile curved across his face. Crazy damn Fletcher. He had the mentality of a flea. "Maybe you're right," he said. "Maybe you're right. Did you get Fuller?"

"Get him?" Fletcher replied. "I talked *at* him, if that's what you mean."

"What'd he say?"

"Nothing," Fletcher answered. "Not a damn word. He just hung up. Maybe he's hoping you'll blow Mason's ass away."

"You want me to call the highway patrol?" Hugh asked.

Frank shook his head. "Not yet."

"What we gon' do?" Fletcher asked.

"Wait," Frank said. He added, "Thirty minutes."

⚫   ⚫   ⚫

It was almost comical, Frank thought, standing at the window, looking out. It *was* like a cowboy movie. He'd seen it a hundred times over. A showdown in the street. Maybe that's what he should do: challenge Mason to a gunfight. Find some boots and cowboy hats and play it out. He could be Wyatt Earp and Mason could be one of the Dalton boys, or somebody from Jesse James's gang, or Billy the Kid. Billy the Kid fit him. Temperamental little absolute asshole. Trying to be Harlan. Trying to do what he thought Harlan would have done, and it never occurring to him that Harlan was dead because he, too, had been an absolute asshole.

The crowd waited nervously, wading in and out of the circle of men who surrounded Mason. He knew they were pumping up their nerve, lying to themselves about what they were going to do. It was like being in a football game. All that butt patting and bragging, the helmet slapping, the spewing of man-making cuss words. Not that way in war, Frank thought. In war, few bragged. The tiniest bullet from the tiniest man could blow your brains out. In war, you covered yourself and the man next to you—no matter who he was—as best you could.

He let his eyes drift to the outer crowd of onlookers, who had gathered a half-block away, curious but uneasy. He could see Keeler Gaines walking among the men, talking. Moving from man to man. He liked Keeler. Keeler was still a boy—like Tom Winter—in many ways, but he was also proud and fearless. The ribbons Keeler had brought back from the war almost matched Frank's own in number, and maybe they should have. Maybe Keeler got shortchanged. Maybe Keeler should have had the parade. Maybe Keeler should be the sheriff.

"How much time?" Fletcher asked nervously.

Frank glanced at his watch. "Ten minutes."

"Shit," Fletcher sighed.

"We better have a plan," Hugh said.

"I do," Frank told him.

"What?" Hugh asked.

"It's called the Fletcher Plan."

"What's that?" Fletcher asked suspiciously.

"In ten more minutes, I'm going to walk outside and go straight up to Mason and slap the slop out of him."

Hugh laughed.

And after a moment, when it struck him, so did Fletcher.

"You about twenty minutes too late," Fletcher said.

"Yeah, I guess," Frank said easily. "But I used to know this boy in the army—Jabbo Lewkowicz—who had his own way of looking at things. He used to say if you got there before it was over, you were on time."

"Was that boy a Jew?" asked Fletcher.

Frank twisted his head to look at Fletcher. "You know, I never asked him," he said. "Could of been. There were a good many times when all of us turned out to be whatever religion rode up in the next Jeep."

"Sounds like a Jew to me," Fletcher said. He unbreeched the shotgun he held and pulled out the shell and examined it, then slipped it back into the barrel.

"Well, all I know is I wish he were in here with us right now," Frank said softly. "He was a hell of a soldier."

Fletcher snapped the gun shut, and the click echoed in the room, causing Goodboy Poole to jump at his desk.

"How much time?" Fletcher asked again.

"Six minutes," Frank answered. He turned to Goodboy. "Why don't you go on out the back door, Goodboy. This ain't part of your job."

Goodboy looked up and smiled. He waved his hand nervously in front of his face. "It's not five o'clock," he said. "I don't get off to five. Besides, you may need me to book somebody."

"Suit yourself," Frank said. He pushed his face closer to the window and looked out. "My God," he whispered.

"What is it?" Fletcher asked fretfully.

"It's Keeler. He's headed this way with a bunch of men," Frank answered.

Fletcher moved to the window beside Frank. "Well, shit," he muttered. "And that ain't all. That's Fuller's car that just pulled up."

"Where?" Frank asked.

Fletcher pointed. "Right up yonder, a block or so up."

"I see it," Frank said.

There were a half-dozen men following Keeler, crossing the yard of the jail in front of Mason and the men with Mason. They walked up the sidewalk and onto the landing that led to the doorway of the jail.

"Better see what that's all about," Frank said. He went to the door, opened it, and stepped outside.

"How's it going, Frank?" Keeler said cheerfully, in a loud voice.

"What're you doing, Keeler?" Frank asked. He glanced over Keeler's shoulder. He could see Fuller Davis making his way slowly down the sidewalk.

Keeler turned to face Mason. A wide smile rested on his face. Almost a clown's smile. "Well, me and some of the boys—You know all these boys, don't you, Frank? J. D. and Charlie and—Well, hell, you know them. Anyway, we been standing up there watching what's going on down here, and it come to us that they wadn't single one of them boys out there with Mason that'd ever been in the army, or the air force, or the marines, or, hell, not even the navy." He paused, looked toward Mason. "And you know what, asshole? The more we thought about it, the more it pissed us off. You come down here telling the best man this county sent off to the war that you gon' waltz right in and take one of his prisoners away from him? I don't think so. Maybe you don't know it, but when you been in a foxhole with a man, you don't never let him down, and it don't make no difference who he is, or where he's from, or what color he is. So, if you want to get to Frank, you got to come through us, and we did a little tally up there on the hill. Between us—not counting Frank—we killed thirty-two men. You think you pissants scare us? Shit."

There was a moment of silence. A stunning, unbelievable moment. And then a restless stirring among the men behind Mason.

"You a nigger-lover?" Mason said to Keeler, the words curling from his throat. "That what you saying? You a nigger-lover?"

Keeler laughed. "You know, Mason, if it was a choice between a nigger and you, I'd take the nigger every time, but that ain't got nothing to do with this. All this is about is this man standing here." He reached out and put his hand on Frank's shoulder. "So, come on, little man," he snarled. "Your thirty minutes are up."

"Wait a minute," Frank said quietly to Keeler. "Mr. Davis just got here. Maybe he can talk some sense to him."

"I hope not," Keeler muttered. "I want to kick his ass, Frank. I really do."

"You may have your chance," Frank whispered. He watched Fuller step from the sidewalk and cross the lawn. He was looking at Mason and George. He seemed weak, walking the way an old man walked when he needed a cane but refused one. He did not stop until he stood in front of Mason. Mason stared at him, a sneer still on his face.

"What're you doing?" Fuller asked in a rough voice.

"I come to get that nigger," Mason answered.

Fuller's hand shot up suddenly, his opened palm catching Mason on the side of the face. The slap was like a rifle shot.

For a moment, Mason's body coiled, and then he was caught from behind by George.

No one spoke.

Fuller turned and walked toward the jail. At the foot of the landing, he looked up at Frank.

"You got the wrong man in there," he said softly. "It was me that killed him."

THIRTY-FIVE

The story that Fuller Davis told was a lie, and Frank knew it—knew it by intuition, knew it by Fuller's hesitant, faltering voice, knew it by Fuller's answers to his questions. And he knew it, he believed, by the evidence in his desk drawer. The shell that he had found in the broom straw was from a twelve-gauge gun; Fuller claimed that he had used his sixteen-gauge, and he could not remember what he had done with the shell. Carried it away with him in his gun. Threw it out the window of his car somewhere between Harlan's home and his own home.

The story was simple. Fuller had arrived late in the afternoon to talk to Harlan. He had found Harlan in the barn loft, drunk. They had argued and Harlan had threatened him. He had fired his gun in self-defense, and then he had left to agonize over killing his son.

"Why'd you have the gun with you?" Frank asked.

Fuller blinked rapidly, then looked away. "I was scared of him," he said. "I was always scared of him."

"Did you know he was dead, right off?"

Fuller nodded. "I could see it."

"Mr. Davis," Frank said softly, "I want to ask you straight out, one time—just between me and you, without your boys being in here: Are you telling me the truth?"

Fuller looked up. His eyes welled with tears. "I'm ready to go to the jail," he whispered.

Frank shook his head. "Well, sir, I didn't put you under arrest yet. But I'd appreciate it if you'd answer my question. Just between us. I promise."

"I got two other boys I got to try to help," Fuller said painfully. "You saw what almost happened out there today."

"All right," Frank said.

Fuller stood. He leaned his hands against Frank's desk for a moment, balancing himself. Then he again said, "I'm ready to go."

"You won't be staying," Frank told him. "We're just gon' book you, like we got to. Then we'll get some bail set, and then you'll be going home."

● ● ●

Nothing was as quiet as disbelief, Frank thought as he watched Fuller Davis's car pull away from the courthouse, followed by Mason and George in their own cars. No one had said anything unnecessary in the presence of Fuller. The silence had been eerie. Even Mason and George had been subdued. Frank had expected them to argue about the arrest, but they did not. George had said, in a voice so low and apologetic it was difficult hearing him, "I guess you had to do it."

Still, Frank knew the silence was only in his presence and in the presence of Fuller. The phone lines would be white-hot.

"Did you hear? It was Fuller that killed Harlan. . . ."

"He must of had all he could take. . . ."

"Poor old man. He's got to be weak in the mind. . . ."

"Them's a sorry lot of boys he's got for sons. . . ."

Frank turned and went back inside to his office. He closed the door and sat, leaning heavily against his swivel-back chair. He took the shotgun shell from his desk drawer and studied it. Fuller had lied. He had lied to protect Mason and George, knowing his sons would not stop until someone—Jule, most likely—paid for the death of their brother, and more people would be hurt, or killed. It was a last desperate act, something that might have been found in the Old Testament—wisdom and sacrifice.

He rolled the shell in his hand and then sniffed it. The smell of gunpowder was becoming faint, and a curious surge of energy washed against his chest. Everything in him—every sensation—told him that he was holding the shell that had killed Harlan Davis. And Pegleg. He had to remember that: Pegleg was also dead. Both Peglegs.

And Fuller Davis had not fired the shell that he held in his hand. He believed he could prove it by comparing the pellets taken from Harlan to the pellets from a sixteen-gauge shell.

But maybe it did not matter. Fuller Davis had confessed to killing his oldest son in order to save his younger sons. It was that simple. He had said, "I got two other boys I got to try to help." And maybe it would help them. Maybe the shock of it would drive some sense into their thick skulls.

Frank dropped the shell into the desk drawer and closed it with a light touch. He would keep the shell, but he knew it was little more than a souvenir. The grand jury would not indict Fuller. The grand jury would decide—collectively—that Harlan deserved what he got, while Fuller deserved only pity. And maybe that was what justice was all about. Maybe.

A light knocking rapped against the closed door to Frank's office.

"Come in," Frank said.

Avery Three opened the door and stepped inside and closed the door behind him. He leaned against the doorjamb. "You know you just booked a man on murder charges who didn't have a damn thing to do with it," Avery said. "He didn't have any more to do with it than Jule did."

"We got his confession," Frank said.

"But nothing else," Avery countered.

"Not at the moment," Frank admitted.

"He didn't do it, and you know that as well as I do," Avery said.

"You got a better candidate?"

"A better candidate? Frank, Porky Pig's a better candidate than Fuller Davis, but if you want a name, how about Alice Davis? According to the Overton County grapevine, Mason and George have been spreading the story that Alice threatened to kill Harlan."

"When did she do that?"

"Who knows? Maybe she's been doing it for years," Avery said. "But from what I hear, it happened the day he was killed. Mason said he talked to Harlan by phone sometime in the early afternoon, and Harlan was laughing about it. I suppose the reason Mason and George haven't made too much of it is because we had Jule locked up."

Frank rocked forward at his desk. "I think if I'd lived with him, I might have made a threat or two myself," he said.

"I did some checking two or three weeks ago," Avery replied. "There were a couple of domestic complaints she'd filed. Dismissed, of course, but still she had the fortitude to file them. One of them was rather interesting. Harlan had to take a shotgun away from her, or so he claimed."

Frank picked up a pencil on his desk, drummed it lightly, thoughtfully, on the desktop. After a moment, he said, "Is that where you'd put your money if you were a betting man?"

"If I were a betting man, sure," Avery said. "She had motive, a history of abuse, and the time to do it, not to mention a pretty select choice of weapons. From what I understand, Harlan had a small arsenal in every corner of the house, but if it really was Jule's gun that was used, she had the chance to steal it. That was an interesting little tidbit about her car being on the road. Maybe she went on to Jule's house, found the gun, and used it."

"I knew about that," Frank said. "She told me. Said she was going down to Reba's house to see what Harlan might of done, then when she saw Jule's car, she turned around and went back home, and then she went over to her mama's house. Anyway, why would she steal Jule's gun?"

"My God, Frank, who did we have in that courtroom today? Alice Davis or Jule Martin? Maybe she'd planned on leaving it in the barn, then changed her mind and hid it somewhere. Maybe it's at her mother's house."

Frank turned the pencil in his hand, pressed his thumbnail into the soft wood, gazed thoughtfully at the nail print. "I don't know," he said after a moment. "She don't seem the type. Seems too skittish."

"Sometimes we call that fragile," Avery countered. "Fragile breaks, Frank. Fragile breaks easily."

"You've got a point," Frank said. "What's going to happen to Jule?"

Avery moved away from the door, began pacing in his lawyer's stroll. "Nothing. Between you and me and the lamppost, we were about to have a mistrial declared, anyway. I talked to the judge a few minutes ago. He'll go through the motions in the morning and dismiss Jule's case, and you can release him."

"What about Fuller?" Frank asked.

"Teasley's going to convene the grand jury next Monday, but I'm guessing—we're both guessing—that's as far as it'll go. The grand jury will declare it a matter of self-defense, then it'll be a closed case, won't it? A hundred years from now, nobody on earth will give a tinker's damn who killed Harlan Davis, and that's why I don't really think there's much reason to put the hounds on Alice, even if I personally believe she took a few liberties with Harlan's efforts to breathe. No reason to torment her. I suspect she's had her share of troubling moments."

"I can't argue with that," Frank said. "You going to have any problem out of the judge over Fuller?"

Avery laughed easily. "One of the most compelling things about the law, Frank, is the need to wrap things up and put a neat little bow on them. My God, man, what do you think a grand jury's for? We put the ball in their hands and they kick it out of sight. Takes the heat off us. The judge knows that better than both of us. He also knows he doesn't want Fuller to come to trial, and he knows how to handle that."

"You're telling me it's over. Is that right?" Frank asked.

"That's pretty much up to you," Avery replied.

Frank dropped the pencil on the desk. "All right," he said. "Handle it your way. I still may do some poking around, though."

"Suit yourself," Avery said. He put his hand on the door handle, paused. "Your lady friend looked great today, Frank."

Frank blushed. "What lady friend?"

Avery laughed and left the office, closing the door behind him. His whistle disappeared down the corridor of the courthouse.

It was out, Frank thought. And now it would be all over the county. Frank and his lady friend.

And what was wrong with it?

Nothing.

He was surprised the rumors were so late in starting, in fact. He had begun seeing Evelyn regularly, even thought of it as official dating. But that was her doing. She had said to him one evening, "Frank, don't you think it's time you quit making up excuses for stopping by to see me? Good heavens, you've asked every question known to mankind about that old sawdust pile, and that break-in by Harlan Davis. What am I going to have to do? Shoot somebody on my front porch to give you more excuses for stopping by? If you want to date me, just say so, because I'd like that. But I want it to be for me, not for some ridiculous sheriff's report."

And he had blushed and mumbled, "I'd like that. I'd like to be seeing you for you, and nothing else."

"Well, take a long, hard look," she had replied. "Because what you see is what you get."

The way she said it—soft, cooing, promising—had made Frank feel faint.

Seeing her had become both obsession and frustration. Obsession to have her, to rip back the sheets of her bed and make love to her as he made love to her in dreams. Frustration over the almost childish ill timing that existed between them. On nights when he was willing to pitch caution to the winds, she would retreat nervously. On nights when she purred for him in a begging voice, he could hear warnings that made him rush away on some pretended business at the jail.

"If we ever get it right, Frank," she had whispered on one such night of pretended business, "it's going to be like riding a tornado. I promise you."

"Straddle or sidesaddle?" Frank had asked foolishly.

"Bareback," Evelyn had teased.

He always blushed remembering the conversation. Teenage damn kids didn't talk such mush. Teenage damn kids said it straight out. And that was another thing that had changed since the war. People were a lot bolder. He could see it in the Mayfair Drug Store. Kids holding hands, secretly stroking each other under the tabletops of the booths, where they gathered in the afternoons for Coca-Colas and milk shakes.

In the middle drawer of his desk, there was a small sign that had been distributed during a peace officers convention in Athens. It was the motto of a retired agent from the Federal Bureau of Investigation, who had lectured at the convention. The sign read: Don't Rush Things.

Every time Frank saw the sign, he thought of Evelyn Carnes.

But maybe it was time for rushing.

There was a message that Mildred had left for him, a late-afternoon call from Evelyn. *Expecting you for supper*, the message read. *Don't be late*. The *Don't be late* had been underlined twice by Mildred.

•　●　◗

The supper had been too filling—fried chicken, a pork roast, green beans, mashed potatoes, fried okra, sliced tomatoes, cantaloupe, a strawberry cobbler—and Frank rubbed his stomach, burped softly, noiselessly, and swallowed again from the glass of iced tea that he had carried with him to the front porch and to the rocker that had begun to fit his body comfortably. Inside, he could hear the running of water and the clicking of dish on dish as Evelyn cleared the table.

He was being spoiled, and he liked it.

And maybe something would happen tonight, he thought. It was in the air, crept over the hair at the back of his neck like a suspicion he sometimes got when questioning people for whatever wrong they might have done, knowing they had done it by their look-aways and by their hemming and hawing. Or like nights in the war, when he could not sleep, believing he could smell gunpowder before guns had been fired.

Something was in the air for sure. Too many things pointed to it.

It had been a fine meal. The kind of meal that celebrates something.

Evelyn still had on the yellow dress. Two top buttons unbuttoned. The yellow dress had flashed at him all day in the courtroom, like Morse code signals. Flashed the same message over and over in the dots and dashes of her slightest body movement: "Touch me, touch me, touch me."

He stretched in the rocker, heard it squeak under his weight. The night was cool for summer, or it seemed cool after the heat of tension from the late afternoon. He inhaled, and the air that he inhaled seemed to be from autumn. The autumn perfume of colors from trees colored in splashes of red and yellow and rust. And cedar. Mixed into the imagined perfume, there was the scent of cedar. He remembered his mother ironing clothes, putting her flatiron on boughs of cedar during pauses as she rolled the clothes over the ironing board. It was the sweetest of memories. He hesitated in his rocking, cocked his head as though listening. He had been in a home with the smell of pressed cedar. Not long ago, he thought. Where? Then he remembered: Reba Martin's home.

He swallowed again from the tea.

His mind jumped. Where was the shotgun that belonged to Jule Martin?

In his desk, there was a tablet. On one sheet was a heading that he had printed: HIDING PLACES.

The rest of the sheet was blank.

Nobody will ever find it, he thought.

It was in the river, most likely. Far downstream. Taken apart. Thrown in piece by piece. Even if somebody—Duck Heller or Grady Sorrells or Henry Hanover or one of the others—took it as a joke on Jule, they would never admit it. Not when there had been so many questions about it. Even if Alice Davis had taken it and killed Harlan with it, as Avery Three believed, it would never be found.

A dog barked from far off. Another answered.

"You got your tea?" Evelyn called from the kitchen.

"I got it," Frank called back.

"You want some more cobbler?"

"I couldn't stuff in another bite with a shoehorn," Frank told her.

Evelyn laughed girlishly. He could hear her walking through the house, toward him.

She opened the door and stepped onto the porch.

"Oh, my," Evelyn cooed. "I may need a sweater, it's so cool out. Must be getting ready to rain. I can feel a little mist in the air."

"We can go in," Frank said.

"No. I like it out here," Evelyn said. She brushed her hand across his face and sat in the rocker beside his. "I don't know about you, but I've still got a good memory of how hot it's been this summer. Still feel it all over me, like I'd been laying in the sun too long and my skin was nothing but a blister." She exaggerated the memory by fanning her palm in front of her face. "Every summer, I think about it, Frank. How it was when I was little. I swear, we were as poor as church mice. It's one of the reasons I always felt sorry for the colored. That was how we lived. Just like the colored. Living hand to mouth, and not ever knowing if whatever we had in the hand would fall out on the way to the mouth. All we did from sunup to sundown was work in somebody's cotton field. Lord, how I hated those cotton fields. My daddy hired us out for Saturdays and Sundays sometimes. I still remember being so cooked out by the sun, I could barely walk." She laughed lightly. "Oh, Lord, I will never forget that sun. Just thinking about it makes me want to rip this yellow dress off and parade around in this cool night air naked as a jaybird."

A rush of blood pumped through Frank. "Well, now, you can't go doing that," he said. "I'd have to put you in jail for indecent exposure."

"Oh, fiddle, you wouldn't dare."

Frank leaned toward her. He whispered, "I guess I could turn the other way."

Evelyn giggled. She reached for Frank's hand, pulled it to her face, kissed his fingers, tipped them with her tongue.

"You're right," Frank said. "Summer's coming back. Must be a hundred out here."

She peered up at him. "You got some business waiting on you back at the jail?"

"None I can think of," he said.

"Ummm, that's good," she purred. She rolled her face in the palm of his hand.

"I'm gon' give you to Christmas to stop that," he moaned.

Evelyn pulled her face from his hand, gazed at him. "Frank," she said softly, "do you want to make love to me?"

Frank swallowed. His heart was racing. He could feel a web of heat over his face. He nodded hesitantly.

"Enough to marry me?" Evelyn said.

The heat left Frank's face. He blinked once. "Ah——" he said.

Evelyn smiled, lifted his hand again, kissed it. "I can't tell you how long I've stayed awake half the night, just imaging what it'd be like, having you there in bed with me," she said. "I never wanted a man until I met you, Frank. Never. Jed was a pig. I married him because I thought I had to, that he'd be the only man who'd ever ask me. Sharecroppers, Frank, that's what we were. I remember living off fatback and gravy and biscuits, and thinking I'd die out there in that sun, in somebody else's cotton field. And then Jed came along, driving a fancy car, bringing me boxes of candy, slipping money and store-bought whiskey to my daddy. I don't even know what making love's all about, but I know what I want it to be, and I know I want it to be with you."

She kissed his hand again. "But, Frank, I've thought about it all day today—sitting there in the courtroom, watching you, being scared to death when Mason pitched his fit—and I know what's been wrong between us, why we can't ever be ready at the same time. It's how we were raised. You've got to marry me first, or I've got to know you're going to. As old as we are, that's good enough for me—just knowing it. I can't just hop in bed, no matter how much I want to." She looked up at him. "I hope you want me as much as I want you."

"Ah——" Frank whispered.

"A girl's not supposed to do the asking, Frank."

"Ah——" Frank said again.

"But I will, if that's the way it has to be. I'll drop down on my knees and beg. I'll beg like that old blind man over in Athens—Blind Willie, they call him. God, if I had a guitar and could play it like he does, I'd do that. I don't want to spend the rest of my life wasting away, standing out here on this front porch day and night, looking for cars to pass by, wondering if it's you. And I think that's what I'd do, Frank.

Stand out here until I needed a wheelchair, or until my eyes failed me, and I couldn't do anything but listen for you. So, damn it, Frank, will you? Will you marry me?"

"Ah——" Frank repeated.

"Frank, I'm begging," Evelyn whimpered.

"Don't," Frank said painfully.

"But I want to, Frank. I really do. I want to beg. I want you to know how much it means to me."

For a moment, Frank did not speak. Then: "But you don't have to beg me. I should be begging you."

"Just——ask me," Evelyn whispered.

Frank swallowed hard. He said, "Will you——marry me?"

"Yes," Evelyn cried. "Oh, God, yes. Yes. When?"

"Ah——"

"Please, Frank, please. Let's not wait. I'm too old to wait. I've been waiting for you from the day I was born. Waiting's for teenagers."

"All right," Frank said quietly. "You tell me. When?"

"Saturday," Evelyn blurted.

"Ah——"

"That's four days away, Frank. God made more than half the world in four days."

"It's——"

"I don't need a big wedding, Frank. We'll just put the word out. Anybody that wants to come can just show up. Have you got a good suit?"

"Ah——I guess."

"Send it to the cleaners first thing in the morning. Tell them you want it out by Friday, and then you just show up. I'll take care of everything else. Call Florence and Jarrell and see if they can come down. I can't wait to meet her. Maybe she'll be my matron of honor."

She pulled his hand to her face, rolled her face in the palm. Frank could feel the lava heat of tears that bubbled from her eyes. She laughed happily. "Listen to me. Blithering on like a chatterbox wound up so tight the springs are about to snap apart. But I can't help it. I feel like that's what's happening." She looked up at him. "I've never been this happy. Never."

"Saturday?" Frank said. "You're sure?"

"Saturday," Evelyn answered. "Yes. I'm sure."

• • •

Frank was numb. His mind was numb. His whole body was numb. He had driven in a crawl from Evelyn's home, aware only of the tingling of numbness. His thoughts were lodged on three words: I'm getting married. Even when he consciously tried to think beyond the words, he could not. They echoed in the caverns of his ears, and he forced himself to think backward, not forward.

Thinking backward, he could not remember agreeing to a Saturday wedding, but he must have. She had squealed with joy, had jumped from her rocker and rolled herself into his lap, burying her body against him. Her mouth had covered his mouth, and a heat that seemed to come from some pit fire burning between her hips blew into him, scorching his tongue and throat and chest.

They had not removed their clothes, had not groped each other, had not wallowed in her bed, but Lord, they had made love. If the groping and wallowing was better, he was not sure he could take it, was not sure the pit fire would not consume him in flames hot enough to melt steel.

He stopped his car in the driveway of his home and sat for a moment, letting the tickling vibration of the idling motor fill his hands from the steering wheel. His hands were still clammy.

Damn, he thought. He turned off the motor and glanced at his watch. It was ten minutes after ten. Earlier than he thought. And then he remembered: Evelyn had insisted that he leave before anything regrettable, anything compromising, happened. She had calls to make, she had insisted. Plans to work out. He licked his lips, tasted the taste of her lipstick. Cherry-flavored, he thought. He got out of his car and walked numbly toward his house.

From the porch, he heard the voice: "Mr. Rucker."

His body jerked. His hand fanned to his side, but he was not wearing his revolver. He turned to the porch. Under the lip of the roof, it was dark. He could not see anyone.

"Mr. Rucker," the voice said again. It was a woman's voice.

"Who is it?" Frank asked sharply.

He saw a figure step to the edge of the porch, at the top step.

"It's Cecily Martin," the voice said quietly.

Frank relaxed, moved toward the porch. He could see Cecily under the moon's spill. Her face seemed to be brushed in silver, the way the light fell over it.

"Anything wrong?" Frank asked cautiously.

"No sir," Cecily said. "I hope it's all right I was waiting."

"It's fine," Frank told her. He walked up the steps to the porch. "You want to sit down? There's some chairs—"

"No sir," Cecily said quickly. She handed him an envelope. "I just come to give you this." She paused. "I thought I'd better not leave it at the door. Somebody might of found it."

"What is it?" Frank asked.

"It's a letter I wrote for Uncle Jule. I went by to see him at the jail. He—can't write, so he wanted me to. Told me what to say and I wrote it down."

Frank turned the envelope in his hand. "Well, I appreciate it. I'll read it right away."

"Yes sir," Cecily said. She did not move.

"How's your mama?" Frank asked. "I know she was worried about today."

"Mama's fine," Cecily answered. "Mr. Fuller's been good to them. I hope he don't go to jail."

"I don't know," Frank said. "There's a good chance he won't."

Cecily did not speak for a moment. She turned her face away, toward the street. She chewed nervously on her lower lip. Then she said, "Mr. Harlan done things to me too."

"I thought so," Frank said gently.

A burst of tears blinked out of Cecily's eyes. "He make me do things to him. Say he gon' kick mama out the house if I don't. I'm glad he's dead."

Frank watched the tears flood across Cecily's silver-brushed face. "I can understand that," he told her. "There's some men that don't know much about how to live."

Cecily rocked her head in a nod. She glanced back at Frank. "I got to go," she said. She walked quickly down the steps.

"Cecily," Frank said.

She stopped and looked back.

"If he hadn't been killed, if he'd been put on trial for what he did to Remona, would you have told what happened to you?" Frank asked.

Her voice was so low it was barely audible: "Some lady that lives next door come over a little while ago, wanting to know why I was here. I told her I'd done some housework for you and was waiting to get paid." She lifted her face to Frank. "Mr. Frank," she said, "I'm colored. You don't know what the colored have to do." She turned and walked away.

Inside his house, at his kitchen table, Frank read the letter.

Sheriff Rucker,

    Cecily's writing what I'm saying.

    You done me a good turn by keeping them people away from me.

    I told you the truth. I didn't kill nobody.

    I don't know where my gun is. I been looking. I can't find it.

    But I know Mr. Fuller didn't kill nobody neither. Not Mr. Fuller.

    I'm writing this to say thank you. Ain't many white men would do what you done. I guess if you hadn't put me in jail, I'd be a dead man now.

    That's all I wanted to say.

                          Jule Martin

Frank folded the letter and slipped it back into its envelope, and then he held the envelope between his fingers and tore it in half. And tore it again. And again.

Jule was right. Fuller Davis had not killed anyone. Not Fuller Davis. Whoever killed Harlan was still free.

Maybe Avery Three had been right. Maybe Alice Davis had taken all she could take. God knows, she had plenty of reason.

He pushed away from the table and went to the trash can on the back porch and dumped the torn-up letter from Jule, written by Cecily. From across the yard, he could hear Eva Kemp practicing the piano. A church hymn. "Church in the Wildwood," he thought. Sometimes, with Eva, one tune sounded much like another. A small, satisfying smile popped on the corners of his mouth. Sharon had wanted to play piano because Eva played piano, but Sharon had run off with the piano player. He wondered how Sharon would feel when word got to her that he had married. Maybe she would talk about it to her husband, if she had not talked her husband into deafness and silence.

It had been a long day, and a hard one.

But it had ended well enough.

Even Eva Kemp's slaughter of "Church in the Wildwood" could not spoil the moment. The taste of cherry was still on his lips.

THIRTY-SIX

On Saturday morning, the men of Crossover gathered at Dodd's General Store, most of them dressed in the suits they wore only on Sunday, and at funerals or weddings. They had been swept from their homes like floor trash, driven away by wives busy with the rushed-up plans for Evelyn Carnes' wedding to Frank Rucker. And they were happy to be floor trash.

"I guaran-damn-tee you I'd put on this monkey suit every day of my life if it'd get my old lady to send me off somewhere," Keeler Gaines vowed. Keeler wore his army helmet from the war, still playing the fool out of merriment over his standoff with Mason Davis, swearing boldly that he was ready to sign up for another tour of duty.

"Well, Lord, Keeler, maybe that's what you ought to do," J. D. Epps advised. "From what I hear tell, things might get a little sticky over there in Korea before too much longer. Give you something worthwhile to do."

Keeler laughed. "Shit, J. D., me'n you and two flatbed trucks of the Georgia National Guard could clean that place up with a Daisy air rifle in two days flat."

"Well, there you go—two days of work and the rest of it a paid-up vacation on Uncle Sam," J. D. said.

The men around them laughed.

"Couldn't be much worse than facing down Mason," J. D. added.

"I was hoping he'd draw back on his daddy," Keeler said. "I was gon' bust his ass if he did. That old man's the salt of the earth."

"I tell you one thing," Arthur Dodd admitted. "I almost dropped my teeth when Fuller said it was him that killed Harlan."

"Well, Goda'mighty, Arthur, you don't believe that for one minute, do you?" asked J. D. Epps.

And the argument about the guilt or innocence of Fuller Davis began again. It was an argument that had started a half-dozen times, had sputtered and ended, an argument of clucking and head shaking and blue-sky guesses.

Fuller was only trying to stop his sons from making a fool of themselves.

If anybody had a reason to kill Harlan—and that list was as long as a donkey's dick, according to Keeler—it was Alice.

Could have been one of the brothers pissed off at him. Mason, most likely. George had too much of his mama and daddy in him, even if he never acted like it.

Could have been Jule, like the charge against him had claimed.

But the argument was harmless. There was too much euphoria in the air to be wiped away by argument. Too much reliving to do. Too much retelling. Frank Rucker's wedding to Evelyn Carnes was part of it. And Keeler was part of it. Keeler had stood up for Frank, and to the men at Dodd's it was like watching Germany and Japan sink to their knees. For a moment, stirring in its intensity, Keeler had taken them all back to World War II, and the music of that moment still played in them. Drums and bugles. March music keeping time with their heartbeat. And then the news of Frank becoming engaged to Evelyn had sparked the mood, put a parade strut in their step.

The jokes about Frank ranged from handcuffs to hard labor.

"Damn fool got sentenced to life without ever going before the jury," Keeler said, peeking out from his helmet.

"Well, daggum, Keeler, that ain't what you'd call a bad-looking woman," Charlie Hazelgrove observed.

"Don't matter, she's a woman," Arthur said sourly. "They all alike. All of them."

The crowd was large and the babble loud by the time Troy pulled his truck to a stop. Tom was with him.

"Well, by God, look what the cat drug in," Keeler said happily as Tom approached the store, dressed in a new gray gabardine suit. "How you doing, Tom?"

"Doing fine," Tom said.

"Lord, boy, you look like you running for governor," Keeler teased. He looked up at Troy, winked. "Next to you, Troy looks like one of them queer waiters I used to see after the war in San Francisco."

A grin bloomed on Tom's face. "Elly picked it out for me. We going to Mrs. Carnes' wedding."

"Yeah, well, you take a good long look at Frank's face during the marrying part," Keeler advised. "He's gon' look sick as a dog on a hot day. That's what it's like, being married. You better remember that look."

The men laughed good-naturedly.

"You know, Tom, if it wasn't for you, none of this never would have happened," Keeler said.

"Huh?" Tom said.

"That's right," Keeler declared. He took his helmet from his head. "Here, you want to wear my helmet?"

Tom blushed. "No sir. I ain't big enough. I'd get my head lost in it."

"What you mean, if it wasn't for Tom none of this wouldn't of happened?" asked J. D.

"Well, good Lord, J. D., where'd it all get started?" Keeler said. "It all got started when Tom and Sonny run off and Tom found that bone. Ain't that right?"

"Well, be damned if that ain't the truth," J. D. replied.

And the talk turned to Tom. A laughing kind of talk that rolled over the events of the summer—the beating and rape of Remona, the break-in on Evelyn Carnes, Harlan's death, Jule's arrest, Keeler's standoff with Mason, Fuller's confession, Frank's wedding—and narrowed them to the runaway of Tom and the discovery of Rody Martin's bones.

It was like the old camp-meeting song, the men concluded: *"... the toe bone connected to the ankle bone ... the ankle bone connected to the leg bone ... the leg bone connected to the knee bone ... the knee bone ..."* The bone Tom Winter pulled from the sawdust pile had led to the discovery of Rody Martin's skeleton and to all the other events that had happened. Connected everything. Fuller Davis was the last part of the connection—the head bone, as the song would declare.

"By God, you ought to be in one of them circus sideshows," J. D. said to Tom.

"I hear tell your mama's making you read the Bible from cover to cover," Charlie said, chuckling. "Next thing we know, you gon' be running off to Egypt. Gon' be down there at the creek with a chinaberry limb, trying to divide the waters."

"Lord, Tom, you wouldn't know the truth if you stepped in it barefooted and it was bigger'n a pile of fresh cow turds," J. D. added. "You'd think all that squishing between your toes was snow."

Tom grinned proudly. He sat on the porch beside Keeler and drank the Coca-Cola that Troy had bought for him. He liked being in the center of the men who teased him, who encouraged him to tell stories. It was like being in the heat of the sun on a cold day. He saw Troy leaning against one of the columns that held up the porch, an amused smirk on his face. He saw the Darby twins, William and Daniel, hanging near the edge of the crowd, glaring at him. The Darby twins were his classmates. No one liked them. They were sneaky and mean. They were not dressed for the wedding. Good, Tom thought.

"What was it you was telling us last week, Tom?" asked Keeler. "Something about finding a tobacco tin stuffed with some Confederate money and a letter signed by Robert E. Lee."

"That's right," Tom said enthusiastically. He glanced up at Troy. Troy wagged his head. "Yeah. Fell out of my pocket when I was crossing Sweetwater Creek. Last I saw it, it was going over some shoals."

The men laughed, punched at one another.

"I'm gon' put it in my will for them to bury me in concrete, Tom, just so you won't be digging me up, hauling me around somewhere," Keeler told him.

"I guess chasing you and Sonny down on that river is something people around here's gon' be talking about for forty or fifty years," J. D. offered. "You a mess, boy."

The men laughed again.

"Talk about Sonny, that looks like him coming down the road," Arthur said, cupping his hand over his eyes to shade out the sun.

Troy pushed himself up on his toes, looked. "Yeah, I think you're right."

"That boy's growing like a weed," Arthur added. "Looks more like a man every day."

Otha Darby, the father of William and Daniel, spat a stream of tobacco over the side of the porch. "Got them nigger genes," he said darkly. "It's the ape in him. I ain't never seen a nigger wadn't like that. Wobbling along, dragging them arms. Looks just like a ape, don't he? I bet he can hambone up a storm." He giggled. William and Daniel giggled.

No one else laughed. No one spoke.

"He's a good boy," Arthur said finally. "Ain't been easy for him this summer. Smart too. I never saw nobody that age—white or colored—that could do figures in his head like he does."

Otha snorted a laugh. "Shit, Arthur, you can teach a ape to count. Just put some bananas in front of him."

Arthur's face flushed with sudden anger. He swallowed. "I guess so," he mumbled. Then: "But I never heard of a ape that could rattle off the multiplication table like he can. Ask your boys. They was over here one day—Tom, you was with them, wadn't you?—and Sonny beat everybody on this porch doing the multiplication table."

"That's right," Tom said eagerly.

"Kicked my butt," Keeler agreed. "That's a smart little scooter."

The men watched Son Jesus approach the store. He was walking slowly, hesitantly.

"How's it going, Sonny?" Arthur called cheerfully. "Your Uncle Jule home yet?"

Son Jesus nodded. "Yes sir," he answered softly.

"Well, you tell him I asked about him," Arthur said. "Where's your mama this morning? She usually drops by on Saturday."

"She helping with Miss Evelyn's wedding," Son Jesus answered. His eyes scanned the men, stopped on Tom, then he looked down.

"Glad somebody with some sense is up there," Arthur said. "Put all the rest of them women in the same room and it ain't gon' be nothing but a hen party."

A few chuckles hummed across the porch.

"Hey, boy, how about doing the hambone for us?" Otha said. He laughed again.

Son Jesus turned his head, looked down the road.

"Leave him alone, Otha," Arthur warned. "Can I get something for you, Sonny?"

Son Jesus licked his lips. He said in a quiet voice, "Mama, she need some flour and fatback." He pulled a dollar out of his pocket, held it tight in his hand.

"Well, you come on in here," Arthur said cheerfully. "I'll fix you right up. In fact, I think I got a jawbreaker that's got your name on it."

Otha bent over from the porch. He slapped his hands against his thigh. "Com'on, boy, give us a little hambone."

"Otha, if you don't leave that boy alone, I'm gon' turn Keeler loose on you," Arthur said, forcing his voice to be light.

"Naw," Troy said easily. "Keeler's sitting down. I'm standing up. You can turn him over to me." He looked at Otha and smiled. The smile was a warning, a dare.

"Well, dang," Otha drawled. "I wadn't doing nothing but cutting up with him. Goda'mighty, Troy, niggers like that."

"Maybe so," Troy replied. "But I don't. Not with this boy."

A grin cracked on Otha's face. "Yeah, I guess you don't. Y'all just about raised him, ain't you?"

For a moment, Troy did not speak, then he said in a flat, even voice, "Just about." He looked at Son Jesus. "Go on in the store with Mr. Dodd, Sonny. He'll get what you need."

"Yeah," Keeler said. He called over his shoulder to Arthur, "Give him a candy bar, on me." He smiled at Son Jesus. "Them jawbreakers been in there for a year. Arthur's just trying to get shed of them."

Son Jesus walked up the steps and into the store.

"Goddang it, Otha, why you want to make fun of that boy?" Keeler said irritably. "That boy ain't done nothing to you."

"Just cutting up," Otha said defensively. He looked around at the men on the porch. None of them spoke. "Shit, I'll pay for his candy bar." He reached in his pocket and pulled out a dime and flipped it to Keeler.

Keeler held the dime between his thumb and forefinger and studied it. "Candy bar?" he said after a moment. "I thought I said I was gon' buy him a Ford car."

A gentle laugh rumbled across the porch.

The men were talking about the two new engines of the 1949 Ford—the V-6 and the V-8—and comparing them to the Jeep station wagon when Arthur came out of the store with Son Jesus. Son Jesus was carrying a small brown bag.

"He give you that candy bar I told him to?" Keeler asked.

"Yes sir," Son Jesus said timidly. His eyes darted to the Darby twins.

"I hope it was a Tootsie Roll," Keeler said. "I like them things."

"That's what it was," Arthur said. He patted Son Jesus on the back. "You tell your mama I hope everything goes all right."

Son Jesus bobbed his head once, slowly, then he walked down the steps and turned to go around the store, toward the woods.

"You gon' cut through them woods, don't let no bears get you," Keeler called.

"Anybody seen one of them new Jeeps?" J. D. asked.

"They was one over in Overton yesterday," Charlie said. "Got all that wood-looking stuff on it. Looked like somebody was driving a tree with a car on its top."

And the men fell back into their gentle quarrel about the good and bad of automobiles. They were not aware of William and Daniel Darby slipping away, following Son Jesus.

Only Tom saw them. He took the last swallow of his Coca-Cola and stood and started into the store.

"Put my bottle up while you're in there," Troy said. He handed Tom his empty bottle. "And don't go getting dirty. Mama'll be all over me if you do."

"I ain't," Tom said defensively. He went into the store and put the bottles in a case, and then he went to the side door of the store and looked out. He could see the Darby twins sneaking after Son Jesus, following a line of trees that bordered a field behind the store. From the front of the store, he heard a sudden burst of laughter. A joke told by Keeler, he thought. He stepped quickly out the side door and rushed toward the trees.

He could hear William's voice: "Hey, boy, wait up a minute."

He squatted beside an oak and watched.

Son Jesus was standing in the edge of the field, his arms wrapped around the grocery sack. William and Daniel were circling him. Tom could hear the taunting.

"Where's that candy bar, boy?" Daniel hissed. "My daddy paid for that candy bar."

"Yeah," William sneered. "It ain't yours. It's ours. Better give it to us."

Tom saw Son Jesus open the paper bag carefully. He reached inside, pulled out the candy bar, and offered it to William.

"It's got nigger on it," William said.

"Yeah," Daniel parroted.

"You think you white, don't you, nigger?" William snapped. He flicked his hand at Son Jesus. Son Jesus closed his eyes. His arms clutched the grocery bag.

"What's the matter, nigger? You scared?" William said. His hand flicked again at Son Jesus. Flicked again. And again. He knocked the candy bar from Son Jesus' hand, then he stepped on it.

"Yeah, nigger, you scared?" Daniel teased. He punched Son Jesus lightly in the shoulder.

"What you got in that bag?" William asked, his hands flicking in front of Son Jesus.

Son Jesus did not move. His arms were tight around the bag. His eyes stayed closed.

"Let me see it," William snapped. He grabbed at the bag, pulled it away from Son Jesus, spilled its contents on the ground.

"Well, by granny, he's got him some flour and some fatback," William crowed. He looked at Daniel, grinned. "Know what I think?" he said.

"What?" Daniel asked gleefully.

"I think we ought to turn this nigger white." He leaned over and ripped open the small bag of flour. A puff of white rose from the ground.

Tom jumped up from behind the oak and sprinted across the field. "Leave him alone," he cried.

William looked up in surprise. Then he laughed. He stood, holding a fistful of flour. "What you gon' do about it, nigger-lover?" he said.

"Leave him alone," Tom said again. "He ain't done nothing."

"He's a nigger," Daniel snapped.

"And you a nigger-lover," William snarled.

"I ain't, neither," Tom said. "Just leave him alone. Go on home, Son Jesus."

William stepped in front of Son Jesus. "You ain't going nowhere, boy, not to I tell you to."

"Yeah," Daniel said. He pushed at Tom with his hand.

"I'm gon' go get Troy," Tom said, his voice trembling.

"What's the matter?" Daniel teased. "You scared of me?"

"I ain't scared of you," Tom said. "Go on home, Son Jesus," he added weakly.

William laughed. He stepped to Son Jesus and threw the flour into his face. Son Jesus did not move. His head was bowed, his eyes closed. The flour coated him. "He don't look much like a nigger now, does he?" William chortled. He picked up the sack of flour and began to claw at it with his hand and to fling the flour over Son Jesus.

A sudden fury blew into Tom. He cried, "Damn you, William Darby," and he dove past Daniel, tackling William. They tumbled to the ground. Tom's arms were pumping frantically, his fists slapping at

William. He could feel William hitting him in his face, and then Daniel was on top of him, punching him in the stomach and chest. He pulled his head back, rolled once, glanced up at Son Jesus. Son Jesus' face was as white as snow.

"Run, Son Jesus," he screamed. "Run."

Son Jesus gazed down at Tom sadly. He touched his face with his fingers, looked at the dots of flour on his fingertips, and then he began to run.

Tom pulled his body into a ball, covering his face with his arms. The fists of the Darby twins rained on him.

THIRTY-SEVEN

The dress that Evelyn Carnes chose for her wedding was the yellow dress. Her lucky dress. Her lucky color. She did not care that she had worn it twice in one week—at a trial and at her wedding. The dress had served her well. It deserved being worn.

She had been nervous, standing beside Frank, facing Reverend Harry Hinton at the altar railing of the Crossover Methodist Church, praying silently that Harry Hinton would not turn her wedding into a revival. But it was over, the ceremony as simple and as dignified as Harry could make it, and now she was standing under the shade of an oak tree in the front yard of the church, surrounded by well-wishers who had already feasted from the dinner-on-the-grounds reception meal that Ada Winter had organized among the women of the church, a meal watched over by Reba and Remona and Lucy Hix.

It was a yard filled with oohs and aahs, of glad laughter, of chirping that sounded like a convention of birds.

Evelyn had known that Frank was uncomfortable. He was not accustomed to the examination of well-wishers in a receiving line, and she had gently pushed him away. "Go play with your little friends," she had teased, and Frank had bloomed red in the face and slipped away, permitting his sister, Florence, to take his place. Florence was a far better companion than Frank in a receiving line. She was bright-eyed and pretty in the way that plain people could be pretty. And most important, she knew how to speak in words of more than one syllable.

For three days, Evelyn had sailed from hour to hour with an energy almost impossible to control. And she had performed miracles. Miracles. Even Ada Winter had said so. Now she was suddenly tired. A happy fatigue, though. She would sleep well tonight, she thought. She had just enough energy in reserve to fulfill her promise to Frank, and then she would cuddle against him and the sleep of joy would flow over her like warm water.

She glanced over the crowd. A deer's look. Quick, complete. She saw Fuller Davis and a small group of men surrounding him. Another group of men, Hugh and Fletcher and Florence's husband, Jarrell, among them, circled Arthur Dodd, listening to something that struck them as humorous. An off-color joke, no doubt. One of Arthur's prize put-downs about women.

Her own mother—the only member of her family to attend the wedding—seemed to fade into the shrubbery lining the church. Her mother was old and bewildered. She held a paper cup of tea, her always sad eyes as bewildered as the eyes of a frightened animal, and Evelyn knew she felt out of place, unworthy. It was a feeling that she understood too well.

Near her mother was a gathering of young girls and, near them, a gathering of young boys. Rachel Jarrett was giggling, cutting glances at Tom Winter. Tom posed, his face turned from Rachel, but his eyes on her. He was wearing his grown-up look—preoccupied, stuffy. His face was bruised, his suit wrinkled. She had heard Ada talking fretfully of a fight Tom had had with the Darby twins. Something over Reba's boy. "That boy's going to send me to an early grave," Ada had sighed in her grumbling over Tom. "And of all the people to mess with, he has to pick that Darby bunch. If you want to find a hornet's nest of trouble, just look up that family. The best they've got are a few horse thieves."

At the side of the church, behind a row of tables hurriedly made of sawhorses and planking covered with paper tablecloths, Evelyn saw Reba and Lucy still serving food, jabbering merrily. Elly and Remona poured tea. Remona did not smile. Evelyn felt sorry for Remona. She, too, knew rape. Not like Remona, but rape still. Rape was the way Jed had made love.

She turned, pushed up on her toes, looked over the shoulder of Harry Hinton, who was prattling to Florence about Overton County's pride in Frank. She saw Frank standing under a pine with Keeler Gaines. She smiled. Crazy Keeler. He was still wearing his army helmet.

A breeze with mist in it swam across her face.

"My goodness," someone near her said. "Looks like rain. We'd better start putting things up."

Evelyn lifted her face to the breeze. "Feels good," she said aloud, but speaking to herself. Everything feels good, she thought. Everything.

• • •

Frank stood, his arms crossed, his face furrowed, listening to Keeler.

"I been playing the fool with the boys over at the store, but I ain't told nobody yet but you, Frank," Keeler said seriously. "But I done it. I signed back up yesterday afternoon over in Athens. I'll be leaving in a week or so."

"Hope it's the right thing," Frank said quietly. He added, "Your wife know?"

"Not yet. I'm gon' tell her tonight, but to be downright honest, I ain't got much of a choice," Keeler replied. "They ain't enough crop in the field to pick or pull, and I'm already on the book to Arthur for almost a thousand dollars. Only way I know to pay him back." He paused, laughed lightly, sadly. "Hell, the army ain't a bad life. Three squares a day, clothes on your back. And we ain't at war with nobody. I guess I can take it." He paused again, removed his helmet from his head and held it, looking at it. "Tell you the truth, it ain't been easy being back here. I guess I picked up some fast feet during the war. They's a lot I'd like to see out there, Frank. A lot of people I ain't met yet."

"Yeah, I know what you mean," Frank admitted. "I think about it sometimes myself. I guess everybody does."

"It wadn't the same when we come back, was it?" Keeler said simply. "Looked the same, but it wadn't."

"I can't argue that," Frank told him.

Keeler glanced across the churchyard, saw Tom. The butterfly of a smile danced across his mouth. "You know who I wish I was?" he said. "I wish I was Tom Winter. Lord, he's got some spunk. If he stays alive long enough to make it out of here, they ain't no telling what kind of trouble he'll stir up."

Frank pivoted his body to look at Tom. Tom was mugging before the gaze of Rachel Jarrett. "You're right about that," he agreed. "Maybe you been around that boy too long, Keeler. Maybe that's what you're about to do. Run away, stir up a little trouble."

"I ought to smuggle him out with me," Keeler said. "I swear he knows where that gold is, Frank. I swear he does."

Frank laughed easily. He saw Evelyn motion to him, and he lifted his hand to wave a message: Be right there.

"You got the boss calling," Keeler said.

"You got that right," Frank replied. He shrugged and started to walk away.

"Frank," Keeler said.

Something in Keeler's voice, something tight, made Frank turn back to him.

"I just wanted to tell you something before I left," Keeler said. He paused, looked up at Frank. "I'm glad I know you," he muttered. "Just wanted you to know that. This county needs a man like you, with all the change that's going on."

"I appreciate that, Keeler," Frank said.

"You better get that woman out of here, before it starts to raining and she messes up her hairdo," Keeler said. "I guaran-damn-tee you, women hate that." He extended his hand and Frank accepted it. The grip was strong. The grip told stories that words could not. "And before you get your dander up, I didn't have nothing to do with tying all them oil cans to your car or painting up the windows with shoe polish. That was Fletcher." He smiled and strolled away, pulling the helmet back over his head.

From a nearby group of men, J. D. Epps called, "Hut, two, three, four."

● ● ●

He had walked for almost six hours, steadily, his shoulders and head bent against the mist that curled off the floor of a low, gray cloud. In some places, the cloud dipped to the ground, leaving damp tracks on the road grass. In the light, the grass looked silver-coated.

His shirt was thin and he was wet from the mist. The sole of his left shoe had a round, worn dot, quarter size, and he had cut a cardboard in the shape of his foot and slipped it into the shoe. He could feel the damp of the road grass seeping through the cardboard and his sock.

On his back was a secondhand Boy Scout knapsack that had been given to him as a Christmas present by Cecily when he was ten. The knapsack was stuffed with the clothes that he owned. Cradled in his left elbow was a wrapped fertilizer sack that he hugged next to his chest.

It was a backroad and he saw few cars, and the cars that did pass him slowed only out of curiosity. White men mostly. One or two driven by blacks. The drivers of the cars casting looks but, not knowing him, driving on. It was not unusual to see a black boy walking a roadside.

It was late in the day. In another hour it would be dark, and he had no idea how far he had yet to walk. Not too far, he thought. Not if the road was the right one, and he was sure that it was. A few miles back, he had passed an old service station that had been closed for many years, its walls and roof covered in the tangle of kudzu vines, like knots of braided hair. The front of the store, with its drooping-eyebrow porch and two small-window eyes and cement-step mouth, had a facelike appearance, covered as it was in vine hair. He remembered the porch from the drive with Duck Heller and his mother. He was on the right road.

• • •

Reba sat at her kitchen table, stroking her fingers over the sheet of paper that she had pressed flat with the heel of her palm, careful not to touch the penciled words. Her eyes were wet from crying. A low moan hummed in her throat.

"Mama, he's just gone to see somebody," Remona said softly, trying to sound assuring. Her voice failed her. She could hear the tremble.

Reba shook her head. Her eyes stayed on the paper. "He gone," she said after a moment. "He took his pack Cecily give him. Took all his clothes. Even when he run off with Thomas, he left that pack home. He ain't coming back."

"I still think that's where he is," Remona replied. "Walked over to see Cecily. Uncle Jule gon' bring him home."

"He gone," Reba repeated.

"He ain't with Cecily, we can get the sheriff," Remona said.

Reba pulled her hands quickly to her face, cupped her fingers over her mouth. "Can't get the sheriff," she said fretfully. "Sheriff put him in jail."

"Mama, no he's not. Look what the sheriff done for us. Sheriff won't put him in jail."

"He put Jule in jail."

"But Uncle Jule's out," Remona said gently. "The sheriff didn't let nobody hurt him."

Reba picked up the sheet of paper and pushed it across the table toward Remona. "Read it to me again, honey."

"It says: 'I got to go off. Don't worry,'" Remona said, without looking at the pencil printing on the paper.

A smile, quickly lost to anguish, fluttered over Reba's face. She reached for the sheet of paper, pulled it to her, gazed at the words she could not read. And she remembered the warning from Conjure Woman: *There be a day when he be leaving.*

"He'll be back, Mama," Remona said. She glanced out the window. Darkness pressed against the trees.

"It's rainy out," Reba said absently.

"Mama, he's all right."

"He just a baby."

"No, Mama, he's not a baby," Remona said. "He's twelve. Mr. Fuller say he work more like a man than a boy. Mr. Fuller say Son Jesus got more sense than most people he knows."

Reba smiled proudly. "He my little man. He all right. Jesus look over him."

"You wait," Remona said. "You wait and see. Uncle Jule gon' drive up any minute. Son Jesus gon' be with him."

•　•　•

He saw the dot of light from the road and remembered it. A single lightbulb in the center of the room. The room he remembered too. Two chairs facing each other under the lightbulb. A single table against one wall. A fireplace. On one wall, a picture of Jesus, his face a rich hue of brown. Not black. Not white. Not yellow. Not red. All the colors puddled together and brushed into the features of a man with gentle, dark eyes that seemed to be gazing at the spot where Conjure Woman sat. From the road, through the window, he believed he could see Conjure Woman sitting in her chair.

He shifted the backpack on his shoulders, turned the fertilizer sack in his hands, and began to walk toward the house.

At the edge of the yard, he stopped and twisted his body to look back. He could not see the road. The night had folded behind him like a curtain, closing off where he had been. A single splinter of light, like the white spew of sudden fire, flashed, and in the flash he could see his mother sitting at her kitchen table beside the soft orange of a burning kerosene lamp, a great sadness covering her face. He blew softly into the darkness, into the image, and the wick of the lamp fluttered, then died, and the image vanished.

He walked up the porch steps to the door, hesitated. From inside, he heard a voice: "Come on in."

He opened the door and stepped inside and closed the door behind him. Conjure Woman sat motionless.

"You see the sign?" she said after a moment. "You see the white face?"

Son Jesus nodded.

"You be leaving?" Conjure Woman said.

Son Jesus nodded again.

"Where you going?"

Son Jesus shook his head.

"Go back on the road," Conjure Woman said. "A car coming by. When it stop, you get in."

"Yes m'am," Son Jesus said quietly.

"Go," Conjure Woman commanded. "You been picked. What be waiting be out there. The world be changing. You one of the changers. The time for breaking be here. You breaking away from all that ever was. Someday, you be famous. People call out your name. I been knowing this since the day you was borned."

Son Jesus ducked his head and began to back away.

"Leave what you got here," Conjure Woman ordered.

He shifted the fertilizer sack in his arms, then he stopped and slipped the backpack off his back and knelt and placed the backpack and the fertilizer sack on the floor.

"You be all right," Conjure Woman said softly.

Son Jesus stood, turned, and walked out the door.

●   ●   ●

Tom heard Jule's car sputter to a stop, and he pulled himself up from his bed to look out the window. His body ached from the beating by the Darby twins. He saw Jule crossing hesitantly to the kitchen door of the house, heard the knock, heard his mother and father at the door speaking with Jule, heard his mother's hurried footsteps leading from the kitchen.

"Tom," his mother said in a fretting voice. "Jule said Sonny's run off, and I want to know if it's got anything to do with that fight you got into with the Darby boys."

"I don't know," Tom answered. "They were picking on him. I told you that."

"I knew I should have gone over to Reba's after the wedding," his mother sighed. "I just knew it."

"They look over at Mr. Davis's farm?" Tom asked.

"They looked there," his mother answered. She wrapped her hands into her apron. "Lord, that poor boy. It's pitch dark out there, and rainy."

"Why'd he run away, Mama?" Tom said.

"I wish I knew." His mother looked sadly at Tom. "But I know where he learned it from. I told you, son, that someday you were going to get somebody in trouble by all that carrying on."

"I quit running away," Tom said.

"Sonny didn't," his mother replied.

"They gon' get the sheriff?" asked Tom.

"That's what I'm about to do right now," his mother answered.

● ● ●

It was Evelyn who answered the telephone, rushing out of bed to catch it on the fourth ring, her yellow silk nightgown barely clinging to her shoulders.

"Evelyn, it's Ada," Ada said. "I sure hate to do this on your wedding night, but I need to talk to Frank."

"I'll get him for you," Evelyn said. She added in a giddy whisper, "It may take a couple of minutes."

"Oh, never mind," Ada said quickly, feeling suddenly embarrassed. "Just tell him that Reba Martin's boy—Sonny—is missing. It looks like he's run away."

"Oh, my," Evelyn sighed in a concerned voice. "Bless Reba's heart. It seems like she just can't get away from trouble, don't it?"

"Looks that way," Ada replied. "Tell him that Hack and Troy will be driving around looking."

"I'll tell him," Evelyn promised.

In the bedroom, Frank rolled to his back, pushed up on one elbow. "Trouble?" he asked.

Evelyn slipped back into the bed next to him, pulled open her gown, wiggled close. The heat of his body was like the heat of a sun-warmed cloth. "Reba Martin's boy run away," she said. "That was Ada." She pushed her head into the cradle of his shoulder.

"Oh, Lord," Frank said. "Ada's boy wadn't with him, was he?"

"She didn't say he was."

"Wonder what that's all about," Frank mused. "That's not like Sonny. Wonder if something happened over at Fuller's place."

"Like what?"

"Wish I knew," Frank said. He stretched, dropped his arm across Evelyn's chest, rubbed her rib cage lightly. "Well, I better go help look."

Evelyn caught his hand, turned her face to his face. "You know," she said, "I saw him earlier today."

"Where?" Frank asked.

"I was coming back to the house about an hour before the wedding—I'd forgot my blue garter—and I saw him just when I was passing that turnoff to the logging road, the one that leads back to where the sawmill was," Evelyn said.

Frank pulled up to a sitting position. "What time?"

"I don't know. About one, I guess."

"You sure it was him? He's grown a lot this year. When I saw him at the courthouse, I almost didn't know who he was."

"Oh, it was him, all right. Looked like he was carrying something."

"What?"

"It was too far away to see good. Maybe a sack, or something. Looked like he had something on his back too."

Frank rolled to the side of the bed and reached for his pants. "Where was he?" he asked again.

"I told you. Coming down that logging road."

"Coming down it, or going up it?"

"Down it, toward the main road."

"Damn," Frank muttered. He stood and stepped into his pants, then reached for his shirt.

"What is it?" Evelyn asked.

"Nothing," Frank said quickly. "He was just a long way from home, that's all. Not like him to wander so far off." He buttoned his shirt quickly.

"I don't know what can be done tonight," Evelyn said. "You can't hardly see your hand in front of your face out there, it's so soupy dark."

"I'll drive around. Maybe he's on the road somewhere," Frank told her.

"Well, I guess I'd better get used to this. Hopping up in the middle of the night. But don't worry. I'll be here, keeping the bed warm. You just come back."

Frank smiled down at her. "I will." He leaned over the bed and kissed her lightly.

In the living room, Frank dialed the telephone, listened to the ringing. A sleep-drugged Hugh answered.

"I need you to meet me over at Reba Martin's house," Frank said.

"What's wrong?" asked Hugh. "You sound like you got the devil chasing you."

"What it feels like," Frank admitted. "There's something—I don't know. We'll talk about it when you get over here." He hung up, then sat back in the chair. A chill crawled across his shoulders.

● ● ●

He had walked to the Athens road in the ink-dark night—a mile, perhaps farther, from the turnoff to Conjure Woman's home—before he saw the lights of a car coming slowly behind him. Two eye-spots of light, cutting into the night.

The car passed him, braked, came to a stop, reversed, stopped again beside him.

"You lost?" a voice asked merrily.

Son Jesus peered into the car. He saw a man with a thin, light-chocolate face covered with a large smile, white teeth flashing. The man was dressed in a close-fitting double breasted suit.

"I hope you know how to talk," the man said.

"Uh—yes sir," Son Jesus replied.

"You lost?" the man asked again.

Son Jesus looked down the road. "No sir," he said. "I was just going on down the road."

"Well, damn, boy, it's too dark and wet to be walking around out there this time of the night," the man said. He laughed. "Crawl in. That's exactly where I'm going—on down the road. Might as well do it together."

"Yes sir," Son Jesus said. He opened the car door and slipped inside. A wave of warm air struck his face.

"What's your name, boy?" the man asked. He pulled the car in gear and started forward.

"Uh—Son Jesus," Son Jesus answered.

The man laughed again. "Well, damn," he exclaimed. He thrust his hand toward Son Jesus. "Son Jesus, meet Isaiah—Isaiah Tanner." His laughter rolled in the car. "Two old Bible boys out on the road—now don't that beat all?" He glanced at Son Jesus. "You running away?"

Son Jesus tucked his head.

"Shoot, boy, don't go feeling shamed about that," Isaiah Tanner said. "I could tell that right off. Got that peeking-back-over-your-shoulder look. Seen it a lot of times. Why I stopped for you. I bet you ain't got two dimes to rub together. Just up and left everything behind. Well, that don't matter. I got some rubbing-together cash stuck down in my shoe. What'd you do to make you run away, anyhow?"

Son Jesus did not answer.

"Stood up to some white man, that it?" Isaiah said. He beamed proudly. "What I done. White boss I was working the fields for up there in South Carolina. Told me he was gon' whip my black ass for breaking a plow stock in them rock patches he was trying to grow cotton on. He pick up a stick and I whop him upside the head, and then I lit out."

Isaiah glanced at Son Jesus. A look of judgment. "When I was about your age, I'd guess. Just took off running and got out. Best thing I ever done. Shook that cotton field dust off my feet and lit out. Yes sir, I seen the world since then." He mugged comically. "At least as far it goes to Cincinnati, Ohio." He nodded like a man listening to music. "What you think I do now, Son Jesus?"

"Don't know," Son Jesus mumbled.

"I'm a traveling baseball man," Isaiah crowed. "Pitcher, shortstop, outfielder. Yes sir, that's what I am. I done played with Satchel Paige and Cool Papa Bell and lots of them other boys. Been up Virginia with a little high-tone girl that loved every ball I got, but I tell you, boy, they ain't no woman alive feel as good as a baseball in your hand. No sir, they ain't." He laughed boyishly. "Had to sneak away in the middle of the night from that woman. Going down to Florida now. Play me some ball down there. They got a bunch of colored teams that play down there, straight into the wintertime. Maybe go on over to Cuba. Gon' play for one of them white teams someday, just like Jackie Robinson."

"Yes sir," Son Jesus said. He had heard Uncle Jule talk about the great ballplayers who played in Florida.

"Long as you just running off, why don't you come on down there with me?" Isaiah suggested. "Get you a job cleaning off tables in one of them fancy resort hotels. Lots of rich people down there, just throwing money around like it was growed on trees."

Son Jesus swallowed. He could see nothing ahead of him but the car lights, like spears thrown against the night. He glanced back. He could see nothing.

"You ever play baseball?" Isaiah asked.

Son Jesus shook his head. He thought of his games with Thomas Winter. "Not real ball," he said.

"Well, you look to me like you got you some long-arm muscle," Isaiah said. "How old you say you was?"

"Uh—fourteen," Son Jesus said, lying, feeling the regret for lying press against him.

"Maybe I'll teach you how to throw my Can't-See-Um pitch."

Son Jesus looked at Isaiah curiously, and Isaiah laughed.

"It come in so fast, ain't nobody see it," Isaiah explained. "Ain't hard. Satchel showed it to me. It's all in whipping your arm around, like a snake striking at a rat." He whipped his arm over the steering wheel. "Sometimes I call it my snake pitch."

"Yes sir," Son Jesus said. He could feel himself spinning away from his home, from Crossover, from Overton County.

"Couple of years, you'll be coming back here leading parades," Isaiah said cheerfully. "Have girls dancing at your feet." He looked at Son Jesus. "You got a girl back home?"

"No sir."

"You got folks?"

Son Jesus bobbed his head hesitantly.

"Well, don't you go thinking about that," Isaiah told him. "We'll send them a postcard from down there in Florida, let them know you all right. One that's got palm trees on it, or maybe some oranges. Dress you up in one of my baseball uniforms and take a snapshot of you and send that back. Put a few dollars in the envelope. That's all they want to know, that you all right. Shoot, boy, we colored. Colored man's got to keep moving or he gon' be plowed under on one of them cotton farms."

Son Jesus settled against the car seat. He thought of his mother, of Remona, of Cecily, of Uncle Jule, of Thomas. They seemed far away.

"Maybe I'll teach you my Fall-Down pitch too," Isaiah said. "Way it come in, it look like it gon' hit you upside the head, and you gon' fall down getting out of the way, but it curve down like it was shot by a gun."

Isaiah laughed again, and there was happiness in his laughter. And promise. Happiness and promise.

○ ● ●

The light of morning, still fog-dull, rubbed against Conjure Woman's home like a cat with an arched back—fur-soft, purring. She raised her face to look at the light, then pushed herself up from her chair. She had not moved, the entire night. She walked to the window, looked out. She could see the phantom reflection of her face in the glass and fog. She closed her eyes, listened. She could hear the peace of deep breathing.

"He sleeping," she said softly.

She turned away from the window and crossed the room to the fertilizer sack, stooped to lift it. Then she brushed away the sawdust still clinging to it. She opened it carefully, deliberately.

And she lifted the shotgun up, like an offering.

"My hand be on him," she whispered.